Breaking the Regime

Third Book of the Promissa Trilogy

E.R. Phoenix

E.R. Phoenix

Contents

Trigger warning: May contain spoilers

The dystopian romance Breaking the Regime takes place in a society where injustice, persecution, and brutality are rampant. Some of the incidents described may be disturbing to some readers.

A few scenes depict torture. There are also instances of gore, alcohol consumption, weapon use, and explicit sexual content. Other topics include mental illness and suicide.

Dedication

To all who feel like giving up,
Embrace the hard parts of life, and make them your own.
Grow from these experiences, and keep fighting.
You are not alone.

—Emily Dickinson, "My Life had stood—a Loaded Gun"

My Life had stood—a Loaded Gun—
In Corners—till a Day
The Owner passed—identified—
And carried Me away—
And now We roam in Sovereign Woods—
And now We hunt the Doe—
And every time I speak for Him—
The Mountains straight reply—
And do I smile, such cordial light
Upon the Valley glow—
It is as a Vesuvian face
Had let it's [sic] pleasure through—
And when at Night—Our good Day done—
I guard My Master's Head—
'Tis better than the Eider Duck's
Deep Pillow—to have shared—
To foe of His—I'm deadly foe—
None stir the second time—
On whom I lay a Yellow Eye—
Or an emphatic Thumb—

Though I than He—may longer live
He longer must—than I—
For I have but the power to kill,
Without—the power to die—
—Emily Dickinson, "My Life had stood—a Loaded Gun"

Chapter 1

Davon

April 7, 2214

Seconds turned to minutes the moment the grenade went airborne. We all turned in unison and ran. The clink was all I heard before I was shoved from behind. A booming crack echoed around me. The floor trembled, and I pulled Abi to me, then covered her body.

The sting of debris cut my skin, but I hauled myself up. Dust filled the air. I couldn't see beyond Abi.

Her left arm rested at a weird angle and reached toward the exit. I couldn't tell if it was broken or dislocated.

I coughed. "Can you move?"

She nodded and pressed her lips together. Tears streamed down her face, and the dirt from the explosion followed their tracks.

She stroked my chin. "You?"

Warmth trickled down my back. I reached behind me. My fingers grazed jagged debris lodged deep into my skin.

"Fuck." The word escaped before I could stop it.

Abi opened her eyes wide.

I sucked in a breath, the air thick and suffocating. "It's nothing serious."

"Are you sure?" Her voice trembled.

I touched my brow to hers. "I'm sure, baby. Now let me take care of your arm." I slid my belt off and looped it behind her neck, then eased her arm into the makeshift sling.

She closed her eyes and flinched.

"Better?"

She nodded, then shifted her gaze toward the hall. "Where's Jimmy?"

I helped her up.

We faced the remnants of the explosion. The whole tunnel had collapsed. A few feet beyond us, I saw him.

Abi's face contorted into one of pure anguish. "Jimmy!"

His hands stretched toward Abi. Half his back was crushed by heavy pieces of concrete. A stabbing ache constricted my chest. *No!*

Abi stared at the debris entombing Jimmy, and her expression filled with agony.

I could tell she knew the gravity of his injury the moment she shook her head and sank by his side.

I started pulling rocks off him, my body surging with adrenaline. I had to save him.

Jimmy reached for her. "Abi?" His voice was raspy.

His deep cough echoed around us. Blood poured out of his mouth.

She caressed the side of his face. "I'm here."

Jimmy covered her hand. "Good."

The strain in my muscles was heavy as I heaved one rock after another off of him.

Please, God, give me the strength.

Abi wept.

"Don't cry." Jimmy wiped her cheek with his thumb.

I couldn't hold my tears back anymore, but I kept going. There had to be a way.

I grunted as I lugged another rock off him, then collapsed to my knees.

His waist was crushed, and a huge hematoma marred his skin. Part of a wall pinned his legs. I bent over him and grabbed the edge of the cement wall, but it wouldn't budge no matter how hard I tried. He was trapped, and I couldn't do anything to save him.

My ribs tightened more with each searing breath. He'd die here, and I couldn't stop it.

This can't be happening!

"Don't leave me, Jimmy. I can't." Her voice cracked. "I can't do this without you."

Jimmy's blue eyes shone with tears. "You can, and you will." He let out a shuddering exhale. "I love you. I always will."

Abi dragged her body closer to him and kissed his temple. "Don't talk like that. Don't say goodbye." She looked up at me, eyes wide. "What are you doing? Why did you stop?"

"Abi, I..." I slumped forward, hands clenched over my thighs. "I can't free him."

She glanced at the slab of concrete covering Jimmy's legs. "No." She shook her head violently and returned her attention to Jimmy, who gasped for air.

She stroked his hair. "Someone will come soon. We'll get you out. I know we can."

Jimmy darted his eyes to me. "Take care of her."

"I will." He must have been the one who pushed me forward as we tried to escape the blast. I'd forever be indebted to him.

Jimmy smiled at Abi. "Make them pay."

His breaths became shorter. Faster.

Abi rested her brow against his and closed her eyes. "I love you, Jimmy. Please don't leave me."

"I never will." He exhaled one last time.

I shut my eyes and offered a silent prayer.

"No!" A guttural growl left Abi. She held on to him. "Don't leave me!"

She kissed his hand and clutched it to her chest.

His blue eyes were open. He almost looked alive.

I sat by her and closed his eyes, then took her in my arms. "I'm sorry, baby."

Her brother was dead. He gave his life for us.

Her sobs broke through the rumbling sound of the collapsing hall.

"It's caving in!" I yelled. "We have to go."

She clung to Jimmy. "We can't leave him!"

I jumped at a crunching sound behind us. I could make out two figures. I squinted. "Matt? Connor?"

The dust settled around them.

Matt stepped back when he saw us, holding his palm over his mouth. His gaze misted with unshed tears.

Connor ran toward Abi but jerked to a stop when he saw Jimmy. He clenched his fists by his sides.

The bunker roared.

Matt grabbed my waist and pulled me up.

I flinched. My whole body ached.

Matt turned me around and raised my shirt. "Your back."

I waved him off. "I'll be all right." I glanced behind him. "Aoki?"

"He went ahead with the citizens."

I exhaled. "Good." He was safe.

Connor crouched beside Abi. "Abi?" He brushed her hair back.

Abi slumped against his shoulder. "She killed them." Her face was etched with pain.

Connor's gaze drifted across the rubble, then to Jimmy. He looked up at me. "Maria?"

I could only nod.

Connor took a deep, shuddering breath. He stood and offered his hand to Abi. "We need to go, or this will become our tomb."

The muffled thud of a bomb reverberated around us. The sound came like a wave until the ground shook. Connor covered Abi.

When it was over, she glanced around, then widened her eyes, as if waking from a nightmare.

Connor tugged at her, but she fought, clutching Jimmy's hand. "We can take him with us!"

"I'm sorry, Abi. There's no time." The cracking sound of the tunnel muffled his voice, and silent tears smudged his face. "Do it for him. Live." He forced her hand open, then pulled her up and cradled her against his chest.

"No!" She winced and struggled against the man who was a father to her. "Jimmy!" she yelled as a thunderous boom rang around us.

Connor passed us. "Follow me!"

I cast one last look toward Jimmy before Matt drew me away. Each step was gut-wrenching. Moving forward but away from them.

Maria and Jimmy didn't deserve to die, nor did the hundreds of soldiers out there. Tears sprang from my eyes as we escaped the collapsing tunnel and followed the emergency lights to the common area.

The clang of heavy boots rang from hall C, and I glanced back in time to see the massive bodies of more than a dozen enhanced NWG soldiers advancing toward us.

We took one of the emergency exits. Blasts followed us out.

Matt kicked the door closed behind us.

We followed Connor downhill, heading north.

Connor put Abi down and took out a trigger mechanism. "Take cover!"

Matt pulled Abi and me to the ground.

The mountain rocked beneath us as a muffled roar rang out. The early morning sky was clouded with dust and debris as our home collapsed.

It was like a knife to the heart. A decade's worth of memories buried forever.

A loud cracking noise startled me, and I followed it to the northeast. A light flashed as another piercing snap echoed around us. A sniper. It took a moment for me to get up again and alert Connor.

I moved a finger to my mouth and pointed to the place.

"Stay with her. We'll go check it out," Connor whispered.

He and Matt left us behind a boulder.

Abi's hands trembled uncontrollably.

"Love?" I wiped away a lone tear and enfolded her in my arms. "I'm so sorry."

She grabbed my shirt. Her breaths were short and labored. "He's gone." She sniffed. Every inhale she took paralleled her anguished sobs.

My throat burned. I'd give anything to take away her pain.

I kept my stare toward the remnants of our base. Tammy would pay for her betrayal. They would all pay for each life they took.

I relaxed my jaw and nuzzled Abi's neck, holding her cocooned against me. "I'm so sorry, love."

A branch snapped in the direction Connor and Matt headed. I drew my gun and pushed Abi behind me.

They were getting closer. *Fuck.* I took a step toward the sound and cocked my gun.

A desperate voice reached us. "Abi? Where are you?"

I didn't recognize it. Who the hell was calling out to her?

"Over there. Behind that boulder."

Matt?

Footsteps rushed toward us, then David came into view. His face covered in dirt, smears from what I could only think were tears marked his cheeks.

I put the gun down, and the tension in my muscles eased. I hadn't seen him since the checkpoint attacks.

He bowed slightly toward me, then squatted in front of Abi.

"David!" Abi caressed his face with her uninjured hand. "You're alive?"

He smiled and placed his hand over hers. "Very much so." He brushed her arm, which she held close to her. "You're hurt." He lowered his eyebrows.

My chest hurt at their closeness. At his endearing touch. Then I remembered Abi telling me about him. Of how close they'd become. I pushed away any negative thoughts and stood by her.

She shook her head. "It's nothing." She threw her arm around him. "David, Maria and Jimmy..." She closed her eyes. "They're gone." Tears streamed down her face.

He hugged her. "Connor just told me." He sobbed against her neck. "Fuck, Abi. I...I'll kill that bitch for what she did."

Their sobs broke through the forest.

My stomach hardened at the way he embraced her. The look he had.

I massaged my jaw, then took two deep breaths, fighting back the urge to separate them. If she needed him now, I'd stand aside. He'd been there for her when I wasn't. When she needed it most.

The booming sound of a mine went off. Rapid fire raged near us.

Matt rushed to my side. "Connor's waiting. David's team cleared a path for us."

I turned my head to the south. "But the soldiers?"

"Katherine's with them. They'll keep engaged until we're all safe. Seth should be on his way with reinforcements." Matt looked at Abi. "We should go."

Abi nodded, then her gaze shifted to me. "Your back." She came to my side.

I sighed. "It's fine."

She lifted my shirt. "There's blood everywhere." She flinched. Her palm was cut by a piece of scrap metal lodged into my side. "Davon!"

Every movement was like being stabbed, but we had to go on. "I'll take care of it once we're safe."

"But..." She clung to my shirt.

I kissed her hand. "I promise. I'm okay."

"Don't worry. I'll make sure to take care of his wounds once we're safe." Matt eyed the makeshift sling holding her arm. "Can I check it?"

Abi nodded. "My elbow hurts, but it's weird. I don't feel much of my forearm."

"Can you move it?"

She moved her shoulder, but her arm hung limp. She grimaced. "Just the shoulder."

Matt nodded. "I'm going to remove this. Use your other hand to hold the arm." He unbuckled the belt.

Abi took a deep breath.

"I'm sorry. I know it hurts." He checked her shoulder and elbow. Frowning, he tilted his head.

David stood beside him. "Is it broken?"

Matt shook his head. "Her elbow is dislocated."

I closed my eyes briefly. A broken arm would have taken months to recover.

Matt held Abi's stare. "I need to set it back, or you could have nerve damage."

"Will it hurt?" Abi winced as he moved her forearm.

Matt gave her a pained look. "It will."

Abi darted her eyes between us, then dropped her gaze. "Do what you have to do."

Matt glanced at me. "Hold her still."

I wrapped my arms around her waist, then carefully eased her back against my chest. "I'm right here. Everything will be okay."

She turned her face to me and nodded. "I'm ready."

Matt grabbed her upper arm, then moved her forearm until there was a soft snap.

Abi cried out. She doubled over and retched.

I patted her back. "That's normal, love. Just let it all out." I held her as she wiped her mouth with her other sleeve.

David offered her some water. "Here."

She took it. "It feels weird. Kind of numb, but it's better now."

Matt nodded. "Good."

"Will she be okay?"

We stepped aside at Connor's commanding voice.

"She will." Matt secured the belt to hold her arm. "When we get to farming, we'll take care of the rest. She'll recover."

Connor stroked Abi's hair, then kissed her temple and embraced her. "I'm so sorry, kiddo."

She slumped against him, tears streaming down her face.

Nodding, Abi sniffed and pulled away. "Thanks for coming back for us."

Connor smiled. "I'll always come back for you." He ruffled her hair. "We should go."

With Matt on one side of me and Abi on the other, we sprinted toward the escape route.

David followed behind.

Five minutes later, we reached David's team and started moving north.

An explosion followed by a roaring sound made me stop. "What was that?" I asked Connor.

"Mark found where the Halcyon troops were coming from. That was him making sure to slow them down."

I glanced uphill. Mark took off his protective gear and stood, an M72 LAW in hand. He held his hand over his eyes as a deep blast echoed through the mountains. He glanced back at us with a thumbs-up, then started downhill.

He caught up with us a moment later.

I grabbed his forearm and pulled him in. "Glad to see you in one piece."

He smiled. "Same here."

Connor patted his back. "Let's get moving."

The sounds of battle resonated from the south, but we went on.

It was almost noon when we stopped on a hilltop.

A heavy fog covered the valley that hid the farming and engineering bunker.

My eyelids were heavy, and my eyes drifted shut for a moment. "We made it."

Abi sagged against me, letting out a huge breath.

I hugged her, and everything that took place a few hours ago surged forward.

The people we lost and the ones who would follow now that war had begun. Each death left a scar on the rebellion, one that would never heal.

I glanced around our group. Our eyes reflected how much we'd lost.

Connor gripped my shoulder. "Do you have a minute?"

Abi was covered with soot, as were the rest of us who witnessed the explosion of our home base, Janus Peak. To see all we'd built crumble to nothingness had been a blow to our spirits.

I stroked her cheek. "Will you be okay?"

Her hazel eyes were dim even as the sun glinted on them.

My heart tugged as she covered my hand with hers.

She nodded.

I brought her to me, careful not to touch her arm, then kissed her brow. "I'm sorry about everything."

She quivered in my arms and held me closer.

I let go of her and darted my eyes to David, who stood beside her. "Thanks for everything out there."

David was the best sniper in the PRF, and what his team did out there saved many.

He nodded. "I was just doing my duty."

"It's good to have you back." I squeezed his arm, then turned to Connor.

The whistling wind was our only witness as Connor and I made our way downhill. The silence that followed what we just encountered was all-encompassing. Suffocating.

Nothing to say. No words of hope to share. There was only one thing to do—take one step after another, and keep moving forward.

"I want to run something by you before giving the order." Connor kept his eyes on the horizon. "As things are going, either we risk the New World Government patrols following us north, or we give them the import bunker. Before all this, it was a plan Seth and I put in place in case Janus Peak was lost."

I pondered about it for a moment. "Pushing the NWG troops west and giving them import might be our only choice. Is there enough space for Seth's people in science?"

"There is, but it's just a temporary arrangement. We'll move everyone here until the cavern system is ready. The preparations are well on their way. It's not safe around here anymore."

I stared at the valley. We'd recruited hundreds of rebels over the last decade. The caverns ran for kilometers and would serve us well. "It's a sound plan."

There was still one missing piece.

I squished my eyebrows. "Have you heard back from Yuxuan and his troops?"

Connor raked his blond hair back. It had grown to his nape since the last time we saw each other. "I sent out a scout a few days ago. Yuxuan lost half his patrol but keeps fighting." He shook his head. "I'm not sure where he and his troops are right now or if they know about the attack."

I took a deep breath. "So we're in the dark."

"He's a seasoned warrior. I'm sure he'll make it."

A stab hit my chest. *What if they already got to him?* "Is there any way to contact him?"

"I can send another scout." Connor arched an eyebrow. "What are you thinking?"

"That we should regroup and plan a strategy. This..." I bowed my head and shook it. "This was a hard hit to the rebellion."

"We lost too many." Connor looked up the hill.

I followed his gaze and saw Abi.

David was holding her close. Too fucking close.

I took a step forward, fists clenched. What the fuck was he doing?

"Davon?"

I stilled.

Connor squeezed my shoulder. "Come on, man. You know she loves you. It's just...when you were away, they became very close. Trust her."

I should have been there for her. Now David had a place in her heart that was his and his alone.

I swallowed my urge to go up there and pull them apart.

That's when Abi's eyes met mine. Her lips parted, and my chest grew light.

She was mine, and I was hers. There was nothing else.

"We're close. Let's go." Deep sorrow replaced the usual strength of Connor's voice.

I'd do anything to help ease his suffering, but I couldn't see how.

I clutched his arm. "We'll push through. We trained for this." I used as much confidence as possible in my tone.

He nodded, and I followed him downhill. The fog dispersed.

My pulse faltered.

She stood in the midst of the chaos. Her swollen womb showed her advanced pregnancy. Deb cared for the wounded outside the bunker.

I wanted to hold her. To beg for forgiveness. To talk to her for hours and comfort her. But that was no longer an option. I put my hands in my pockets and stopped. How would I ever breach this wall between us?

Connor sighed. "She'll forgive you. Give her some time."

"I hope so." I lowered my gaze to the person Deb was helping, and everything stopped. My whole vision darkened.

No. It can't be.

Chapter 2

Abi

April 7, 2214

Davon followed Connor downhill, our two generals.

We'd made it but lost so many. I looked south, wondering about those still fighting.

I peeked at the heavens, and his blue eyes stared back at me, asking me to leave him. I'd never see those eyes again or hear his voice. I'd never catch the scent of wood and forest that he always carried or see the wind ruffle his dirty-blond hair as he smiled.

Time slowed, and my vision blurred. There was not enough air.

David's warm hand enveloped mine in a strong hold. His glimmering hazel eyes were set on me. He captured my trembling chin and brushed away the tears that slid down my face. He grabbed my nape and pulled me to him in an embrace, resting his chin on top of my head. "I'm so sorry, Abi. I wish I could go and get them back. I wish none would have died. I wish so many things."

His gentle voice filled the emptiness in my heart. It was like a brick that was crushing my chest was suddenly lifted, and air filled my heavy lungs.

He caressed my hair. "I should have been there. For Maria. For Jimmy. For you." He bent down and hid his face in the crook of my neck, sobbing silently. "I'd never forgive myself if anything happened to you."

I sobbed in his arms and let it all out. The tension I'd been through in the last couple of weeks. The stress that had taken over my life while working next to Jordan Niles. The realization that I'd lost Maria and Jimmy forever.

I allowed it all to flood through my veins till agony transformed into wrath. Until my mind became consumed with a desire for justice for what we had lost.

I grabbed his face with my free hand and stroked his cheek.

The pain etched into his features broke me. His tanned skin glistened with sweat and tears, his hair falling over his eyes, hiding the inevitable truth—we'd lost them. We'd never see them again.

"David. Please look at me."

He tucked his hair behind his ears, and I caught his gaze.

I searched deep within for the courage to speak, to push down all the pain and help this man who had allowed me into his life. "No one could have done anything differently. It just...happened."

He nodded, and our eyes met in a silent stare. He held my shoulders. "We'll get them for this. Every single one of them."

His words were stern. Clear.

A sense of calm overtook me, and I could breathe easy again.

There was no doubt in my mind that he'd avenge our friends. He'd take them down. No different than the promise I'd made that dreadful night. We'd take our revenge. Jimmy, Maria, and all who'd died would rest in peace, knowing we'd taken the New World Government down.

A sudden awareness made me look downhill. A jolt ran through my body the instant I stared into Davon's deep, dark eyes.

The air was charged between us. My body urged me to run into his arms, knowing that with his touch, all the turmoil within me would quiet down. That only he could give me the peace I sought.

David stepped back and darted his eyes between Davon and me before starting downhill.

I followed him.

Sarah guided people inside the bunker. I pressed a palm to my heart. She was safe.

Countless wounded lay across the valley. Other citizens helped them up or carried them inside on gurneys.

"No!" Matt's scream echoed around us as he sprinted toward one group.

Mark was not far behind him.

When I saw who they ran to, my body turned cold.

His long, dark hair hung from the side of the gurney, and Deb was calling for help.

No. It can't be.

Davon and I exchanged a pained look. My heart thundered as we rushed toward our friend.

Connor and David followed behind.

Matt slid to a stop next to his husband. We stood just behind him.

"Give them space!" Deb didn't notice me as she spoke to the soldiers by her side.

I wanted to hug her. To run into her arms and tell her how much I had missed her, but Aoki was hurt, and I couldn't move.

"Aoki?" Matt grabbed Aoki's hand, but he didn't respond.

Mark was already by his side. He looked over his shoulder. "What happened?"

Deb shook her head. "I don't know. They carried him all the way here. He's bleeding a lot."

Crimson stained his gurney. The back of his cream shirt was covered in blood. A hand strangled my heart. I ached to reach for him.

Matt checked him. A torrent of tears slid down his face. His hands trembled as he put his fingers against Aoki's neck and exhaled.

Deb gripped Matt's hand. "Breathe, Matt. You need to be calm. Aoki needs you."

Davon crouched next to the gurney. "Tell me what to do."

The moment Deb saw Davon she stumbled back. Her terrified gaze broke something in me. Her eyes bulged, and her chin quivered. I'd never seen her so scared.

My heart hammered against my chest, and I walked to her and grabbed her shoulders.

Her eyes widened, and tears sprang from her eyes. "Abi?"

I smiled. "I'm here."

She cupped my face. "Is it really you?" Her voice shook.

I nodded.

She grabbed me by the nape and pulled me into a fierce hug.

She was here. Alive and well, and the last three years flashed through my mind in an instant. All the suffering and hopelessness had brought us to this moment. We were finally together.

Matt's desperate voice cried behind us, taking us back to Aoki's predicament. I would have given anything to have had a happier reunion. But here we were, with our friend gravely injured and the rebellion hanging in the balance.

"Help me move him," Matt told Davon.

They turned him sideways.

Matt scrunched his face. "No, no, no."

"What's wrong with him?" Deb took the words out of my mouth.

Matt's body tensed as he glanced backward. "He's been shot. We need to get him inside ASAP."

Davon's eyes were downcast.

Matt went to Deb. "I'm sorry we're meeting like this." He looked at her belly. "You shouldn't be here. Get inside, and ask Steven for an operating room, then stay in your room."

Connor moved to Deb's side. "You should let Zachary take care of Aoki."

Matt frowned. "You have no say in this."

Connor grasped his arm. "Matt, you're in no state to do this, and you know it."

Matt grabbed Connor's shirt by the lapels, his face inches from him. "Like hell I'll let someone else operate on my husband!" He took a calming breath and let go of Connor. "I can do it. I can save him."

Anger flickered in Connor's gaze, but concern replaced it. He softened his features. "At least let him be by your side. We're with you. Don't push us away."

Matt took two shuddering breaths, then nodded.

Connor touched his shoulder. "I'll make sure everything is set." With one last glance at us, he draped his arm around Deb's shoulders and kissed her head. "Let's get back inside."

Deb leaned into him and allowed him to lead her inside.

Matt grabbed hold of the gurney. David and a couple of soldiers helped him.

That's when I noticed a backpack, and it was moving. It was abandoned about a meter away from Aoki.

I took it, and a hiss hinted at who waited inside. I unzipped it enough to peek within. Shirokuro's black-and-white face greeted me. Meowing desperately.

Aoki saved him.

"Everything will be okay. Daddy's going to make it." I petted his head, then closed the backpack and put it over my right shoulder.

I turned toward Davon, who'd followed me. He massaged my waist. "Do you need help carrying him?"

I adjusted the backpack as best I could. "I can manage." A shot of pain coursed through my left arm, but I didn't flinch. I had to be strong.

"Come on." Davon gently pressed the small of my back, and we followed the others.

Mayhem was insufficient to describe what was going on. Blood stained the floor and walls. Citizens helped as much as they could, while doctors and nurses attended the injured.

Someone bumped into me, and I cried out.

Davon squeezed my waist. "You're okay?"

I nodded.

Aoki moaned loudly. "Matt?"

We all stopped.

Matt took Aoki's hand. "Love? Can you hear me?"

Aoki's eyes fluttered open. "Matt?" The corner of his mouth curved up in a tender smile that quickly changed into a frown. "My whole body hurts."

My throat burned.

We couldn't lose him. Not here. Not now.

His breathing was slow and weak. He looked around. "Where are we?"

Matt grabbed his hand. "You're safe. We're in the farming and engineering bunker."

Aoki nodded. "Mark?"

"He's out front, making way for us," Matt said.

Aoki was pale, and his eyes closed again.

"We need to hurry!" I screamed.

Mark looked back, his eyes frenzied as he ran toward us. He bent toward Aoki. His eyebrows drew together as he stroked his brother's temple. "I'm here."

We were stuck in the middle of the turmoil.

"Matt!" someone called from the end of the hall.

Matt followed the voice. "It's Steven. He's out front." He kissed Aoki's temple. "Hold on, love."

At the end of the hall, Dr. Lewis waited for us beside Steven.

Steven looked haggard. His ash-brown hair was tousled and his eyes sunken. He held open a door to our right.

Dr. Lewis rushed to check Aoki, then fixed his glasses. "Get him inside. It's not much, but it's clean. Rachel already brought what's needed."

Davon followed everyone in. I was right behind him.

Shirokuro meowed.

"What was that?" Steven asked from the door.

I pulled the backpack up, but this time I couldn't stop myself from wincing. "It's Aoki's cat."

"We have a place for all the pets that are coming in. If you'd like, I can take him."

I took off the backpack. "Thank you."

He grabbed it. "We'll take care of him until Aoki is better." He pointed to my arm. "You should take care of that."

I shook my head. "I want to stay."

Davon and Matt moved Aoki onto the bed and laid him on his stomach. Rachel grabbed a pair of scissors to cut through his shirt, exposing his back.

I gasped.

Dr. Lewis, who was putting on sterile gloves, turned to me, then glanced around the room. "Everyone should leave. We need to keep the room as sterile as possible."

Davon stayed next to the bed. "But I'm a universal donor. I can give him blood."

David came to his side, hiding the bed with his body. "You have wounds to take care of. My blood is the same as yours. I can stay."

I took a tentative step forward, wanting to catch a glimpse of my friend.

Matt worked on Aoki's back as blood gushed from the bullet hole.

I grabbed hold of Dr. Lewis's blue T-shirt. "Will he be okay, Dr. Lewis?" My heart clenched at the possibility of losing Aoki.

His stormy-gray eyes said more than words could. "Aoki was hit by a bullet close to his backbone. We don't know the extent of the damage."

Aoki was in trouble.

"Please save him." I let go of his shirt.

"We'll do everything we can." He walked me to the door, then glanced at my injured arm. "Take care of that. We'll let you know as soon as the surgery is over. And please call me Zachary."

With everything going on, I'd never spoken to him so directly. He was Matt's senior but not by much.

"Zachary! I need you!" Matt's yells echoed across the room.

Zachary tilted his head toward him, then back at me. He raked his ebony hair back and grabbed his nape. "I have to go." He entered the room.

The world spun around me. I stretched my arm and gripped the doorframe to steady myself. *What's wrong with me?*

At that same moment, Davon came out, followed by Mark. He caught me. "Are you okay?"

I held on to him. "Yeah. Just a bit dizzy."

He snaked his arm around my waist and took me down the hall. "Let's go find a doctor. We need to take care of our wounds."

We went through the crowd. Everything was blurred, but I kept going. *This doesn't feel right.*

"Davon!" someone yelled.

Davon stood on his tiptoes and searched for the voice. "C'mon, baby. Dani's down the hall."

Danielle Walters, councilperson of the farming and engineering bunker, was a good friend to Davon. We last saw her before we left Janus Peak almost half a year ago.

I couldn't see a thing as Davon pulled me through the throng of people that was either passing, helping the injured, or calling for a doctor.

When we reached Dani, she was talking through a small device in her ear. "Anyone who knows at least something about medicine will do. There are too many injured and not enough hands." She found us and held up a hand. "Sure, Michael. Thanks." She closed her eyes. "I love you too."

Dani's concern for her partner was palpable.

I hoped science was safe as well as its councilmembers, Jess and Michael.

She tapped her ear, wiped her face with her sleeve, then hugged Davon, making him almost fall over.

Davon flinched.

"Thank God you're safe." She shivered against his chest. "I'm scared. We don't have enough hands. Michael is sending as many people as he can, but it's not enough."

"Everything will be all right." He caressed her long, wavy, dark hair.

With so many injured, we'd have to recruit civilians to help.

After a moment, she released Davon and shook her head. "I'm sorry." She pinched her nose and darted her eyes to me. She opened them wide and held my shoulders. "Abi? What happened?"

She examined my arm, and I winced. "We need to stabilize this." She checked Davon, then grabbed his arm and twisted him, exposing his back. "What the hell happened to you?"

He gestured dismissively. "It's nothing."

"Nothing?" Dani clasped his hand. "Your back is covered in shrapnel!" She searched the area around us. "Follow me."

We went down another hall, then through the doors to her office.

She pulled out two chairs. "Sit."

Davon grimaced as he sat.

"Wait for me here. I'll get someone to help," Dani said.

The moment she closed the door the world turned on itself. Everything came back to me—Tammy's face as she sneered, Maria's mutilated body, Aoki coming in and out of consciousness, Jimmy trapped under the debris, his last words...

My breathing came short and fast. My throat burned, and an anguished sob left me. I couldn't hold it in anymore, and I burst into tears.

Maria... I wouldn't be able to talk to her anymore. To joke around with her and hear her laugh. She'd never pester me again about training or push me to become a stronger woman.

And Jimmy... I'd never feel the warmth of his embrace or hear his gentle voice as he urged me to keep going. To hold on.

All the time lost with him... I'd never get it back.

Davon covered the side of my face and pulled me in.

I cried until I was empty inside, and by the shivers coming from Davon, he was as broken as I was.

We held on to each other until there were no more tears. Then came the emptiness. The unwanted knowledge that we could lose everything. That even at this moment our soldiers were still fighting.

How could we dare to believe we could do it? How could we hope to get our city back when we'd lost so much?

As fast as those thoughts came, I recalled Matt's beaming smile, Davon's loving caresses, and Aoki's uplifting words. I remembered Connor and Deb in that wedding picture and David's bright eyes when we shared a beer. Sarah, who had endured so much suffering but kept pushing forward. There were Rebecca, Peter, Lisa, and Frank, who'd decided to go against all odds to aid us. I thought of Paul and all the others still trapped inside Electi.

Then I saw Jordan. His dark and penetrating aura enveloping all. His smile that concealed so much evil. His eyes that held so much cruelty.

The roaring in my ears was deafening. I could see him sneering as he received news of the attack. Taking his time to plan how he'd assault us next.

I remembered Rebecca and wondered if she had tried to defend us. If she had, there was no telling what Jordan would do to her. He was calculating and vile and would stop at nothing to destroy us all. To hurt Davon.

Davon held me so tight that there wasn't any space between us. We were one. "We have to fight, love. We can't give up. Not now. Not ever. Even if we die in the process, we'll take Promissa back and destroy him. For our family."

Our minds were one. Our goal the only option.

A fire kindled inside of me for all we had lost. I imagined Mom and Dad smiling at me. They didn't speak, but their voices echoed in my soul: *You will fight, and you will win.*

Chapter 3

Davon

April 7, 2214

All the people we'd lost would forever be etched into my mind. Their faces ran like a film, again and again, and at the end, there was always him. His mocking sneer teased us as we took the blow.

Jordan Niles. My own father. The architect of this nightmare.

The last shred of love I had for him had decayed into nothing. The memories I guarded, ones that kept me clinging to hope, had darkened into oblivion, becoming no more than shadows of a man who was no more. I had no father. No love left for that man.

I'm glad he suffered knowing his own son betrayed him. I would've given anything to see him crumbling down at that moment.

Even as the impossibility of winning faced us, I wouldn't back down. We'd fight and welcome death with open arms if it brought our freedom. He'd pay for every single one of the souls he'd taken.

The door squeaked. Dani stopped for a moment as Abi and I came out of our embrace, then entered, Rachel behind her.

Rachel's usual bun was especially disheveled, with her highlighted curls falling to the sides of her face.

"Rachel?" I asked.

She was just with Aoki. What if...?

In two long strides, she reached Abi and put a first aid box in front of her.

She looked at me. "Aoki is still in surgery. Matt told me they had everything under control and asked me to help you guys." She wiped her hands on her blood-spattered jeans, then took gloves out of the kit and put them on. "So here I am."

I exhaled and settled back into my chair, wincing as whatever was on my back dug into me.

Her light-brown eyes traveled between us, and she pushed the kit toward Dani. "Put gloves on, and use clean rags to clean Davon's wounds while I check Abi's arm. Antiseptic will do for now until we get more supplies from science. Don't touch any shrapnel. I'll extirpate them once I'm done with her."

Dani pulled her black hair back into a loose bun, then put the gloves on. "Please sit facing the backrest."

I did as I was told.

She patted my shoulder. "I'll help you remove your shirt."

The fabric stuck to my skin. I suppressed a flinch.

"I'm sorry."

I shook my head. "Don't worry."

Dani tentatively brushed my skin with the rag.

I twisted enough to catch her gaze. "Think of it as a way to get back at me for all the times I drove you crazy."

She gave me a small smile. "How can you make jokes at a time like this?"

I covered her trembling hand. "I'll be all right. Do your worst." I took a deep breath and looked at Abi to get my mind off the burning in my back.

Rachel checked her arm. "It's still set. We just need to immobilize it." Her demeanor shifted for a moment before she turned back to Dani.

"Michael sent in some new sleeves this past week to Janus. It's a new tech. We'll need one for her arm. Did you receive them too?"

"We did."

I flinched as Dani lightly grazed what I would guess was a piece of metal.

She hissed. "Sorry." She stepped away from me. "I did all I could, but there's so much damage." She discarded the bloody rag and her gloves. "I'll fetch the sleeve." She left in a hurry.

"Let's see to your back." Rachel stood behind me. "We risk infection if I don't get this shit out."

"Do you need any help?" Abi sat next to me.

I put my hand on her thigh. I needed her touch. Her warmth. My back was fucked up, and it would hurt like hell.

"Here, hold this for me." Rachel handed Abi a metal tray full of medical instruments.

Abi held it with her right arm.

"This will hurt." Rachel took the pincers. "We'll be here for a while."

I arched my back as she extracted the first piece of shrapnel, and I squeezed Abi's thigh. "Fuck."

I was not sure how much time passed, but it certainly wasn't a stroll through the park. Every piece she extirpated hurt as much as the last one. By the end of it, sweat trickled off my temples, and I clenched my fists to hide my quivering hands.

"Almost done." Rachel stitched another open wound. She'd repeated the process again and again.

"Hey, sorry it took so long. We're almost out of supplies." Dani stood by me.

"I'm almost done," Rachel said.

I frowned as Rachel pulled out one last fragment. The slide of the rag against my skin made me recoil.

She tapped my shoulder. "All done." She took the tray from Abi. "Thanks."

I stood and put on a clean shirt Dani offered.

Rachel set the tray down and wrapped the sleeve around Abi's left arm.

Dani passed her a pack of some bluish liquid, and Rachel connected it to a valve on the top part of the sleeve.

Rachel squeezed, and the liquid filled it. "Stay still for at least five minutes until it hardens. Then you're good to go. This resin will mold to the area and keep it immobile. It's waterproof, so you can continue your regular life. Wear it for a week, then you can start therapy. You'll be fine in no time."

I'd seen similar technologies in Electi. Warmth spread through my chest at the breakthroughs we'd achieved with so little.

"I need to help out there." Rachel made to leave.

I grabbed her arm. "Tell me about Aoki. How grave is it?"

Rachel pressed her lips together. "As I said, Matt was still operating when I left." She shook her head. "They're doing their best."

Dani scrunched her eyebrows. Her dark eyes held my stare. "What happened to Aoki?"

"I'm sorry. I have to go." Rachel left the room.

I took Dani's hands in mine. She was Aoki's friend too. "Aoki was shot. It's his back."

Dani took a step back, her hands trembling.

Abi grabbed my hand.

I squeezed it, and after a deep breath, I let the words out. "Matt fears the bullet struck his spinal column." The pain that hit my chest was unbearable. A rising ache filled me to the core. The risks of such an injury were abysmal.

"But..." Dani blinked. "Does that mean...?"

I shook my head. "We still don't know. It depends on where the bullet hit and whether it got to the cord or not. Matt and Zachary are doing what they can."

God. I pressed my hands against my eyes.

Abi hugged me, and I succumbed to her hold. I interlaced my fingers through her curls and covered her waist with my other arm, pulling her close.

"If anyone can help Aoki, it's Matt. I'm sure he'll do everything he can to save him." Abi stroked my hair.

I let out a pent-up breath. "Thank you." I nuzzled her neck, then kissed it before letting go.

Dani touched my arm. "I need to continue dealing with the emergency, but please let me know how the surgery goes." Her eyes were filled with pain and doubt.

"I will."

I was about to follow Dani out when Abi grabbed my arm. I faced her.

She bit her lip. "Davon, when Aoki woke, I remember he said his whole body hurt. Isn't that a good sign?"

Even in the darkest moments, her hope never faltered. My chest swelled at the woman who'd given me her heart and taught me day by day to walk in the light.

I brushed my thumb over the corner of her lip, lifted her chin, and smiled. "I think so."

Her face brightened, and she leaned into my touch, then followed me out. The hall was even more crowded than before.

Abi ran ahead of me. "Abraham?"

Mr. Jackson was crouched in front of Nina, holding a bloody gauze to her temple. He was bleeding from several places too but seemed okay.

"Abigail!" He stood and hugged her.

Warmth traveled through my veins as he held her like a father would his daughter. I was so thankful she'd found him. Someone who could remind her that all was not lost. That Jacob's memory lived on.

Abraham cupped her cheeks. "Thank God you're okay." He darted his eyes to me. "Thanks for keeping her safe."

I nodded. "Always."

I had met Mr. Jackson many times but never as Jacob's father. Jacob's execution had turned Abi's life upside down. To lose the man she loved, to watch as they killed him had marked her deeply.

I looked at Nina, then back at him. "Are you both all right?"

"We're okay." Nina removed the gauze. She had a large slash on the side of her forehead. She folded the cloth over itself and pushed it against the wound.

"We got attacked by an NWG soldier on our way out. She hit Nina's head and then tried to stab me." Abraham pulled his sleeve down and covered his bloody arm.

Abi grabbed it. "This is deep, Abraham. It needs sutures."

He squeezed her hand. "It's no big deal."

"It is." Abi went to Nina. "And you?"

Nina showed Abi her cut, but it wasn't as deep as Abraham's.

Abi looked around and waved at a citizen who held a first aid case. "Hey! Can you lend me that?" She took what she needed and cleaned the wound.

I held Abraham's arm while she sutured it.

Abi was in her element, and my heart swelled at watching her. She was so much stronger than the woman I met in the outskirts.

I jumped as someone tapped my back.

"Davon, Abi, Connor wants to show you something." Steven captured our attention.

Abi raised an eyebrow. "I'm almost done." She cut the string with her teeth.

"Thank you," Abraham said.

Abi smiled.

She cleaned Nina's wound and came to my side. "Do you know why he wants us?"

Steven swallowed hard. "It's better if you see it for yourself."

My heart skipped a beat. For Connor to summon us at a moment like this meant it was urgent. But what could it be?

We followed Steven down a corridor. After passing through a huge room that was being used as a makeshift hospital ward, we crossed through double doors and came into another hall. We went into the first room on our right.

Connor stood in front of a computer screen, arms crossed.

There was a huge computer monitor on the wall opposite the entrance, with a sofa to the right and a door I could only think was a bathroom to the left. A table sat in the middle. The room looked like a resting or entertainment area of some sort.

The moment we stepped inside his pained gaze met us. "I'm sorry, but there's something you both need to see."

We stood with him in front of the screen. My email account was open with a message from my father. My blood chilled at the subject line: *To my dear son, Davon, and my daughter, Abigail.*

Abi's breaths came hard and fast.

I grabbed her hand and continued reading.

Hello, Abigail. How did you like the surprise? Did you truly believe I didn't know your true intentions? Did you think I was stupid enough to not know what was happening in front of my eyes?

My arms trembled, and I clenched my fists in an attempt to hide it. My muscles tightened.

Did he always know?

Abi's face turned ashen.

When you told me about Deborah Davis being the leader of the rebellion, I dug deeper into her family history, and, alas, I found her younger sister's file. The resemblance you shared with her sister was uncanny, but I gave you the benefit of the doubt.

The puzzle pieces started to align during the meeting we had about the spy. I'll never forget your glazed eyes and how you fought to keep a strong countenance. I can still taste your fear, and it was so very sweet.

My bodyguards followed you after that meeting, and to my surprise, they saw you with someone in the lobby.

Abi squeezed my hand. "Uncle Scott."

I was curious about your encounter and asked for Bayat. When she came to my office a week later, she told me about your conversation with your dear uncle, confirming my suspicions. Gabrielle Jones was a spy, and her real name was Abigail Davis. Rest assured, my dear Abigail, your uncle is staying in a very comfortable place at the moment. He's doing quite well.

I tensed. He had him.

I glanced down at Abi.

Her lips quivered, and I swallowed hard to keep up a front. She needed me to be strong, but this was beyond twisted. I could have lost her.

Do you have any idea of the control I had to muster to not grab your little neck and squeeze the life out of you? But after thinking it over, I decided to play along. After all, you went through so much trouble getting here. What harm would it do to keep it up so I'd find out who was helping you?

I suspected you were working with Matt since he hates my guts, but I still needed to know if Davon was part of your scheme.

Son, you proved yourself again and again, so I thought you were blind to what was happening. After all, how could my own blood betray me?

I planned to call you both in for a meeting tomorrow and reveal the true face of Gabrielle. My guards were ordered to arrest her the moment she stepped out of my office.

I only needed a couple of hours, but everything went to hell.

Your mother was with me the moment I got the call. When I found out you had betrayed me, the strangest thing happened. She said you were only trying to help Promissa. That I needed to understand. Then she pleaded for your life.

Imagine my surprise at finding that not only my son but also my wife betrayed me. The two people I loved most in this world. The only ones I trusted were playing me all along. But rest assured, you'll both think twice before messing with me again.

The pounding of my heart reached my ears. *Mom.*

I let out a guttural roar. I grabbed the first thing I found and hurled it across the room. I saw red as I lunged for the monitor.

Connor grabbed me from behind.

I elbowed his stomach, but he kept me restrained. I threw my head back and made contact, but he locked his arms around my neck in a choke hold.

He squeezed, and my vision blurred. "You either calm the fuck down, or I will make you. You'll gain nothing from losing your shit."

I fought his hold until I saw Abi. She was in a corner, Steven guarding her. Her wide eyes and trembling chin made me pause.

Everything came into focus as the rush of adrenaline dropped. The room was askew, as if a tornado had gone through it. Papers and equipment were scattered all across the floor.

I furrowed my brow. Had I done all this?

I closed my eyes and breathed deeply. If my father harmed my mother, it would be the end of him.

Connor let me go.

I opened my eyes to Abi's tender touch. To her beautiful face. She hugged me until my breathing became stable.

Abi brushed her fingers through my hair in an intimate caress. "She'll be all right. He won't harm her."

I caught her hand and kissed her palm. "Sorry for scaring you, love."

She shook her head. "It's okay."

I cupped her face with both hands. "It's not. I'm sorry."

I leaned into her, letting my brow touch hers as we both breathed together.

"There's more."

We shifted our gazes toward Connor and faced the monitor.

I knew Ms. Gibson would follow through. After all, she had the best teacher. After I got her message, I sent out my troops, followed by the enhanced army, to the coordinates she gave. There was no better punishment than to destroy your home.

What you did to me, son, I will never forgive. I'll see you lose all you've built with those traitors, and I'll enjoy every minute of it, every loss you suffer, every death of each of your precious rebel friends. Then I will hunt you down and catch you both. I will break you until there's nothing left of your previous selves. I've told you before and am telling you again. No one opposes me and lives to see through it.

Welcome to my little game.

Love,

Jordan

Abi covered her mouth. "I'm going to be sick."

I grabbed her and followed Steven as he pointed to the adjoining room.

"Come on." I rushed her inside and held her hair back as she retched.

I helped her up. She searched the sink cabinet, found mouthwash, and rinsed her mouth. She soaped her face, then splashed water all over it. After closing the faucet, she stayed bent over, breathing hard for a moment before gazing at her reflection.

The circles under her eyes evidenced the heaviness of the last couple of hours.

I passed her a towel. "Are you better now?"

She nodded through her reflection, and I put my arms around her. She turned and cuddled into my neck. We stayed there for a long time until our tremulous minds quieted.

I thought about our family back in Electi and about the rebels still giving their all out there.

There was no turning back now.

Chapter 4

Abi

April 7, 2214

Jordan's words sank in as we basked in the silence of our own little world. He could have taken me at any moment.

Davon's fears were real, and I was so full of myself that I thought I was smarter than Jordan. I was so close to getting caught. A day away from losing it all and never again seeing the light of day. Now we were blind again, unknowing of his next move.

What would he do to Uncle Scott? To Rebecca? What if he knew about Lisa, Frank, or Peter? How many lives had we put in danger because of our mission? I shivered at the thought.

Davon held my chin up and searched my eyes. "Are you sure you're all right?"

My heart melted. This man, even after reading that message, worried about me first.

I moved my thumb over his chapped lips, then grabbed his nape and pulled him to me.

Our mouths met, and my mind calmed at the intimate touch. He deepened the kiss, and I pushed myself against him.

We stumbled back against the wall.

He gripped my hair and tilted my head back, tasting the sensitive flesh beneath my ear. He nipped at my neck, and goosebumps rose all over the left side of my body.

I grew feverish at his intimate touch. He was so strong yet so gentle.

Ever so slowly, he moved his right hand down my chest, his left holding me by the nape. "I will kill him before I let him touch you." Rage swirled behind his dark irises.

His ominous tone stirred something deep inside me. A knowledge that he'd always be there to protect me. That he'd destroy anyone who dared harm me and would make Jordan pay for all he'd done.

It wasn't an empty threat. It was a fact. And even as it awakened my need for revenge, I couldn't ignore the reality that part of the person Davon was today came from the love and education Jordan had given him as a child.

I remembered the moments I lived next to Jordan when he welcomed me into his family. The laughter during meals. The caring manner in which he talked to me. The glimpses of Davon I sometimes caught through his eyes.

Jordan was a dichotomy and a dangerous one.

Davon's thundering heart beat against my ear as he clutched me to his chest. I prayed he wouldn't have to be the one to end Jordan because no matter what he'd done, he was still his father.

Someone knocked on the door.

"Abi, Davon, it's about Aoki," Steven said.

Our hands reached the door handle at the same time, and Davon let me open it.

Connor stood beside Steven. "Aoki made it through the surgery."

I looked to the heavens. *Thank God*.

"Do they know if...?" Davon said.

A chair screeched behind Connor, and I caught a glimpse of Deb. She sat in front of the monitor, but her gaze was fixed on Davon. She gripped the chair handles.

When did she get here?

"She shouldn't be here," I murmured.

Davon shuffled back. "I should go."

"Stay." Connor held his hand up and turned to Deb. "You okay?"

She paused for a second, then nodded.

There was movement beside her, and a huge dog came to her side. It looked like a wolf but smaller. Its fur was white with blond patches, and an ethereal blue painted its eyes.

Deb petted it and exhaled slowly.

With a sigh, Connor turned back to me. "She brought the news about Aoki, and when I told her you were here, she stayed. Zachary should be here soon to check on her. She hasn't been sleeping well."

Deb had shadows under her eyes, and blood smeared her uniform.

I squeezed Davon's arm. "Be back in a sec."

Davon kissed my brow. "Okay."

Deb pulled me into her arms. "I can't believe you're really here. I missed you."

Her hair smelled like lavender, and her warmth eased my tormented soul. I took a step back to look at her, then played with one of her curls, like I did when I was a child. Her eyes shone. She was radiant.

"Three years lost to me. You've grown." She cupped my face.

"There's so much I want to tell you." I looked at her womb, then glanced up and swallowed hard.

She smiled. Laugh lines were etched around her eyes. "We're doing all right. He's due anytime."

I touched her womb. "How about you?"

She glanced at Davon. "I still have a long way to go." She scrunched her eyes with her fingers and shook her head.

I jumped as the dog licked my hand.

Deb chuckled. "This is Aspen, my service dog. She's a sweetheart and helps me calm down."

I petted her chin, and her tail wagged happily. "She's pretty."

Deb rubbed Aspen's ears. "I'm glad Aoki is out of danger."

I twisted toward the guys, who were deep in conversation. "Yeah, but Davon told me about his injury, and I worry about permanent damage."

Deb tensed. Was it because of Davon or Aoki?

I looked back to find Davon's eyes on us.

Connor stopped talking and nodded at Deb.

She bowed her head back.

Connor said something to Davon, and they came to us.

I stepped aside.

"Deb?" Davon's voice was low and unsure. "How are you?"

Deb took a shaky breath.

Connor held her hand.

She closed her eyes for a second before settling them back on Davon. "I'm taking it one day at a time."

Davon reached out to her, then pulled back.

I seized his hand.

He was lost on the verge of tears. "I don't know what to say. I'm just...so sorry."

Deb's chin quivered, and she dropped her head and held it with both hands. Her breaths came hard, ragged.

I inched toward her. "Deb?"

She pushed me away and launched herself at Davon.

Connor caught her just in time.

"You're sorry?" She bared her teeth, struggling against Connor's hold. "You're fucking sorry?"

Aspen was by her side, growling at Davon.

Steven grabbed the dog by its collar, keeping her at bay, then hurried out.

Davon moved farther back.

Deb's chest heaved. "I should have killed you. I should have ended you that night." She snarled, her face tight.

It was as if another person had taken control of Deb's body.

I stepped between them.

"Abi!" Davon reached for me.

Deb recoiled in Connor's arms, then darted her eyes between us. They swelled with tears. "How can you be with him? He's a monster, just like his father."

My throat tightened. "I'm so sorry, Deb. But he's not your enemy. Everything he did was to get you out. He didn't have a choice."

She sneered. "He broke me, Abi! He fucking broke me!" Her wails reverberated across the room.

My heart shattered for her. For Davon. How could we move forward from this?

She fought Connor's hold. "I'll never forgive you, Davon. Never!"

Davon stood in silence, staring at the floor. His shoulders curled over his chest.

Hope of fixing things slithered away from me. Whatever happened in that prison had marked them both, and neither seemed able to push through.

Zachary rushed into the room, followed by Steven.

Sarah bolted inside after them. Her hair was matted with blood.

Zachary plunged a syringe into Deb's upper arm.

Connor held her until her breathing slowed and her body slumped. He laid her on the sofa.

I walked toward them. "Will she be okay?"

Zachary checked her vitals. "She and the baby are fine. I gave her a mild sedative. She'll be up in a few minutes."

Sarah embraced me. "Thank God you're back. I was looking for you, but others needed me." She glanced at Deb, then Connor. "What happened?"

Connor raked his hair back. "I thought she was ready. We talked about it."

Zachary furrowed his brow. "About what?"

"About her meeting Davon," Connor said.

Sarah crouched beside Deb and brushed her hair back. She gave Connor a pinched look. "What the hell were you thinking?"

"Sarah." Connor creased his brow. His tone was stern.

She shook her head. "I'm sorry. It's just—"

"It was a decision we both made," Connor said.

She looked at me, then at Davon. "The wound is still too fresh. We've been working on her accepting you two are together, but to have Davon meet her... She's not ready for that. I don't know if she'll ever be."

My stomach plummeted at the certainty of her words. "But we must try."

Sarah softened her gaze. "You wouldn't understand."

I bit my lip and moved to her side. "Then tell me. Make me see."

"Come on. Let's give them some privacy." Connor gestured for Davon to follow him out.

Zachary and Steven left too.

I'd need a whole journal to express my emotions at this moment. How many times had the hope of seeing my sisters saved me when I was alone and at the point of giving up? To be here with them in the flesh seemed surreal.

I'd give anything for this reunion to be a happy one, but this was our life now. Joyful moments were scarce. And this was not one of them.

Sarah faced me. "Do you have any idea what she went through when she was inside that prison?"

Silence. That's all I could offer my sister because, in truth, I never asked for the details. Not even once.

I imagined different scenarios but never could see Davon hurting Deb in my mind. It was an impossible task and one I didn't want to confront.

She jerked her face toward Deb. "Look at her nose."

It had a bump it didn't have before.

"That's from when Davon broke it." Sarah took Deb's left hand—her pinky finger was gone. "He cut off her finger, and after that, since she wouldn't speak, he waterboarded her. She almost died that night."

I covered my mouth as nausea overtook me.

She grabbed Deb's other hand. "When she got here, all her nails were gone from this hand." She shook her head. "She even has some missing molars. I couldn't count the bruises on her body nor her scars."

I trembled.

She had pink spaces on her arms where skin was growing back, burns on her arms that appeared blotched, and in the right corner of her chest, a mark was burned into her skin: the crowned silver snake with the acronym NWG. We were like cattle to them, their property.

She stood and showed me the same spot on her chest. "That wasn't Davon. They mark all the prisoners." She took my hand in hers. "Abi, what happened in there was a nightmare and more so because her best friend, her own brother, did it to her. Her scars are not only those we can see, but most are rooted deep within her in the dark recesses of her mind. To move on from that is almost impossible, and no matter how much we try to tell her it was for the mission, she can't seem to grasp it. For Deb, Davon is a monster, and she can't assimilate his old self with the evil counterpart she met out there."

This was why Davon believed there was no redemption for him. Why he told me he'd never be able to atone for what he'd done. His father had made him into a beast, and at last I understood what he tried to convey so many times. That no matter how much he tried to make up for his sins, he'd never forgive himself.

How could I ask Deb to push it away and accept him back into her life?

Sarah stepped closer to me, her head slightly tilted, trying to catch my gaze. "That's not the worst part. The only reason she held on was for her baby. Imagine her shock when she found out who the father was. She didn't talk for a week after Connor told her, then one day she said she'd keep it." She faced Deb for a second. "I don't know what will happen when he's born. When she's actually holding Jordan Niles's son in her arms." Her green eyes met mine. "How do you think she'll react?"

She'd lose it.

Deb's pregnancy was part of what Jordan Niles called the Prometheus Project. It was a genetic enhancement program with the objective to create a super race that would dominate others with two goals in mind—to purge the Promissa citizens from the face of the earth and to dominate the rest of the continent. Deb was impregnated without her consent while she was in prison along with others. Their babies grew at an accelerated rate, and at only four months of pregnancy, Davon's baby brother was about to be born.

Deb stirred.

I crouched next to her. "Hey."

Deb shook her head and forced her eyes shut before opening them again. She sat up, holding her head. "It hurts."

I ran my thumb over her hand.

Deb squished her eyebrows. "Sarah?"

Sarah sat by her feet. "I'm here. Zachary gave you some medicine so you'd calm down."

Deb glanced around and rubbed her brow. "What happened?"

A huge weight pressed against my chest. What did she mean?

I frowned. "Don't you remember?"

Deb blinked slowly. "What do you mean?"

Sarah avoided my gaze.

The room suddenly seemed smaller. What was wrong with her?

"You attacked Davon," I said.

Deb bolted off the sofa. "Did I hurt him?"

"No. He's okay." The pressure that had grown inside of me eased as I came to the realization that Deb *did* care about him. There was hope.

She held my hands. "I'm sorry. I thought I was ready."

Sarah came to Deb's side. "There's nothing to be sorry about. It's expected. You should have asked us before meeting him. You weren't ready."

"I just hoped…" She closed her eyes and covered her face. "Why can't I remember?"

"I told you already. It's called dissociation. It's a natural response." Sarah stroked Deb's back.

"So I'm crazy." Deb shrugged her off. "What happens if I kill him one day? What kind of life will I have after murdering my best friend? After losing my sister?"

It couldn't be that bad. Could it? She'd never… My thoughts wandered to that night when I almost lost Davon to her attack.

I shook my head. "That's not going to happen."

"For God's sake, Abi. I almost killed him once and now this." Deb paced, then grabbed her hair and grunted. "This is so frustrating. I want to move forward. I do. I just…" Her watery gaze moved between us. "So much happened in that room."

I hugged her, and Sarah pulled us into her embrace.

What a bittersweet reunion.

I swallowed my pain and buried the wrath that had taken root inside of me. We were each broken in our own way, but I'd make it right. My family would be whole again.

Deb's sobs subsided. "I'm so sorry about everything. I'll keep trying."

I hugged her tight. "The important thing is we're back together."

No matter how long it took, I'd be there for her. I'd help her move forward.

She took our hands. "I can't believe we're together at last." Her eyes glowed. "The only one missing is Jimmy. He helped me so much when I got back."

Sarah wrinkled her brow. "It's weird. I haven't seen him." She turned to me. "I thought he'd be with you for sure. He was so anxious to see you." She scrubbed a hand over her face and stared at her feet. "Last time I saw him, we were all in command. Maria left to get Tammy but hadn't returned, so he went after her." Her hands shook, and she put them inside her pockets. "I tried to stop him. I did. But the place was in chaos."

They didn't know. Jimmy…

"Jimmy didn't…" The words got stuck in my throat.

Two walls crushed my chest. How could I tell them? What if Deb lost it again?

Sarah grabbed me. "Didn't what? Did something happen to him?"

I gasped at the strength of her hold.

Deb patted her shoulder. "Give her some space."

Sarah took two long breaths, then let go.

Deb brushed my arm. "Are you okay?"

I tried to breathe, but I choked.

Not now.

"What's wrong?" Deb's voice shook.

"I think she's having a panic attack. Help me get her to the sofa." Sarah's voice was distant.

Everything was hazy.

"Stay with her."

"Breathe with me. I'm here." Deb's mellow voice reached me over the violent pounding of my heart.

I pressed a palm against my chest, but everything went out of focus.

It hurt! Was I dying?

"Come with me, honey." A huge shadow stood over Deb.

"But what about Abi?" Deb's pleading voice was like a murmur as she walked away.

I squeezed my eyes shut.

Jimmy's dead. He died, and I left him there. Like Jacob.

Warmth wrapped around me. "Come here, love."

I opened my eyes.

Davon's musky scent enveloped me as he gathered me into his arms. "Breathe."

"Give her this." Matt passed something to him.

Davon pushed a pill into my mouth, then held a cup to my lips.

I drank.

Davon rocked me gently. "What happened?" He looked at Matt and Sarah.

Sarah slouched. "It's my fault." She wouldn't meet Davon's gaze. "Abi was calm until I asked about Jimmy."

Matt rubbed his neck. "God." He gestured toward the door. "Come with me. We need to talk." He glanced back at Davon. "I'll lock the door so no one bothers you."

Davon nodded. When they left, he cradled me against his chest. "How can I fix this?" A strangled sob followed. "It's all fucked up."

I lost track of time as a hollowness grew inside me and my body went numb.

I needed to move on. But how?

Chapter 5

Davon

April 7, 2214

Abi's body sagged on top of mine. Her breathing had calmed a while back, and now she slept.

We were on the floor. I clenched my jaw at my fucking uselessness. At the lack of control I had over this situation. This had been her worst panic attack yet, and I couldn't do much else but hold her.

To see her this lost crumbled the last of my reserves. How could I protect her from her own mind?

Then there was Deb. Her words hurt worse than the stab she gave me the night I helped her escape. The trust and friendship we held for a decade was wrenched from me the moment I agreed to this mission, and getting it back seemed like trying to keep a sinking boat afloat. Like I was drowning in a dark sea and there was no light to guide me to the surface. Deb taught me to fight for what was right. She was not only my sister but my mentor, and now I'd lost her, and I might never be able to get her back.

It was midafternoon when Abi stirred. She opened her eyes and sat up. "Shit." She covered her face. "I'm sorry."

"There's nothing to be sorry about, love. It's..." I shook my head. "I wish I could turn back time and save them." I ran a hand down her back.

"Sarah asked me about Jimmy. My head went back to the bunker, and then it hit me." Her hazel eyes locked on me. "I'll never see him again or Maria."

My throat hurt, but I pushed back my tears.

Maria didn't deserve that death. To be killed by the one you love. I couldn't imagine the hurt. The pain she went through during those last moments.

And Jimmy...

I shoved down the urge to scream at the injustice of it all. Leslie would pay for every single life she had taken from the rebellion.

I brushed the back of my hand against Abi's cheek, and she leaned into it.

"I lost so much time being mad at him. I should have forgiven him earlier." Her eyes flooded with tears, but she wiped them away with her shirt. "Now it's too late."

"Don't torture yourself with what-ifs. Tammy's the one who killed him. You couldn't have known." I massaged her neck.

She stiffened.

I stilled. "What is it?"

"It's not. I can't..." She ran a hand through her hair, then grabbed her nape. "Sarah told me about Deb. The state she was in when she arrived."

Fuck. My stomach sank at her words. She knew it was bad, but to actually see it was another thing. What I did in that room sickened me.

Her gaze traveled fast across my features, almost like the night we met. "I know it was part of the mission, but what you did to her..." She dropped her head and closed her eyes. "Sarah said you almost killed her."

I planned to tell Abi so many times, but I was a coward. Terrified she'd leave me.

How could she not? After all, Deb was her sister, and I was the son of her sworn enemy.

I withdrew my hand. My heart was about to pop out of my chest.

I destroyed Deb to appease my father's twisted games. To get intel she'd never provide and convince him to trust me.

Sure, I helped her flee the prison. I finished the mission. But to what end?

She was damaged beyond repair. Abused not just physically but mentally. Not only that, but she was carrying my baby brother. A pregnancy she didn't ask for but had accepted. That was the kind of woman Deb was. She'd always protect the innocent even if it killed her inside.

Abi scurried off me and hugged her knees.

I curled my shoulders and looked down. "I should've told you what went on in there."

An eerie silence settled between us.

A lump formed in my throat.

She wouldn't look at me.

There was nothing else to do. She deserved an explanation.

"Every time I had to torture someone, I escaped into a dark place and did what was asked. I learned to dissociate myself from my actions a long time ago. It was the only way to satisfy his demands."

I swallowed hard. "Sometimes I'd only accept what I'd done after the session was over, when I rubbed off the blood, or when I scrubbed my tools. Other times I pushed everything to the back of my mind and kept going as if nothing had happened, only to have my victims join me in my nightmares."

I interlaced my fingers. Nausea assaulted me at the memories of the first man I'd killed. My father made me take off all his nails and skin his left arm.

Father talked me through it, but I made a mess. "You'll learn with time, son. This is what you're meant to be. Feared by all."

I beat the man to death with a bat afterward, swallowing the urge to cry. To retch at the thudding sound of his flesh as the bat connected. At the snapping of his bones when they broke. I hid my emotions and continued without pause. He was long dead when my father took the bat from me. I hadn't even noticed when it happened.

My father sneered at the butchered corpse, then put an arm around me. "Well done, son. You've made me proud."

I was only sixteen.

I took a shuddering breath. "I've killed countless rebels just to keep my cover. Some were my friends. Images of their abused bodies and empty eyes still haunt me."

I glanced up.

Abi was silent. Her attention rapt on me. Her gaze soft.

"Every time I entered that room, I put away the Davon you know and brought out the devil Father raised. The difference was that with Deb, I couldn't disconnect. I had to know when to stop so I wouldn't kill her or her child. I was there the whole time. I remember it all."

I stood and turned away from Abi.

My gut wrenched. I could still see her pleading eyes. Hear her anguished screams. They echoed in my mind continually.

I covered my ears and let out a guttural roar, then punched the desk. The pain from my knuckles was a good reprieve from the agony that burned inside me.

Abi wrapped her arms around me, and I gasped at her warmth.

A sharp pain hit my chest. I wept for all the lost souls. For all the people I'd broken. For the suffering I was putting Abi through. For the light I extinguished inside Deb.

There was no absolution. No way in hell I'd ever forgive myself. There was only darkness and pain, a void I'd never be able to fill again.

Abi moved around me and cupped my face. She didn't utter a word as she drew me in.

I closed my eyes against her neck.

She brushed my hair, holding me close. "We'll figure this out."

I shook my head. "Deb needs you now." It was hard to breathe, but I'd made up my mind. "I'm leaving."

She took a step back, her arm hanging loose by her side. "What do you mean?" Her chin quivered.

I stepped into her. "Your sister needs you, and I don't think my presence helps. I talked to Connor about it. I'm going with him to science. Our scouts just came in. Seth and Katherine managed to bait the troops west as planned, but hundreds of enhanced soldiers stayed behind. We need to make sure we're safe."

"But..." She blinked. "You'll be back, right?"

I sighed. My soul screamed for me to stay. "As soon as we deal with the problem."

She gripped my shirt. "I can go with you. I can fight."

Her pleading voice was breaking through my defenses.

I covered her sleeved arm. "You're in no condition. You need time to heal."

"But..." Her voice broke.

I embraced her and kissed the top of her head. "You have your sisters. David too. You're not alone. Deb needs you. I'm trying to do something for you."

"By leaving me?" She scoffed and turned away.

I pulled her to me. "Don't you think for even a second that this isn't killing me too. Deb and you need time to heal, and I need to go out there and kill the bastards who did this. They murdered our friends." I shook my head. "I can't just stay here with my arms crossed."

She tried to put distance between us, but I caught her chin and kissed her. It was not a gentle kiss.

We were breathing hard by the end. Her eyes seemed lighter than usual, with a yellowish hue spreading away from her irises.

"I'll be back in no time. Please. I'm doing this for you."

"You say that, but I know there's something more." Her voice trembled.

I shifted in place. "You need time to think about what you need right now. You've been hanging on to the promise you made to me, but now that you know what I'm truly capable of, I want to give you a chance to decide."

She squished her eyebrows. "To decide what?"

I clenched my fists to hide my shaking limbs. "If you want to stay with me or not."

She shuffled back a step. "What the fuck are you talking about?"

I reached out to her, but she slapped my hand away.

I pocketed my hands. "You've been holding on to me because of that promise. How can you be with me after all I did? You need this."

Abi closed the space between us, merely inches from my face. "Who do you think you are to tell me what I need or don't need?" She grabbed my waist. "I fucking need you. Flaws and strengths. All of you. Only you. I love you."

I looked down. "I..." My chest was cleaved in two by her words. *How can she love a man like me?*

"Look at me." She stroked my stubble. "You can leave now, but that won't change a thing. I'm not with you because of a promise. You're the man I love. My everything. And no matter what happened out there, my feelings won't change. We'll work through this."

I didn't deserve her.

I touched my brow to hers. "This is for the best. Fix things with Deb, then we'll figure things out."

She gave me a soft smile. "There's nothing to figure out." She wrapped her hand behind my back and pulled me flush against her. "Please stop doing this to yourself. You're the most caring man I know. You've given your all for this community."

I was on the verge of tears. "I can't, Abi."

"You can't what?"

I shook my head and breathed in her comforting scent. "I can't go on without at least giving you this chance."

She sighed, then stepped back and put a hand over my heart. "Then do this for me. Take this time to work on yourself and accept that all you've been through is part of who you are. I need you to be the man I fell in love with. To own what you did for the rebellion and pull through. I already accepted it. I love you whole." She slowly lowered her hand to my abdomen. "I'll be waiting for you. Loving you just as I do now." Her touch turned my skin to fire.

I took in a shuddering breath. "What are you doing?" My voice was raspy.

"Making sure you don't forget how much I love you." Her hand snaked down until... "All of you," she whispered against my ear.

Her touch ignited every single inch of my body.

I gasped. "You have no idea what you do to me."

Her eyes shone with desire. "Show me."

I grabbed her and picked her up.

She wrapped her legs around me.

Our tongues clashed in a rough kiss. Tasting. Devouring.

I couldn't take it anymore and backed her up against a wall.

I pressed my body against her, letting her feel what she did to me.

Abi moaned, and I clasped her breast and squeezed.

She let her head fall back as I nipped her neck, then licked her flushed skin, savoring every inch of my way back to her luscious mouth.

She whimpered against me.

I kissed her deeply and unwrapped her legs from my waist. I unbuttoned her pants and slipped my hand in.

"Wait. What if someone enters?" She was breathless, her desire running through my fingers.

"Don't worry. The door is locked." I rubbed my hand against her center, making her writhe.

She buckled against me.

I drowned her cry with my mouth and held her as she came undone.

I couldn't get enough of her.

Hanging by my last shred of control, I stepped away just enough to pull her pants off.

The moment I unbuttoned mine, she stroked me, sending a rippling current down my body.

"Take me." Her sultry voice was my undoing.

I grabbed one of her legs and pulled her up. "Are you ready?"

She kissed me. "Always."

I sank into her. I was home.

My body ached with need as I thrust into her soft center.

Abi's moans drove me wild. She was my everything.

"Harder!" she pleaded.

I conceded, slamming wildly into her.

If there was a heaven, this had to be it.

Our bodies joined in the most desperate way. The sound of our lovemaking echoed around the room. It was perfect.

I increased my rhythm, and in only seconds, her walls tightened around me.

"Davon!" She gasped.

Pleasure built within me. It spread like lightning, and my whole body quivered with need. I couldn't hold back anymore.

I grabbed her flush against me until my muscles stiffened, and then I let go. "Fuck!"

My body shuddered against her, and I came hard, pushing into her, again and again, until I was empty, exhausted, and *complete*.

In that moment, there was no war. No deaths. Nothing to fix.

Only us and our love.

"I love you," she mumbled against my chest.

I nuzzled her neck. "I love you too."

The farming and engineering bunker would serve as the command center for the People's Revolutionary Front until everyone was moved to the caverns as planned. We'd keep ourselves hidden, and soldiers would be positioned around the mountains to take down any drone that managed to enter the area. We couldn't risk the enemy finding our location.

It would take time to recover from the NWG's attack, time we didn't have. Father would make sure of it.

They'd made a storage room into the new headquarters.

Nina sat in front of multiple monitors, her desk set in a corner next to the conference room.

Mark was sending off runners to scout the area. Other soldiers were dispatched to aid in eliminating what was left of the NWG forces in the periphery of Janus Peak.

The transfer to the caverns would start soon, led by Councilmember Faez, who, after losing the energy bunker, was put in charge of that operation. The move would start with the children and citizens who were in good shape. For the others, farming would act as a makeshift hospital, and citizens would travel north in groups once their health was stable.

The conference room was full of high-ranked soldiers. Connor presided over the meeting to my right, Corporal Mathews opposite. Mark sat by my side.

Faez, Steven, and Dani were also here.

Connor put his palms on the table. "During our leave, Captain Mark Ito will serve as temporary general of the PRF, with Deborah by his side." He looked at Mark. "We'll have an assembly after this meeting. Sarah is already gathering everyone. People need to know what happened."

So that's why Sarah wasn't here.

Matt was also missing.

When I left Abi with Deb at the infirmary, Connor and I visited him. He explained that Aoki received damage to his spinal column but that the cord was not severed. He appeared in his element, but I worried. It was not like him to be this calm, more so after almost losing Aoki. I needed to go see him later. Alone.

Connor ordered Matt to stay here and help Mark, but we all knew it was to give him time to be with his husband. He couldn't fight without knowing how Aoki would fare.

Nina brought in a cup of water and set it in front of Connor. Next to it, she left a note.

He sipped from the cup, then read the note. He furrowed his brow and nodded to her.

Nina sat next to Mathews.

"Most of you are aware that Leslie Gibson, code name Tammy McGregor, gave away our location." Connor took a cleansing breath. "She killed General Maria Diaz and, before leaving the bunker, tossed a grenade inside, causing Jimmy Thompson's death."

There was a moment of silence before he continued. "We lost hundreds who fought so our people could escape. Each of them died as heroes, and we stand here thanks to them. Many are still fighting out there. Once this situation is under control, at least for the time being, we'll have a memorial to honor them."

Connor stretched his hand toward Nina.

She passed him a tablet.

He showed us the screen. "This is what we're dealing with."

The silence that overtook the room was eerie. The video was from one of our drones. Hundreds of enhanced soldiers made their way through the forest, killing everything in their path. Death was everywhere. Countless bodies lay on the ground. Their blood smeared the snow beneath them.

I covered my mouth with my fist.

Corporal Mathews clenched his hands over the edge of the table.

It was a massacre.

"We just received intel that Major General Yuxuan Li and his soldiers bombarded the area around Janus Peak, forcing the NWG forces west."

I widened my eyes. This must have been what the note was about.

Connor passed the tablet back to Nina. "Katherine and Seth baited the soldiers west, and with Yuxuan guarding the back, I'm sure our plan will work."

"What's the plan?" Mathews asked.

"To give them import. By now, the civilians must be on their way to science via our transport routes. Davon and I are going out to aid them and to kill any enhanced soldier troops that stayed behind. We need to buy enough time to move our people to science."

"Is there room for one more on your team?" Mathews lifted an eyebrow.

Connor dipped his chin. "Of course, you're welcome to join us."

Mathews nodded.

Mark cleared his throat. "With all due respect, we all know about Davon's mission, but what will we tell the citizens? Everyone has stayed quiet because of your orders, but people have many questions."

Everyone turned their gazes to me.

Connor pushed his shoulders back. "We'll tell everyone the truth—that he infiltrated the government on my orders to catch the spy. That thanks to him we saved the people of energy, saved Deb, and found out who the spy was."

"And what about the other spy?" I asked.

Connor lowered his head, then gazed at each of us. "There's nothing to do. Protecting our people is the priority, so we'll keep our eyes open, our senses sharp, and hope to hell they left Janus Peak with Leslie. Because if the enemy is still with us, we may lose it all."

It was nighttime when I went to see Matt.

Zachary told me he was running on adrenaline throughout the surgery and that he worried Matt would break down at any moment.

After I knocked several times, Matt opened the door. His vivid green eyes were dull. His usual smile gone. Before I had the chance to step inside, he crashed into me.

My brother.

I wrapped my arms around him, and he crumpled into me. As much as I tried to console him, he wouldn't stop crying.

"I'm scared. What if I hadn't been here in time? What if he died?"

There was a quiver in his voice. I'd never experienced this desperation from him. This agony.

There were no words because if the same happened to Abi, I didn't know how I would deal with it. I'd destroy everything in my path.

Too many friends died today, and as it was, I couldn't wait to go out there and annihilate the sons of bitches who did this.

Matt let go. "He hasn't opened his eyes yet, but it's expected." His pained stare went to the bed behind him.

The surgery was over, but until Aoki woke, the world seemed dull and empty. It had lost its luster.

The air was heavy, but Aoki looked serene. At peace.

I went to his side. "Will he walk again?" I was unable to stop the words. It was a hard question, but I needed to know.

Matt came to the bed and held his husband's hand. "I don't know. With Electi's technology, I think he would, but out here, as things are, I'm not sure."

I fisted my hands at my sides, containing the raging thoughts that swarmed my mind. They'd pay for this.

The assembly went off without a hitch. Connor made it clear that I was innocent and entered Electi on his orders. I explained how I joined my father's council voluntarily as an undercover agent to free Deb and find out who the real spy was. We hid nothing except for the measures I had to take to free Deb.

I would carry that weight alone.

The names of all the citizens who died in the attack were spoken. Cries and sobs filled the mess hall, and a moment of silence was offered for all the lost souls. At the end, Connor asked the citizens to vote for my reinstatement as general of the PRF.

My heart rate picked up as the loud thumping of their feet made the room vibrate. I leaned against the table, looking around the mess hall, then blinked, finding Abi out there, smiling. How could they just accept and forgive me? How could they still want me as their leader?

My chest expanded, and the fire within me rekindled at their acceptance.

I stepped back and joined Connor. His hand settled on my shoulder, giving it a gentle squeeze. I was home.

I met Abi outside the bunker. The valley was empty, as opposed to when we arrived. Not a single star shone above us, as if the sky itself mourned the fallen. A freezing drizzle fell upon us.

Abi pulled down her hood.

I touched my khukuri and my gun, then secured my vest. We were about to leave, using the night as our cover.

Abi hugged me. "Be safe out there."

I wrapped my arms around her. She was so small. So delicate. But within, she was a formidable force. Whoever messed with her would face hell. "I'll be back in no time."

After we made love, she made me swear I'd come back as soon as everyone was safe. That we'd work things out together.

I couldn't deny her.

Connor cleared his throat. "Ready to go?" He'd donned camouflage clothes and tactical gear. A rifle hung on his back, a gun holstered on his right hip.

I nodded.

Abi hugged Connor. "Take care out there."

He gave her a dashing smile. "Take care of yourself. And Deb." He kissed her cheek.

When he turned, she squeezed my hand. "I'll be waiting."

"I'll make it back. I swear. I love you." I kissed her.

A string pulled at me to stay, but I needed to do this. It was the least I could do, and deep inside, I knew she'd be all right. She was strong. And if all else failed, David would protect her with his life.

I recalled the look in David's eyes when he was with her and how it matched hers.

It hurt to know Abi could feel this strongly about someone else. I'd accepted Jimmy as her brother, but this... I feared it was somehow different. Deeper.

Dangerous thoughts flashed through me, but I pushed them back. I remembered her words this afternoon. Our lovemaking. Her moans as I thrust deep within her. The love that burned between us with each touch. With each kiss.

She's mine, and I'm hers. That's all there is.

I took a deep breath and followed Connor.

"How did she take your leaving?" he asked when I reached him.

"We worked things out."

"I'm glad." Connor smiled. "Now let's go kill some sons of bitches."

Chapter 6

Abi

April 8, 2214

After Davon left, I tried to reason with his way of thinking, but it was fucking hard.

Did he truly believe I stayed with him only because of a promise? Could he hate himself so much to think he couldn't be loved?

Before we even reached Janus Peak that first time, I'd sworn I'd push through whatever he was hiding from me. The possibility of leaving him never entered my mind.

In truth, the moment he told me who he was, I clung to that promise to push through. I stayed because I told him I would no matter what he said. But I quickly learned having Jordan Niles as a father didn't mean Davon was the same. He'd proven to be a kind soul again and again.

Aoki and Matt told me countless times about how much he dwelled on his past. And the remorse that lay deep within him.

I understood the depth of his feelings. He despised the man he'd become, and unless he forgave himself, he would never deem himself worthy of love.

When the people reinstated him as their general, he almost lost his footing, as if he didn't expect everyone to take him back. I just needed to make him see all he'd done. Not the dark parts he focused on but the good ones. The lives he saved. The army he created. The rebellion he built. I'd make him see that even though he carried his father's name, he was his own person. That his past didn't define him.

"Can't sleep?" David's voice filtered through the snores and sounds of the dozens of people who shared our room.

Earlier, Dani and Steven divided the citizens and handed out cots to each.

David was very tired after giving a pint of blood to Aoki, so I decided to stay by his side.

Zachary said Deb needed time to adjust to the new situation, so she stayed in the infirmary under observation. Both she and Sarah were devastated by the news of Maria's and Jimmy's deaths, and Sarah chose to stay with Deb.

I tried to make out David's features in the darkened room. It had to be past midnight.

I sighed. "I'm worried about Davon."

David covered my hand with his. "Talk to me."

"Everything's so fucked up that I can't see a way through." A gloom had taken hold of my mind, and I was always battling to not fall into it. "I'm lost."

"Me too. It's like I'm back in that room, barely holding on." His voice broke.

I squeezed his hand. He'd suffered so much and now this.

He moved closer. "I trained with them. Davon is a warrior, and with Connor by his side, they'll be unstoppable. I'm sure they'll be safe."

"I know that. It's just..." I paused. Could I tell him about it? David was the only friend I had by my side right now.

I couldn't talk to Deb or Sarah about this even if they were by my side. As for Matt and Aoki, they had their own problems to deal with.

"Have you ever been with someone who doesn't believe themselves worthy of love? Of happiness?"

David slid away from me and turned his face up. He took a long breath and smoothed his hair back, then used his arm as his pillow. "I had someone. His name was Jonathan."

I furrowed my brow. He'd told me he had a girlfriend before the regime. "I didn't know."

"That I like men? Not many do." He caught my stare before turning back to look at the ceiling. "I'm bi, by the way, same as Aoki."

Aoki had told me about a woman he met at the facilities. She was his first love, but they ended things before graduation. She believed all the bullshit they fed her, and Aoki couldn't live with that.

"He and Matt and a handful of others are the only ones who know. I like to keep my life private, but with Jonathan, it was different. I wanted to let others know about us. To make a life with him."

I propped myself up on my right elbow. "What happened?"

"He wanted our relationship to be a secret." His voice quivered. "He couldn't accept who he was."

"For real?" That was wrong in so many ways.

Hundreds of years ago, gender distinctions were erased from the system, and all laws and legislations applied equally to all individuals. This ensured everyone was protected and had the same rights and access to healthcare.

In terms of relationships, all individuals were protected regardless of gender or the number of people involved. In Promissa, before everything went to hell, society valued each individual based on their character and actions, something we maintained inside the PRF.

So this made me question why. Why would he deny who he truly was?

"Jonathan had been raised differently. His family lived in the past and convinced him there was something wrong with him. That it wasn't natural." David fell silent for a moment. "He left for import a year ago, said he needed to distance himself from me. I haven't heard from him since." He covered his eyes.

Was he crying?

My heart ached for him. He deserved happiness.

I squeezed his hand. "Do you still love him?"

"I don't think so." He fixed his gaze on me. "I've moved on." He shrugged. "And it doesn't matter either way. I can't be with a man who can't accept himself for who he is." He shook his head. "I'm sorry. Here I'm blabbing about my problems, and you were telling me about yours."

He shifted sideways, mirroring me.

"It's Davon. He can't seem to accept that I love him after all he did."

David sighed. "It can't be easy for him. Even more so after all that happened." He tangled one of my curls around his finger.

My pulse steadied at his touch. "But what if he can't push through it? What if *we* can't move past this?"

He let my hair go. "Aoki told me how he's changed. That he seemed happier. I can't even remember seeing him smile. You've helped him, and I'm sure you'll make it through this. But you need to give him time and make him see the gift he has in you." He stroked my cheek with his thumb. His touch was delicate. Loving.

For a moment, I thought he'd say something else, but then he put some distance between us. "You'll work things out. I know you will."

"Thank you." I smiled.

David lay on his back. "Don't thank me. I'm just calling it as I see it." He elbowed me playfully. "Now sleep. I already decided what to do to keep our minds busy."

I widened my eyes. "Why do I get the feeling I won't like it?"

He smirked. "Because you won't. We'll go outside to hunt in a couple of hours, and you'll be doing the shooting."

I slapped his shoulder. "You're joking, right? I'm terrible with guns as it is. Imagine how bad it will be with only one functional arm."

He sighed. "First of all, you're great with a sniper rifle, so don't talk down to yourself. Second, we're using rifles tomorrow for the hunt, but we'll also work on target practice with handguns. Third, that's exactly why we're doing it. I'll make sure this time you learn to shoot with any type of weapon. You need to be able to defend yourself against these monsters with all you've got. When they come, you'll be ready."

I shivered at the thought, but David was right. I needed to be ready because I'd meet them out there. That was a certainty.

I plunge the khukuri through his belly, my face inches from his pleading eyes. "Their names were Jacob and Bonnie."

Warmth spreads through my limbs, and I look down. My hands are covered in blood.

The man gurgles. Blood spews from his mouth, and I twist the khukuri inside his belly.

I glance into his almost dead eyes and smile. "I hope you rot in hell for all that you did." I pull my blade out.

His entrails gush out of his belly, and a thick, dark torrent of blood covers my blade and arms.

I slash at his neck with all my strength, and he falls sideways. His head hangs at a weird angle.

I smile inside. He's dead at last.

His dark eyes fade into bluish ones, and Jimmy is there. Dead.

I scream.

"Abi!" Someone is screaming for me, but it's so far away.

"We can take him with us!" My body shakes, but Jimmy's dead eyes watch me.

"Don't leave me," he says.

"There's no time." Someone pulls me away.

"No!"

I jerked awake, covered in sweat.

David shook my shoulders, and the moment our gazes met, he pulled me into him. "It's just a nightmare. I'm here."

My night terrors were back. With everything that happened, I buried what I did yesterday.

I breathed heavily.

I murdered the man who took everything from me three years ago, and I enjoyed every second of it. Rage clawed through me as I made that final slash, and for a moment, a sense of calm took its place. Then reality hit me. I killed a man in cold blood. I gutted him and relished his suffering.

Jordan and this fucked-up world he'd created turned me into a killer.

"Do you want to talk?" David's soothing voice broke through my violent thoughts.

I shook my head and settled into his embrace.

I'd be all right and would make it through. I just needed to make peace with who I was. With this new reality.

I basked in his warmth and rested in the crook of his shoulder, then let myself drift back to sleep.

David raked his dark hair back. "That's the third deer you've missed."

I huffed. "I don't understand why I keep missing. I've shot men before."

An image of Jimmy sprawled on the forest floor hit me, and I shook. I held my chest.

David gripped my shoulder. "Listen to me. I'm here. Breathe."

I focused on his hazel eyes and regained my control.

He bent over, bringing his gaze level with mine. "What just happened?"

"I just remembered the last man I shot was Jimmy." I pushed the words out.

David darted his eyes from the rifle in my hand to me. "I thought Davon did it."

"I was the one who shot him." I could almost hear the gunshot. "Jimmy had already shot Davon once. If I didn't stop him, he would have shot a second time and killed him. That's why I couldn't deal with Jimmy before. Now I've lost him."

David took me in his arms. "I'm sorry. I didn't know. Let's go back."

"No. We stay. We practice."

He took a step back. "But—"

"Please. Teach me. I couldn't hit Tammy yesterday. Maybe if I had, Jimmy wouldn't be dead." If I'd hit her, she wouldn't have thrown that grenade. "I want to protect our people."

David nodded. "Okay, but forget about hunting. We'll do target practice first and move on as you progress."

I passed him the rifle. "Ready when you are."

We practiced for a couple of hours, then Steven summoned us to his office, where we drank from a keg of David's brew.

Steven sat at his desk. He wiped the foam from his mouth. "How did the hunt go?"

We sat close to one another.

"David took down a deer." I swallowed, letting the chilled liquid flood my senses.

"And you?" Steven asked.

David's thigh touched mine. A simple gesture that centered me.

"I'm sure you didn't ask us here to chat about our day," he said.

Steven relaxed and propped his elbows on his desk. "I wanted to talk to you about security. Matt said you were the best. Can I count on you?"

David nodded. "Tell us what you need."

"We need snipers on the periphery of the bunker but especially on the way to the caverns."

"Done," David said.

"Good." Steven took another sip from his mug.

There was something I was itching to ask. "How are we managing with resources?"

About five hundred people arrived yesterday. What if the food became scarce? The move to the caverns would start soon, but with so many wounded, how could farming sustain the citizens?

Steven dipped his chin. "We're good. Since we supply all the bunkers, food won't be a problem. In terms of medicines and doctors, we're waiting for science."

David leaned forward. "When are you expecting them?"

"Hopefully soon. It's one of the reasons we had to send a troop out west. To make sure their way is safe."

I fiddled with my mug.

My skin prickled at the fact the NWG troops were this deep into the mountains. How safe were we really?

I caught David's eyes on me when I glanced up.

Steven watched us both. "They'll be okay, Abi. You haven't seen Connor in battle. They'll make it back."

I nodded, praying their strength was enough to face our enemy.

One day we were fine, and the next we almost lost everything. Nothing was guaranteed. Everything hung in a balance that was slowly turning against us.

I trailed my fingers down Aoki's long, black hair. I came so close to losing him. Seeing him this frail and vulnerable as opposed to his normally joyful self broke something inside me.

"Don't fuss over me." Aoki's serene voice filtered through my restless mind. He took my hand. "I'm okay."

A tear slid down my cheek. "I know. But..." I moved my gaze down his body.

He squeezed my hand. "I'm alive. And Matt says I might regain my movement eventually. I just need to work hard."

"But there's no guarantee."

He couldn't walk.

I came as soon as the meeting with Steven was over. David stayed with him to go through the details about security.

Before leaving to get us lunch, Matt explained there were treatments for this type of medical situation. He believed Aoki could regain movement with them, but they were only available in Electi.

A wave of nausea hit me. All this bullshit made me sick. I hadn't been able to keep anything down since last night.

Aoki glanced down at his legs. His eyes shone with unshed tears. "I'll make it through."

The doorknob rattled, and Matt entered. "Hey, I brought some of the good stuff."

I grabbed the coffee he offered.

He dropped a bag on the bedside table, then kissed Aoki, lingering close to his face. "How are you doing?" His voice was soft. Loving.

Aoki stroked his cheek. "Better now that you're here."

Matt smiled.

He hadn't left Aoki's side since yesterday. The only sign of the pain he'd been through after watching his husband almost die was the dark shadows under his eyes.

Matt sipped his coffee and closed his eyes. He groaned. "This stuff is good."

Something about fresh-brewed coffee made it hit just the right way. "Yeah."

Matt moved a chair next to Aoki, facing me. "I just saw David in the mess hall. He told me you were training."

"Yeah. Guns. We did some target practice." I lowered my head and skimmed my fingers around the rim of my cup. "I'm a mess, but he promised he'd be patient."

Matt chuckled. "As expected. David would do anything for you."

I tilted my head toward him.

Matt gave me a half smile and looked at Aoki.

I raised an eyebrow. "I don't understand."

Matt furrowed his brow. "You really haven't noticed?"

I darted my eyes between them. "What are you talking about?"

"David is head over heels for you," Matt said.

What the fuck? My eyes almost bulged out of my face. I would have noticed, wouldn't I?

Aoki shook his head. "Poor guy."

I jerked back. "You can't be serious."

I went through our moments together. The way we'd connected over the months Davon and I had been apart. The way he reacted when he found out I was leaving. The small moments we shared. How could I be that blind?

Matt's expression became solemn. "Sorry, Abi, but it's the truth. We all see it, and I'm sure Davon does too. David's a good guy. He'll never cross that line with either of you, but that doesn't change his feelings."

I covered my head with both hands. "God."

Aoki tapped the bed. "Come here."

I sat.

He patted my thigh. "Nothing has changed."

I slumped my shoulders. "But I don't want to hurt him. He's important to me."

How could I put it?

I cared about David. I could tell him anything, and he'd never judge or try to change me. He was always there, listening. We took care of each other.

Matt cleared his throat. "We understand. He was there when you most needed him, and I'm sure you were there for him too. Did he tell you about Jonathan?"

I nodded.

"I was here when Jonathan left him," Aoki said. "David was destroyed. He became very guarded. Reclusive even. Wouldn't talk to anyone. That's why Connor sent him to checkpoint one. After he met you, we all saw it."

Matt stood. "You brought him back, just as you did with Davon. You gave him something to fight for." He softened his features and offered me a small smile.

"He's my friend, but it's somehow deeper. Like what I had with..." I couldn't say his name.

"Jimmy?" Aoki's voice was low. Gentle. "Matt told me. I'm sorry."

"It's okay." Hearing his name tugged at my heart, but I took a deep breath.

For a moment, I tried to make sense of it all. I never really thought about it, but now that I did, it was very confusing.

Could Matt and Aoki understand? Could Davon and David accept it?

"Do you think it's wrong? To love him?" I whispered.

Aoki and Matt widened their eyes.

I shook my head and held my hands up. "It's not what you think. It's...different." I clutched Davon's sapphire pendant, the one he gave me on my birthday. "My love for Davon is much deeper. At a different level. My soul calls to him, and nothing will ever change that."

I loved Davon. My heart ached when we were apart, and my soul was set ablaze when he was near me. It was something primal. Real. A love rooted so deep inside of me that it had no beginning and no end. I needed him like I needed air. Longed for him. Lived for him.

But I loved David too. I thought about his easygoing attitude. About all the moments we'd shared. All the joy and pain we'd seen through together. His smile. His comforting touch. His warm voice. The sense of self I had with him. It was like we were connected. Like we were destined to meet.

"David's like a lifeline. I know no matter what happens he'll always be there. That I can count on him. And I know it's the same for Davon, but..."

"But Davon has his own problems?" Aoki asked. "You think you burden us all, but it's not true. We all get it, and Davon would do anything for you."

"I know, but..."

Matt gripped the handrails. "But what? We don't compare? You know we're here for you too. And Davon."

My throat burned. Now I'd hurt Matt. "I'm sorry."

The bed squeaked. Aoki shifted toward me and groaned.

Matt was by my side in a second, holding Aoki down. "Don't move, love. You'll hurt yourself."

Aoki gave him a hard look, then squeezed my knee. "You love them both. You keep them both. Davon as your partner and lover. David as your close friend. Talk to them. Make things clear. They'll understand."

Aoki's kind words soothed me, and I covered his hand. "Thank you."

Matt curled his shoulders and swallowed hard. "I'm sorry. I overreacted."

Aoki sighed heavily, then took Matt's hand. "We all love differently. Feel differently. Each of us is unique in their own way."

Matt nodded, then set his emerald eyes on me. "I don't know what came over me." He pulled me into a hug. His gentle breath stroked my neck. "You can always come to us. Always."

Whatever tension there had been between us dissipated in that moment. We were all under a lot of stress.

He cupped my cheek with his calloused hand. "There's nothing wrong with what you feel. You've created a bond with David, and that's all right. I understand. I think Davon already does. But you should talk to them both."

I smoothed back one of Matt's golden curls. He was such a beautiful man, inside and out. "I will, and thank you. You know you're my family. I love you so much."

Matt leaned into my touch. "I love you too."

"What about me?" Aoki asked.

"What's not to love?" I giggled.

Aoki hit my arm playfully, his smile wide.

Matt's eyes glistened as he looked at him.

My heart was full. Matt and Aoki always filled me with ease. They gave me so much strength.

The moment was broken by a knock on the door.

"I'll get it." Matt turned.

My stomach growled.

Aoki snickered.

I huffed. "I'll set up lunch." I took the bag Matt brought and walked to a counter. Mashed potatoes with shredded chicken. I put Aoki's plate next to mine on the bedside table.

"Came to see your man."

I jumped.

David shifted his gaze to me. "You good?"

I noticed then that I was staring at him. I shook my head. "Sure, I'm just tired."

David walked to the other side of the bed and gave me one of his smiles.

I smiled back, knowing everything would be okay between us.

"Hey, man." He gripped Aoki's pale hand with his tanned one. "How's that blood flowing?"

Aoki shrugged. "I don't know if it's working. I feel like shit."

David hit Aoki's shoulder. "Que cabrón eres."

Aoki laughed. "You can't take a joke."

David narrowed his eyes, but they were filled with mirth.

"I'm feeling good. For real. Thanks for what you did."

"Always." David's tone became serious. "Are you sure you're all right?"

Aoki nodded. "As good as new."

"Good." He raised the paper bag he held. "Who's up for some chocolate chip cookies?"

I closed my mouth as soon as I realized I was gawking at the cookies, but David had already noticed.

He grinned. "I was ready to leave the mess hall when Rosa called me back and offered me fresh cookies. She made them for everyone."

"How's she doing?" Aoki asked.

"Good. She sends her regards."

"Who's Rosa?" I asked as I fed a spoonful of mashed potatoes to Aoki.

"She's the cook here." Matt ripped the bag from David's hand and hurried to me.

"Hey!" David ran after him.

Matt held the bag high, and David, being shorter than him, couldn't reach.

It was funny as fuck.

Matt took out a cookie and had a bite. "You said it was for everybody."

David doubled over, panting. "Whatever, man."

We all laughed before sitting down for lunch with Aoki. It appeared almost normal. As if there was nothing wrong with the world.

Chapter 7

Davon

April 8, 2214

My mind wandered to Abi, to the citizens who were injured, and to those who still fought. I closed my eyes and focused on the mission. We managed to help Michael cross over to farming, but now we were in no-man's-land, clearing the way for the soldiers who'd been fighting nonstop since last night.

Corporal Mathews stayed behind with four hundred strong, who joined our forces from science and technology. They were gathering RPGs and explosives for the battle in Promissa.

Michael also provided our troops with new armor, but he didn't have enough for all the soldiers. This attack had come by surprise, and he'd only recently started working on it. Hopefully, they'd be ready before we finally entered Promissa.

Connor and I went ahead with fifty of our strongest to take out any scouting NWG troops.

Once Mathews and his troops joined us, we'd rush west to make sure everything went as planned.

"Up ahead. Eleven o'clock." Connor pointed to his side.

The crunching of boots as soldiers took their positions was almost imperceptible.

A group of NWG soldiers scoured the area ahead of us. Their dark, armored uniforms revealed we were dealing with an enhanced NWG troop.

I took out my khukuri.

Connor brushed his favorite gun, a 9mm Sig Sauer P226, then moved his hand to the stacked leather handle of his KA-BAR combat knife. He unsheathed it and held it by his side as we crouched and moved to our objective.

We called them reapers. Their vicious ways and their stealthy assaults gained them that nickname. These assholes were freakishly strong and, as Matt said, fucking hard to kill.

They didn't feel pain or fear. And if you gave them the chance, they'd kill you with their bare hands, laughing as they broke you. It didn't take long to see some of them were sadistic sons of bitches who basked in the death of their opponents.

We got a few of them after we left science but not before they decimated seventeen of our men. They not only killed but savored ripping apart their enemies. It was a gruesome sight to behold.

Earlier, before I plunged my khukuri through the weak side of an enhanced soldier's armor, she cackled as she gutted one of my men even after he was already dead. It was sickening, and it fueled my wrath.

When it was over, Connor and I were bathed in enemy blood, and it took some time before our rage subsided and we were us again.

We determined the best way to kill them at close range was with blades, using ambush as our main strategy. It was risky given the proximity, but it ensured the kill.

Guns blasted up front, and we ran toward the sound. It worked—the reapers focused on the shooting soldiers as we rushed in with half our troop. I jumped on one's back, ripped off his helmet, and gripped his hair, exposing his neck. I slashed his throat with the dhaar of my khukuri. The crack and spray of blood told me I'd severed his head. I jumped down and rushed to the next target, who repeatedly shot one of our soldiers. His body was a dreadful palette of gore and violence.

When I was about to strike, Connor charged into her, gripping his dagger with both hands as he plunged it into the back of her neck. The soldier regurgitated on top of our man and fell topside, dead. Connor eyed me, eyebrows furrowed, teeth bared as thick drops of blood fell down his chin.

How many had he killed already?

Connor wiped his eyes and searched the forest. He darted toward his next victim and went down into a sweep kick. The massive man fell back like a block, and Connor thrust his knife into his Adam's apple. A gurgling sound followed by silence marked his horrific death.

This was the general I sparred with when it all started, a Connor I hadn't seen in a long time, not since I was sent on my mission to find Abi. My limbs quivered at his show of strength. I'd witnessed him fight before, and he was strong as fuck, but this... When fighting these assholes, he went berserk, and it was better to steer clear of his path. The man was a monster on the battlefield.

A sudden blow across my lower back sent me flying headfirst into a boulder. Warmth trickled down the side of my face, and I couldn't focus. I touched my temple. The skin was open and tender to the touch, and the searing pain split my head in two.

Get up!

The ground vibrated beneath me, and I used the boulder to pull myself up. When my vision cleared, a succession of gunfire hit the most massive reaper I'd ever seen. His nostrils flared, and he clenched a metal mace in his right hand.

The throbbing pain in my back was unbearable as I gaped at the weapon he used against me. I shook as I witnessed its blunt body and heavy hexagonal head.

Thank God they gave us a new set of armor in science and technology; otherwise, my back would have broken from the impact.

The reaper grunted as several soldiers continued rapid fire to get him off his path. His goal—me.

One of the soldiers rushed in, but before he could reach him, the reaper grabbed the man by the neck, tore his throat out as if it was nothing, then dropped him. Bile rose into my mouth, but I kept pushing myself up. He was only a few feet away from me.

The reaper cracked his neck from side to side, rolling his shoulders back as if nothing had happened.

A guttural roar burst across the forest, and Connor was there. He grabbed the arm that held the mace as I got my bearings and struck the fucker's side with my khukuri.

The recoil from the armor was enough to make me drop my blade. "Fuck!" I'd missed the weak point.

The reaper swung Connor as if he was a ragdoll, but Connor wouldn't let go.

A clink hit the ground, and smoke covered the area. A soldier must have thrown our last smoke bomb. Earlier we used all but one in our encounter with these fuckers.

"Connor! Shoot his hand!" I hoped to hell Connor was still holding on to his arm.

The round from Connor's gun was followed by a heavy thud. I reached blindly toward the sound and grabbed the mace.

Using all my strength, I picked it up.

"Do it!" Connor dropped to the ground.

I swung the mace and struck the massive soldier's head until he fell. I kept hitting until someone grabbed my arm, stopping it midway.

"He's dead," Connor said.

I came back to my senses. The armored helmet was dented halfway into the enhanced soldier's head, and brain matter splattered the forest floor.

I surveyed the area. We'd done it, but with the reapers lay more than a dozen men donning the PRF gray uniform. I closed my eyes and offered a silent prayer for them.

I dropped the mace, but Connor grabbed it and wiped the bloody remnants against the dead reaper. He unhooked the harness from the man's back, put it on, and placed the mace in it. It fit perfectly.

Then he grabbed a machine gun from the reaper's uniform and holstered it. "Grab everything you can. We'll arm our troops with the dead's weapons."

While the soldiers scavenged the bodies, I retrieved my khukuri and sheathed it.

I sauntered away and crouched next to a tree, then retched. It was just like the time when I had my first kill. I lost control of my senses and beat the hell out of him without noticing he was already dead. It was sick.

Someone approached from my right, and I wiped my mouth with my sleeve as Connor reached me. His blond hair was matted with the blood of dozens of men. His dark-gray uniform was soaked in enemy blood.

He pocketed his hands. "You did well."

Here was my general and friend, unfazed and proud of what I did, while my arms trembled as I cursed the monster that lurked within me. "I couldn't stop. I...lost myself for a moment there."

"We did what was needed, Davon. There's no other way to beat them. We become animals to fight animals." He reached down toward me.

I grabbed his arm and pulled myself up. "But..." My stomach churned again, and I swallowed it down.

"Use all he taught you against him. Make him see that the man he trained to kill us all is his nemesis. Be strong and own it. This is who you are."

His words resonated with Abi's and how I needed to accept myself for who I was.

The truth of his words burned within me. My father changed me, made me into this. He took pride in who I had become.

I'd make him see. At the end of it all, he'd dread the day he broke me.

We encountered two more groups of enhanced soldiers, then stopped to regroup with Corporal Mathews's troops. Weapons and gear were distributed among our forces.

Scouts scoured the perimeter as we took a moment to rest. We were almost there. In one or maybe two hours, we'd reach the import area perimeter. Once we confirmed the NWG troops had moved into it, we'd turn back. We couldn't fight them all. Not now.

Mathews brought back explosives with neuromuscular blocking agents (NMBAs), more smoke bombs, and RPGs. With those and the equipment we were taking from the dead, we might be able to enter Promissa soon. Last night's attack pushed the PRF into a corner, and we needed to get back in the game. Knowing Father, he kept most of his troops inside Promissa. With the threat from the Liberty Enclave, he wouldn't risk leaving Electi and Promissa unprotected.

So many fucking dead.

I thought back to yesterday's events and couldn't help the nagging feeling that Father wouldn't just sit in wait. That he'd make another play, and we were blind to it.

I thought of Abi, praying nothing would happen until I was back.

My stomach roiled, but I took a swig from the vodka Mathews offered, letting its bite wash over me. I shouldn't have left.

Connor allowed us one small drink. After what we just went through, it was the only reprieve he could provide, given we needed to be ready to fight again if the time came.

"You all right?" Mathews propped his elbows on his thighs as we stared west.

With a shrug, I drank and let the burning sensation numb my senses. I passed the flask back to him.

He took a swig. "We saw the dead on our way here."

I stared down at my empty hands. "They killed so many."

"But you took them down." He refilled the flask and held it between us. "To our brothers and sisters and to small victories." He drank, then handed it over.

"To small victories." I drank.

"You guys ready to go?" Connor carried a thermos with him. "Finish that, and drink some of this. We need to be alert."

We finished our drinks and reached out.

Connor filled two mugs with coffee, then put the thermos aside and crouched next to a stream. He splashed water on his head. Dark rivulets went downstream as he cleaned off the remnants of battle.

Mathews grasped his mug with both hands and blew the steam lazily. "We were toasting your victories today. The soldiers told me you were fearless out there, taking out most of the reapers by yourself."

Connor faced us. "You call that a victory?" He grimaced. "No, that was no victory." He cupped water in both hands and bent, scratching the blood from his hair aggressively.

My hands shook as I downed my coffee in one swallow, attempting to soothe the ache at the back of my throat. We lost thirty-seven today. And they were small hostile forces.

Connor rinsed his hands and stood. "I did what was needed to defend my people. These monsters were made to annihilate us, and I will not cower before them." He walked back to camp. "Let's go. The clock is ticking."

Mathews and I finished our coffee and followed our leader.

Smoke rose around the import bunker. Among the NWG soldiers, three men donned the black uniform of the higher-ups.

"I only see NWG troops and their captains. Do you think they made it out?" I passed the binoculars to Connor.

Connor grabbed them. "There would be more dead if not." He adjusted the lenses, and his mouth went agape. "He's here."

"Who's here?"

He passed the binoculars back and pointed toward an area northeast of the bunker. "With him down there, we can rest easy. He'll make sure they don't follow."

A lone figure clad in black gave orders to soldiers, and they rushed inside the bunker. *Peter?*

He waited for them to leave his side, then ran north.

"We turn back." Connor said.

I grabbed his arm, followed the direction Peter took, and froze. "Wait!"

Yuxuan, jian in hand, fought about a dozen enhanced soldiers by himself in an isolated area north of the bunker. I checked south. The main troops marched through the area, all ignorant of what was happening except for Peter.

He was running to Yuxuan's aid.

"Yuxuan is out there."

His movements were like a dance, sleek but with so much strength that each strike made even the enhanced soldiers lose their step. He sliced through the weak side of the armors, then circled back and finished each. Blood streaked around him like ribbons. It was like watching a masterpiece in its making, but against so many, he'd die.

Connor snatched the binoculars. "Fuck!"

"What do we do?"

It was an impossible choice. If our troops aided them, we risked the enemy catching our presence, and we couldn't fight against this many.

Connor shook his head. "We can't risk our people."

I furrowed my brow. "So we just leave them there?"

Hundreds of NWG soldiers stood between us and them, but if a few of us went to their aid, approaching quietly through the forest, maybe we'd have a chance.

Connor sighed heavily. "Abi will kill me."

My heart skipped a beat.

"I only do this because I'm sure even if I say no, you'll find a way to go and save your mentors." Connor caught my shoulders. "You need to be stealthy, and we both know how good they are with their senses. I don't know how they haven't noticed what's going on in that area. I can only guess the reapers caught him escaping not long ago. If that's true, they could call for reinforcements at any second."

"Peter is there. He'll help me." It would be risky, but I couldn't abandon my two mentors. There was no way. "I can do it."

"I'll go with him." Corporal Mathews stood beside me.

Connor cursed and rubbed his nape. "Okay, but if things go south, run. I can't go with you. The wounded need care. We'll meet in science."

I extended my hand.

He pulled me into a hug. "I'm not joking. If you don't make it back, I'll fucking kill you with my own hands." He patted my back.

"We'll make it back." Mathews held out his hand.

Connor took it. "Take all you need. If you can paralyze them, do so. You can carry Yuxuan back."

We both nodded and went to get our gear.

Mathews moved ahead and hid behind a pine tree.

I did the same. Yuxuan fought less than twenty feet away. Eight reapers were still standing.

"Stop this. It's an order." Peter's commanding voice traveled throughout the forest. "We need to take him alive."

Two soldiers stopped, while the other six sneered and continued fighting.

So they didn't have complete control. This was what Matt warned us about. That they were having cognitive issues and some killed for the thrill of it. They were crazed when it came to blood.

How could Father risk this much for this little experiment? They could easily turn against him. Maybe if we captured one alive, we could learn more. Maybe there was a way to use them against him.

I shook my head and followed Yuxuan's movements. He was heavily wounded. I couldn't discern how much of the blood was from him or from his enemies. He continued without pause, but his attacks were slower, lazier.

I signaled Mathews, and he threw the canister.

The soldiers didn't react until it hit the ground, then all hell broke loose. The two who listened to Peter turned to us, weapons in hand, ready to defend their general. They stopped suddenly, a dagger protruding from each of their throats. Lavigne stood behind them, his arms twisting, then pulling back his daggers. They fell limp.

Peter put on a mask, then went to help Yuxuan.

My heart thumped wildly, and my arms tingled with adrenaline. Time to kill some motherfuckers.

Mathews and I dashed in, our masks secured.

Yuxuan stood still the moment he saw Peter engage the soldiers, then glanced toward me. When I nodded, he swung his jian toward a reaper who was going for Peter's head and stopped it just in time but not before the recoil threw him back.

Mathews hurried to his aid.

We had no idea how long it would take for the NMBAs to affect them, so we had to fight until then. I just hoped it didn't take that long.

I skidded through the terrain and squatted between two reapers. I grunted as one kicked my thigh but maintained my stance and elbowed him with all of my strength before slashing his side. Blood stained my khukuri, but he didn't budge. He pushed me against the other soldier.

He held my arms. "You fuckers. Do you think you can win against us?"

This was the first time I'd heard them talk. I mean, they were human, but in my mind, they were thoughtless beasts.

He chuckled as the other one approached.

"How about we show this one who's the boss here?" the one who pushed me said.

I fought the reaper's grip, but it was in vain. The other one cracked his knuckles less than three feet away from me.

I couldn't see behind his helmet, but I bet he was sneering.

The initial strike took my breath away. By the second blow, the metallic taste of blood entered my mouth. The punches kept coming, and the more I struggled to get free, the more he hit me. Blood spewed from my mouth. Every punch was agony.

When will this paralyzing shit take effect?

The sounds around me faded, and my vision turned cloudy. I was losing consciousness. I fell, and the punches stopped.

Abi... I couldn't give up. I had to make it back. I used my elbows to push myself up and looked around. The reapers were beside me. Unmoving.

Finally.

There was rustling next to me.

Someone ripped off my helmet and covered my face. "Don't die on me now."

That voice. She shouldn't be here. I pried my eyes open.

Soldiers surrounded us. No one wore masks. It seemed the agent had dissipated.

"At ease, soldiers." Mathews's voice sounded distant.

Katherine prompted them to put their weapons down.

"Katherine?" I coughed out.

Her dark eyes were inches away from mine. "Davon!" She scrunched her eyebrows, then threw herself over me.

I grunted.

"Sorry. I'm just glad you're alive."

"What are you doing here?" A burning sensation filled my throat, and the words didn't sound right.

"We don't have time for questions. Can you walk?"

I tried to move, but my body wouldn't cooperate.

I glanced at Peter. His arms were up as two PRF soldiers pointed their guns at him.

I stretched my arm out. "Stop!" A shot of pain traveled through my chest. I flinched. "He's with us." My voice was hoarse.

"What Davon says is true." Mathews humphed.

Katherine came close to my ear, her voice low. "I understand, Davon, but the people don't know. Maybe it's better to keep him locked away until we decide how we'll proceed." She shook her head. "After what he did to energy, people may not understand and may even hurt him. But I'm sure they'll listen to Connor when the time is right."

Her words were true. People only knew Peter as a villain. As the general who had attacked us countless times. We'd need to take it to the council.

"We need to go now!" Mathews's words were final.

Katherine signaled her soldiers. "Take him into custody, but he's not to be harmed."

Peter complied as the soldiers handcuffed him and took him away.

It's for the best.

Mathews carried the lifeless body of Yuxuan.

My heart faltered. *No.*

The pounding in my head was relentless and the weight on my chest agonizing. We were too late.

Katherine pulled me up, and I struggled to stand. She grabbed my waist, and we started moving. Every step was torture, but I carried on.

I don't remember how much time passed as we walked in silence. My body was numb from the cool wind. I stumbled.

Katherine held me strong. "We're almost there."

"Kathy?"

Seth?

Seth ran to us. "Are you okay, buddy?"

I curled my lip up. "Been worse."

Seth's gaze moved to Katherine. "And you? Are you hurt?"

Katherine shook her head. "I'm good."

Seth brushed her arm. "Are you sure?"

She smiled. "I am."

There was a closeness between them that wasn't there before. Could it be...?

The right side of my body burst with pain as Seth wrapped his arm around my waist. "I'll take you from here."

He darted his eyes toward Mathews, who passed Yuxuan's body to two soldiers.

"What happened out there?"

Mathews rolled his shoulders back. "Yuxuan is paralyzed and heavily wounded. Davon was beaten pretty badly. The agent took over five minutes to take effect on the reapers."

I sighed. The burden in my chest lifted. Yuxuan was alive.

"Reapers?" Seth asked.

"That's what we call these monsters." My chest hurt just from speaking.

"Hold on a bit longer." Seth followed Katherine toward a tent.

I spied Peter as he was taken into another tent. Behind him, more than six PRF soldiers carried three cots, each with a massive reaper sprawled on top.

I opened my eyes wide. "You took them?"

Katherine looked in their direction. "It was my call. We need to know how they work. They're heavily sedated."

Reapers.

Seth's eyes grew huge. "Is that who I think it is?"

I nodded.

"I'll make sure he's safe," Seth said.

I turned my gaze to Seth. "Thank you."

"Let's get them inside." Katherine opened the flap, then helped Seth set me down on a cot. "I'll get someone to check on them." She bent over me. "We'll talk later."

I was on the floor next to Yuxuan. His hands twitched, and he opened his eyes.

"You all right?"

"I..." Yuxuan cleared his throat. "What the fuck was that gas?"

"A paralyzing agent. Science prepared it."

Yuxuan grimaced. "Brilliant." He chuckled. "A fucking nightmare but brilliant."

A medical soldier examined me after stitching my temple. "It appears no bones were broken, but you should take it easy once we arrive at science. I think there may be internal damage." She injected me. "For the pain."

I grimaced. "When are we leaving?"

"In the next hour or so. We stopped because Councilmember Williams ordered us to. But we need to be in science before night arrives. It's not safe out here."

So Katherine did it for Yuxuan. I smiled inside. She trained with us countless times. Thank God she turned back.

The entrance of the tent flapped open.

Katherine came in with a couple of soldiers. "How are they doing?"

"Major General Li received a stab wound near his clavicle, and his left arm isn't responding, but he'll make it."

The moment Yuxuan learned his arm wouldn't move he inhaled sharply and slumped back. He was left-handed.

I glanced sideways. He was sleeping after asking for meds.

I swallowed hard. He wouldn't be able to hit the battlegrounds for some time, and for a man like him, that could be worse than death.

The soldier finished putting her medical supplies away. "I sutured the wounds that needed more attention. General Niles should be kept under observation once we arrive at the bunker. He appears to be fine, but we need to make sure there's no internal damage."

Katherine sighed, then faced her soldiers. "Grab your stuff, and bring in two sheets. We can carry them the rest of the way."

I started to sit up once we were alone.

Katherine held a hand to my chest. "Don't try to be brave now." Her voice was stern, but her eyes were glazed. "You've done enough."

I squeezed her hand. "I'm okay. I can stand." I clenched my jaw.

I'd been beaten before countless times. I knew how to suppress my pain and go on. Father had made sure of that.

Katherine humphed. "You never listen." She crouched beside me. "Put your arm around me."

My muscles strained at the movement, but I stood.

"Thank you." I brushed my hand over her arm before letting go of her. "Thanks for coming back for us."

Her eyes misted. "I'm glad I did."

Purplish bruises marked my chest and sides.

Katherine helped me put on my shirt.

I touched my face and winced. Fucking bastard messed me up good.

She helped me put on the rest of my uniform, never overstepping or hinting at our past relationship. I was glad to be on good terms with her after our last encounter. I mean, no one could blame her. We'd spent years together, and when we last met, she wanted our relationship to continue. I told her I had Abi, and that was it. She was furious at the time. I wondered what had changed.

"What will happen to Peter?" I asked.

Katherine darted her eyes toward the tent opening, then she shifted closer to me. "He's already been taken care of. His wounds weren't as bad as yours."

We walked outside. The last rays of sunlight bathed the forest, illuminating the faces of the citizens. Most dragged their feet, picking up their belongings as they went while looking back at their lost home.

"Come on! We don't have much time till sundown." Seth stood in the middle of the area, shouting orders, until he saw me. "What the fuck are you doing up?" He strode over, red-faced and angry as hell.

Katherine raised her hands and shook her head. "Stubborn asshole won't follow orders."

I chuckled. "Guys, I'm good. Trust me. Sure, those reapers did a number on me, but I'm still standing, aren't I?"

"Learning from Matt, are you?" Seth grunted. "I'm not going to even try to convince you otherwise. It's a waste of time." He gripped my shoulder. "Now for the real question. What the hell are you doing here?"

Right, we decided to come after they'd already left. "Connor, Mathews, and I scouted west with some troops to clear the way for science and you. We wanted to make sure you made it out. Then we saw Yuxuan fighting. Do you know why he was there alone?"

Seth gazed at the tent, then shook his head. "I don't know. My best guess is he stayed behind to cover our escape."

Exactly what I would expect from him. He'd give his life for any of us without hesitation.

"Is the way clear, then?" Seth asked.

I nodded. "We took care of it."

"And Connor?" Seth furrowed his brow.

"On his way to science with what's left of our troops."

He dipped his head. "How many did we lose?"

I tried to recall their faces. "Thirty-seven who marched with us. Hundreds back in Janus. And you?" I tensed.

Seth glanced up. His eyelids were heavy. "Too many to count." He scratched the back of his neck.

I tightened my fists. "Fuck."

He straightened. "Any good news?"

"Science gave us soldiers. Four hundred strong. They also gave us new weapons and armor."

"Good." He took a deep, cleansing breath.

I shifted in place. I couldn't find the words to say the rest.

"Just tell us. Who's the traitor? Who's the fucker who brought them in?" Katherine asked.

I'd almost forgotten she was by my side.

"It was Tammy. Tammy McGreggor." A sour taste rose in my mouth. That fucking bitch.

Her forehead wrinkled. "Maria's partner?"

I nodded.

"Did you get her?"

I squeezed my eyes shut and angled my face away from them. The pain was too close to the surface.

She clasped my forearm. "What happened?"

Seth stood behind her, his rapt attention solely on me.

Maria's body. Leslie's fucking sneer before throwing that grenade. Jimmy's last words. Abi's cries. It all came back to me.

I swallowed the lump in my throat and faced them. "She killed Maria and Jimmy."

Katherine stumbled back a step and covered her mouth.

Seth put an arm around her. His eyes mirrored her pain.

Katherine's cries broke through the shuffling sounds of the citizens, and everyone stopped to look at their leaders.

Sobs broke throughout the campsite as word of Jimmy's and Maria's deaths spread.

We all trained with Maria at some point. She was important to us all. A good friend and a kind soul.

Jimmy, being the contact between the bunkers, was known by everyone. Loved and respected by many. He never said no and lived for the rebellion.

As I stood there, surrounded by my people, their pain overwhelmed me. Their sorrow merged with mine, and the blow was nearly physical. Sharp claws tore at my chest, leaving it raw. Open. Bleeding.

Chapter 8

Abi

April 8, 2214

"These are delicious." Deb closed her eyes, savoring the chocolate chip cookies I brought. "Who made them?"

"Rosa did," I said. "David brought them from the mess hall."

"Why didn't he come? I saw him yesterday, but with all the shit that went on, I didn't have time to talk to him. By the way, he talks a lot about you. It seems you two are close."

My ears went impossibly hot. Did everyone notice? I bit my lip. "Yeah. We kind of connected when we started training together, but it's not..."

Deb waved her hand. "I know, Abi. There's no need to explain. You need all the friends you can get, and he's a good guy." She swallowed the last of her cookie.

She got me.

I passed her a glass of milk. "How are you feeling?"

"Still trying to make peace with all that happened. I can't believe she betrayed us." She looked at her glass.

Tammy.

"I know. She was a good friend." All those moments I spent with her during my time away from Davon. Each of them a lie. It hurt, but most of all, it broke the faith I had in people. With a spy still at large and how things went with Tammy, who could we trust?

"Did you know she was the one who talked me into going out to save Sarah?"

All other thoughts left me. "Tammy?"

Deb nodded.

I furrowed my brow. Was that part of her mission from the beginning? "Do you think she sent you in so they could arrest you?"

"Everyone knows who I am." Deb was lost in thought. "I bet she did. A desperate attempt to get the intel out. What she didn't know is that I'd never talk, no matter what."

It only took an instant to imagine her back inside that room. With Davon.

I shook the thoughts away.

Deb's face grew solemn. "I couldn't believe Sarah when she came to tell me last night. Tammy was my best friend. After I came back, she visited daily to talk and bring me sweets." She pursed her lips. "She lied to me the whole time, then killed our family." Her eyes glazed. "I can't believe Maria and Jimmy are lost to us."

I swallowed back my tears.

I couldn't wrap my mind around the fact that Tammy had a hand in Sarah's rescue. "Does Connor know about Tammy's part in the rescue mission?"

"No. With everything that happened, I didn't think it was important."

"I'll tell him about it." Something seemed off.

Deb turned her wedding band around her finger. "He's very stressed. Things have been difficult lately, with the baby and all."

Were they having problems? Connor seemed so centered.

She rubbed her belly absentmindedly. "You know." She sighed. "I do love this baby. I know you all worry it will change, but he's been with me through my worst moments. He's given me the strength to keep fighting." Her face brightened. "He's mine."

My heart was full.

She pressed my hand to her stomach.

I widened my eyes at a soft thud against it.

"Did you feel that?" She smiled, a genuine full smile. "This little guy is kicking the heck out of me." She took a deep breath. "Connor will love him too. I'm sure of it. We just need to work on it, but we'll be all right."

So that was it. Connor couldn't make peace with the pregnancy. I couldn't judge him, not after all we'd lived through.

Even for me, it was hard to come to terms with Jordan being the father. But if I could do it for Davon, I would for this baby. He didn't have to pay for his father's sins.

We both turned as Sarah entered. We were in a room Dani prepared for Connor and Deb.

Sarah looked at our joined hands over Deb's belly. "I see you've met Douglas?" She sat next to Deb, who lay in bed. Her smile was beautiful when she touched Deb's belly.

My eyes welled. She named him after Dad.

"Ah! He kicked me!" Sarah's eyes glimmered.

Deb chuckled and took our hands in hers. "I wish Mom and Dad were here."

I thought back to our family picture and Sarah's sketch of the three of us. The last two remnants of my family, burned down with my home.

Deb moved her hand to my watch. "He still watches over us."

"I know." A surge of hope ran through my veins. *Dad.*

"I wish Charlie was here," Sarah said.

The moment turned somber.

"How old should he be right now?" Deb asked.

"He's ten. He was born on January 6, 2204." She fiddled with a piece of cloth she took from her pocket. "I'll meet him soon."

The firmness in her voice sparked my hope.

Deb and I exchanged a glance.

"Do you have intel? Did someone find him?" I blurted out.

Sarah darted her eyes between us, then shook her head. "No." She tightened her fingers around the yellow cloth she held.

Could that be Charlie's?

"Sorry. I just mean we'll soon find him, right? When we get the city back?" She put it away.

I touched her arm. "You know we will. I'll help you find him."

Sarah blinked. "I'll be right back. I have something to show you."

"Do you think she's all right?" I asked Deb the moment the door closed behind Sarah.

Deb watched the door. "She's different. When I went to rescue her, she was already like this. Talking as if she was about to see her child. Maybe it was her way of dealing with what she went through in that prison." Deb twisted her face away from me. "You have no idea how it is in there."

"I'm sorry about everything. I truly am." I wanted to fix things between Davon and Deb, but how?

"We'll work things out." She squeezed my hand. "Give us some time to heal."

I pinched my lips together and was about to respond when Sarah entered, holding some papers.

She gave me a picture. It was the one of our family I'd held on to for all these years. The one I thought I lost.

I hugged it to my chest.

"I went to your room on my way out when the attack started." She held out the other paper toward me. "Jimmy kicked the door open so I could get inside." She slumped her shoulders. "I can't believe he's gone."

I swallowed back my tears and unfolded the paper. It was the sketch she drew of the three of us.

I threw myself into her arms and held her fast. "Thank you." My voice broke. "Thank you for this."

She tightened her hold. "I'd do anything for you. Anything for my family."

I was home.

April 9, 2214

Two days had passed since Davon left. He'd told me it would take some time, but I'd give everything to at least know he was okay.

Michael arrived yesterday with many doctors and nurses. Medicine also. He'd told me Davon and Connor helped them, then moved on.

The bunker was quiet today. Faez started the journey toward the caverns with about three hundred civilians and one hundred soldiers. Abraham and many others were on their way to safety. The ones who stayed behind needed medical attention.

As for David, he left before dawn with part of our sniper team. He forbade me to go with him since my arm was still healing.

Everyone was out and about. Matt left earlier to help Mark with something. I was bringing breakfast when Aoki was urging him to go.

"I'll be right here when you come back. Just go and do your thing. Our people need you."

Matt left reluctantly after giving him a scorching kiss.

I wished David could find someone who reciprocated his feelings. That would give him what he needed. Because deep down, I knew our love was different. It wasn't romantic but rather protective. As if you were guarding a piece of your soul.

He deserved a love like Davon's and mine. Strong enough to overcome any barrier. So deeply rooted that you had no idea where you ended and the other began. One in which you couldn't fathom life without the other.

"How's your wristband going?" Aoki asked, bringing me back to the present. He was always so at peace.

Matt helped sit him up this morning, and I did his long, black hair into a side braid.

I was sitting next to his bed, preparing something for Davon and enduring a long battle with Shirokuro, who was obsessed with the leather strings I was binding together. It was difficult with the sleeve, but I had a lot of time on my hands. I wanted Davon to have a piece of me, so I broke a couple of my hair ties, the ones he used to confiscate when we first met, and made them into a black-and-white leather bracelet.

Aoki brushed his fingers over the leather. "It's beautiful. Light and dark. Day and night. Just like you two."

After the latest events, I wondered how much darker I had become.

Shirokuro put himself between Aoki's hand and the bracelet, then started purring as Aoki gave him the attention he demanded.

We both laughed.

I gazed into Aoki's obsidian eyes. "I can't stop thinking about Davon and Connor out there." My stomach roiled at the possibility of them being wounded and alone. "Do you think they're okay?"

Aoki put his shakyo away. "I'm sure they are." He gave my hands a squeeze. "I know it isn't easy. Sitting and waiting for our strong-ass men to be back from their never-ending missions is hard, but we have to trust they're okay. I'm sure we'll receive some news soon."

Hours later, Rachel came to check on us. Her honey-brown eyes were brighter, her semblance livelier than the day of the attack.

Rachel examined my arm. "Everything appears to be better. We'll take that off in a day or two and start therapy."

She continued to stretch and bend Aoki's legs. She came in twice a day to do it. "Michael and his investigation team started working on the stimulation device Matt wants to implant in your spinal cord. I'm sure they can do it."

Electi's medical facilities were equipped with technology to aid with this kind of injury, technology we didn't have, but that didn't mean it couldn't be created. Matt had not given up on getting Aoki to walk, and as soon as Michael arrived, he gave him all the instructions he needed to develop this device. It sent electrical signals through the spinal cord to restore movement in paralyzed muscles. We were hopeful it would work.

The door banged open.

"Fuck. Sorry." Nina tossed her head sideways to get her blue bangs out of her face and dashed over to me. "Connor sent me to get you. He just arrived."

I gripped the bracelet and ran out.

Nina hollered my name, but I ignored her.

I arrived at Connor's temporary office just as Mark rushed out. "Abi!"

"What happened?"

Mark fixed his glasses. His hands shook. "I...have to go. They're waiting for you inside." He continued down the hall without looking back.

My heart beat fast. Could something have happened?

I opened the door.

Connor was talking to Matt over some files, then closed them the moment I entered.

I sought Davon, but he was nowhere. "Where is he?" The pounding of my heart reached my throat.

Matt was with me in a second. "He's alive. In science. Recovering." He held my shoulders. "He's getting the help he needs and will be here as soon as he's better."

"Recovering?" I jerked my head toward Connor. "What happened to him?"

Connor rubbed his eyes, then put his hands on the steel desk. "It was crazy out there, but we made it to import. Just as we were about to leave, Davon saw something."

I stepped away from Matt to face him.

"Lavigne was out there, running to an area north of the bunker. That's when Davon saw Yuxuan. He was fighting against a group of reapers." Connor raked back his blond, disheveled hair. "Davon couldn't abandon his mentors, and he went to aid them. I'm sorry I couldn't go with him. The injured needed to be taken to safety."

God. Peter was like a father to Davon, and Yuxuan was his teacher. He looked up to them both. But what did Connor mean by reapers?

I scrunched my eyebrows. "Reapers?"

"Enhanced soldiers." Matt fisted his hands to his sides. "That's what they call these monsters."

The room was still as a tomb before he continued. "If Davon hadn't gone back, we fear both would've died. These soldiers can't be trusted. They're not stable. Some thirst for violence and lose control during combat even against their own."

Connor lowered his shoulders. "They all made it, but Yuxuan and Davon were badly beaten. Katherine got there just in time."

Katherine? My stomach dropped at the mention of her name. When I last met her, she'd somehow changed, but with Davon back... I shook my head. I needed to focus on what was important—Davon.

I clasped my hand around Connor's. "How bad is it?"

"Davon's heavily bruised. He had some internal damage, but he's receiving the best medical care we can offer. He woke up this morning and wanted to come back, but they need to keep him under observation for some time."

My stomach plummeted, and my hands shook. "I should go to him. Please let me go to him."

Connor squeezed my hand. "He asked me about it too, but I'd prefer you stayed. It's still dangerous out there, and your arm isn't healed. He'll be back in no time. Take this time to get better and be with Deb. He's in good hands."

I raked my hair back. He was right. Even after my practice with David, I couldn't shoot straight. "Okay, I'll stay. But if they take this off and he's still out there, I'm going to get him."

Connor held his arms in front of his chest in surrender. "Understood, Ms. Davis."

I shook my head.

I hadn't even asked how Connor and Mathews fared or the other soldiers. "And you? The troops?"

"Not good." He slumped back in his chair. "I'm sorry. I just...can't talk about it now."

Connor was not a man to lose his words.

How many had we lost?

I stepped away from the desk. "I understand."

Matt cleared his throat. "I'll call for an emergency meeting this afternoon as you requested."

Connor nodded. "Perfect." He caught my stare. "I want you to be there. It's time you were brought into the council."

My brain short-circuited for a moment. "What do you mean?"

"I mean exactly what I said." Connor tapped the desk, then straightened. His commanding presence dominated the room. "Deb wants to step down. We had a meeting in science before I left, and the results were unanimous."

I chuckled nervously. "You're joking. Right?"

"I'm being serious here, Abi." Connor crossed his arms.

"A councilmember? Me?" I shifted in place. "But I don't know anything about being a leader." I was ignorant of a lot of the inner workings of the PRF. "I think you're biased. You're family. If you nominated me, they will follow the general of the army. It's expected."

"It wasn't me who nominated you."

I tilted my head. "Then who?"

"Katherine Williams," Matt said.

I gasped. Didn't she hate my guts?

I gestured dismissively. "You're messing with me."

Was Matt serious?

I turned to Connor. His stern pose never wavered.

"You're not joking." I lowered my arms to my sides.

What are they thinking? I just got here. How could they want me as one of their leaders?

I wiped a bead of sweat from my brow. Why was it so hot in here?

Connor approached me. "Don't you see it? In the short time you've been here, you've worked tirelessly for the rebellion. You've met all the councilmembers and gained the respect of your fellow citizens. For God's sake, you weren't even rescued at first. You found us and have fought nonstop for our cause ever since. You're strong, stubborn, and you sure as hell never give up. You're ready for this."

I took a step back and shook my head. "But—"

"You went out there, got on Jordan's good side, and gathered intel for us. You risked your life to secure allies and bring our spies into the fold. We need you. The rebellion needs you."

My chest swelled. "But I don't want this."

"And that's why you must be the one. Do you think any of us wanted this? We all were in your place once, but we stepped up for our people."

To have so many souls counting on me. What if I wasn't good enough?

I pocketed my quivering hands, and Katherine came to mind. She was not my friend. I wouldn't even call her a colleague, but if she believed in me, then maybe... "I don't know what to say."

"I'll be right by your side." Connor's gaze turned tender.

Matt put his hand on my back. "Just accept it. He won't back down."

I took a second to think it through. I wanted change. I craved it. To free our people and end this regime. To see Promissa shine again.

I caught Connor's stare. "Tell me what to do."

That night the PRF stood outside the bunker, facing south toward Janus Peak. The valley was full of citizens. Some carried flowers they'd picked, while others brought mementos of their loved ones. Saying goodbye to all the people we lost was necessary. We needed to move on.

Steven made a small garden outside with a metal box that would be buried after everyone put something inside for each soul who had left us.

It was the best we could do without the bodies. A small reminder of their lives and a place for those memories to be kept safe.

My throat burned as I gripped the yellow wildflowers I picked earlier, ones I'd found were Jimmy's favorite out here. Their scent reminded me of the ones he'd given Sarah after she lost Carlos. It was surreal that now Jimmy was the one gone.

David stood by my side, holding a piece of cloth.

I couldn't make out what it was. "Is that for Maria?"

He slid his gaze toward me, then nodded and showed me what he held. It was a small flag. It had white and red stripes and a blue triangle on the left with a white star in the middle.

I didn't recognize it. Throughout my life, I'd only known Promissa, but Abraham had taught us about some other countries on the continent like ours. Cities that were left to fend for themselves after the wars. When the NWG took control of Promissa, history was lost to us all.

"It's a flag from our ancestors. Many generations have passed since we migrated here. I remember Dad had one. Maria had kept hers, and when we met, we found we came from the same place. We don't know much about what happened to Puerto Rico after the wars for resources and got stuck here without any way to find out."

"I'm sorry about that. We've been in the dark for so long that sometimes I forget how everything was before all this. So much history has been lost." I touched the flag. "It's amazing you still carry this. I knew you were Hispanic, but I didn't know where you came from. It's nice you and Maria found each other out here."

His eyes misted, and he looked to Connor, who read the names of the deceased one by one. "It is. We found in each other an anchor to our past, and she became like a sister to me."

"James Thompson."

My heart skipped a beat. I stepped toward the box, then kissed the flowers before putting them on top of the hundreds of mementos the other citizens had left for their loved ones.

Sarah and Deb stood by my side.

Sarah grabbed the edge of the box, and her fingers paled with the strength of her grip. "I'm so sorry, Jimmy. I shouldn't have let you go in there alone. I should have stopped you. You wouldn't have died."

Deb covered Sarah's hand. "There's nothing you could have done to stop this, Sarah. Tammy betrayed us all. You couldn't have known."

I squeezed Sarah's other hand, and she sobbed quietly. "I'm so sorry."

Connor softened his gaze and came to Deb's side. He kissed her temple. No words needed to be spoken. He just stayed with us, offered a small prayer for Jimmy's soul, then returned to his place.

"Maria Diaz."

David stepped forward.

I went with him to pay my respects to my friend. "Never forget you were loved by all," I whispered.

My chest hurt as I let go of the drawing I made for her, one of a lone red rose similar to the ones on her tattoo. I still couldn't fathom the pain she went through during those final moments. I wished I could have had more time with her.

David took my hand and put the flag inside. "Descansa en paz, amiga. La encontraremos y pagará por lo que te hizo. Dalo por hecho."

His tone was stern, but I wouldn't ask. Those words were for Maria only.

The memorial continued until all names were spoken, then the box was buried and covered with more flowers.

"May we never forget our mission," we said in unison before everyone left in silence.

Chapter 9

Davon

April 10, 2214

"Abi?"

The radio crackled.

"Davon?"

I took a moment to savor the sweetness of her voice. It traveled through my body like a salve, fixing every part of me that needed mending, igniting my soul with that fire only she could spark within me.

"I'm here, baby." I let out a long exhale. "Glad to hear your voice."

"God, Davon, I..." Silence stretched over the radio Jess had given me.

Jess was not only a councilmember of science, but she was a dear friend. Well, more like that crazy aunt each family had. I loved her for it, but she could be intense. She'd been taking care of me since I arrived, always checking on me like a mother hen to her chick.

I pressed the button. "Are you still there?"

"Yes, sorry. I'm just happy." A sniffing sound reached me.

My throat thickened. I should be holding her at this moment, not stuck miles away in a bed.

Jess wouldn't let me leave until, and I quote, "Your sorry ass learns some respect and listens to the doctor's orders."

On my way here, I did myself more harm than good, and I collapsed from blood loss. My internal hemorrhage was fixed in surgery. I asked Connor not to go into any details. I wanted to be the one to tell her.

"Are you okay? And Deb?"

"We're good." She sighed. "I was so worried. You sure you're all right?"

"I am now, but I wanted to talk to you about something."

Before I could continue, there was a commotion outside, and then, like a tornado, Jess entered the room.

She took the talkie from me. "Hey, hon! How are things going?"I rolled my eyes as Jess did her usual thing.

Everything was radio silent for a moment before the static of the talkie reached us. "Jess?" Abi seemed confused.

"Hey!"

I rubbed my brow.

"I'm glad we could finally reach you. Davon was about to escape if we didn't connect you. For being such a giant, he's such a baby."

I reached out to grab the talkie, but Jess took a step away from the bed.

Abi's deep chuckle reached me, and my heart fluttered to life.

"Has he been misbehaving?" Abi asked.

I shook my head at Jess's smirk.

"Yeah. Ever since his surgery, he's been bothering anyone who comes near."

At the mention of the surgery, I almost fell out of my cot, reaching for the talkie.

Jess furrowed her brow and gestured with her free hand as to what I wanted, but it was too late.

"Surgery? What surgery?"

"Oh! Someone's calling." Jess threw the talkie at me, mouthed "I'm sorry," then escaped the room. She was just as childish as Matt. It was difficult to believe she was my senior.

"Babe, listen to me. I was just about to tell you when she entered." I kept my tone as calm as possible, knowing Abi was about to burst.

"Did you tell Connor to lie to me?" Her tone was low. Hurt.

I rubbed my face and gripped my neck. I'd fucking kill Jess. "No, baby. I told him to let me be the one to explain it to you."

The silence on the other end was eerie.

"Love, I'm fine. I just pushed myself too much, and there was bleeding inside, so they had to fix it. It was nothing grave."

"Nothing grave!" Her tone hit me square in the chest. Gone was her soft alto. "You had surgery, Davon. That by definition is grave. Would you really have told me if Jess didn't interrupt? Or would I still believe everything was all right because my sweet-ass boyfriend decided to keep the truth from me?"

"So I'm your sweet-ass boyfriend?" After a long minute, I decided to break the silence. "Baby, I'm telling the truth. We promised to not keep secrets from each other. I just wanted to be the one to break the news so you'd hear in my voice that everything was well."

Static came from the talkie. "You promise you're all right?" Her voice was sweet. Comforting.

I smiled. "I am."

"And when will you be back?"

I humphed. I'd give everything to go back to her this minute, but the doctors ordered me to rest until I recovered to ensure I was ready to go out there again. "In a week or so."

"Okay." There was a pause. "I'm coming over."

I looked up to the heavens and asked for guidance. "Baby, even though all I want at this moment is you in my arms, I'm sure Connor already told you not to come out here."

"But..." Her pleading tone was almost my undoing.

"Please, love. We'll be together soon. Don't take risks coming here. Also, think about your position. The people need their new councilmember with them."

"They'll manage without me."

I shook my head. "I'm aware of the upcoming meetings. We need to plan our offensive before my father attacks again. You know it's only a matter of time."

"I can join the meeting from science by your side."

God, she is so stubborn. "I'm well taken care of and will be on my way as soon as the doctor gives me the go."

A large exhale came from her side. "All right, but promise you'll follow the orders."

"I do. I promise." I would give everything to be with her now. "God, I want to hold you."

Abi's sigh reached me through the radio. "Me too."

I held the radio to my chest and breathed deeply to quell the heaviness of my heart. Being away from her was driving me insane. "Is everyone really okay?"

"Yes. Michael and Matt are working on a device to help Aoki walk again, and Mark is moving people north into the caverns. Deb and Sarah are calm, and David is teaching me to shoot."

"And you?" She was the kind of person to put others first, and I worried if she had the support she needed with all the shit that was going on.

"I'm better. They'll soon get my sleeve off to start therapy. Aoki and David have helped."

"David?" Hearing his name was like a punch to my gut no matter how hard I tried to be at peace with their relationship.

I should've been with her instead of stuck here.

"It's not what you think."

I swallowed hard, pushing away the jealousy that started boiling through my veins. "You don't have to explain, love. I wasn't there for you when you most needed, and I understand if you need some time to..."

An annoyed huff reached me. "I'm going to stop you right there, and you will listen to me very carefully. David is my best friend, and I love him, but it doesn't compare to how I feel for you. I can assure you that any doubts you have are wrong. Sure, I want you both in my life, not one without the other. But you...you're my everything. No one can take the place you hold in my heart. I love you more than life itself. It goes beyond my comprehension. I'm yours, and you're mine. There's no one else."

The raging storm that had been brewing inside me since I saw them together after the battle calmed at her words. Sure, hearing her say she loved him turned my stomach to stone, but I'd cling to her words.

Every day out here, I'd wondered if she took my advice and used our time apart to rethink our relationship. She was in her right, and I had pushed her to do it. It was the reason I left. Just from watching them together, I'd seen they loved each other. What I didn't know was what kind of love, and that killed me inside. The thought of her asking me to accept him as another partner in our lives had crossed my mind. I loved Frank and Lisa, but I wasn't sure I could do it.

Nevertheless, her remarks reassured me things were not as I had imagined. "I love you, Abi."

"I know."

"So, Councilmember Davis. It's sexy now that you're kind of my superior. You need to wear those glasses for the meetings, and you're set." I snickered.

There was a huff on the other side of the line. "I'm freaking out, and you're joking about it?"

I chuckled. "Okay, okay. But for real, how are your new duties going?"

She sighed. "I don't know what the hell I'm doing."

I rolled my eyes. Couldn't she see how fucking amazing she was? "You're the best for the job. Did Connor tell you Katherine was the one who nominated you?"

"He did. What the fuck, Davon? Doesn't she hate my guts?"

The first time they met Katherine was all over me. I'd been in a relationship with her for two years, and when I came back with Abi, even though we'd broken up, Katherine wouldn't give up. It was the first time I'd seen Abi jealous.

I raised an eyebrow because I'd thought the same thing, but she had changed. "She's different. I can't pinpoint what happened, but she's been cordial and hasn't stepped out of line for even a moment. I have my suspicions, though."

"Suspicions?"

We sounded like children gossiping.

There was no harm in telling her. "I think Seth and Katherine are a thing."

"Wait, what? Seth, who's like a teddy bear, with Katherine, who's such a badass."

I laughed. "I know, though I can assure you Seth isn't a teddy bear. He's quite the warrior."

The man was a beast on the battlefield, just like Connor. His body was built like a tank.

"I know. It's just that he's always so sweet to me that I see him like that."
She giggled, and the sound of it lightened my soul. "If it's true, I'm happy
for them both."

"Yeah. I'm glad we could move on from that."

"Give me a sec." A couple of minutes passed before I heard the click from
Abi's side. "I have to go. Connor called for an emergency meeting. I'll let
you know what happened as soon as I can. Love you."

Before I had a chance to answer, the radio went silent.

I hung my arm to the side and took a deep, cleansing breath. Staying here
for another week would be fucking hard.

"I'm sorry." Jess's face was comical, peeking from behind the door.

"I don't know what I did to deserve people like you and Matt in my life,"
I said nonchalantly, when in truth, I didn't think I deserved such awesome
friends in the first place. They were too good to me.

Jess threw the door open. "Well, it's not a walk in the park with you
either. Was she mad?"

I shrugged. "You know it."

"I'm sorry. I thought you'd already told her." She took the walkie from
me.

"No worries. Everything turned out fine."

She checked my incision wounds from the laparoscopy. "These are already healed. I think you'll be ready to go in a week or so."

I hoped earlier.

April 25, 2214

One week turned into two.

The doctors asked me to stay. They wanted to make sure I was strong enough for the journey after so much blood loss. I was not happy about it, and neither was Abi, but it was the right call. I'd been exhausted and slowly getting up to exercise, but there was a heaviness in my body and limbs that wasn't there before, one I needed to work through.

"Scouts say the troops are regrouping between Janus and import," Katherine said from the head of the table.

Seth sat by her side. "We already sent out Lavigne's propped pictures. Your father must have them by now. Here are the copies."

I took them.

Who knew artists and doctors could be so good at getting someone to look like that? Thick makeup that appeared to be real wounds and blood, messy clothes, and a pale countenance did the trick. Father had to think he was our prisoner, then we'd announce his demise.

Connor and I had talked about it, and we both agreed that pushing Father's limits might go in our favor. Good decisions were never made with despair, and losing his general of the army would do just that. It could go both ways, but we were willing to take the chance.

"What about the envoy from Empire City? Has there been any other news?" Mathews asked.

After our call, Abi had reached out to Jess. The envoy Connor sent out about two months ago contacted us. They were granted an audience with their council and already had a liaison in Empire City. Her name was Jules Sinclair. She was a general in Empire City and the person responsible for sabotaging Father's trade system.

I looked at the computer screen, where Connor, Abi, and the rest of the councilmembers watched us from the farming conference room. Matt and Mark were there also. Faez was on-screen too, direct from the caverns.

Connor tapped his fingers rhythmically on the table. "Still nothing."

I clenched my jaw. We were running on fumes as it was. Scouts still fought out there to keep the troops away. An explosion here and there. Camps set out deep in the mountains. Scattered minefields to confuse their militia. It was working and giving us time to stand again, but the moment to strike was closing in.

I watched the faces on the monitor, then darted my eyes around our table. Most stared down at their hands. Others shifted their gazes around the room like me, as if looking for answers. Spirits were low even after two weeks had passed.

I propped my elbows on the table and interlaced my fingers, then covered my mouth. We couldn't win this way. We needed to be awake and push through.

Katherine stood and pointed to the map projected behind her. "We already sent our best miners to the tunnels." She indicated the spot where Matt, Abi, and I had to stop on the way here. "It's collapsed all the way into the forest, so they need at least two more weeks to make it viable for our soldiers."

"What about the rebels inside the city?" Jess asked.

"Aleczander Constantine, the head of Promissa's rebel cells, has made contact via checkpoint one's dead drop," Connor said. "He's been gathering more people to our cause and has started communicating with our spies in the government center. Martial law has been implemented throughout Promissa, but Electi's citizens seem to be unaware of the current situation."

Thank God they hadn't found that drop.

Connor and I spoke before the meeting. Constantine informed him he had NWG soldiers working for him. Peter and Abi's uncle assured us we had many supporters, but hearing it from the rebel faction's head gave me hope.

Countless soldiers worked for Constantine, and they were infiltrated deep within their ranks.

I thought back to Scott Davis. We knew he was being held but hadn't heard from Muñoz since our escape.

As for Mom, there was no way of knowing. I just hoped the love my father had for her was stronger than his rage.

I moved my hands over my face and pulled my hair back, grabbing it by the nape. God, if he dared put a finger on her, I'd lose it.

Connor rummaged through some papers and passed them around. "Constantine alerted the council of a situation occurring inside Promissa. There have been disappearances throughout the city. Citizens are being taken away to work on a new train. Constantine lost some of his people too, but he says he has enough to aid us when the time comes." He shared his screen. "A spy took pictures of the blueprints, and it appears to be weaponized."

I hid my fists under the table. I'd already told Connor about the initiative I suggested during my first council meeting, but to see it realized this soon shook me.

The screen showed a heavily armored train, with machine guns installed at different locations and modern cannons placed throughout it. Various compartments occupied the roof, which I could only assume were for missiles. A train made for war.

Father was not playing games. Whatever plans he had for this war machine sent chills down my spine. I was sure he had given it a lot of thought and had recruited the best engineers to work on it. The weapons appeared to be exceptional at first glance, and we had no idea what was hidden inside.

"We think his next step will be to take the war to the skies. We've all heard about the accounts of the last strike from our military before we lost the war. They took down most of the NWG's airfields in their last assault."

Connor changed the screen, and there were aerial shots of an airfield full of workers and half-built jets. "This airfield lies at the northern limits of Halcyon. Joe found this intel in the cloud. It came from Halcyon, possibly from one of our own. One of many we've lost contact with."

My chest expanded. Having a spy inside Halcyon could give us an incredible advantage. "How do you know this?"

"It was encrypted with our own cypher, but we haven't found anything else. We won't pursue it. We should focus on what we have."

I nodded. "Understood." Looking for a spy was like searching for a needle in a haystack. They were like ghosts, and we didn't have time to chase them. Still, I hoped one day we'd find a way to reach them.

Connor cleared his throat and changed the picture. Jets were parked next to the airstrip, their construction almost complete. "We believe these jets will be taking over the skies in no time. We need to act soon, or we'll lose our opportunity to win."

My blood thickened. Father had taken this one step forward. This was my initiative, and he'd used the workforce not only to finish the train but to take on the skies.

Connor switched the screen back to the image of their conference room in farming. "I already had some intel about this, but it far surpasses what we initially expected. I ask General Niles to please address the council on this matter." His gaze was set on me.

We knew the time would come when I had to explain what transpired while I was part of the council. When I first told him, he was enraged but understood it had to be done to secure my place at Father's side. I just hoped the others would also understand.

I looked at Matt and Abi over the screen. They gave me a small nod of reassurance. We'd been through it together, and no secrets stood between us.

My throat tightened, and I swallowed forcefully. "This was my initiative."

The tension in the room was palpable. Curses came from the monitor and whispers from all sides.

Abi's gaze did not leave mine, giving me strength.

Katherine planted her palms on the table, her penetrating gaze holding me in place. "What do you mean?"

"I had to get Father to trust me." I intertwined my hands on the table. "I had hopes we'd attack before he started collecting workers."

"You should have thought harder before making the decision to put innocent people in his hands," David said through the monitor.

Connor invited him to the meeting since his sniper team was key for our attack.

I gritted my teeth. "You wouldn't know. You weren't there." I looked at Abi, then Matt. There were choices we made out there that broke us. Impossible ones.

David flexed his fingers on the table and made them into fists. "At least I know I'd never use citizens as pawns."

I tightened my jaw. "And what the fuck do you think I should have done?" Who the hell did he think he was talking to?

David stood, and his chair fell to the floor.

Connor punched the table. "Sit, Martinez."

I stared into David's eyes.

A silent threat passed between us before he picked up the chair and sat, fists clenched on the table.

Connor shook his head. "We can't turn against each other now. Either you work through your differences, or you're both suspended for a week."

Abi sat opposite David and glared at him.

David reached for her but pulled his hand back when she lowered her head and shook it softly. She looked at the camera and nodded at me.

Connor squared his shoulders. "General Niles, once we all regroup in farming, you will be expected to give a full report on your time as part of the NWG council."

I straightened. "It will be done, sir."

He nodded. "I know you already briefed me about this, but the council needs to know. You need to recall every single conversation from all the council meetings you attended. It's time for war, and we can't leave any stone unturned."

Chapter 10

Abi

April 26, 2214

"Enter." Connor's voice filtered outside.

The door to his office squeaked as I opened it.

He gestured for me to come in. "We're almost done."

Matt and Zachary sat in front of the desk.

Matt turned toward me. His ashen complexion made me stop for a moment before I approached.

I touched his shoulder. "You okay?"

Matt raised an eyebrow, then nodded.

What had him on edge? Aoki was doing better, so it couldn't be that. Had something happened to Davon?

No. He was coming back today, and they would have told me the moment I came in. It had to be something else.

Zachary stood and moved aside, offering his seat. "Please."

I waved dismissively. "I'll stand. Thanks." I wanted to ask what was happening, but it was not my place, so I stayed silent, waiting for them to finish.

Zachary stayed up. The shadows under his eyes marked another hard night.

It hadn't taken long to find out Doctor Zachary Lewis lived for his job.

I went to the infirmary daily to lend a hand, and most patients were doing much better, but many were still on the road to recovery, especially those who had lost limbs or had gone through surgery.

Zachary was almost living in his office at the infirmary, taking breaks only when another doctor made him, who was usually Matt. Both men looked on the verge of exhaustion.

Connor put away his tablet. "That will be all. We'll reconvene tonight after Davon gets back." He looked at me. "I want you here also."

"Sure." My pulse peaked for a moment.

I came to talk to Connor, not knowing he was in a meeting. Nina just showed me in, and now I was being summoned to another meeting later. One that, by the look of the men in this room, appeared important. It seemed like they'd been here for hours, and it was only 7:00 a.m.

Matt came to my side. "Breakfast?"

I smiled. "Later. I want to talk to Connor about something."

He nodded. "All right. See you later." He followed Zachary out.

Connor motioned toward the seat Matt had vacated. "Sit. What brings you here?"

I sat. "Sorry for interrupting. Nina said I could come in." With everything going on, I hadn't had time to talk to him about Tammy's involvement in Sarah's rescue.

Connor smiled. "No need to apologize. My office is always open to you. You're family." He put away the files that covered his desk and gave me his undivided attention. "Tell me, what's got you winded?"

The weight I'd been carrying lessened at his endearing words. Just knowing he was here for me filled me with peace. Even though we hadn't had much time to talk lately, he was family, and his presence centered me.

I swallowed dryly. "Has Deb talked to you about Tammy?" Saying her name brought a sour taste to my mouth.

Connor raised an eyebrow, then leaned back in his chair, tracing the curve of his wedding ring with his thumb. "She did."

"And what do you think?" I held my breath.

He grimaced. "I'm thinking of all the ways I can kill Tammy."

I sat forward. "Do you think it was an attempt to get the intel out?"

"It's obvious." He pressed his lips together. "Fucking bitch." He rubbed his eyes furiously. "She'll suffer for this."

The door opened, and Nina came in with two mugs of coffee. "I thought you both might want some."

Connor took one. "You're a lifesaver."

Nina grinned as she handed me the other.

I sucked down my nausea and waved my hand. "It's fine. I just had some."

She left with it.

The truth was I hadn't been able to drink coffee for a week. Maybe it was because of Davon's situation or everything that was going on, but I couldn't keep anything down. I was surviving on protein and potatoes and avoided everything else like the plague.

This whole thing had started in Electi, and I thought it was because of Jordan and the mission. Maybe with everything that was happening, my anxiety had taken hold and affected my body.

He looked down at his mug. "By the way, I was about to call Nina to get you. I wanted to talk to you about something."

Something about the way he averted his gaze made me pause.

I hunched forward, clasping my hands together in an attempt to calm my nerves. "Sure. What is it?"

"It's about Davon and you. About your mission out there."

I interlaced my fingers. "What about it?"

He met my gaze. "I want you both to see a therapist. You should work with her before we go to war."

I settled back and rubbed a hand over my face. "Therapy? Are you serious?" *God.* I didn't have time for this shit. In truth, I didn't think anyone could help erase the stuff we had to do out there.

He took a sip of coffee. "You went in there, pretending to be someone else, and were forced to harm our people. I know what you did affected you deeply."

Our hands were tainted with the blood of our fellow rebels. I shuddered when I thought of Thomas and Joanne. Our mission had claimed Thomas's life and possibly Joanne's. But that was our problem, not his or the doctor's.

"With what time? Tell me, Connor. How are we supposed to pull ourselves together with the enemy at our doorstep? We'll swallow our pain and push through. There's no other way."

"We can't continue ignoring what you went through out there. David told me about the nightmares. About the flashbacks." Connor's tone was stern.

I humphed. *Traitor.*

"Listen to me, Abigail."

So he was using my full name now.

I rolled my eyes. "Do you think I don't know where things stand?"

I wanted to shake some sense into him. Everything was going to hell out there, and here he was, trying to push therapy on us. Hell, everyone in here needed it after the attack. We'd all lost a part of ourselves out there.

"Davon will be back today. You both need to figure things out. I need you to be 100 percent when you're out there."

I crossed my arms. "We *will* be. Just trust us."

He furrowed his brow. "I won't back down. Just one session—that's all I ask for. If you don't accept, you'll be removed from your duties till further notice."

I hissed. "You're such a hypocrite."

Connor widened his eyes.

Fuck! Did I just say that out loud?

He rolled his chair away from the desk and clenched his hands over his thighs. "Say that again."

I loved Connor, but he had to stop this nonsense. "You're one to talk when you can't accept what you were dealt. When you're abandoning Deb and her child. You prefer to drown in work rather than deal with the problems at home. I don't think I'm the only one who needs help."

He blanched and propped his elbows on his lap, then hid his face in his hands. "That's different."

I walked to his side and put my hand on his back. "How is it different?"

He slumped back in his chair and sighed heavily. "How long have you known?"

I sighed. "Deb told me about it. She appears calm, but I know she's hurting."

"I just can't fathom that he's Niles's son. What if he's evil like his father? He's a mutation. Not human." His voice quivered.

"Connor." I stroked his arm. "Davon is your brother, and he's also Jordan's son."

He exhaled hard. "Don't compare them."

My stomach hardened. How could he be so...? Argh! "This is bullshit, and you know it. Tell me, how are they different?"

Connor punched the desk, and I jumped back. "They violated her. They took away her will and impregnated her while she was unconscious. How can I just sit here and accept this creature as my own?"

A chill swept over me. I hadn't stopped to think how it was for him. The three of us were out there together, helping each other push through, while he was all alone in here, trying to make sense of it all. And knowing him, he didn't tell a soul. He just kept pushing, setting aside his feelings, and being the general everyone needed him to be.

But what about Connor Harris, Deb's husband, the twenty-eight-year-old man who carried the heaviest burden of all—to lead the rebellion?

My throat burned, and tears threatened to leave my eyes. "I'm sorry I wasn't here for you. I'm sorry about everything."

"Don't be." He shook his head and kept his gaze down.

I wanted to reach for him. To give him the comfort he craved during all those months. "Connor, please. I'm here for you."

His glassy eyes found mine. "You wouldn't understand."

This was the man who helped me through my worst moments, and now he needed me. I shifted his chair so he faced me, then pulled him to me.

He hesitated for a moment before he put his arms around my waist and sobbed.

I stroked his hair, holding him fast against me. "I'm sorry this happened to you."

His hot tears wet my uniform. "I know I'm wrong. I just... She came back different. They took away her light, and I don't know how to get things back the way they were."

Connor always appeared strong, but the weight he carried on his shoulders was massive, and he was as broken as the rest of us.

I kneeled before him and cupped his cheek. "Start by being there for her."

He leaned into my hand as the last of his tears dried. "I'll try."

My mind traveled to the morning the baby kicked. "Did you know she named him Douglas?"

His eyes softened, and he nodded. "Deb told me. Like your father."

I offered him a small smile. "She doesn't see Jordan Niles's son. She sees hope in the soul that was with her in her darkest hours. She survived for him. For you."

Connor's Adam's apple bobbed as he swallowed hard.

I touched my temple to his. "Don't give up on her. Don't let hate hinder your love."

He grabbed my hands. "I'll do my best and visit the doctor also."

I sighed.

Maybe it was time Davon and I looked at ourselves. We were all damaged. Broken. And we needed to fix it.

I shot the target and reloaded. Practice made perfect, and David ordered me to go out every afternoon to the valley and practice shooting for at least an hour. This was my second hour.

I'd been pushing myself more than usual to fight the constant exhaustion that had taken over my body. The rebellion needed every able body, and I would not fail my family.

I jolted as two muscular arms closed around me from behind. By the feel of it, the attacker was much bigger than I was.

My brain went into high gear, and I shifted my weight forward, just like Jacob had taught me. Using all my strength, I struck back with my elbow. The grunt told me I hit the spot. I cocked my gun and spun around.

Davon was bent over, holding his abdomen with both hands.

His surgery!

I put the safety on and went to him.

"Davon?" I tried to see the harm I'd done, but he wouldn't let me. "Please, love. Talk to me."

What did I do?

He put a hand up, gasping for air.

God. I fucked it all up. "Stay here. I'll go get Matt." All else faded as I started toward the bunker.

He gripped my arm, holding me midstep. "I'm all right."

I turned back to find him still clutching his stomach. "Did I hurt you?"

"No, it just took my air." He chuckled and looked up. "Hell. You almost knocked me down."

"Don't laugh. I could have hurt you. What were you thinking?"

He shrugged. "About how much I missed my woman and how good she looks in uniform."

I couldn't help but smile. "Are you sure you're all right? What about the surgery?"

"It's okay. It's on the other side, and it doesn't hurt. I'm good." He stepped into me and gave me a sultry smile, then grazed his fingers down my arm, took my gun, and holstered it inside my waist.

His touch electrified me down to my core. God, I missed him.

I hugged him fiercely, savoring the feel of his arms around me as he picked me up.

I wrapped my legs around him and buried my face in the crook of his neck, taking in his musky, leathery scent. "I missed you."

He kissed my neck and nipped my earlobe, which sent shivers down my body. "I see they got that sleeve off."

"Yeah." I pulled him closer and giggled as he rubbed his stubble against my neck. "Why do you insist on surprising me while I'm armed?"

He laughed deeply and touched his brow to mine. His dark eyes were full of mirth. "You look sexy when you're in your element." He smirked. "I just can't resist."

I played with one of his wavy locks. "You're crazy."

"Maybe I am." He raised an eyebrow. "Now, how about I properly kiss you?"

I grinned and pressed my hips against him. "Be my guest."

It wasn't proper at all.

We entered the bunker and ran into David.

He looked at our joined hands, then up at Davon. "You're back." Gone was the caring voice I was used to. It now had a rough edge to it. A dangerous one.

Davon squared his shoulders and squeezed my hand. "I am." His tone was stern, like that of a general to a soldier. His grip was strong.

Was he doing it because of David?

The tension between them was palpable, and I held my breath, hoping to hell this didn't end badly.

David took a step back and pocketed his hands. "Sorry about yesterday. I shouldn't have overstepped."

Davon relaxed his hold. "Let's let bygones be bygones."

My whole body relaxed at once. I hadn't noticed how tense I was until the standoff between them ended.

David shifted in place. "Well, I'm off. I'm training the new recruits from science."

"Wait!" Davon called after him just before he reached the exit. He let go of me and walked to him, then gripped his shoulder. "Thanks."

David furrowed his brow. "For what?"

Davon jerked his head my way. "For keeping her safe."

"Always." David smiled at me. "She can drive me crazy at times, but it's worth it. Abi is a force to be reckoned with. I pity the souls who fall on her bad side."

Davon raised his eyebrows. "Believe me, I know."

My worries eased. We'd work things out.

David darted his gaze my way. "See you later?"

I nodded. "Sure."

Davon walked back to me and rested his arm over my shoulders. "Can we go somewhere private?" he whispered next to my ear.

Goosebumps rose on my left side. "Yeah."

I grabbed his hand and guided him to my room, one I was assigned after being named as councilmember.

A familiar fire burned within me when Davon locked the door.

He claimed my mouth, then started kneeling.

I stopped him midway. "My turn."

I pushed him against the wall and removed his shirt. Then I saw it, the scar from the surgery. It was on his left side, opposite the one Deb had given him. I grazed my fingers over it, and he took a shuddering breath.

I pulled my hand away. "Does it hurt?"

He shook his head and drew my hand back until it touched his skin again. "Don't stop."

His plea was my undoing, and I kissed the contour of his phoenix tattoo, nibbling and teasing as I made my way down. His scent sent a current straight to my center, and I melted for him.

"Abi," he murmured breathlessly as I kneeled.

He strained against his jeans, and I freed him.

I took him in my mouth. His musky scent filled me with need, and it made me crave him even more.

He fisted his hands against the wall.

Having this kind of control over him made me bolder, and I increased the momentum.

"Love, I can't take much more." His erratic movements told me he was close, and I took all of him.

"Fuck, Abi!" He grabbed the back of my head and held me to him, then buckled against me.

His essence filled me. It was bliss as wave after wave crashed into me. He was mine.

He pulled me up and kissed me. "That was amazing," he whispered between kisses, then pushed me back until we reached the bed. He gave me a seductive smile. "My turn."

I fell back onto it, and he removed my uniform.

I arched up as his warm breath reached my center. The feel of his tongue on me drove me wild, and I grabbed hold of the sheets, squirming for more.

He was relentless. Unwavering. And it kindled something inside me that grew and grew until my whole world shattered around him.

He stayed there until the storm passed, his rhythm worshiping and intimate. He kissed his way up until he climbed on top of me. "I want to feel you." He slid into me in one strong thrust.

Our moans echoed around the room, and I pulled him deeper.

His grunts, the push of his hips, his bulging muscles, and the weight of his body against mine rekindled my ecstasy.

He grabbed my shoulder with one hand and lifted my hips with the other, increasing his pace until my pleasure skyrocketed. With one last stroke from him, my core contracted. I cried out as pleasure ripped through me and I lost my sense of time and space.

He stilled within me, mouth open in a silent scream, and came undone again.

Still holding my hip, he moved his other hand toward my nape and brought me up to him, angling me so he could kiss me passionately, still as one.

The moment was intimate and tender, our love permeating from our bodies. It was something else. Something deeper.

We collapsed on the bed, exhausted.

I threw my leg over him. "Can I assume by what just happened that you no longer have doubts about us?" I made circles with my fingers on his chest.

He chuckled. "I guess so." He held me close.

I took a deep breath. "God, I missed your scent."

He faced me, eyebrows squished together. "What are you talking about?"

I looked up from the crook of his shoulder and placed kisses along his stubble until I reached his lips. "Mmm. It's your natural scent. Musky. Leathery."

I widened my eyes, remembering something. I climbed on top of him to make my way to the side table.

He started tickling me.

"Hey! Stop it!" I hit his chest and squirmed, struggling to open the drawer.

The rumble of his laughter vibrated below me, but I grabbed what I was looking for.

I sat up, straddling him. "I made this for you."

He took the bracelet and smiled.

I grinned, unable to hide my glee at his reaction. "Aoki helped me."

He passed it back. "Will you do the honors?"

I clasped the bracelet around his wrist. "Do you like it?"

"I love it." He kissed me. When it ended, his calloused hand covered my cheek. "I love you so much." His eyes were bright. His voice cracked with emotion.

"And I you." I let myself fall into his embrace. Into the peace only he could give me.

Chapter 11

Abi

April 26, 2214

When we entered Connor's office, Matt was standing beside him, both staring earnestly at a computer.

Zachary sat in front of the desk.

Matt peeked at us from underneath his blond curls. "Good, you're here. You have to see this."

He turned the computer. It showed blueprints of some kind of facility.

"Is this Frank's intel?" Davon asked.

"It is," Connor said.

Matt opened another window.

A list popped up, each entry with a word written by its side, medical jargon I didn't understand.

I pointed at the screen. "What are these?"

Matt scrolled down the list. "These are diagnoses and quantity of supplements or medicines to administer to each enhanced soldier."

Was this why Connor called us in? To talk about the enhanced soldiers?

I browsed through the list. No names were written down. My pulse quickened. They were just numbers to them.

I jerked my face toward Matt. "Medicines?" Did their creations come defective in terms of health? Weren't they supposed to be superior?

Matt straightened and walked around the desk. "Remember, we talked about some of them having cognitive problems?"

I nodded.

Matt sneered. "It appears their little experiment has also led to other situations. No matter how much you alter a body, it always has a limit. They hit these creatures with large dosages of a chemical Dad developed with a team of experts."

Connor clicked on a picture of an enhanced soldier as a doctor plugged some kind of device into his body. It was set on his forearm and fit into his skin, with a small circle that opened to the outside.

"These chemicals boost their metabolism, and the other supplements keep their bodies running," Zachary said.

I faced him. I almost forgot he was sitting to my right.

Zachary fixed his glasses. "These devices check their body chemistry periodically and automatically administer what each one needs. They last about a week or two, then they need to be replenished. Each soldier carries extra doses so they can change it on the battlefield."

"So without these, what happens to them?" Davon asked.

"They would eventually collapse," Zachary said.

"You see, humans aren't supposed to be this way." Matt paced around the office. "I was just telling Connor maybe we should send Constantine's rebels to take down these supplement facilities. Our scouts can watch for any incoming shipment of these supplements. Either way, these creatures are an abomination. They are monsters programmed to kill, not to feel. We should block these supplements and take them down."

What the hell? My stomach roiled at Matt's assumption.

"I understand where you're coming from and the harm they've done, but we can't assume they're incapable of feeling." I grabbed the edge of the desk. "They're still humans, after all."

Matt raked his hair back. "Look, Abi. I'm not talking about the children they've created from Promissa's genetic pool. Maybe they do have hope. But these freaks from Halcyon." He shook his head. "They're something else."

"They're not at fault for what those assholes did to them." My hands hurt from the strength I was using to grip the desk.

Davon shook his head and sighed. "You haven't seen them. They're not human."

I widened my eyes at him. "There has to be a way to save them."

Davon rubbed the small of my back. "I don't see a way to fix them, love."

I frowned, then jerked away. How could he jump to conclusions without even trying? "We won't know unless we try." I darted my eyes between the two men I adored and saw only disdain in their features. A hate that made my skin crawl. "You can't be serious."

"We are." Matt came to my side. "We can't risk not taking them down. Our community will be endangered if we let them in."

I shook my head. "At least try. Take one or two. Talk to them. See if there's a way of reasoning with them, of changing their alliance."

Connor rubbed his stubble absentmindedly. "Abi does have a point." He took out a tablet from his desk and tapped it.

We all turned to him.

Matt stepped forward, blocking my view. "No! You know how I feel about this. We already tried. It's useless."

Zachary stood and faced Matt head on. "It's not! We have an opportunity here that we must take." He flexed his fingers into a fist.

Davon wrapped his arm around my waist and pulled me away from them.

My heart thrummed in my ears as the tension in the room skyrocketed.

Connor slammed his palm on the desk with such force that we all jumped. "I won't tolerate this kind of behavior in my office. Either you calm the fuck down, or you can both leave."

Both men breathed heavily but stood down. Zachary sat, while Matt leaned against the wall.

Connor passed me the tablet.

A video feed from an enclosed room showed a man in his twenties. He was massive, much bigger than Connor, who was built like a tank. His dark-brown hair was cropped short, and his muscles strained against the gray fabric of his shirt and pants. He sat on his cot with his elbows propped on his knees, eyes set eerily on the camera. It was a live feed.

I lifted my gaze to Davon. "Is he one of them?"

Davon eyed the tablet from behind me. "Yeah. That's one of the enhanced soldiers who beat the crap out of me."

I gripped the tablet hard.

In one of our calls, Davon told me they'd taken some of the enhanced soldiers hostage.

I shook away the violent thoughts that rushed through me. The urge to hurt the man on the screen. To make him pay for what he did.

I took a deep, cleansing breath, trying to contain my burning rage and think this through. I put aside my wrath and focused on the real culprit, Jordan Niles. These men were just his victims, the same as all of us. They were brainwashed. Created with a sole purpose—to kill and destroy.

I'd only seen them from afar, but they were incredibly strong and relentless.

"When did they arrive?" Davon asked.

Connor sank back into his chair. "Two days ago."

Davon grunted. "What do you plan to do?"

"Interrogate them. Matt and Zachary came up with a way to control them," Connor said.

I focused on the video feed and caught the soldier studying the room. His fingers twitched, and he rubbed his hands down his pants. The camera followed his movement, and he tilted his head toward it. He raised an eyebrow as he gazed into it. It was as if he was looking right at me, and I couldn't shake the feeling that he was a very intelligent man, not a mindless monster like Matt suggested.

Davon shook his head. "I get what you're trying to do here, Connor, but do you think they can be trusted?" His gaze hardened. "For God's sake, they ripped apart our soldiers." He looked at me for a moment before exhaling heavily. "They're beasts."

I brought his hand to my chest. "Let's hear Connor out." My heart ached for Davon and all he'd been through, but as Zachary said, this was a chance we couldn't lose.

Connor rested his arm on the side of his chair and leaned into it. He rubbed his chin, his fingertips tracing his lower lip before pulling away. "We want to see if they can be reasoned with and find out what they're made of to get an idea of what we're going up against."

The soldier had something inserted in his upper left arm. It looked like the mechanism we discussed earlier. Some kind of medical cuff was secured around each wrist but not to each other, so his arms were free to move.

I pointed to the circle in his upper arm. "Is that the device that releases chemicals?"

"It is. The three of them have it," Zachary said from my right. "We already recreated the supplements and are giving them what they need."

"And the cuffs?" Davon asked.

"They're designed to track their vitals and neurological responses," Zachary said. "They suppress adrenaline surges at any spike of aggression."

Matt approached Connor's desk. "That's what Zachary and I created to manage them if they lose control. It keeps them in check. They'll save your life if he tries anything while you're in there." His gaze never left Connor.

I shuddered at his statement.

"What do you mean while she's in there?" Davon's voice carried a menacing tone, one directed toward Connor.

Connor looked down at his hands. "Matt tried to talk to him to no avail and ended up making it worse by hitting him the moment he misspoke. I have no mind to go in there after all I've witnessed. This one is the only one who has talked to us even though it hasn't been amicable. I thought maybe Abi could speak to him."

Davon was about to talk back, but I grabbed his arm. The veins in his arms were popping out. He took a deep breath and stepped back, giving me the space I silently asked for.

I gulped. "Why me?"

Connor's soft gaze caught mine. "Because I know you. You never give up and always see the best in people. Something tells me you'll find a way. I promise you'll be safe."

"What if he attacks her?" Matt clenched his hands on the desk.

Zachary mirrored him. "You know the cuffs will take care of that."

"I don't like this." Matt huffed and shook his head.

Davon stood beside him. "Me neither. I can go in. I can make that motherfucker talk in no time."

"And that's why I'm not sending you in. Rachel has been treating him, and he's shown no sign of violence toward her. She wanted to be the one to interrogate him, but I prefer a councilmember in there, someone who has all the information." He gave me a fond smile. "I would never put you in harm's way. You know you're like a daughter to me, and I would be the first to stop you if I didn't think it was safe."

I swallowed the lump in my throat because even though I considered him like a father to me, it was the first time hearing the words from him.

Connor cleared his throat, then shifted his gaze to Davon. "Look, I know what these monsters are capable of. I've fought them. But we need another approach if we want to find out how their minds work."

"Another approach?" Matt's tone was hard. "This one almost killed Davon. They shot Aoki and took almost half our forces down, and you want to get to know them? That's bullshit."

Connor stood, fists grounded on his desk. "Don't you think I know what they did?" He tilted his face away from us, shook his head, then faced Matt straight on. "Fuck, Matt. I know every person we lost out there. Each one of their lives meant something to me, and I couldn't do shit to protect them. But maybe this way we can look for a way to get back. Who knows what we can achieve?"

My stomach quivered, and I tried to shake away the feeling that something was terribly wrong about his statement. There could only be one thing he was thinking of. "So you want to use them? Is that your plan?"

Connor grunted and pushed away from the desk. He stood and crossed his arms. "I don't know what the fuck I'm doing, Abi. But we have to try something. Otherwise, we're in the dark. We need to understand how they work. What they did to them. How deep their hold is on them and if they can be turned against their creators. There has to be a way to get through to them."

Maybe if we got to know them, we could learn from it, but using them... "I'll do it but on one condition."

Davon grabbed my arm gently. "Are you sure about this?"

I covered his hand. "Do you trust me?"

Davon nodded and let go of me.

My chest swelled at his understanding because, knowing him, he was fighting the urge to take me away from all this.

I put the tablet down and rolled my shoulders back, my mind set on what needed to be done.

Connor moved his hands to his back. "Go ahead."

If they fought alongside the rebellion, it would be because they wanted to, not because we made them do it. "If we're successful, we take them in, not as our possessions or weapons but as part of the PRF. We let them incorporate into the community and give them the choice to fight or not."

Connor shook his head. "Abi—"

I raised my voice. "I won't follow in the NWG's footsteps. I won't be like him." Using them as weapons would make us just like them. I wouldn't do it. Not ever.

Connor let out a hard exhale. "If you're successful and they do show some humanity, I'll give them a chance, but I can't promise anything."

The pounding in my ears quieted down, and I relaxed. "Thank you."

Matt took my hand. "I will stand by you, but please be safe."

I squeezed his hand, feeling the tension between us disappear. My brother was with me too.

Connor slumped into his chair. "I promise you'll be protected. I'll make it so you're never alone. Soldiers will be just outside the door, and Rachel will be by your side at all times in case he makes a move. The cuffs should take care of him, but if they fail, she'll have a tranquilizer gun with heavy sedatives at the ready."

I nodded.

"Then it's settled. We'll get everything ready and let you know when we'll start." The room went silent for a moment before Connor continued.

"If we're successful, we'll use the same facilities they used against us to reeducate them. We'll offer them a chance at life after all of this."

A light flared inside me. "Yeah. We can make a program, some kind of system where we readapt them to our way of life."

"But what if they can't readapt?" Davon asked.

"Let's not cross that bridge until we reach it," Connor said.

Zachary stretched his hand toward Connor. "I'll take my leave, then. I have to attend to some of my patients."

Connor shook it. "Thank you for your hard work. We'll talk later."

Zachary nodded, then left.

Davon squeezed my hip. "Maybe we should go. It's late."

My stomach growled. It was past nine, and we hadn't had dinner.

"Wait." Matt tapped the computer screen. "Before you leave, there's something I wanted to show you." He moved the computer so we could all see it. "It's better if you all read it."

Son,

There aren't enough actions to make up for every sin I've committed during this regime. I won't deny that at first, I paralleled or maybe surpassed Jordan's vileness. The truth of it all is that this whole genetic program and the idea of controlling the population once we took power was my own. I convinced Jordan as well as General Thorne Steele that it was the right move to make.

It was only when Lisa threw one of my files in my face that I understood the gravity of my actions. You were only eight, and she'd found you making doodles on a file inside my study. When she went to scold you, she opened it.

I never thought I'd feel so ashamed of my work, but having the woman I loved calling me a sick monster changed everything. She made me see the truth.

I was drowning in power and never stopped to think that the people who were here before us were human beings. I was broken inside, but there was nothing to do. I tried to sabotage the project in Halcyon, but Thorne Steele was—excuse the redundancy—a thorn in my side. He was obsessed with the project and learned how to run it. He was vigilant. Guarding it like it was his, and it became his once Jordan and I moved into Electi.

Then it was my time to make amends. I want you to understand that the children who have been created through the Elysium and Apex Projects from the Promissa gene pool do not have their genes altered. I lied in the files you found. They are just like us, except for the ones who are part of the Prometheus Project. Those will be enhanced humans and will need supplements through-out their lives, but you can still save them. If I survive this, I'll help you with the ones growing inside the facilities in Electi. They aren't at fault for what I did.

Jordan doesn't suspect, but if he finds out, he will destroy everything. Please protect them if anything happens to me. I attached a map of the locations of their holding facilities.

Once you go into Electi, I urge you to take control of the in-vitro facilities. They'll be the only guarantee for future generations. I included a detailed account of everything we hold inside.

Please be safe, and count on me for whatever you need.

Love,

Dad

"He sabotaged the projects." Davon sighed. "God, if Father finds out."

Matt took a deep breath, then let it out hard. "Dad dies."

I stood frozen in place. Frank had risked it all for his family, and we could lose him in a second the moment Jordan discovered his betrayal.

I remembered his charismatic ways. The love he had for his son and for Lisa. The caring way in which he always treated Davon and me. If anything happened to him, my heart would break.

We needed to protect him. It couldn't wait. "Can we get a hold of Frank?"

Connor seemed lost in thought for a moment, then he propped his elbow on the armrest and rubbed his stubble. "Maybe we can get a note in through the hospital facility inside Promissa. We have people there. It'll be dangerous, but we can create a dead drop somewhere inside."

"Let's do that." I put my palm next to the computer. "Put him in contact with Constantine's people. He may prove helpful on the inside." I clenched my fists. "We need to get him out after our attack begins. We'll assign a troop to take over his rescue once inside. He'll be in danger, and we can't risk him."

Connor's eyes gleamed. "Who are you, and what have you done with Abigail Davis?"

I laughed, then sobered when I caught Matt's and Davon's perplexed expressions. "What?"

Matt took my hand. "Thank you."

I chuckled nervously. "It's nothing. He's one of us."

Davon's hand pressed against the small of my back.

Connor clicked the keyboard, and a map appeared. "Let's make a plan."

By the time we were done, it was past midnight. Nina had brought in sandwiches and refreshments earlier, so we went straight to bed. Just as I snuggled against Davon's chest, there was an urgent pounding on our door.

Davon was up in an instant, gun in hand.

I lowered his arm and drew him back into bed. "Relax. I'll go see who it is." I slipped on his T-shirt, which hung down to my knees, and opened the door.

Sarah's green eyes met mine. "It's the baby. It's coming."

I was awake in a second, my heart threatening to break out of my chest. "Is Deb okay?"

Sarah grabbed my hand. "She's all right. Zachary is already with her in the operating room. Connor too."

"We'll be right there."

Sarah nodded. "I'll go get Rachel." She ran down the hall.

"What happened? It sounded urgent."

I turned to see Davon already pulling on his jeans.

My breath caught for a second. "It's Deb. She's having the baby." I wanted to scream for joy, but worry for her well-being had me grounded. There were too many risks to ignore.

Davon froze for a moment. "My brother."

We both went into high gear and were ready within five minutes.

"Where is this operating room?" Davon followed me out.

"We prepared a hall for surgeries and emergencies. It's the same hall where Aoki is staying."

My heart thundered as we made our way through the web of passageways I'd grown accustomed to. What if something went wrong?

David stood in front of a door when we got there, Sarah next to him.

"That must be it," I said.

We were panting by the time we reached them.

"How is she doing?" I asked David.

"She's doing good. Zachary and Rachel are with her, and Connor just went inside." He brushed my arm lightly before withdrawing his hand.

Davon snaked his arm around my waist and yawned. "Come on. Let's sit."

We sat in a waiting area with David and Sarah.

Rosa came in with a tray full of coffee mugs.

"You're an angel." David helped her pass them around. He gave me a mug.

When I smelled the aroma that had once given me so much comfort, nausea churned in my gut. *I hate this.*

I put the mug on the side table.

Davon touched my thigh. "You're not having any?"

I waved dismissively. "I'll have some later. I'm just not in the mood."

He pulled our brows together. "Deb's strong. She'll make it. My brother too." He gave me a quick peck on my temple.

I took in a comforting breath and let myself fall into the crook of his shoulder. Soon I'd meet my nephew.

Douglas was about to be born.

Chapter 12

Davon

April 26, 2214

A soft hum carried through the hall, followed by the rhythm of rushing footsteps. The double doors swung open.

Matt pushed Aoki's wheelchair into the waiting room.

Aoki's gaze swept across the space, and he smiled as he found us.

I nodded at them.

Matt came around the wheelchair and crouched in front of his husband. "I'll be right back, love." He gripped Aoki's thighs.

Aoki cupped Matt's face with both hands. "She'll be all right. You're the best."

Matt kissed Aoki's hand.

Aoki grasped Matt's silver necklace and brushed the back of its yin-yang pendant with his thumb. "Have I told you how much I love this?"

A jolt ran through me at the memories of that night. We gave that pendant to Matt on his birthday. It had an infinity symbol engraved on its back with their initials. That was the last dinner we had as a family. The last time I saw my mother. I shuddered and closed my eyes, praying my father's devotion to her was greater than his thirst for vengeance.

I opened my eyes and hugged Abi to me.

Abi squeezed my hand, lightening the load that had fallen onto my shoulders.

There were so many people to protect. So many things that could go wrong.

I twisted my head enough to capture her gaze. With her soft smile, all the fog in my mind cleared, and I relaxed.

"Countless times," Matt said, getting our attention back to our friends.

"Well, I do love it." Aoki tugged the necklace to him, drawing Matt's lips to his in a lingering kiss, then he whispered something in his husband's ear.

Matt blushed and chuckled. "I'll hold you to that."

Hope blossomed as I watched my two best friends. This was what we were fighting for. Our family. Our right to live our lives to the fullest without a regime pressing down on us. If their devotion to each other wasn't reason enough to stand and fight, then nothing would be.

Aoki stroked Matt's cheek, caressing down to his neck.

Matt caught his hand and kissed it. He offered Aoki a roguish smile. His fingers slid down Aoki's long, dark hair, which hung loose, till they reached his waist and squeezed it. "I love you."

Aoki smiled. "And I you." He slapped Matt's butt. "Now go. Do your thing."

Matt kissed him one last time, then dashed inside the delivery room.

I made to stand, but Aoki gestured for me to stop.

"I can do it myself." He pushed the wheels of the chair until he faced Abi, then he jerked his face toward the door, curving his lip up in a mischievous smile. "He's so hot when he's in his element."

I snickered. "I don't know about that." I shook my head. "He's always looked like an asshole to me no matter what."

Abi kicked my ankle, but Aoki laughed out loud.

I clasped Aoki's shoulder. "Sorry about the procedure."

After our meeting, Matt explained the device they'd created didn't work. They'd tried the procedure a week ago, and there was still no movement in Aoki's legs. Michael said he'd make some adjustments to the device in a week or so.

My blood boiled at what they'd done to my friend. Aoki was a soul who should roam freely, and to see him bound to a chair fueled my anger toward my father. So many innocent people were dead or permanently damaged by his indiscriminate attack.

Aoki waved nonchalantly. "Ah, no worries. We knew it might not work."

"But Matt said they'd keep trying," Abi said. "We're not giving up on you."

"I know." Aoki's eyes glistened with tears he'd never shed. That was just him, a man who refused to let others see his spirit crumble.

Aoki raised both eyebrows. "Any news?"

I took my coffee from the side table, my gaze set on the double doors. "We just got here."

Abi offered her mug to Aoki. "Here. Have mine."

We both watched her.

She took his hand and put the mug in it. "Just take it."

Aoki stared blankly at her. His perplexed look mirrored mine.

I furrowed my brow. "Are you okay? This isn't like you. You never refuse coffee."

Abi propped her elbows on her thighs.

I caressed her back. "Are you sick again?"

"It's been happening lately. I'm anxious. That's all." She took three deep breaths and sat up straight. Then she took something from her pocket and bit it.

I pointed at her hand. "What's that?"

She opened it. It was a ginger root. "Rosa gave it to me yesterday. She was worried that I'm not eating much because of the nausea. I told her I'm just anxious, but she insisted on giving me this. She also said I should visit the doctor, but I'm sure it'll go away. I'm almost certain it's because of all that's happened." She pocketed what was left of the ginger, then patted my knee. "I feel better. Don't worry."

She'd been this way since Electi. I attributed it to my father's presence and the stress she was under. But now... "Are you sure?"

She cast me a sidelong glance. "Positive." Her ashen complexion said the opposite.

I was suddenly aware of every single time Abi had run out of a room after mentioning Father. Of the times she'd been sick after we got here. Now this...skipping coffee? My heart lurched. Could it be that...?

I caught her hand and brought it between us. "Say you'll go see Zachary after this."

She watched me with an unsure gaze. "I don't know. I don't want to bother him."

I kissed her knuckles. "Just do it for me."

She hesitated for a second, then nodded.

Zachary was an obstetrician before all this started. That's why he took care of Deb personally. If what I suspected was right, he was our best shot.

My chest expanded at the prospect of having a family. I couldn't dwell on the hows and whys, but if it was true, I'd raze the world to keep them safe. I would protect them with my life.

Sarah and David went out to ask about Deb's status.

We waited for them for quite some time. Abi's eyes started to close.

I kissed her temple. "Sleep. I'll wake you if anything happens."

"Okay." Her voice was but a whisper. She leaned into me.

I hugged her to my side, and she drifted off to sleep.

Long minutes passed in silence before Aoki gave me his empty cup. "Are you thinking what I'm thinking?"

A moment of understanding passed between us.

I raked my hair back. "Yeah. I don't understand how, but it's a possibility. She's been like this since Electi."

Aoki nodded and darted his gaze between us. "Have you been taking your pills?"

"I have. That's why I don't understand." I'd been cautious. I was free of antibiotics when we decided to sleep together for the first time after the attack.

Aoki sighed. "Nothing is 100 percent effective. And it doesn't have to be that. It might be stress induced."

I sighed. "It's not that I wouldn't be happy. It's just the timing." I clenched my free hand on my thigh. My stomach roiled as a dark thought passed through my mind.

She'd never agree to stay behind. She was set on going out there to fight. How could I protect her from herself?

Aoki patted my knee. "Let's not rush into it. Maybe it's nothing."

Sarah dashed inside, and a baby's cry filled the quiet room.

My pulse quickened at the sound.

Abi woke instantly.

Sarah smiled. "They're both okay."

We rushed to the hall and found Connor holding his baby. My brother.

Connor's smile said everything. This was his child. He'd protect him with all he had.

I stepped forward, unable to hold myself back.

Connor's eyes met mine. "Want to hold him?"

He pushed the bundle into my hands, and I thought I'd break him. He was so delicate, so small. Dark hair covered his small head. His olive skin, just like mine, reminded me of my mother and father. This was my brother. My blood.

Abi caught his chubby hand. "He's beautiful."

I smiled as the baby pressed his mouth against my chest. I darted my gaze to Connor.

Connor took him from me and put his finger in the baby's mouth.

My brother started sucking.

"Hungry already?" Connor chuckled.

I looked sideways to find Abi's stunning smile set on her nephew. "How's Deb?"

"Matt and Zachary are finishing up with her. The C-section was a success, and she was never in danger. She already saw the baby." His expression sobered for a moment, then he swallowed and smiled. "She'll be okay."

For an instant, a shadow loomed over Connor, and I couldn't help but worry. What was he hiding? Was Deb truly okay?

"Can I hold him?" Sarah asked.

"Sure." Connor put the baby in her arms.

Abi went to her sister, a smile plastered on both their faces as they fussed over the baby.

Love surged through me at the sight. My brother would live a happy life with a family who loved him.

Then reality seeped in, and I saw my father's reflection in him. I thought of the moment he told me about his child. About his creation.

I wouldn't let Father get his claws on Douglas. I wouldn't let him break my brother the way he shattered me. I'd do whatever was needed to protect him.

It took everything in me not to go into Deb's room when everyone entered, but it wasn't time. We weren't ready.

I paced the hallway for some time before I decided to go to the room where we read Father's email. Two soldiers watched the video feed from around the perimeter. No reapers were in sight. No attacks coming.

The soldiers turned and nodded as I went to the computer in the corner of the large desk. I clicked on my email. No response.

I sent a message to Father the second I woke from my surgery. One with a video file of Lavigne after being *tortured*. I expected an outburst from him, but it never came.

My fingers itched to write another email. I wanted him to know he couldn't keep us down. That he hadn't won yet. I swallowed my rage and closed the computer. It was not time.

In a week, we'd send him a picture of Lavigne's massacred body. We needed him to believe we'd killed his trusted general.

I prayed it would be enough to convince him because I wanted him to lose it. We were entering dangerous territory, but he made harsh decisions when put in a corner, and that might work in our favor.

I went down the hall and took a right.

A soldier stood guard over the cell block. He saluted. "General Niles."

"I'm here to see General Lavigne." The man to whom we owed our lives.

"He's in the last cell on the left." The soldier wrote down my name and let me pass.

The thud of my boots echoed around the empty hall. I found Peter sitting on his cot, fiddling with his wedding band. He must miss Suzanne.

His light-blue eyes widened when they found me. It broke me to see him this way.

We'd met many times since he came with us, but after much consideration, the council decided to keep him as a prisoner until we could explain his alliance to the rest of the community. After all, he was known for the horrific deeds he did for my father, and we needed to explain before letting him roam free.

I grabbed a chair and sat. "How are you doing?"

He shrugged. "I've been treated worse."

In science, he was under guard by Seth and Katherine, but when he arrived at farming, something happened.

The soldiers here had lived through the worst of the attack, and when they saw Lavigne, they were out for vengeance. Some sneaked into the prison the night he arrived and beat him badly. Connor reprimanded them and gave the order that he was not to be touched. Some protested, but no one dared oppose our general.

Matt checked Peter afterward. He was heavily bruised, but there wasn't any permanent damage.

Peter rubbed his jawline. A dark bruise had started to show. His eyes were swollen. "I deserve worse."

I shook my head. "You had no choice."

He nodded toward me. "And you? Do you forgive yourself for all you've done? Can you live with the evil deeds you've carried out for him?" He chuckled ruefully. "No, boy, there's no redemption for us. No forgiveness."

The weight on my chest grew heavy as the truth of his words sank in. Some good news might help his morale. "Carol will be here in a day or two." She had already moved to the caves, but Faez gave her permission to come to us.

He was at the bars in a second. "And the child?"

I shook my head. "Mark opposed it. He will not risk Diane."

Peter nodded. "I understand. Will I get to meet him?"

"I'll tell him to come by."

He let go of the bars. "Thanks."

"Tomorrow we'll have an assembly with the caves via satellite. We'll tell everyone you're an ally. After that, you can roam the bunker freely, and the council will take you in as an advisor."

I had talked to Connor about it, and he understood Lavigne was our best option against the NWG. Having their general on our side raised our odds of winning exponentially. Also, I needed him. He was the man who held me together when my life was upside down. I wouldn't have anyone else by my side during these difficult times.

Peter went back to his cot. "Let's hope all goes well." He met my gaze. "Did you start with the tunnels?"

I nodded. "We're on it. We think they should be cleared out in a few weeks."

His eyes gleamed. "And you will attack then?"

I cracked my neck. To hold back on the attack could be dangerous, but we weren't ready. "Not yet. First, we'll move everyone to the caverns, then we'll plan out how we'll approach this war. The soldiers need time to heal, so we keep pushing their forces away by any means possible until we're ready. If we rush the attack, we might lose everything."

He dropped his gaze. "Have you heard back from the Liberty Enclave?"

I pressed my lips together. "No news yet. Our group should've already met with their council. We can only wait."

There was too much hanging in the balance. We needed more. We'd lost too many.

The pit in my stomach grew by the day. Without their aid, taking back Promissa would be possible but harder. Sure, we were working on better weapons and armor, but from what Father said, the Liberty Enclave army was a force to be reckoned with, and having them on our side could be just what we needed to win.

"They'll answer your call." For a brief moment, Peter's expression was distant. "What about the cells inside the city?"

I couldn't help but smirk. "They're ready. Waiting for our orders." Knowing they were with us gave me solace.

"That's good." Lavigne rubbed his growing stubble.

He was always an elegant man, clean-shaven and with an air of grandeur. What you would expect of one of the most powerful figures in the NWG. But now his unkempt appearance seemed unnatural. Almost like I was talking to another man.

He gripped his shoulder, rolling it back, then grimaced. "Have you heard about your soldiers?"

Dozens of soldiers were missing. We weren't ready to give up on them, but my hope was dwindling as time passed. "Still nothing."

"He has them." Peter's tone was stern.

I propped my elbows on my knees and massaged my temples. "I'm positive he does."

My mind traveled to that morning. To Anna killing that reaper and Pedro's impaled body. She was one of the missing soldiers.

"We will get them back. Have you heard from your man?"

Muñoz...

I shook my head. "No, but I'm hopeful."

We'd sent Constantine the locations of two dead drops we had around the city, including the new one at the hospital. He'd sent in his people to check them. If they weren't compromised, he'd reach out to Muñoz.

I cracked my knuckles. Muñoz had proven to be one of our best agents, and I couldn't lose him.

The right side of my head started pounding. I gritted my teeth. I had to stay strong.

Peter tilted his head toward me, his eyes dead serious. "Focus, Davon. We regroup. We strategize. And we take Jordan down. We leave no room for doubt. We go in and win. There's no other option."

I left the hall with renewed faith. We'd make it.

April 28, 2214

"I'll take care of her," David said from outside our door.

Abi, who stood between us, nudged him with her elbow. "I can take care of myself, you know."

David gave her a smile that made me shift in place. A smile not given by a friend. His eyes glinted with something much stronger.

I stepped closer to Abi and caressed her back, my fingers grazing the skin between her tank top and the seam of her cargo pants. "We know, love. Be safe out there." I pulled her to me by the curve of her hip, kissing her temple.

Her hazel eyes met mine in a feverish gaze.

The warmth of her skin brought back memories from this morning. Of her cries of pleasure as I grabbed her hips. Of her hands grasping the bed against my heavy thrusts. Of her hair between my fingers as our bodies clashed against each other.

Memories of her silent scream as her body contracted around me, pushing me closer to the edge. Of her scent when I pulled her up. Her back slick against my chest as I gently wrapped my hand around her and grabbed her breast, eliciting a moan from her luscious lips.

My lips tingled at the memory of her smoldering kiss as her storm passed and mine was about to begin. The warmth of my palm as I reached down to cover her center, then thrust deeper into her, again and again.

"Fuck, Davon." I could almost hear her voice. Watch her as her limbs weakened and she almost fell forward onto the bed.

My muscles strained to keep her up against me as I pushed deeper into her. My fingers stroking that place that turned her body into fire.

"Yes!" She covered my hand with hers, pushing herself over the limit for the second time.

Her body went taut against mine, and I quivered as my ecstasy reached its limits and I couldn't hold it anymore. I came hard, letting myself go into her.

"I love you," I whispered in her ear after all was over, then peppered kisses across her nape when her head leaned against my chest.

Her glazed eyes met mine in a satisfied gaze.

I eased out of her, then hugged her and lay her on the bed. Her breathing evened out as I caressed her navel, bringing her body back from that place where we forgot about everything and let our love run wild. Free. Raw.

The moment was gone when David cleared his throat.

I frowned and came back to the present.

David left first, giving us some privacy.

"I'll see you later." Abi pulled me down, then kissed my chin, my cheek, until her lips met mine in a gentle kiss, one that promised so much more.

Comms came in hours later when they reached the halfway checkpoint.

"Phoenix to Falcon. On our way back."

I sighed at the sound of her voice. "Copy that."

Every time someone left the safety of the bunker, dark thoughts swallowed me, more so when it was Abi. I trusted David implicitly, knowing he'd never put her in harm's way, but still...

I walked back to our apartment to find Peter and Mark already in deep conversation over some beers David had left.

Yesterday's assembly had been heated. The rage harbored toward the NWG grew when they were presented with their general. Many hours passed before they finally conceded that he was an ally. We presented all he'd done and how, thanks to him, we'd found the spy.

The heartbreak of being betrayed by Tammy was still palpable among our citizens. The wound still too close to the surface.

Peter Lavigne renounced his position in the NWG and took an oath to protect the PRF and fight the enemy. He'd be an advisor to the council but would be just one more soldier in our army. Nevertheless, in no time, he'd be respected and followed. He was just that kind of man.

Mark passed me a beer when I joined them at the table. Abi and I decided to use our room, preferring a more intimate setting for what was about to happen.

Peter clutched his mug. "Thanks again, Mark, for making this possible and for taking care of my daughter."

Mark shook his head. "There's no need to thank me. You both deserve this." He took a sip of his beer. "When Carol arrived, she was a broken woman. It took a long time for her to trust me with who she really was, and she missed you dearly. I think if it wasn't for Diane, she wouldn't have moved forward. I somehow knew you had to be good because she adored you no matter what and always had hopes that you'd find each other someday."

"After she escaped, I vowed to live a better life. To make her proud no matter where she was." Peter closed his eyes for a moment. "The day we found your base I spent hours searching." He tilted his head and clenched his jaw. "I thought I'd find her corpse among so many." A lone tear escaped his eye. "I'm so sorry. There were so many dead. So many families just lying there, lifeless at my feet. Murdered by the orders of a psychopath, and I couldn't do shit." He abandoned his beer and fisted his hands on the table. "I'll never be able to make up for that day. I'll never forgive myself for the genocide that took place because of my orders."

The heaviness of his words drilled deep within me. The atrocities we had to commit to appease my father's twisted desires would forever haunt us.

Mark gripped Peter's hand. "You're here now. That's what's important. Whatever you did out there stays in the past." His gaze darted between us. "You were both his victims but in a different way than ours. I'm just glad you're here with us now."

Mark's words eased the pain that grew inside me. When I glanced at Peter, he'd covered Mark's hand with his.

"Thank you." Peter's lips curved up in a half smile. "This seems surreal. That I'm actually meeting Carol after so many years of leaving flowers at her grave. After thinking I'd never see her again."

Mark patted Peter's hand. "She'll be thrilled to see you."

There was a knock on the door, and Peter's chair almost tumbled over as he stood.

I put my beer down. "I'll get it." I opened the door but stopped halfway.

"It'll be all right, Carol. Just go in there. You have no idea how much he's waited for this moment." Abi's soft voice lingered as Carol's hands shook.

They were holding hands.

"It's been so long. What do I say?" Her eyes misted, gaze set on their joined hands.

Abi squeezed her hands. "And who says you have to say something? Just go in there. Peter has mourned your loss for so long. He's never given up hope."

A couple of tears slid down Carol's cheeks. "But that's it. I abandoned my parents without even saying goodbye. I was so mad and scared that I didn't wait to think of the consequences. Of all I'd miss."

I opened the door wide and stepped outside, careful to close it behind me so she didn't feel exposed.

She opened her eyes wide. "Is he...?"

I nodded. "He's in there with Mark."

Abi let go of her hands so Carol could face our room.

"Carol, there's no better time than now to mend the past and start over. Forget about the time missed, and cherish today. You have your father, and he's done nothing but long for this moment since he lost you."

My chest ached at the knowledge that I'd never have this. Peter had changed the moment he saw the error in his ways. Frank too. But Father... I shook my head. There was no sense in even thinking about it. He'd already gone too far. He was lost to me.

I grabbed her hand and smiled. "Come on. Your father can't wait to see you."

She took one step, then another until only the door stood between her and her father. She reached for the handle and turned it.

Peter was standing right there. His eyes gleamed as he studied the woman standing in front of him. He took a tentative step forward.

"Dad." Carol's voice broke, and I let go of her.

"It's really you." He took a shaky breath and bowed his head. "I'm sorry for all you went through. For not being brave enough to stand for what was right." His chin quivered as he looked up. "For pushing you away." His voice cracked.

I fought back my tears as the burn at the back of my throat rendered me speechless. The person who had brought me up like his own son. The man who showed me how to push through and not let myself be bullied or changed by the evil that was my father was bowing down to his daughter and asking forgiveness for all his deeds. He had renounced his old life to defend our cause.

Carol burst forward and into her father's arms. Her sobs mirrored those of a child who clung to her father like a lifeline.

Peter's hands shook, as if not daring to move, but then he wrapped them around her and buried his face in her neck.

Their cries echoed across the room, and I took a step back at the force of the emotion that burned throughout the area.

Abi grabbed my hand. Her eyes shone with unshed tears as she pulled me to the door, giving them the privacy they deserved.

Before leaving, I glanced back to find Mark, glasses in hand, wiping away his tears at the scene that appeared before us. A reunion that was long overdue.

A spark flew across the darkness that had overshadowed my mind, reminding me of what we fought for. Family. Community. And love.

April 30, 2214

"Can you pass me a bun?" Carol stretched her hand toward Matt's side of the table.

"Sure." Matt grabbed a bun and passed it over.

"Your food is something else, Aoki. I haven't been able to keep much down lately with all that's going on, but this..." Abi munched on her steamed bun, then moaned. "This is something else."

Aoki bowed over the table. "Glad to be of service."

The buns were filled with vegetables and cooked to perfection. It had been a long time since Aoki had prepared something like this, and it was the first time he had cooked since his surgery. Carol had helped him.

I took a bite of my teriyaki chicken. It melted in my mouth. When its sweetness hit my taste buds, fireworks exploded in my mouth.

Carol pursed her lips. "I didn't know you were feeling off."

Abi waved dismissively. "It's nothing."

Carol drew her eyebrows together. "If you say so, but maybe you should go for a checkup."

Abi sagged in her seat. "Okay. I'll do it. But, really, it's nothing."

I sighed inwardly. I'd been trying to get her to see the doctor. I couldn't get my mind off the conversation I had with Aoki. We even talked in therapy about it, but Abi insisted it was nothing.

We were having dinner with Peter, Carol, and Mark. Connor had lent us the conference room so we could have our privacy.

Carol and Peter's reunion had been heartbreaking. To see the man I considered my father crumble into tears at the sight of his long-lost daughter had moved me deeply.

Peter clinked his metal mug with his fork. It was filled with beer, as were the ones each of us held. "I have a few words."

He stood. "First of all, I wanted to thank you all for joining us tonight. Looking into my daughter's eyes after so many years is a blessing I hadn't expected to get during these trying times. Thanks for keeping her safe, and even though Suzanne isn't here, I'm sure she'd be ecstatic to know I finally found her."

Carol's crystal-blue eyes misted, and she brushed her father's forearm.

He smiled at her, then looked at Mark by her side. "Thanks, Mark, for taking care of my family. I..." His voice shook, and he captured our gazes, one by one.

Abi was sitting beside him and covered his hand.

He swallowed hard and returned her gesture. "Thank you for giving me back my hope."

Peter stayed silent for a moment, then raised his mug.

Matt stood. "I also have a few words."

Aoki smiled from his wheelchair beside him.

"God, no." I raised my mug. "Peter, go ahead and clink your glass against mine. I can't take another one of Matt's toasts."

Peter chuckled.

"Well, since Peter has no complaint, I'll ignore Davon's plea and follow him in his toast. When I found out you were our ally, I couldn't have been more relieved. To have to fight you out there would have killed me." Matt glanced at me. "It would have killed us both." He returned his gaze to Peter. "We're glad you're here and will always be thankful for what you did for us out there." He lifted his mug. "Welcome to our family. Cheers!"

We all drank.

Matt put on a solemn face. "Most importantly, I want to thank you for being around, especially because of Davon."

I rolled my eyes. "And there he goes."

Abi snickered beside me, knowing exactly what was coming.

"He's been an asshole for the longest time, and dealing with him has been one of the most difficult tests we've had to endure. Abi has helped."

He tipped his mug toward her. "You're an angel, hon, but it's not enough." His gaze returned to Peter. "We need you because you've always been able to put up with him. We trust that in your hands, he'll be able to reach maturity at last so we can endure his presence a little bit longer."

I choked on my beer, and everyone burst out laughing. Matt just grinned and winked at me.

I held up my mug toward him and nodded. "I love you, man. Even when you're being an annoying prick."

Only he could bring joy in such challenging times.

We clinked our mugs and drank wholeheartedly.

My heart hitched as I took in everyone at the table. My family. I prayed we'd all make it through to the end.

Chapter 13

Abi

May 3, 2214

"We can't wait much longer. While we're here, our soldiers are trapped God knows where. They may already be dead or about to talk." David's harsh words were directed at Davon, who'd just announced we were going to give our envoy in the north a few more weeks to reach out to us. "You know better than anyone what happens in there."

I stroked Davon's thigh under the table, noticing his muscles tense, then gaped at David. Everyone at this table knew about Davon's job in Electi, but using it to prove his point was a punch to the gut. "The tunnels into Promissa aren't clear yet. We can wait a bit longer."

David clenched his fists on the table. "For how long?" He lowered his head, then let out a long, quivering breath. "I'm scared for our people. Who knows what Niles is planning for them or what may already be happening inside our city? We're blind right now, and they're suffering."

We all carried that same fear. Jordan was a monster, and he would stop at nothing to destroy us. What if he hurt Rebecca? Sure, he adored her, but I'd seen him lose it before, and the possibility that he could harm her didn't escape me. Then there was Uncle Scott. I shivered just thinking of the things he'd be going through because of his treason. I squeezed Davon's thigh, seeking the comfort only he could give me.

Davon covered my hand under the table. "I understand, Captain Martinez, but we can't make rash decisions. As Councilmember Davis said, the tunnels aren't clear yet. If we don't hear from them by then, we'll attack."

Attack. War. All would come to an end soon, and we needed all the help we could get. I closed my eyes, silently praying the Liberty Enclave would answer our call before the tunnels into Promissa were cleared. Their army made Jordan nervous from what Davon told me, and if true, its presence could be crucial for our victory.

Then there was the reaper waiting for me inside that room. The one I'd talk to after this meeting. My legs quivered at the thought. Nina showed me the video feeds of them out there. The way they fought was savage, and facing one had me rethinking why I accepted Connor's offer. If I could somehow get him to understand our pledge, maybe, just maybe, he'd decide to fight by our side.

David darted his eyes between us and nodded.

Connor promoted him to captain just yesterday after Mark was promoted to colonel.

David had a team of snipers and soldiers under him. I was part of that team, which he personally requested. We'd been strategizing nonstop about how to enter the city. We decided where we'd hide and how we'd wreak havoc so the government troops would move into the most advantageous positions for ambushes.

David was a pure soul, and he, like Davon, lived for the rebellion. Last night we talked over some beers, and he told me it was proving impossible for him to just sit back and do nothing. He said if it wasn't for his loyalty to the PRF, he'd have already disobeyed orders and gone inside the city.

"We have intel that might ease your worries, but first, we need to talk about Aleczander Constantine," Connor said from the head of the conference table.

We all turned to him.

He passed a file to David, and when he opened it, something stirred in his gaze. "So this is the leader of the rebel factions."

Connor nodded. "As you all know, we investigate all citizens in order to ensure our safety. After processing Mr. Constantine, we found some interesting intel about his past. It's all in this file."

David passed a page. "It says here that he's an elite trained by General Thorne Steele."

Davon took his hand away from mine. "Steele?"

The room grew quiet and my leg restless. To be trained by the second most powerful man in the NWG was not something to be ignored. This man could be dangerous, and I wondered what made him turn against his people.

"He came from Halcyon when they arrived, a lieutenant at a young age," Connor said.

David creased his brow. "Do you know why he became a rebel?"

Connor sighed. "It was because of love." He tapped his pen on the desk. "After much digging, we found intel that he fell in love with a Promissa citizen, one who opposed the regime. When Constantine's superior found out, they executed his lover in cold blood. They made a spectacle of it, breaking his bones one by one before finally cutting his throat open. Constantine deserted the NWG militia after that, set on ending their tyranny. It's all in the file."

David turned a page and recoiled for a moment before gripping his throat.

Nina, who sat next to him, covered her mouth and turned away.

David shook his head, then pressed his eyes together before relaxing his grip on the file. His menacing gaze turned to Connor. "When did this happen?"

"Ten years ago when Minister Niles implemented the regime in Promissa. We all know fear and cruelty reigned during those early days. Many died trying to resist him."

David held the file up, showing us a picture of a massacred man on a pole. "This is what we stand against."

Blood drenched the front of his body, and his limbs rested in weird positions.

Gasps erupted across the room as we witnessed the cruelty of our enemy. I thought back to my parents. To their cold-blooded execution. To Sarah's trauma. I pictured their bodies lying on the street, forgotten, as if their lives meant nothing.

I shivered, thinking of what could be happening to our people right now. To how Jordan might respond to our betrayal. To the vile things he could do just to spite us.

After a moment, Connor continued. "Now, as to why I brought him up, Constantine finally accessed one of the dead drops that connects us to the prison. Muñoz left a note."

David turned another page, then widened his eyes. "The soldiers."

"Can I see it?" Davon asked.

David extended the file across the table, and Davon took it. He put it between us. Muñoz didn't write much, just a sentence: *They're alive.*

A list of names followed. My heart skipped when I saw my uncle's name. He was alive, as were Anna and about a dozen of our soldiers. But many names were missing. Did that mean they were already dead?

Davon slumped back in his seat, and I took the file.

A picture fell out. A handsome black man in a navy-blue suit stared back at me. He had perfectly trimmed stubble, and his eyes were so dark you couldn't make out the pupils. There was something about him, a promise behind his intense gaze.

"Is this him?" I held the picture up to Connor.

"It is." Connor's expression turned sour.

"What are you not telling us?" Seth shifted in his seat next to David.

Both he and Katherine sat with us today, having arrived yesterday with the rest of the science citizens. We were slowly vacating the bunkers, preparing for our move to the caverns.

As for Yuxuan, he had left early to train our forces. Because of his injury, he would not be able to fight on the battlefield for some time, so he was assigned to the protection of our civilians once the war started. He was also training our new recruits in hand-to-hand combat and close-quarters combat. Connor wanted our soldiers prepared to defend the bunker and, in time, the caves.

Connor clasped his hands on the table. "Constantine informed us that a new curfew has been put into effect. Anyone found outside during these hours will be killed on sight."

I stilled. *Killed on sight?*

Our happy moment lasted but a minute before everything tumbled down.

Did Jordan decide to push the purge forward? Had our citizens already proven unnecessary? Or did Jordan finally lose it?

Time slowed as we waited for our general to continue.

"He estimates more than a hundred have already been killed. Constantine has been using the tunnel system Davon discovered to move his people inside the city, but Promissa is drowned in chaos."

My blood chilled. Our people were being kept prisoner inside their own homes.

A chair screeched.

"Will we not retaliate?" Corporal Mathews gripped the edge of the table. His muscles bunched beneath his uniform.

"When the time comes." Connor took the file from Davon.

"You're saying we'll just sit here and do nothing while our people die?" Mathews pointed outside. "They're killing them, and you plan to do nothing?"

Connor stood. "I won't tolerate insubordination at this table. You either sit or leave, but once you're out, you're suspended till further notice." His tone was terse, his voice unwavering.

I dared a look at Mathews. His breaths rushed in and out, and he slowly sat.

Connor glared around the table. "If for a minute any of you think what we're doing isn't enough, you can come up here and take my seat. If any of you know of a better way to confront this, I'll gladly step down."

I was rooted to my seat by his words. Never had I seen Connor like this.

The room was dead silent.

I hid my trembling hands under the table, and Davon wrapped his hand around mine.

Connor sat. "We will retaliate with force once the tunnels are clear. Even if our people inside the Liberty Enclave haven't communicated by then, we will attack." He turned toward Matt, who sat at the other end. "Lieutenant General Anderson, will you please explain our strategy to the council?"

Matt rose. "Yes, sir."

The meeting was calm after that, everyone's attention raptly on Matt. All had ideas that were noted down. Our strategy could work even with small numbers.

The rebels inside the city were taking on recruits and arming themselves with the help of the disloyal NWG soldiers. They'd wait for our orders to engage.

Once our spies inside Electi took the minister of transportation hostage, our attack could start. Most of our plan depended on this since we needed control over the train to stop the government from sending in enemy reinforcements from Electi, especially the reapers.

The sniper team would enter using the tunnels to reach different buildings inside Promissa. Part of our armed forces would wait inside the tunnels till the time came to attack.

Constantine's troops would plant bombs inside part of the supplement facilities. Their detonation would mark the start of the attack.

After the explosions, Joe would hack the system and broadcast a message from Connor, unveiling all the lies the NWG had told over the years and calling for action. Thanks to Joe, I was able to get inside the government's system without endangering our cover, and now he was in charge of making sure we could get through the system. He'd also control the train once we had access.

Snipers would start taking down NWG officers all around the city, then our soldiers would come out of the tunnels, taking advantage of the confusion.

The other half of our troops would come in from the forest. We needed the NWG to think we had many, and attacking the city from all sides was our best shot.

Our first objective was to take down the government center. We were still working on the logistics and everything that came after once we moved into Electi.

This plan started over some beers at David's, and now it was finally ready to be put into action. We had a lot of work ahead of us. I just hoped everything worked out the way we intended.

A double mirror showed us a complete view of the space. White walls surrounded the room, with a cot lying in a corner and, next to it, a small bathroom, which had little privacy.

Davon grabbed my hand just as I gripped the door handle. "I don't feel good about this."

I let go of the knob and faced him. "It'll be all right. You and Matt are right here, and Rachel will be inside with the tranquilizer."

Matt furrowed his brow while watching the reaper intently. "I still don't like it."

I sighed.

"Guys, you need to let go of your macho-man attitude and trust we'll be all right. Lucas hasn't been violent toward us, unlike how some of us have been." Rachel stared at Matt.

He raised an eyebrow. "So he has a name now?"

Rachel stepped forward and clenched her jaw. "Why wouldn't I give him a name?" Her skin flushed beet red. "Or are you planning to do to him what those bastards did?"

"Sorry." Matt put his hands up.

Rachel hissed. "Ever since he came, I've been assigned his routine checkups. I would have talked to him, but Connor was adamant the interrogation be run by one of the higher-ups. He's been nothing but gentle toward me and hasn't shown any sign of violence." She raised her eyebrows. "That is until a certain person went in there with another plan in mind."

Matt shifted in place. "In my defense, he was looking at me the wrong way, and I thought he would attack."

Rachel tsked. "Whatever you say."

"Okay, guys. Stop the bickering, and let's get this started. I have to go with David to secure the way to the caves for the next group moving out, and we're losing time." I grabbed the knob, and the man inside turned his attention to the door.

Davon hugged me, then kissed the top of my head. "Be careful in there."

Some of the pent-up stress eased off my chest. I nodded.

Matt gave Rachel the tranquilizer gun. "At the first sign of aggression, you pull the trigger. You won't kill him. He'll just sleep for a while."

Rachel huffed, then took the gun and put it inside her gray nursing uniform, hand secured on the trigger. "It won't come to that."

Davon grabbed her arm. "Rachel, that man in there is a monster. Put it inside your head. Don't think for a second he won't attack if he feels threatened. Hell, from what I've seen out there, he'll attack while you sing him a lullaby."

Rachel bowed her head. "Understood."

Matt took both my hands in his. "Be cautious, keep your distance, and don't trust him."

"I will." I turned the knob.

An eerie silence enveloped me the moment I crossed the threshold. A shiver ran down my spine when I glanced into his crystal-blue eyes. His cold stare didn't leave me until Rachel stepped in. He took a small breath, then his posture relaxed, as did his gaze. It was almost imperceptible had it not been for Davon teaching me in Electi how to catch it. Body language would tell you a lot about a person, and from what Rachel had said outside and his actions, I believed there was some kind of connection between them.

I stretched my hand toward him. "Hello. My name is Dr. Davis."

I held a file in my left hand and gripped it against my white coat. Even my name was embroidered on it.

Connor didn't want him to know I was a soldier. The reaction to our uniform might prove violent, and he wouldn't risk it.

The enhanced soldier didn't take my hand.

I took it back. "Do you have a name?"

He arched an eyebrow. "412." He darted his eyes toward Rachel, who stood by the door. "But she calls me Lucas."

Numbers. They were just numbers. How could we expect them to be calm and rational when they weren't even treated like humans?

I breathed slowly to calm my raging heart. "And which do you prefer?"

He nodded toward Rachel. "She can call me Lucas." He turned a hard gaze toward me. "But for you, I'm 412. That's what all of your kind called me."

Frank had told us they were used to having doctors around.

"Okay." I opened the file. "Based on your biometrics, you should be between eighteen to nineteen years old."

He groaned. "I'm twenty-one."

So he was from the first batch of soldiers the NWG created. "And you were sent here by General Steele?"

"I don't know names. I just follow orders." His tone carried some threat.

I quieted my nerves for the next question. "Do you know where you are?"

"I only know you're my enemy." He didn't flinch, nor did his body react in any way. He was stating a fact.

"If you believe this, then how come we're taking care of you? Why are we keeping you alive?" I kept my tone as flat as possible, reining back my treacherous nerves.

He shrugged. "Strategy. Benefit. You name it."

I closed the file. "We are not your enemy. We want to help you."

He frowned. "If you're not, then why put these on me?" He raised his arms. "What do they do? What do you intend to do with us?"

I took a deep breath and controlled my desire to look back at the mirror. To tell Rachel to grab her gun. "We're just monitoring you. I hope you understand."

He straightened and put his arms down. "I'm just a soldier. I follow orders. I kill. And the People's Revolutionary Front is my enemy. That's all there is."

My skin crawled at the finality of his words.

I nodded. "We'll continue this conversation later. It was a pleasure meeting you, Lucas."

He widened his eyes but quickly recovered.

Connor's orders were to start a conversation. Small steps would eventually gain us the intel we needed, and for today, this was enough.

I offered my hand again, and his arm twitched for a moment before it went still.

I smiled and backed toward the door. "See you later."

I'd make him understand we weren't them no matter how long it took. That he would not be treated as an experiment but as one of us.

Wildflowers bloomed all around us as the trees returned from their slumber to fill the forest with green. David and I sat in a spot we'd found after coming back from securing the road north toward the caverns.

The relocation to the caves would take some weeks, leaving only soldiers and some staff in the farming bunker. We'd take everything, using Seth's vehicles, which had been moved here long ago as a precaution.

I passed David a protein bar. "I know we're going through a lot, but you've been irritated lately. Is there something going on that has you like this?"

We hadn't been able to talk much after Davon came back, and with my new responsibilities as a councilmember and with the enhanced soldier, I didn't have much free time.

He propped his elbows on his knees. "I feel like I'm losing it."

I leaned closer. "Is it because of what's happening in Promissa? Or is it something personal?"

Something had to be going on with him. Something had rattled him.

"It's both." He slumped and took a bite from his protein bar. Then he watched the horizon.

It was a clear day, no clouds in sight.

David rested his head between his knees. "I'm worried about you and about all the shit that's going on in Promissa. But there's something else." He sighed. "It's Jonathan. He's back."

I widened my eyes. "Your ex?" He must have come from import and traveled with Davon and the others. "Are you okay?"

He shook his head. "He came to me last night. He wanted to talk."

"And?"

David shrugged. "He said he was sorry. That he regretted letting me go. That he was ready for something more."

I furrowed my brow. Wasn't Jonathan the one who ended things? "What are you going to do? Are you going to give him a chance?"

Maybe during their time apart, he saw all he was losing. Maybe he found himself and finally accepted who he was.

David clenched his fists. "Why would I? He never bothered to contact me after leaving. Not even a note. Now he wants me again? As if nothing happened?" He shook his head. "I told him I moved on, but he insisted we try again." He sat back. "I don't want to deal with him right now."

Breaking with imposed beliefs could be scary, and accepting fully who you were was daring. For some people, it was easy, but for others, it took time. Aoki had only gone out with girls until he met Matt, not because his parents were against it, like Jonathan's, but because he hadn't met the right person. For him, it took some time to explore these new feelings. For Jonathan, having to go against his family had to be hard, but if I put myself in David's shoes, could I forgive him?

I rubbed my nape. "Maybe in time he'll back away. Or maybe you'll come to forgive him. You never know." I brushed his arm, but he jerked away.

"Por favor, no me toques así."

I took my hand away. "What did you just say?"

"I said, please don't touch me that way." He set his intense gaze on me. "Don't you understand?" His tone was harsh.

My pulse soared. "Understand what?"

He took a deep breath, then captured my arm and pulled me to him. His face was mere inches from me. "That when I say I moved on, it's because of you. I want nothing to do with him."

I took a shuddering breath and traveled back to my conversation with Aoki and Matt.

He closed his eyes, then softened his hold and rested his temple against mine. "I care for you, Abi, much deeper than a friend would. You're that part of my soul I lost out there." He shook his head without letting go of me. "I need you."

When he exhaled, goosebumps rose all around my nape.

I came to my senses and pushed away from him. "David," I whispered ever so softly.

I loved him, and I wanted him in my life but not like this. Not like he wanted.

He took both of my hands and kissed them tenderly, then put them over his heart. "I know you feel something for me, or you'd be walking away right now."

I opened my hand over his heart. "I do love you. There's a connection between us that can't be denied, something that draws me to you, but it's not romantic." I looked down. "It's not like what I feel for Davon. For me, there's only him."

David seized my chin so his eyes met mine. "Are you sure?" His pupils dilated.

My brain went into high alert. Was he going to kiss me?

I stilled and leaned away. "This isn't right, David. I can't."

His eyes misted. "We can come to an arrangement. We can work something out."

I frowned. "What do you mean?"

He brushed his thumb down my jaw. "We can talk to Davon. Get to know each other, and see if there's a way we can both be with you."

His words didn't hit me wrong. Open relationships were not frowned upon. Frank and Lisa were an example of that. And a polyamorous relationship maybe worked for him but not for Davon and me.

I cupped his cheek. "I'm sorry. I wish I could give you what you need."

I truly wished I could because the hurt in his eyes cut like a blade in my chest. He was hurting, and I was the reason why.

He closed his eyes, then kissed my palm. "I understand."

"I hope you can find someone who makes you whole in all the ways you need, but I'm not that person." I hugged him.

He whispered near my ear, "I don't think anyone will ever live up to you."

As we parted, he kissed my cheek, nearly touching my lips, then took a deep breath and let me go.

We stayed in silence for a long time until he stood and extended his hand to help me up.

We made our way into the bunker, and I spied Davon sending away some soldiers.

As if sensing me, he turned and made his way toward us. He greeted David with a strong forearm hold. "I hope there are no hard feelings between us."

I remembered the tension between them at the meeting this morning.

"None at all." David glanced at his watch. "I have to go. Mark wants me to train the group that came from science." His eyes met mine for an instant before he nodded and left.

Davon put his arm around my waist and kissed the top of my head. "We have some time before it's our turn to take care of Doug. Maybe we can find something to do." His eyes shone with mischief.

I gave him a sensuous smile. "And what do you have in mind?"

He leaned over me, brushing his lips across my ear. His warm breath electrified every fiber of my being. "Why don't I show you?"

I wanted to tell him about David, but I couldn't think straight when his lips traveled down and he nipped that sensitive spot beneath my ear, sending a wave of pleasure throughout my body.

Davon grabbed my hand, and I couldn't do more than follow his long strides toward the bunker.

An hour later, we knocked on Matt and Aoki's door.

"Coming!" Matt said as Doug's cries filtered out.

Ever since the birth, Deb had refused to see the baby. I didn't know what changed after the birth, but she had abandoned her son.

Zachary said it was probably postpartum depression and that, in time, she might accept the baby, but Matt had his doubts, as did Sarah. They both believed because of Deb's trauma, she might not accept him ever. It was one thing to feel him inside but another to see the uncanny resemblance he shared with his father. Even as a baby, the Niles genes were strong, and he was a picture of Jordan. Of Davon.

Deb told Matt and Aoki to take him away. Connor and I tried to talk some sense into her, but she refused, and even though we wished she'd accept him, she was in her right. The child wasn't hers. The pregnancy was forced upon her, violating her rights.

A couple of days ago, I opened the door to Deb's room, only to find Connor seated on her bed, kissing her passionately.

I covered my heart at the scene before me. *They're okay.*

I tried to close the door, but before I could, both of them jerked in unison toward me.

My cheeks burned, and I averted my gaze.

Connor's chuckle rang throughout the room. "Remember when Abi used to catch us like this? She was just a little girl, and she was always appearing when we least expected."

Deb laughed, and its sound filled my soul. "I remember her face going red just like right now."

My eyes prickled with tears as I recalled the days back in Promissa before my life was turned upside down.

Deb patted the empty space beside her. "Come on, Abi. We're all adults here."

I grinned. "That doesn't mean I want to witness my sister and her husband all over each other." I moved to her side as Connor stood.

He kissed Deb. "I'll be back later."

She gave him a yearning look before pulling him in for a not so gentle kiss.

I covered my face. "Guys!"

They both laughed, and when I turned my gaze toward them, Deb's beaming expression was like a sunrise, and it was only for him.

Connor brushed his thumb down the side of her cheek, grazing her mouth. "I love you."

She stroked his stubble with adoration. "I love you too."

After Connor left, I asked her about the baby.

Her demeanor changed immediately, and the sadness that usually consumed her came back with a punch. She'd smile for Connor, but when he wasn't around, a dark gloom took over the room.

She reaffirmed the same thing she had said after the birth: "I can't be his mother. Every time I look at him I see Jordan. I can't..." Tears flowed down her cheeks. "I can't deal with him."

Connor had worked hard to accept their situation, and now he was lost between accepting the baby and giving him away. He and Deb were all right as long as he didn't bring up the baby.

Connor still had hopes, which was why he took care of baby Douglas whenever he could, but most of the time Doug stayed with Aoki and Matt. The baby slept every night in their apartment, and we helped them during the day so they had some alone time.

Matt opened the door. "Come in. Aoki is almost done feeding Doug."

Deb didn't produce milk, and Zachary explained it was likely because of the type of pregnancy. Her body had gone through a lot of stress, and her hormones were crazy.

Aoki held Doug in one arm and a bottle in the other as the baby hungrily sucked the formula down.

Yesterday Michael and Matt had worked on fixing the stimulation spinal device, and we were anxiously waiting for the results. Aoki had tried yesterday to move his legs to no avail, but Matt said it could take some time.

"How's our bundle of joy behaving today?" Davon went to Aoki's side and lovingly brushed his brother's hair. He bent and kissed his small head.

The baby frowned but kept feeding.

Aoki watched over him with a smile plastered on his face. The love that radiated from him toward the boy was palpable.

"He's just like his big brother—hungry all the time and annoying as fuck." Matt couldn't hide his smirk.

I wouldn't have thought Matt would take the baby in, based on when he first found out about the pregnancy. He had always leaned toward Deb aborting him, but that was history now. Both he and Aoki cared deeply for the baby and had even offered to take him in. To be his fathers.

Connor hadn't answered, but I believed it would be for the best. Matt and Aoki would be incredible parents. The baby wouldn't lack a thing, and we all would help. Time would tell.

I walked over as the baby stopped feeding. The noises coming from him and his flushed face told me something was coming.

Davon winced as the stench filled the space around Aoki. "That went down fast."

Aoki chuckled. He wheeled his chair toward the bed, and I arranged the changing pad.

Aoki changed his cloth diaper with care. "Who's Daddy's stinky little boy?" he said sweetly, using a playful child voice, then he froze and looked at me. "Sorry, that slipped."

"Don't worry." I understood where it came from. After all, they were the ones taking care of Douglas most of the time.

Matt clasped Aoki's shoulder, and Aoki leaned into him.

"We've grown close to him." Matt sighed heavily. "But we understand if Connor and Deb want to keep him."

My heart was torn between my sister and Connor and my dear friends. I prayed that whatever happened they'd be strong.

"Come here." Davon took the baby in his arms and patted his back.

The baby burped, throwing up milk all over his shoulder.

"Glad I could be of help." Davon chuckled, then held the baby away as I wiped off the vomit.

I put a cloth over Davon's shoulder. "There."

Davon smiled at me and hugged the baby to him, humming lovingly and dancing in place.

I couldn't hide my smile as I thought what a loving father he would be. I hoped it would happen. That someday we'd have a family, a normal life.

Shirokuro passed between my legs, purred, and circled Aoki's wheel-chair, rubbing his fur on his feet.

Time stopped. A small movement, almost imperceptible, came from Aoki's right foot.

He froze.

I stepped forward. "Do it again."

His toes moved again, this time on both feet.

Light filled my soul. He'd walk again.

"Matt!" Aoki beamed with a huge smile.

Matt, who'd been standing just behind him, clasped the push bars of the wheelchair, his hands pale from the strength of his hold. "It worked—it actually worked."

Aoki laughed.

"What worked?" Davon had been rocking the baby, concentrating on making him feel better.

I grinned at him. "Love, it's Aoki."

His dark gaze settled on Aoki's moving feet. In two strides, he was next to Aoki, holding Doug with one hand, the other clasping his own hair back. "God," was all that left his lips as tears streamed down his face.

This man, one of the fiercest I'd ever met, was brought to tears by the healing of his brother.

Matt and Aoki left after a while, eager to tell Michael and Zachary about it and to start therapies.

The baby slept in the crib as we lounged on their taupe sofa.

I rested on Davon's thighs while he played with my hair.

His hand stopped. "Can we talk?"

I opened my eyes, aware of a shift in the room. His downcast attitude made me sit up. "Sure. What is it?"

"I saw you."

I studied him, confused by his statement, then I gasped. I forgot to tell him about what had transpired between David and me.

"Is there something going on between you two?" He sounded lost, his voice trembling.

I sat up and held his face until his eyes met mine. "There's nothing going on." I shook my head. "I'd never go behind your back. I'd never betray our love."

"But the way he held you, the way you let him touch you. I..." He gritted his teeth. "I wanted to hurt him." His eyes appeared darker, but he quickly recovered. "I can't be like that. I won't let him touch you again. If you want to end things between us, I'll step aside. But tell me now because I won't be able to stop myself if I catch him kissing you like that again."

"It's not what you think." My heart beat wildly. "I wanted to tell you right away, but, well...things got a bit carried away." I cupped his cheek. "There's nothing romantic between David and me. He just told me how he felt and asked if there was any way we could be together. That I didn't have to leave you. That we could work something out."

Before I could finish, Davon gripped my waist possessively and pulled me onto his lap. His muscles bunched beneath his clothes, his hands holding me in an iron grip. "I will never share you."

I held his stare. "And I wouldn't want you to. I told him no, that I didn't feel that way about him."

He hugged me, pressing his body against mine. "So there's nothing between you?"

"I made it clear that you're the only one for me."

Davon frowned. "And what did he say to that?"

"He understands."

His eyes clouded for a second before he nodded.

I kissed him then before he had a chance to react.

The kiss became heated. His taste was intoxicating, like sin itself. I grabbed his loose hair and pulled it back, bending over him so I could deepen the kiss. I ground my hips against him, but then a cry took over the room.

"The baby!" I yelled. "I forgot about the baby."

I pushed away from Davon, noticing my shirt was opened halfway.

"What the hell?" I buttoned it up.

Davon laughed as I hit him in the chest.

"Don't laugh." I stood frantically and headed for the crib.

I turned to Davon, baby in my arms, holding my finger to his mouth as he sucked on it. The baby calmed.

"If you could see yourself, you'd be laughing too." He adjusted himself, then went to prepare Doug's bottle.

He shook the bottle. "Give him to me."

"I can feed him." I suppressed a flinch as I passed the baby from my left arm to my right.

He tilted his head. "I know it still hurts, more so after your mission this morning. Pass him over and rest."

I humphed but did as I was told.

He took the bundle into his arms and fed him as he bounced lightly.

My heart swelled with love for them both.

Chapter 14

Davon

May 6, 2214

Connor stood by the desk when we entered his office.

Matt and I sat.

"Why did you call us?" I asked.

He took his seat and pushed a note toward us. "We received another message from Aleczander."

I read through it. "Good. He's ready to take down the facilities when the time comes." I met Connor's gaze. "Have you heard from the scouts?" I passed the note to Matt.

The attack on the facilities would mark the beginning of the attack in Promissa. Constantine's forces would take down part of the facilities that produced the supplements for the enhanced soldiers. We'd save the other half in case we were successful in getting the reapers to fight for us.

Because of this decision, we needed to make sure, for the time being, that supplements wouldn't reach the enhanced soldiers already settled inside the forest. They were a threat at our doorstep, and we believed the NWG would try to send supplements in before they collapsed. As of now, thousands of NWG soldiers roamed the western and southern areas of the forest, and we weren't sure how many of them were reapers, so we had to find a way to block these shipments.

Connor nodded. "They haven't seen anything come in. Maybe they took precautions and carried extra supplies. What worries me more is they reported a massive move north. The NWG soldiers are following Seth's tracks. We knew they'd take over that bunker and suspected it was only a matter of time before they took over the whole area, but we thought we'd have more time."

I massaged my temples. One more week. One more week until the tunnels were ready.

Matt clutched his chair's armrests. "When will they reach us?"

Connor pointed at a map stretched over his desk. "They're approaching science. I'm guessing they'll take their time there to investigate." He made a fist. "We have a week. Two at most."

"Fuck." Matt stood to check the map. "We need to go." He looked over his shoulder at me. "Have you talked to David?"

I was the officer in charge of David's group. We never talked about Abi, and he never overstepped again. A soldier through and through.

"I think we can work with that. David and his team have been working nonstop, and most of the civilians have been moved to the caverns." I took out the ledger. "Here's the list of all the citizens who have moved already. We have two, maybe three hundred left. Mostly soldiers." I passed him the letter David gave me this morning. "This is for you. David brought it back from his last trip to the caverns."

Connor broke the seal and read through it. He folded the letter and gave it to me.

"It's from Faez. The caverns are ready to shelter the rest of the citizens. Get everything prepared. We're leaving before the week is over."

I entered our room and followed Abi's retching sounds into the bathroom. She was crouched over the toilet seat, her hair tied back in a messy bun. Her red-rimmed eyes met mine.

She wiped her mouth. "I'm okay. I'll be out in a minute."

"Nonsense." I sat next to her on the floor. "Did you go see Zachary?"

She nodded.

She'd promised after our therapy session this morning that she'd go see him. She was still feeling under the weather, and whatever she was going through, we needed to know. Her glossy eyes met mine, and they reminded me of the first time I saw her. She was scared.

I massaged her neck. "Tell me. What did he say?"

"I'm..." She closed her eyes and swallowed hard. "I'm pregnant."

Even though she only confirmed what I already suspected, her words hit me like a brick to my stomach. With all that was happening, it should have been the worst news possible. But then heat radiated through my chest, and a sense of weightlessness took over me. I cradled her in my arms and cried, not out of sadness but out of joy.

She sobbed quietly. "I skipped two periods, but I've always been irregular. I didn't think it was important until recently." Her beautiful eyes met mine.

I shook my head. "It's my fault. I don't know what happened. I was taking my pills."

She touched my cheek. "I asked Zachary about it. Then I confirmed with Matt. He thinks it might have been after Deb's attack when you were on heavy antibiotics. They can reduce the effectiveness of the pills. He..."

I tried to remember. "But I'd already finished treatment a week before."

"I know. I told him the same." Abi looked down for a second and flinched. "Matt's furious at himself. The antibiotic they used on you can reduce the effectiveness of birth control for a month after the treatment is over. He was quite distraught. He said he should've explained this to us, but it slipped his mind with all the shit going on."

I raked my hair back, clutching it tightly at my nape almost to the point of pain. "I thought it was safe."

Abi's soft caress brought me back.

I sighed. "I'm sorry. It still shouldn't have happened. I should have asked."

A tear slid down her cheek. "Do you want to stop it?"

The mention of abortion struck like a powerful blow.

I helped her stand, and we walked to the bed. I gave her a cup of water.

She took a sip, then pushed it away. "I can't."

I insisted. "But you need to hydrate."

She pointed toward her nightstand. "Matt gave me some natural pills to help. There's also some electrolytes."

I was back in a second. She chewed the pill and then drank.

I waited for her to finish the drink, then put it back where it was.

She dropped her head. "Please say something."

That's when I realized I hadn't answered her question. I sat beside her and held her hands, then lifted her chin until her eyes met mine. "I can't remember the last time I've been this happy." I shrugged. "Well, maybe when I finally kissed you or that time we danced. Then there's every time we've made love." I counted with my fingers.

She nudged my shoulder playfully. "I'm serious, Davon."

"As am I. Nothing can compare to the joy I'm feeling right now. But I know the time isn't right, and if you feel it's better to stop the pregnancy,

I'll be by your side." I touched my temple to hers, taking in a long, shuddering breath. "Tell me, love. How do you feel about this?"

"I've always dreamed of having a family, and since I met you, the thought of having your children has entered my mind many times." She sighed. "I know it's a bad moment, but I want to keep it." She closed her eyes briefly before setting them back on me. "I can't see myself getting rid of it."

I grabbed her trembling chin and kissed her softly. "I feel the same way." I wrapped my arms around her. "We'll figure it out."

May 7, 2214

"Rachel, I'm about to start."

We'd been at this on a daily basis and still hadn't achieved much.

Lucas was cooperative and nonaggressive, but he still believed we were his enemies.

I wanted him to understand that all they taught him in those facilities was a lie. To see the NWG for what it truly was. To realize the real monsters were the ones that created them. I'd shown him countless videos with Rachel's help, who was the only one he actually talked to outside of me.

Davon suggested that Rachel should be in charge of the interrogation, but Connor said she was too close to Lucas and could be manipulated.

Now that I saw them together, I got what he said. There was something in the way he looked at her, some kind of emotion that cracked through the wall he'd erected around him, and I only saw it when he was with Rachel.

Rachel put the laptop away, and when she walked toward me, he grabbed her arm.

He frowned, then withdrew.

It was the first time I'd seen this kind of reaction.

Rachel glared at the mirror and crouched in front of Lucas. "I'm sorry. Does it hurt?"

Lucas shook his head and darted his eyes from the mirror to the woman at his feet. His gaze mellowed, and he shook his head. "No. It just feels...weird." He touched his head. "It's nothing. I just wanted to ask if you'd be back today. I'd like to know more about the wars."

My heart did a somersault. He'd never asked for more. Never showed an interest in history till now. What could have changed?

Rachel put her hand on his knee, then pushed herself up. She smiled at him. "Sure. I'll ask permission to come down later."

Lucas nodded. "I would like that."

I had never heard that tone from him before. A soft one. One very close to the way Davon would talk to me.

Could he have feelings for Rachel? If so, this meant they were not that different from us.

Rachel walked to the door, and I caught Lucas as he languidly brushed the area where she had touched him.

"Morning, Lucas." I grabbed the file from the side of the mirror, then walked closer. "How are we doing today?"

He raised an eyebrow and smirked. He actually smirked. "Cut the bullshit, *Miss Davis*. I already know you're not a doctor."

I froze, clutching the file to my chest. "I don't know what you mean."

He made to stand before me but stopped midway. He frowned and watched the cuffs, then continued up until he was fully standing. He towered before me, not more than a meter away.

I stood readily, maintaining eye contact, and pushed my shoulders back. If he wanted to intimidate me, he wouldn't get the satisfaction, even though on the inside, I wanted to run out that door.

There was shuffling behind me, and Rachel moved to my side, tranquilizer gun in hand. "Lucas, don't make me do this. I don't want to hurt you."

He tilted his head, and his nostrils flared. His biceps tightened beneath his shirt as he stretched his hands in front of him. "What exactly do these do? I feel weird."

I dropped the file. I didn't want to lose him, not now that I saw a possibility of him understanding our stand in this war. "They suppress your adrenaline so you're not violent toward us."

He sneered. "And you say you're here to help?"

I sighed. "I'm truly sorry about those, but we can't risk it."

He gritted his teeth. "We've been at this for a week." He touched his temple. "Everything inside me tells me to attack. To just get it over with and end you all." He glanced at Rachel and shook his head. He squeezed his eyes shut.

When he opened them, they were filled with tears. "I know there's something wrong with me. I can't think straight. I want to stop the violent thoughts that roam through me, but then the voices tell me to kill. To destroy."

I ventured closer to him, knowing Matt and Davon would lash out at me the moment I stepped outside. But I had to try. "We're not here to hurt you."

A moment passed before Lucas relaxed.

"Please sit." I gestured toward the cot. "I just want to talk."

He looked at Rachel.

Her hands shook for a moment before she steadied them, keeping her aim locked on him. "It's all right." She paused and took a deep, calming breath. "Please just do as she says."

He took a step back and sat.

I exhaled hard, feeling a burn in my throat as if I'd been holding that breath forever.

I took off the lab coat and threw it at the door. "You're right. I'm not a doctor. I'm Councilmember Davis from the People's Revolutionary Front. I was sent here by General Harris to get to know you. To try to understand what you're all about." I motioned at the cuffs. "Those cuffs are a precaution. You know very well what you've done to our soldiers."

His blue eyes grew intense. "We were following orders."

I crossed my arms. "I've seen the videos. You enjoy killing. You rip apart your prey like it's a sport."

He humphed. "Not all of us enjoy it."

I dropped my arms. "What do you mean?"

"I can't explain it, but it's like my brain tells me to kill. But when all is done, after the heat of the moment passes, everything I've done crashes down on me. I get dizzy and nauseous." He pressed his fingers over the implant in his forearm. "But it goes away when I push this, and I go numb. As long as I follow orders, they give me what I need, so I just keep doing what they say."

He closed his eyes again and swallowed hard. "But there's something wrong. Ever since you brought me here, I've been sick. The headaches won't stop, and the nausea is overwhelming. I know the real doctors are keeping this shit full, but I miss the high. The rush that came with every kill. The surging energy that traveled through my veins whenever I pushed this. Now I'm just sick and engulfed by memories of the ones I've killed."

I widened my eyes at his declaration and glanced back at the mirror. Were they drugging them? Was there something in the formula that Frank missed?

He clenched his fists. "What is it you want from me?"

I walked to him, breaking all the protocol Matt had drilled into me when we started. I sat by his side. "We want to help you break away from their hold. We want to give you the life you deserve without being controlled by them."

He relaxed his hands and rested them on his thighs. "Then fix me. I'll listen to you if you make the pain go away."

I nodded. "We'll start working on that right away. I promise we'll get you the help you need." I offered him my hand, praying this would be the beginning of what we all wanted—peace. "Do we have a deal?"

He looked at my hand, then at me. He moved his hand closer and shook mine. His grip was strong but measured. "Deal."

I stood and walked away, then the thought of him alone here, trapped in his pain, made me pause. I turned. "Do you have a hobby?"

He furrowed his brow. "What's a hobby?"

My heart broke for this man and all of the creations of the NWG. They deserved much more. "Something you like to do. Something to get your mind off the pain you're going through."

He glanced at Rachel. "I like the books she brings and when she reads to me."

I smiled. "Then she'll be back with more later."

His eyes glinted before I turned to leave.

Rachel followed me out.

Davon and Matt were beet red, their nostrils flaring like beasts.

"What the hell was that?" Davon's severe tone was the same as when he first came across me in that abandoned building.

I raised one eyebrow. "That was me being humane. That was me treating Lucas as what he is, a human."

"You were reckless." Matt pressed his lips together. "He could have killed you."

I squared my shoulders. "But he didn't."

Matt humphed and dropped into his chair, facing the double mirror.

Davon stepped into me. "He could've hurt you."

I lifted my head toward his gaze, but before I could say anything, he wrapped his arms around me.

"Don't ever do something like that again." His voice quivered, and my chest tightened.

I hugged him back. "I was just following my instincts. I'm sorry."

He kissed the top of my head.

The door swung open. Connor stormed toward me, and Davon moved to the side without letting go of my hand.

Connor's brown eyes were hard and his face flushed. "What the hell happened in there?" He grabbed my shoulders. "He could have killed you in an instant. How could you be so careless?"

"Let her go." Davon stepped between us and pushed him away. He held a palm against Connor's chest. "Breathe, brother."

Connor's chest rose and fell in quick, uneven breaths. He shook his head. "I'm sorry." His voice was soft. "What were you thinking?"

I let out a shaky breath. "What's done is done, and I'm sorry if I scared you. I had to try a softer approach. To talk to him as I would to any of you. It was risky, but it worked. Now we know the NWG is controlling them with some kind of drug. We just have to find out why Frank doesn't know about it."

Connor nodded, then after a long breath, he put his hands in his pockets and faced Matt. "Do you have any idea of what they might be giving them and why your father didn't know?"

Matt appeared lost in thought. "I'll meet with Michael and the science team. They took blood samples when the reapers arrived at science, but we need more tests if we're to find out what we missed." He rubbed the back of his neck. "We're going to need to take more reapers in and study their blood."

Connor nodded. "Understood. I'll tell the scouts to capture them alive if they encounter any."

Matt raked his golden curls back. "About Dad, these soldiers are from Halcyon, and as he said, General Steele took control of the project after Dad hinted at shutting it down. Maybe they created something far stronger to get better results."

"But why keep that from the minister of health?" Connor asked.

"I fear it could be worse than that." Davon moved to Connor's side. "I've met Thorne Steele before, and I fear he might be working on his own on this one. My father has always fought to maintain a tight leash on Steele, but he's never been able to control him completely. He lets him make decisions on his own as long as they follow Father's wishes."

Connor placed his hands on the desk and stared at Lucas. "We'll start by weaning our hostages off whatever they were using and ask them to join our side. We'll take as many enhanced soldiers as we can. Our soldiers will carry the paralyzing substance, not just with explosives but also with tranquilizer weapons. They only need to hit the right spot. Once we figure out what they're using, we might be able to help them better."

The room went silent for a moment before Connor pushed away from the desk. He looked at Rachel. "I'll lend you some books to read to him."

Rachel bowed her head. "Thank you, sir."

He put a hand on Matt's shoulder. "The cuffs stay on." He stared at Lucas. "I still don't trust him."

Matt nodded.

Without another word, Connor turned and walked out.

"Take only what you need," Abi told Rosa.

Their voices reached me out in the hall. News about the imminent move to the caverns spread through the bunker like wildfire.

I glanced inside the kitchen.

"But I need to take everything. Who knows what awaits me in those caverns?" Rosa shoved more kitchenware into her duffel bag.

"Rosa, Abraham said the kitchen is set with everything you need. You know there's a chef up there, and people are already living inside the caverns, right?" Abi took some stuff out of the bag.

Rosa humphed. "Okay. I believe you. Now help me get my baking stuff. I want to make cookies for the kids."

Abi chuckled and followed her deeper into the kitchen.

The citizens were nervous. Many thought they were losing what was left of their pasts with this move. I understood, I truly did, but there was no other option. Their safety was our priority.

I was about to go help Abi with Rosa when someone clasped my arm.

"Davon."

I turned toward Peter. His grip was strong, almost to the point of pain.

He let go reluctantly. "A file arrived. It's protected by a password. We think it's from him."

Father.

My heart lurched, and an urge to grab Abi hit me, but when I turned, she was already gone. I made a silent prayer and followed Peter. What the hell had Father done now?

In the computer room, Connor was bent over the computer as Nina worked her magic. But password after password failed.

I gripped her seat. "Let me try."

I tried their anniversary, the day they won the war, my mother's birthday, and mine. Nothing worked.

Could it be?

I wrote down a date only he and I knew, my first kill: 03162202.

My heart stopped when a green light appeared the moment I pressed enter. It was a video.

My fingers itched as the download reached 100 percent.

Static filled the screen until the image was clear. A soldier was tied to the same chair I used for Deb. Her body was a wreck, covered in burns and scars. Her blouse was ripped apart, and her raw flesh was peeled at the breasts. Bile rose into my throat. They'd skinned her.

The person holding the camera stood close to the prisoner, grabbed her chin, and made her look into it.

Her eyes were swollen. Tears marked their way through the blood gushing from a hit to her temple. Her skin was split open, but she was conscious. My hands hurt from the hold I had on the desk.

Anna.

The camera was flipped, and there he was. His menacing stare the same as always. "Hello, son."

My skin crawled at his sinister sneer.

His eyes moved away from the camera, and the image changed again. "Miss Walker here has been indulging in our hospitality. I decided since you were so good to Peter, I might as well return the favor. You see, this one killed a dozen of my enhanced soldiers before they took her down."

Anna whimpered. Father grabbed her face, and the smack of his hand against her cheek cracked through the monitor. She spit blood into the camera.

My father's chuckle traveled through me like poison. He cleaned the lens. "She's as feisty as her predecessor, so I decided to take my time with her." He squeezed her jaw, making her open her mouth, then spit into it.

She jerked violently.

"What, you don't like it?" He hit her again with the back of his hand. The crack was so loud that I was sure her jaw broke. "That will teach you some respect."

She fell unconscious.

"Sick bastard." Connor snarled.

The camera zoomed in on Anna's slumped body. "Too bad. I hoped she'd take a little bit more before taking her leave, but no worries. I'll make sure she doesn't die and will keep you posted on her progress."

The video shifted to a room full of monitors that showed a street in Promissa. Citizens were gathered around four bodies that were hanging in gibbets. The soldiers were badly beaten, crying for food and water. Officers donning the white NWG uniform guarded the perimeter. Then the camera focused on a lone figure hung on a post in the middle of it all. He also wore the NWG uniform, his rank of lieutenant clearly visible.

"No!" I punched the desk at the sight of his dead, mutilated body. His jaw was ripped off, and his legs hung limply. The word *traitor* was carved in blood on his chest.

The image flickered, and my father appeared, seated at his desk. Suit on. Hair polished back. The epitome of the tyrant he was.

"I hope you're enjoying this, dear Abigail. I took special pleasure in seeing your uncle break." His voice dripped with cruelty.

I growled as her name slipped past his lips.

"As for you, son, I hope I get to see you soon. Your mother asks for you daily." His tone turned menacing, and his unblinking stare pierced my soul. "I'll never forgive you for turning her against me. You'll rue the day you decided to betray me."

I clenched my fists. "I'll kill him."

He jerked his face to the side, then looked down at his hands, which he clasped together on the desk. His sneer met me as he returned his gaze to the camera. "I'm afraid you've forgotten who's in charge, so I prepared a little surprise for you."

He leaned back. "I have my methods of finding intel. A little bird passed me the coordinates of your current location." He shrugged. "I'm a fair adversary, so I'm sending just a little taste of what you'll face if you dare to breach the city."

I stood in alarm.

Connor was by my side in a second.

"Let's see what my treacherous son is capable of." Father eyed his watch. "You see, the moment you opened this file, my troops received a signal." He smiled. "I hope you're ready for what's coming."

The monitor turned dark. A sound wave hit me. The whole bunker shook.

They're here.

Chapter 15

Abi

May 7, 2214

There was a rumble before the ground shook with force.

"What's happening?" I lost my balance.

Matt stopped my fall. "Take cover!" He wrapped his arms around me and pushed me down a corridor. "It's an attack!"

The sirens blared around us, and the bunker went dark. The emergency lights came on, and a red gloom engulfed the halls.

"All civilians move to the secure areas. Soldiers, get ready to fight." Connor's voice boomed around the bunker.

Soldiers started running toward the armory, while civilians moved down another hall.

Matt grabbed my shoulders. "You heard Connor. Go to the secure area. You'll be safe there."

I rooted my feet. "If they're here, I want to fight!"

Matt looked at my belly.

I scowled. "Don't get all macho on me. I need to do this."

Matt humphed but let go of me. "Davon's going to kill me."

"Abi! Abi, where are you?" David's screams reached us.

"She's here!" Matt gripped David's arm. "Guard her with your life out there."

David nodded. "You know I will."

If David knew about the baby, he'd argue with me about my decision to fight, but he didn't.

Matt squeezed my hand. His emerald eyes met mine for a second before he dashed down the hall.

David seized my hand, and we ran toward the armory, catching our team.

"Soldiers, grab your gear. We're being attacked," David yelled.

I followed him and changed into the new armor Michael brought from science. I retrieved my sniper and the rest of my weapons, then ran with our team toward the exit that led to the forested area east. We climbed the trees, using the steps imbedded in them. Once we reached our spots, we made ready.

I looked through the scope. Hundreds of enhanced soldiers lined our perimeter. The bombs caused a large area to burn. They had missed us by half a mile.

Yuxuan was out there, giving them hell with his soldiers. Smoke filled the area as, one after another, the mines on the perimeter exploded.

Davon was out there, following Connor and Lavigne into battle. Matt was not far behind.

My heart was about to burst out of my chest, but I breathed in. They'd be okay.

"You ready?" David eyed me over his shoulder.

I nodded, aligned the scope, and exhaled slowly. I took my first shot. The reaper went down. The bullet struck through its neck. It was a clean shot.

My mouth fell open, and a rush of adrenaline coursed through my veins. *I took one down.*

I turned my focus to another soldier, but I wasn't as lucky. The shot pushed it back a step before the reaper growled loudly and started running ahead. I covered my ears at the blast of one of the launchers from Mark's team.

A cloud of dirt followed the explosion. Half a dozen reapers were sprawled on the ground. Their formation was heavily affected by the continued attacks, but they kept pushing forward.

I settled back into position, aligned the scope, and fired again. My body fell into a routine, almost on instinct. We needed to keep at it, and maybe we'd have a chance to win this.

I lost track of time after a while, but we continued pushing. There was no escape for our people. If we let them get closer, they'd kill us all.

"Ready to go down there?" David laid down his sniper.

We were out of ammo, and our troops needed help.

I swiped my hand over the side of my helmet, which closed the gas mask over my face. With comms built in, this new technology allowed us to communicate more effectively and have a wider range of visibility while also having a gas mask built in and ready when needed.

On the battlefield, Davon and his group fought dozens of reapers. Some were already paralyzed, but they'd taken measures, and many were donning protection just like us.

Matt was also down there with his troop. Their machine guns slowed the enemy's advance so our soldiers could get closer.

Taking them down would be a group effort.

"Let's have a taste of some reaper blood." David offered me a huge smile.

We started down.

He grabbed my shoulders the moment my boots touched the ground. "Stay by my side. Don't take any risks."

I shook my head. "You know I can't promise that." I'd never stand down again.

He breathed out heavily. "Why can't you let me protect you for once?"

"Because I can protect myself." I touched his arm. "Trust me."

He nodded, then stepped back and drew his gun.

I grabbed mine and took a moment to breathe.

I silenced everything but the battleground, focusing on the orders coming from our comms and David, who was up ahead. I pushed back the fear that once had stopped me from defending my loved ones and ran ahead toward the screams and into the storm.

It was time to fight.

"Take cover!" a soldier shouted.

Countless NWG soldiers flew back as a grenade exploded within their formation. They were breaching the perimeter, and the fight now was to stop them from doing so.

David hadn't left my side, and we covered each other. We went after our comrades and into the fray, launching ourselves against the reaper forces, which were advancing toward the bunker.

David shoved me aside as a berserk soldier charged at us. His shoulder struck David squarely in the chest, which sent him flying into a pine tree as if he weighed nothing.

For a moment, I thought he was unconscious, but then he opened his eyes and faced his opponent.

A strong force crashed into my back. I sprawled to the ground. The reaper's weight was crushing me, and I fought for air as he rammed my head into the muddy ground. I pushed my hips up, then shifted until I was facing him. Air rushed into my screaming lungs. I unsheathed Jacob's trench knife and drove it into the reaper's side between the creases of his armor. I twisted it, yanked it out, then, with a guttural scream, used all my strength to place a hand on his chest and push him up just enough to see his neck. I stabbed it.

Blood drenched my face, drowning my mouth in its metallic taste. Nausea overtook me, but I spit it out and squirmed away from his limp body.

My arms trembled as I pushed myself up. I ground my teeth. A thousand bricks rested on my back, and I staggered before regaining my balance. I hobbled about, wiping the blood off my face, to find David fighting for his life. The reaper stormed toward him, slashing him countless times with his dagger, the tree the only thing holding David up.

I ran forward as the enhanced soldier swung a metal mace up and prepared to hit David.

David's eyes bulged. "Get down!"

I dropped without question. It was instilled in me after countless hours of training. You didn't question your superior's orders—you just followed.

The rapid fire of a machine gun blazed around me, and I hugged the ground. The shots hit both David and the reaper.

Multiple gunshots struck David's bulletproof armor, and he staggered, grunting in pain.

My scream stuck in my throat.

The attacking reaper jerked as the bullets hit him, but he kept his mace up, aiming toward David.

The reaper with the machine gun emerged from the forest. She hadn't noticed me, and I pushed myself up on my elbows, praying my bullet reached its target: the hand that held the gun.

The shot grazed her shoulder.

She turned toward me. I could make out her vicious smirk behind her protective helmet. I kneeled, held my arms as steady as I could manage, then shot again. This time I hit her below her helmet. She lost her footing and struck the ground with one knee, her blood dripping down the side of her dark-gray uniform.

Adrenaline surged through me. I didn't have time to think, just act, as the other one was about to hit David with a mortal blow from his mace.

I focused my aim on the hand holding the mace and pulled the trigger. The bullet hit its hand, and the mace fell with a heavy thump. David plunged his dagger under the reaper's arm, then into its throat. Blood rained on his face as the reaper stumbled and fell.

David collapsed beside him, holding his chest plate.

I was about to go to David but jerked at the sound of muddy footsteps coming from behind me. The reaper I shot was standing a few feet from me, her gun aimed at my head.

My breath caught. I wouldn't die here. Not today.

My vision turned red, and without hesitation, I dashed around her and climbed up her back. The shots from her gun fired aimlessly around us as I choked her, trying to remove her helmet. I gripped her chin and pulled hard, but it wouldn't budge, so I hit her with the butt of my dagger again and again.

"Abi!"

My heart jumped. I'd recognize Connor's voice anywhere.

He aimed a missile launcher toward the monster. "Let go!"

I leapt off and rolled over as Maria had taught me. The wheezing sound of the launcher was followed by the reaper's body being rocketed into a tree.

I pressed the button to retract the gas mask mechanism.

Connor did the same, and his caring eyes met mine. "I'm glad I found you." He offered his hand.

I clasped it and stood. "Thanks."

He stared at David, a shadow already cast over his dark eyes.

"He's alive. Just knocked down. That asshole filled him with bullets."

Connor turned his gaze toward me, then squeezed my arm. "Stay with him."

I nodded and grasped his shoulder. "Be careful out there."

"I will." He cupped my chin. "Stay safe. I'll come back for—"

I screamed at the top of my lungs as a stiletto pierced his throat. Its sharp, bleeding edge was just inches away from me.

His brown eyes widened, then he stroked his thumb across my cheek. His breathing was labored. "Live," he gurgled. His face was ashen. "Fight."

A booming blast deafened me, and a bullet exited through the front of his helmet. A streak of blood ran down his face. The light left his eyes, and his body collapsed to the ground.

"No!" A guttural roar left me, and blood rushed to my ears.

The pressure in my chest was so strong I thought I'd die, but I breathed in and remembered the words he told me once inside the memorial center. "We can't let this go on."

No more. You will no longer run.

They have to die.

My pain turned to rage, and I let it take over me. It burst through my pores, burning my soul as I turned toward Connor's attacker. The smoking barrel of the reaper's rifle was pointed straight at me. Its acrid scent filled my nostrils.

Violence ripped through me, begging me to let it loose.

I seized my khukuri and charged straight at him. I slid between his knees and slashed my blade across the gap between them, praying there was no armor to protect him. If they were able to feel pain, his shriek would have carried for miles, but he just started shooting as a torrent of blood rained down on me.

I jumped onto his back, locked my legs around his chest, then ripped his helmet off with inhuman strength. I plunged my blade through the top of his skull.

The reaper collapsed, and I squatted over him, cutting him mercilessly until we were both lying on a bed of guts and blood. His body was open, and the reek of human waste assaulted my senses as I came to.

I removed my helmet before puking over the reaper's side. I dropped the khukuri and pressed my palm to my stomach. After the ache lessened, I crawled over to Connor and cradled him.

"Connor!" I took him in my arms.

His eyes were now dull and empty.

He's dead.

This was one of the most important men in my life. He'd been with me during my ups and downs, and now I'd lost him.

My mind wailed as a rush of memories flooded me. An emptiness grabbed me and yanked me into a dark place, one I had succumbed to only once before.

Deb... She didn't deserve any of this. How would she take it? Three months was all she got before Jordan stole the love of her life away. Sarah jumped into my mind and those days after she lost Carlos.

I cried my lungs out, not caring about the thud of boots approaching. A shadow cast over me. Death could take me because I had no fight left within me.

"Abi?" Matt's voice broke through the sounds of battle.

I looked up. The moment his eyes found Connor's body he collapsed to his knees, dropping his gun by his side. He started trembling.

Another set of footsteps echoed from behind him, and Davon came into view. The battlefield seemed to go silent as he took in the scene.

Davon ran to us and seized Connor's shoulders. "Connor!" His anguished screams traveled through the valley. "Wake up! You can't fucking die."

He shrieked, shaking Connor's body, then collapsed over his brother and cried. His sobs were so deep and heartbreaking, so raw and desperate, that it was as if the whole world stood still to witness his grief.

I pulled him up, my own pain reflected in his eyes. The lump in my throat kept my voice trapped within me. I couldn't see the world in the same light again.

I grabbed Davon's face and stroked his stubble lightly, then drew him to me. His quiet tears merged with the blood and tears that streaked my face. The results of our fight and sorrow dripped on our leader. Our friend. Our family.

That's when Davon noticed the blood on me. He touched me, then my belly. "Are you hurt?"

I shook my head. "It's not my blood."

He frowned as if knowing I was keeping something from him.

The constant pain in my belly was a reminder that something was off.

I exhaled hard. "I was attacked by a reaper, but other than some discomfort, I think I'm okay."

He caressed my belly. "Does it hurt?"

I covered his hand. "It's nothing. I'll go to Zachary once everything passes."

He grazed my cheek with his thumb. "How about going to him the moment we get to the bunker?"

I nodded, very aware of the danger I could be putting the baby in if I didn't.

Davon glanced around, then let out a huge breath. The battle raged still, but it sounded distant.

He cupped the side of my face. His eyes moved so quickly I could almost palpate his despair. "Are you sure you're okay?"

I grasped the back of his neck and pulled his brow to mine. "I promise. We're okay."

Matt stood in alarm, then cocked his Glock.

A rhythmic thump grew around us. The noise intensified until a whirring bellow filled the air above us. I glanced up as the sky darkened. A chopping thud was followed by a deafening roar. A black helicopter flew over us, its frame walled by weaponry. I held my breath at the sharp whistling sound of two large missiles passing above us. Dread washed over me.

Were these from the NWG? I wanted to run, but my body wouldn't cooperate. I stayed there, accepting my fate. In less than a second, Davon was on top of me, holding himself up by the elbows. I glanced sideways to find Matt running toward David. He covered his limp body as Davon did with mine.

A series of explosions boomed around us. The ground under us rocked furiously.

"Hold on!" Davon yelled as another helicopter flew over us.

A symbol was etched on its side. A rising sun behind a great city.

Explosive cracks resounded across the skies, and the distant rumble of missiles echoed around us until there was silence.

Davon guided me to David. "Stay here."

Matt rushed over to Connor's body.

David, who I'd thought was still unconscious, grabbed my hand, and I helped him up.

I clasped my hands around his neck and pulled him tight, crying as I drew his raw strength to me, one he always gave freely. "He's gone." His warm scent carried a subtle sweetness that gave me comfort.

David didn't speak. He kissed the top of my head and pressed me to his chest.

I trembled at the thought of never having a conversation with Connor again. Of his ever-present support. His even personality. His love. How would life be without him?

Then his words filtered through my mind. It was the day after my parents were executed. Deb just stared from the room's entrance as he sat by my bed and cupped my face, his light-brown irises glazed with tears and something else—determination.

"You will push through this and live your life so that theirs was not lost in vain. They will be with you even if you don't see them." He took my arms and turned them up. "Their blood flows through you. No one will ever take their legacy from you. Guard it. Take from it what you need, and become fierce. Rise up from the pain, and make their memory your strength. What you live by."

I closed my eyes and took a deep breath, then let go of David. He removed his armor. The memory of him being shot at came back like a bullet. I touched his chest, and he flinched back.

I raised my eyebrows. "You're hurt."

He waved his hand. "It's nothing."

I humphed. "Nothing?" I sighed. "I saw you go down."

I fought him to lift his shirt, and he eventually let me. His chest and abdominal area were heavily bruised. His sides bled from the stab wounds he'd received, but they appeared superficial. Hematomas covered everything.

He pulled his shirt down. "I told you. It's nothing."

I let go. "Promise you'll see a doctor when we get back."

David sighed. "Okay." He brushed my cheek. "But only if you do the same." He bent over. "I can sense something's off with you, and I know you want to be strong, but there are people here who care for you."

How the hell did he know? "I'll go. I already promised Davon."

He nodded, then went to retrieve his stuff.

"Ready to go back?" A shadow cast over Davon, his eyes swollen and red, as he held Connor's body from one side, Matt from the other.

My chin trembled at the sight, and my throat burned to the point of pain, but I swallowed my tears and followed them back to the bunker.

Chapter 16

Davon

May 7, 2214

They were here. The Liberty Enclave had answered our call.

I left Abi in David's care. No matter the differences we had, I was thankful for his presence.

I grabbed the HK416 from the reaper's hands, and from the way his chest was stabbed and his guts spilled around him, I could only guess this was the monster who killed Connor and Abi's victim.

Matt lifted Connor to a sitting position and looked at me. "We can't leave him."

"Of course not. I'll help you." I grabbed the other side.

A void grew within me. He was not only my general but my friend. My brother.

The rebellion would suffer from his loss.

I took a deep breath and hauled him up with all my strength. His limp body proved almost impossible to carry. His boots dragged against the ground, but it was the least he deserved—to be taken back standing. A hero.

Bodies from both sides covered the forest floor as we made our way into the clearing. Father thought this would stop us, but he was greatly mistaken. He'd only thrown fuel onto the fire, and now there was no stopping it. He'd pay for this.

The valley around the bunker was full of our people, most taking care of the wounded.

I sighed. The bunker was safe.

I glanced at Peter. His PRF uniform was stained with the remains from the battle. His sleeve was slashed, and blood seeped from a deep gash in his forearm.

He found us and sprinted our way. "Davon? Is he...?"

I shook my head.

Zachary ran to us and touched Connor's neck, looking for a pulse. He jerked his hand back. Pain etched his eyes as he called for a cot. The soldiers who came to aid us gasped at the sight of their dead general. We laid him down, and Zachary used a sheet to cover his body.

"Do you have somewhere safe where we can leave him until we deal with the emergency?" Matt asked.

"Take him to my room." Zachary dropped his keys into my hand. "Lock him inside until you decide what the next steps will be and how we'll tell the others. Word will spread of his death, and the people will need a new leader."

His eyes stayed on me as he said it, and I understood that as general, I was the next in line to take his place. But I couldn't fathom that at the moment, so I just nodded.

A yell broke away from the crowd.

"Abi!" Sarah ran to her. "You're safe!"

Abi looked down. Her shoulders shook.

"What's wrong?" Sarah darted her gaze around. Her eyes locked on the covered body. She stiffened. "Who's that?"

Abi sobbed. "It's..." She shook her head. "Connor's dead."

I stopped myself from going to her. Abi's pain burned right through me, but they needed this moment.

Sarah took a step back. "No." She crashed to the ground. Her screams filled the air. "No! This can't..." She started shaking, her hands fisted on the ground, scraping the dirt.

Abi kneeled and took her in her arms.

"I don't understand." She started mumbling stuff under her breath. Whispers I couldn't make out from back here.

She pushed Abi away and looked around the valley. Her eyes grew wide, and she hugged herself, then scratched her skin raw, drawing blood from her arms.

I took a step forward.

"Don't!" Abi grabbed her arms. "Stop that! You're hurting yourself."

Sarah shoved her hard, and Abi stumbled back.

I ran to her.

When Sarah saw me, she scrambled away, her eyes never leaving Connor's lifeless body. She shook her head, blurting out senseless words, then stood. "I'm sorry." She dashed into the forest.

I helped Abi up, and she flinched.

I furrowed my brow. "Are you hurt?"

She shook her head.

I'd tell Zachary to check on her and the baby as soon as this hell was over.

Abi tried to follow Sarah, but I grasped her arm. "Let her go. She needs her space."

Abi slumped against me. "What's wrong with her?"

The way one handled death was not the same for everyone. If Sarah needed her space, it was better to let her be. She had nowhere to run.

I pressed her to me. "I'll send soldiers to get her if she doesn't come back by nightfall."

"Why?" she murmured. "Why does this keep happening to us?" Abi's anguished cries traveled through the forest.

My chest was ripped open. A piece of my heart was torn from me, and all I could do was hold her.

When she calmed, I prayed for strength and held her at arm's length. "Is the pain better?" Even with everything going on, I couldn't help but worry about Abi and the babe.

She wiped her tears. "It's better."

I nodded, and the tension in my body eased a bit. "I'm going to help get Connor inside, but after everything is done, remember to go to Zachary. We can't be too careful. Also, there's something I want to talk to you about." I had to tell her about the video, but first, I needed to be sure she was all right.

I looked around for David. He was talking to Yuxuan in the distance. I waved at him to come.

Soldiers spread throughout the perimeter, setting up traps and mines again. It was our first victory against the NWG but a narrow one.

Katherine passed orders. "Make sure the doctors sedate each, then take them to the secured area."

Cot after cot was carried inside, all holding enhanced soldiers.

Peter gripped my shoulder. "Are you all right?" I nodded absentmindedly.

"I'm sorry about Connor." He squeezed my shoulder. "He was a good man."

It was as if the world was engulfed in a dense fog. Nothing was certain anymore.

"Go with Katherine. We'll be okay." My voice was nothing but a whisper, but he nodded and left.

When I glanced back at Abi, David was by her side.

"Will you stay with her?" I asked him.

He nodded. "Of course."

Abi looked to where Matt stood next to Connor's body. "Where are you taking him?"

I held her hand. "Zachary offered his room. We'll keep him there until we take care of the emergency."

"Okay." Abi squeezed it.

I kissed her temple. "I love you."

"Me too." She covered my chest with her palm. "Go. I'll be all right."

David guided her inside.

Seeing her go tore at my chest. There was nowhere else I'd rather be than by her side, but I had a duty to fulfill.

I ran back to Matt and lifted the cot.

Inside, Deb was nowhere to be found, and I let out a hard exhale. I didn't know what would happen when she found out. She was staying in a room in the infirmary hall. She'd taken a lot of time to recover from her surgery and was coming back from her postpartum depression. Connor had been key to that recovery, but now...

I pushed away the thought. I'd help Deb in whatever way I could. She wouldn't be alone.

We locked Connor inside Zachary's room, then bumped into Abi and David when we exited to the hall.

"Come on, David. We need to get you to the infirmary," Matt said.

David hugged Abi, tipped his head toward me, and followed Matt.

"You should go with them," I told Abi.

She stayed by my side. "I will, but first, I wanted to talk to you about something." She took my hands in hers. "It's about the rebellion."

My stomach sank. She could only be referring to one thing.

"Will you do what's needed? Will you take his place?" The strength in her plea made me shift in place. She would not back down. As a councilmember, she'd taken her responsibility to the PRF to heart, and in her mind, protecting it was a priority.

I shook my head and took a deep, shuddering breath. "I'm lost. I never thought we'd lose him. It never even crossed my mind."

He was the face of the rebellion. The one who led us from the start.

I always ran away from this, but now that Connor was gone, I stood alone. I couldn't run anymore.

Abi moved her thumbs over my hands. "His last words urged me to fight. To live. We need to move on and watch over our people. You were his right hand, and I know he would have wanted you to take his place and lead the PRF."

I swallowed hard. "Okay, but as soon as the emergency is over, we'll have a general assembly. The people will choose who their leader will be."

Her hand cupped my cheek. "And will you step up if they pick you?"

Abi's words held me still.

If that occurred, there were no more excuses to run away from my responsibilities. They had already accepted me after everything that happened.

"I will."

Abi straightened. "You won't be alone. I'll be by your side no matter what comes our way."

"Davon!" Dani caught me off guard and threw herself at me. "Thank God you're all right." She cried into my heavy armor.

She glanced around. "Where's Connor? The people are going crazy with worry. The bombings. The helicopters. What the hell is happening?"

Abi touched her wrist and slid her fingers across the watch she always wore. It was her father's watch, which Connor had kept for her. Her eyes were filled with anguish.

I brushed her fingers with a feathery touch, lending her some of my strength.

Connor was my brother. My kin. We went through so much shit together to create this community, this safe haven for all who opposed the regime.

My body burned with ire at the thought of never hearing his voice again. Of knowing our banters were over. Those moments when we went head-to-head in making the decisions. I'd never witness his calming presence again or hear his advice. He was such a force. Such a general. Even giving it my all, I'd never be able to take his place. He was born for this, and they'd taken him away from his people.

Abi adjusted her sleeves, covering the watch. "Connor is dead." Her level voice and even countenance shook something in me.

She had changed, had learned to put on a mask and hide her sorrow. I wanted to take her in my arms. To tell her we'd make everything good again. I wanted her to let go of this front with me.

Dani's eyes glazed as she looked between us, then she took a step back.

I grabbed her arm. "I need to address the people."

The loud whirring of the helicopters' blades thumped against my ears.

The people around us glanced at one another in question. Others shuffled to their feet, ready to fight.

The Liberty Enclave's presence was classified, and many asked what was happening.

Dani wiped away her tears and rummaged through a bag she carried. "Here." She passed me the handset we used to talk through the sound system set around the bunker. She looked at the injured. "We need help in the hospital ward. There aren't enough hands."

"I can help." Abi stroked my free hand with her thumb. "You can do this."

I brought our intertwined hands to my lips and kissed hers. "Thank you." I touched her belly. "Talk to Zachary."

Her smile was radiant. "I will."

After they left, I turned on the device. "I need your attention, please." My voice was hoarse as I tried to speak up.

One of the cadets who was assigned as medical staff offered me some water. "Here, sir."

I glanced down at a girl who couldn't be older than sixteen. I frowned at the blood stains that covered the staff and the key on the PRF uniform, a symbol our own enemy had created.

She gave me the canteen. Her hands trembled.

I softened my gaze. "Thank you, miss?"

"Lloyd, but everyone calls me Rebecca. Becky for short."

An irregular beat hit my chest at the name she shared with my mother, and my thoughts traveled to her. To Father's words in his video. Was she his prisoner? Could he be torturing her?

"Sir?" she said.

I smiled and took a sip. The water eased my dry throat, and I passed it back. "Keep up the good work."

Becky smiled and went to the next person in need.

"Your attention, please."

The hall was swamped with the wounded, their eyes locked on me, their general.

"We received a major blow from our enemy. We knew this could happen but thought we'd have more time." I looked down and took two deep breaths, praying to God not to cry. "I have dire news and what we hope is a good one."

Murmurs filled the space.

I resolved my countenance. "Our general of the army is dead."

Gasps erupted around me. I let the people have a minute to process what I just said. Everyone loved Connor.

"There will be time to grieve, but right now, we need to stand strong. Today we lost many, but we had our first victory. The missiles that took our enemy down are from who we hope are allies. During my mission, my father told me about a country up north called the Liberty Enclave. They're enemies of the New World Government too. They were part of the same country as Promissa, which existed before the wars. The Liberty Enclave is the last bastion of that old government, and now they want to fight back."

"But what guarantees they won't take Promissa from us? What if they're as bad as the NWG?" a soldier asked from the back.

His question was the same as mine. We all had doubts about their true intentions.

"Many share your concern. That's why two months ago, General Harris sent an envoy to their capital, Empire City."

"So the helicopters are theirs? You're sure of this?" Steven asked from the far left.

"I am. Father told me about their symbol. A rising sun behind a great city. It was drawn on the helicopters' tails."

Steven nodded, and the people started calming down.

I swallowed hard. "I will take Connor's place temporarily so we can talk to the people from the Liberty Enclave."

I expected some opposition, but everyone simply hung on my every word. Their unwavering gazes removed all unease I had about their acceptance, boosting my resolve.

"I will go out there with Lieutenant General Anderson to receive them. Please rest assured we have only the People's Revolutionary Front's agenda in mind. We will take back Promissa. We will have our vengeance and our freedom."

Whoops erupted all around the bunker, and I fought back my tears. We were still standing strong. And we would win, whatever it took.

Outside, I met Matt and David.

"Are you all right?" I asked David. I didn't expect him to join us.

"Matt just cleared me." He stood at attention. "I want to meet them if you'll allow it."

"Come with us. We should show all the strength we can."

I had no idea who these people were, but I wouldn't risk appearing weak even though they just saved us. We had to show them we were ready to take back our city. And that we wouldn't back away from anyone, no matter what.

I looked at Matt. "Aoki?"

Matt smiled. "He's safe. The baby too."

Aoki's procedure had worked, and with therapies, he was already moving around with crutches. It had been a miracle of science, one I never doubted Michael could achieve. After all, he was an amazing scientist and medic.

"Good." I exhaled.

The surprise attack could have easily been our doom.

"It was a close call. There's no doubt in my mind that the second spy is still among us."

Matt shifted in place. "Definitely. Someone provided Jordan with the coordinates. Good thing they missed us by half a mile; otherwise, the story would be different."

"We were too lenient," David grumbled.

I didn't answer back because he wasn't wrong. After we moved here, we'd lost the control we had at Janus Peak for some time, only to have the security back up a week later. I could only deduce the spy used this time to pass the information to Father. I was just glad they mistook our coordinates. I'd investigate it further, but there was another issue nagging at my mind.

"Deb?" My voice wavered for a second.

The comfort I couldn't give was eating me whole. The pain she'd have to endure was not fair. She never deserved any of this.

Matt squeezed my hand. "She still doesn't know. When the bunker shook, she became violent and wanted to go out and fight. Sarah calmed her and convinced her to take some calming medications. She's still sleeping."

I shut my eyes, then let go of Matt and scraped my nails across my head. "Fuck! This isn't right."

How would she overcome this huge loss? How would her mind and spirit survive it?

I wanted to scream at the top of my lungs. To cry until there were no more tears. My hands trembled as I slid my obsidian ring off and let it fall to the ground. I stepped on it, smashing it again and again until dirt covered it, then I sauntered over to where the helicopters were landing.

You'll pay for this, Father.

The motors shut down, and a high-ranking officer stepped out. Her black-and-red uniform was distinct from the others, with a silver insignia and a long coat. She was an attractive woman, her face outlined like a statue. Her stony expression gave a sense of unyielding resolve.

She adjusted her hat, which was also adorned in silver, and her striking red hair was held in a tight low ponytail. It reminded me of Grace's, but something told me it was the only thing they had in common.

"Who's in charge here?" Her imposing attitude evidenced her ranking.

David huffed, and she gave him a stern glare that stayed with him for some time. He didn't flinch.

I stepped up, and her blue eyes leveled with mine. "I am the general of the army, Davon Niles. These are Lieutenant General Anderson and Captain Martinez. And you are?"

"Niles?" She hissed, ignoring my outstretched hand. "I was supposed to meet General Connor Harris."

I took my hand back and stood at attention. "He went down in battle. I'm taking his place for the time being."

"So you're Jordan Niles's son?" She clenched her jaw. "Your people told us about you." She examined me, her hard stance unchanged. "I'm sorry to hear about General Harris. I was looking forward to meeting him."

She stretched her arm, and I shook her hand. "General Sinclair from the Liberty Enclave." She looked around the area. "What happened here?"

I gritted my teeth. "My father happened." I sighed. "We were hopeful the two spies in our ranks had left after the attack, but it appears there's still one among us. They gave him the coordinates."

She lifted an eyebrow. "So he already knows we're here."

I swallowed hard. "All communications were shut down the moment of the attack. Nothing will go out of or come into the system."

She nodded. "You made the right call, but you'll have to move soon. We eliminated all their troops, but when he gets news of this loss, there's no knowing what he'll do. Do you have a place?"

I nodded. "We'll move as soon as possible and strengthen our system, ensuring that only my closest officials have access."

I'd tell Nina to encrypt the system so only Matt, Mark, and I had access to it, at least for the time being.

She pocketed her hands. "And you trust these people?"

I kept her stare. "With my life."

General Sinclair nodded. "Good." She headed toward the bunker. "Let's get inside. There's much to discuss."

The three of us stared dumbfounded at each other, then I shrugged, and we followed her inside.

Chapter 17

Abi

May 7, 2214

Davon's heartfelt words traveled through the bunker as I helped Dani and Michael with the wounded. Their wails had stopped the moment his voice boomed from the sound system. Hope had sparked in their eyes when he said those last words.

A sliver of hope also grew within me. I touched my belly. Helping the injured had somehow made the pain bearable, so I decided to talk to Zachary after the emergency passed.

"Abi! I need you to hold him."

I rushed to Michael and stopped in my tracks. My stomach plummeted. I hadn't seen him since before the battle, but I assumed he was outside dealing with the aftereffects of the attack, not here, fighting for his life. "Tell me what to do."

"Just put pressure on the wound. He was stabbed and needs surgery. I'll go get Zachary." Michael dashed out.

I held gauze to his abdomen. Soon it was useless, as spurts of blood continued gushing out. "Mark! Stay with me."

He was pale, and his eyes were closed.

"No! Listen to my voice! We'll fix this. You're going to make it."

God, I couldn't lose him too. My hands were soaked in the darkest blood I'd ever seen.

He's going to die.

Tears streamed down my face as I pressed harder, willing the blood to stop.

"Tell Carol." He swallowed hard. "Tell her I love her." He coughed. "Tell her to go on. Diane needs her."

"No. Don't do this. Don't say goodbye." My voice shook.

This couldn't be happening.

The double doors of the room swung open, and Zachary was beside me in an instant, Rachel and Michael with him.

I stepped away. My hands trembled. Blood dripped on the floor, each drop marking Mark's impending doom.

"He needs blood." Rachel grabbed Michael's shoulder. "Check our records, and find out who's a match for him."

Michael nodded.

"We need to get him into an operating room." Zachary's eyes fell on me. "Get David. He's a universal donor. Mark's lost too much blood, and I can't risk the wait."

"Okay." I rushed out to find my friend.

Sweat dripped from my temples, the pounding of my heart growing louder as I searched hall after hall to no avail.

He was nowhere inside.

I stepped on a chair and looked in a circle. I had to find him, or we'd lose Mark.

An imposing figure opened the doors that led outside, then David, Matt, and Davon followed her in.

I ran to them, bypassing whoever this officer was.

"David!" I tugged at his hands. "Come with me."

He resisted. "But—"

"There's no time." I pulled him harder. "You need to come. Now!"

Davon gripped my shoulder. "What happened?"

Matt stood beside him, mirroring his expression.

The woman who entered with them stood in wait, watching with a raised eyebrow. She had an air of authority about her. Her black-and-red uniform had the same symbol as the helicopters.

I shook my head. "It's Mark."

Davon gasped.

"What happened to him?" Matt stared at my bloody hands. "Where is he?"

"He's badly injured. Zachary took him into surgery." My hands trembled. "There was so much blood."

"Matt, get Seth and Katherine from the prison, and tell them to come to the conference room. The three of us will brief General Sinclair. You go to Aoki. He needs to know." Davon cupped my face, his large hands wiping away my tears. "Can you handle this without me?"

I nodded.

"I need to stay, but I'll come to you as soon as I'm done. Wait for me."

The touch of his lips against my temple sent a calming wave through my body.

"David, go with her."

David nodded, and we bolted to the operating room.

"It's been hours." Carol's knee shook.

She sat by my side and Aoki on the other, holding baby Doug's sleeping form.

When I told Carol about Mark, she'd almost broken into the operating room. If it wasn't for Peter, she might have entered. He held her, murmuring into her ear, and she stopped struggling and relaxed into his embrace.

Peter went into the operating room after that. When he came out, he explained that Mark had received a stab wound that perforated his liver. "They're trying to save whatever they can from his liver. Zachary and Michael say it will take time."

David gave his blood along with another matching citizen, but two hours had passed, and we were on edge.

The waiting room was filled to the brim with people. The most critical cases were brought in, and doctors from science had taken over them. Many patients were cleared, but there was nothing from Mark yet.

David and Matt left a while back, wanting to be part of the meeting with the Liberty Enclave.

It was hard to stay calm. We'd lost Connor, Sarah hadn't come back, and I still had to face Deb and tell her the news.

I turned my attention to the door, and Peter's tall figure entered the room. He had dark circles under his striking blue eyes, but they shone with something more—hope.

I clenched my hands and buried my nails into my bloody uniform.

"He made it!" He sighed. "He's in recovery."

Aoki's eyes brightened.

I squeezed his hand.

His sweet smile met mine.

The darkness that had overtaken the room vanished.

Carol stood and hugged her father. "Thank God." Her eyes gleamed. "When can I see him?"

Lavigne held the side of her face delicately, his adoring eyes filled with love. "Soon. Zachary wants to keep him under observation for an hour."

"Okay," Carol said.

Douglas stirred.

"Can I?" I asked Aoki.

"You never have to ask," he said.

As I stared into Douglas's dark, almond-shaped eyes, hope burned within me.

Maybe we could make it after all.

"Deb?" I entered the room she'd been staying in.

After a week and a half, she still refused to leave. She only stood to go to the bathroom and had lost a lot of weight. Her skin stuck to her bones. Her smile was long gone except when Connor came to visit.

A sudden pang struck my heart, and I held a hand over my chest, trying to even out my breathing. I'd never be in the same room with him again. I'd never feel his arms around me as he tried to comfort me no matter how much he'd been going through himself.

If it was this hard for me, I couldn't fathom how it would be for Deb. How would she push through without him?

"Come in." The soft rustle of the sheets almost muted her tired voice.

I hesitated. Then I turned on the light.

The stale smell hit me. Even with the wildflowers I'd brought her, the room reeked of illness. Of misery.

Deb grunted and grabbed her stomach, then used her elbows to sit up. Aspen watched me for a moment before settling back at her feet.

"Hey, sis. How are you doing?" I wiped my sweaty palms on my uniform.

She widened her eyes. "Why are you covered in blood?"

I hugged myself, squeezing until the pressure stung. I needed to drown out the growing ache inside me.

"Something happened." Her eyes grew larger. "Tell me."

I sat next to her and brought her hands onto my lap. "I'm sorry, Deb."

She shook her head. "What are you...?" Her eyes clouded, and her nostrils flared before she shook her head faster, pulling away from me. "Where's Connor?"

I drew strength from his last words and let them fill me with the courage I needed. "He's gone." My chest caved in the moment I said the words.

Her eyes filled with tears, and she held her shaking hand over her mouth. "No."

I clasped my empty hands on my lap and swallowed to keep my burning tears from flowing. I had to be strong.

"Not Connor." Her sobs were silent until her shaking became violent and she screamed.

Her grief-stricken howl pierced my heart, and I wrapped my arms around her trembling body. I closed my eyes.

Why? What did we do to deserve this pain?

After a long while, the silence was broken by her shattered voice. "How?"

I breathed deeply. "A reaper took him. He was saving me."

Deb nodded mutely.

"He died in my arms. He...wasn't alone." I was numb all over, but I wanted her to know he was with someone he loved when it happened.

"He said to live. To fight." She needed to know what he stood for, that in his last moments he urged us not to give up. To go on without him.

Deb held her breath for a moment before deflating in my arms. "Thank you."

The door rattled. Davon came in, followed by Matt. They must have heard her scream.

Deb didn't flinch at Davon. Neither did she back away.

He stayed by the door when her eyes met his, then he looked down.

Matt came to her side. "I'm so sorry, Deb. I have no words."

She nodded and watched Davon. "Come."

I stilled, and my racing heartbeat reached my ears.

Davon lifted his gaze but did not move.

"Please come." Her voice was nothing but a whisper.

Davon slowly made his way to the bed.

Was it happening at last? Would she finally accept him back into her life?

She took his hands in hers. "I'm sorry." Her lower lip quivered. "Connor loved you so much."

Davon breathed fast, then his resolve broke, and he let out a soft wail.

Deb grabbed his nape, then hugged him.

The bed creaked when he sat on it, holding Deb to him as if his life depended on it. "I'm sorry for everything."

"I know." Deb buried her face in the crook of his neck.

They held on to each other.

Their soft moans drilled into my heart, and I stepped away from the bed.

Connor was here, making sure that in his absence, his family was complete.

I closed my eyes. "Thank you."

Even in death, he was our strength.

"Let's give them some space." Matt touched my back.

I glanced at him, then back at them. "Will they be okay?" I whispered.

"They will." He grabbed Aspen by her collar, and we left the room.

Once out, Matt pulled me into a hug. "I'm sorry, honey. I can't believe he's gone."

The pressure that had subsided suddenly bounced back. "I'm sorry too. We all loved him."

His eyes glazed, then he caught my hand between his and kissed it. "I need to go help with the wounded, but if you need to talk, just say it."

"I will." I took Aspen's leash. "I'll take her with me."

"Okay." He gave me a sad smile. "See you later."

"Matt!" I called after him.

He was halfway down the hall and turned. "Yes?"

I swallowed my words. "It's nothing." I'd talk to him later.

He took a step toward me. "Are you sure?"

I waved him off. "Yeah. We'll talk later."

He nodded and left.

A question had kept pestering me since the bunker shook. Just as I had gone deeper into the kitchen with Rosa, I'd heard something about a file, and I could swear it was Peter's voice. When I'd come back, Davon was gone, and a few minutes later, we were attacked.

What happened after Peter took Davon away? Maybe he took him to the room where we'd seen Jordan's video, where we usually went when a file arrived.

I made my way to that room, Aspen by my side.

When I entered, everything lay as if a storm had passed through it, and a computer monitor was paused. A dropping sensation swept over me. It was Jordan's face staring back at me.

A chill ran through my body as I made my way to it. I moved the cursor and played it from the beginning.

Bile rose from my stomach. Anna was at his mercy, and he was out for vengeance.

The video feed changed, showing the streets of Promissa.

I paused the video. Uncle Scott's mutilated body hung limply on a pole.

The world darkened around me, and whatever peace I had achieved after watching Davon and Deb make up was destroyed in an instant.

All those years he'd been fighting for us, silently serving the rebellion. Doing whatever he could to help. He didn't deserve this.

My hands shook violently, then I doubled over as a sharp pain tore at my belly.

I gripped the desk for dear life. "Help!"

I breathed through it, but something was definitely wrong. I made my way to the door. Maybe someone would hear me if I could get to it.

Chapter 18

Davon

May 7, 2214

I'd lost my brother and had my sister back. My hands trembled as I held on to her. Our soft cries finally subsided.

"I missed you," I whispered next to her ear, then let go.

A final tear slid down her cheek. "I...missed you too."

I could sense by her pause how she still struggled with the trauma I'd brought down on her.

I gazed into her eyes, ones so similar to Abi's. "Tell me what to do. How can I fix things?" I couldn't let go of everything that went on in that room. It was eating me away from the inside—how I broke her.

She grasped my shoulders. "There's nothing to do but go on." She touched my cheek. "Connor would have wanted us to make up. To be reasonable. Let's do that. Let's make it up as we go." She smiled. "I think this is a good start."

My vision blurred, and I leaned into her touch.

"We built this together. The three of us." Her lips trembled, and she burst into tears again. "I can't believe he's gone."

I cradled her nape and held her to my chest, kissing the top of her head. "He shouldn't have died. I don't know how to go on without him."

Everything was quiet when I reached the computer room hall.

My head was pounding, but I had to make sure everything was in order before going to the infirmary to get some pills and then turning in for the night.

I hadn't seen Matt or Abi, but, surely, they'd gone to bed by now.

I sighed. With all that had gone on, I didn't get a chance to ask her if she talked to a doctor. I was looking for her when we heard Deb's scream. Then we rushed inside, and when Deb finally accepted me back into her life, all else faded.

Now I had to tell Abi. I wanted her to know about her uncle before I told the rest of the council.

A loud bark filtered across the hall. It sounded frantic.

There were a couple of dogs here, but only one came to mind.

"Aspen?"

I followed the sound all the way to the computer room. When I pushed the door open, Aspen ran into me, stopping the door midway.

"It's okay." I took a step back and lowered my open palm. "I won't harm you."

She sniffed it and barked, glancing at me, then inside the room.

Was Matt here? I thought I saw him take Aspen from Deb's room.

"Matt?"

There was no answer.

It was dark inside, with the monitor paused on Scott Davis's hanging body.

I furrowed my brow.

Aspen's insistent barks caught my attention again. Her ears perked up, her eyes wide as she darted toward the middle of the room.

Abi was crouching on the floor, holding her belly.

My whole world stopped.

I hurried to her. My heart leapt into my throat. "Abi?"

Her body shuddered.

I wrapped my arms around her. "What's wrong?"

"I think it's the baby."

No! Not them. A heavy weight pressed against my chest, but I leveled my breathing. I had to help them.

Her eyes brimmed with tears. "I'm sorry. I thought…"

"Shh. Don't worry. I'll take you to the infirmary. Everything will be all right."

I took her in my arms and rushed to the infirmary, hoping to hell I was right. The halls were empty except for a few guards.

I rammed my shoulder into the double doors. They swung wide. The room was full of patients, but I dashed to an empty cot.

"Matt! Zachary!" I screamed at the top of my lungs. "Anyone. Help!"

Abi flinched, then grabbed her belly. She wailed in pain.

"Tell me, baby. What can I do?" I wiped the sweat from her brow.

Matt was by my side in an instant. "What happened?"

"She's been in pain since the attack, but she told me her symptoms were better." I raked my hair back. "I found her in the computer room. I think she saw the video feed."

I'd briefed him during the meeting with Sinclair as well as David. We all agreed to tell Abi about it, but the time never came.

"God." Matt sighed heavily and moved closer to Abi. "Hon, I need to know when the symptoms started again and what exactly you're feeling."

Abi's pained eyes settled on Matt. "They never truly went away, not completely. I thought since they mellowed, maybe it was just a reaction to all that happened. Then when I watched the video, the sharp pain became unbearable."

She squished her eyebrows together, squeezing my hand.

Another wave of pain.

Her breathing slowed after a minute, and she relaxed her hold. "It gets a bit better, then hits again."

My heart lurched forward. "Shit, baby."

She cupped my cheek, gently rubbing my stubble. "I should have asked Zachary, but so much shit was going on."

"I know." *Fuck.*

She'd swallowed her pain and kept pushing.

What if we were too late?

She'd been through hell. Abi lost her best friend a month ago and now her father, because that was what Connor was to her.

I touched my temple to hers. "It's okay, love."

Her chin trembled. "I don't want to lose the baby."

I squeezed her hand. "That won't happen." I prayed my words were true. I didn't want her to go into heartache again. It would be too much to bear.

"Is she okay?" My hands shook as Matt examined her.

Matt stepped back. "I'll be right back." He looked around the room. "Megan, can you draw some blood while I grab the ultrasound? We need to run some tests. Also, bring her something for the contractions."

My muscles tensed, pressure seeping through my pores. Was she having the baby? It was too damn early.

I gripped Matt's arm. "Wait. What do you mean by contractions?"

Matt covered my hand. "Listen to me. I don't see bleeding, and that's good. I think she's going through uterine spasms, which can be caused by stress." He shook his head. "She's been through a lot. I need to make sure, but I think both the baby and Abi will be fine."

I didn't let go.

Matt pulled my hand away. "Please, Davon."

I stepped back hesitantly, then turned to the cot.

The nurse was taking her blood.

"It hurts so much." Abi scrunched her eyes shut.

The nurse passed her a mug and two pills. "Take them. They'll help."

I helped her up, and Abi took them.

Matt came back, pushing an ultrasound machine, with Zachary by his side.

"I'm here, Abi," Zachary said, and Matt moved aside.

Zachary lifted her shirt. "This will feel cold." He put some kind of gel on her stomach.

Abi jerked when he pressed an instrument on her belly, then looked at the monitor. "Is the baby okay?"

I glanced at the screen and held my palm to my mouth. There it was. Its small body moved, and my chest swelled. I held Abi's hand as Zachary repositioned the instrument. "It's perfect."

He let out a huge exhale. "Everything's okay."

"But the pain?" Abi gritted her teeth.

"You don't need to worry. The combination of stress and physical exertion can trigger these spasms, but they're harmless. After the blood tests are back, you can rest and continue as normal. I'm sure it was just a scare. But so you're calmer, listen to this." He pushed a button on the machine.

A rapid thump resounded from it.

My mind went blank. "Is that...?"

"Her heartbeat," Matt said.

A girl. My heart fluttered, and I kissed Abi's temple. There was nothing more beautiful than this moment. Nothing that could take away the bliss of hearing my child's heartbeat. Of knowing Abi would be okay.

Abi smiled at me, then turned to Zachary, her eyes alight with joy. "Wait. Did you just say...?"

Matt smiled wide. "You're having a girl!"

"Excuse me, General." A soft voice broke through my exhaustion.

My head rested on Abi's cot, her hand burrowed within mine.

I sat up slowly, not wanting to wake her.

After the news, she'd quickly fallen asleep as the medication streamed into her system.

"The blood tests are back. Dr. Anderson wants to talk to you. He's waiting in his office."

My pulse picked up.

Talk to me? Could something be wrong?

I glanced at Abi.

"I'll stay with her," the nurse said.

"Thanks." I let go of Abi's hand, then hurried into Matt's small office.

Matt examined some papers behind the desk. "I'm sorry I couldn't go to you. Zachary was exhausted, and I took his shift. I have a lot of tests to go through. So many were injured."

I fidgeted with the leather bracelet Abi made for me. "It's okay. Just cut to the point. Is she all right?"

Matt slumped back in his chair. "The blood tests came out fine. She's a bit dehydrated, but that's easily fixed. You're free to leave."

I took a long, deep breath. "Thank you."

Matt drummed his fingers against her file. "She's dealing with a lot, but she's strong. The baby too."

I propped my elbow on his metal desk. "I don't know how to keep her out of the fight. Her mind is set on going out there."

Matt pushed the papers away. "You need to let her go."

My stomach recoiled. How could he ask this of me?

He leaned forward. "You should, Davon. She has the same right to fight as we do, even more so."

I wouldn't risk them. "But the baby."

"You're going to need to trust they'll be all right. She's planned this for too long. She built this strategy from scratch. This is her fight as well as ours."

I bent over the desk, holding my head between my hands. From day one, she'd been longing for this moment. For taking revenge.

"Fuck."

Matt chuckled. "Your woman is fierce. I don't think there's a force on earth that can stop her from going out there. Now more than ever."

God help me.

May 9, 2214

The clock had reached its limit. Our time was up.

As I darted my gaze around the crowded valley outside farming, my mind took me back to the meeting with General Sinclair two days ago.

Katherine and Seth were by my side, while Sinclair sat with two of her officials at the other.

Sinclair rolled her shoulders back, her blue eyes guarded. "Shall we begin?"

I met her stare and nodded. "Of course. First, we want to thank you for coming to our aid. This attack..." I took a deep breath, pushing away the lump in my throat at all we'd lost. "It took a lot from us, and if it weren't for your choppers, it would have been much worse."

Sinclair leaned forward. "I'm sorry about your general. I was very keen on meeting him."

I bowed my head. "Thank you for your words."

She interlaced her hands on the table. "I know you have questions. So do we, so let's cut to the chase. I'm here because we have the same goal—to destroy the NWG once and for all. To break the hold they've kept on our territory for decades."

I kept my rapt attention on her and mirrored her pose. "I know about your intentions to retake Halcyon. Father told me. What I want to know is what your intentions are toward us."

She straightened. "We have known about Promissa for a while now, as it serves as a refuge for some of your citizens, but our main focus is recovering Halcyon."

My phone beeped. "I'm sorry. I have to take this."

"Go ahead." She sat back.

My heart was in my throat. "Matt?"

"Everything's okay."

I sighed. Losing Mark was not an option. I couldn't bear losing another friend.

"Tell him not to worry. To focus on the meeting." Abi's melodic voice sounded close.

"Okay, okay. I will."

Matt's muffled voice made me smile for a moment, as I imagined Abi trying earnestly to listen to our call. "Tell her everything's fine."

"He says everything's fine."

Everything went quiet for a moment.

"Can we come to the meeting? David says he feels fine, and Zachary and Michael seem to have everything under control."

The load on my shoulders lightened. "Sure."

"Perfect. We'll be there in a minute."

I put the phone down. "My lieutenant general and captain will be here in a moment. Do you mind if we wait?"

She shook her head. "Not at all."

I nodded. My leg shook as minutes passed in awkward silence.

"Is Mark okay?" Katherine asked.

I nodded.

Seth sighed. "Good."

"If you want, you can leave when Matt and David get here. I know you have a lot on your hands with the hostages."

Seth and Katherine agreed, and once Matt and David entered, they both left hurriedly.

Once everyone settled, I continued. "As I was saying, I understand your intentions toward retaking the city of Halcyon, but my question stands. What do you want from us?"

She crossed her arms. "Information."

David leaned his arm on the desk. "What kind of information?"

Sinclair pursed her lips. "Who are you again?"

David clenched his jaw. "I'm Captain David Martinez, leader of the sniper team of the PRF."

I understood David's lack of trust, as I too had doubts about their intentions. But we had to tread lightly. I had the feeling Sinclair wasn't someone to mess with.

She narrowed her eyes at David but quickly regained her calm expression. "Nice to meet you, Captain." Her tone was guarded. "To be fair, I'll also present myself. I am General Jules Sinclair of Empire City, capital of the Liberty Enclave. I'm the person who welcomed your envoy and the one who took your plea to our high council."

I cleared my throat, as their passive-aggressive banter was getting out of hand. "Thank you for your efforts, but we'd appreciate it if you could answer our question. What kind of information do you want from us?"

Sinclair shrugged. "It's simple. You've been with the enemy. You're his son, for God's sake. We want to know what we're dealing with."

"And what do we get in return?" Matt said from my right.

Sinclair watched him closely. "That would depend on the intel we get."

My body went hot, and I clenched my jaw. This was not what Connor wanted. "We need to have some kind of assurance that you'll help us if we give you that intel."

Sinclair raised an eyebrow. "We already gave you our aid, or did you forget what happened today?"

Fuck. She was right.

I rolled my shoulders back, trying to relax my stiff neck. Maybe we were being stubborn, but I couldn't ignore the power of their army. What if they saved us just to gain our trust? What if after everything went down, they took Promissa from us?

"I assure you our intentions are just. I could ask the same question of you." Sinclair's chair screeched as she stood. "How do I know you'll keep your end of the bargain?"

The officers at her side followed suit.

We'd reached a stalemate.

I pushed myself up, as did Matt and David. "Our priority right now is to get everyone out before the New World Government attacks again. Once we reconvene at the cavern system we prepared, we'll meet with the rest of the council to continue this discussion. If they agree, we'll share our intel. Does that meet your expectations?" I swallowed hard, trying to calm my thundering heart.

If she declined, we'd lose a powerful ally.

After a long pause, she nodded. "It does, and as a token of our goodwill, we'll help you move the wounded to this place. My choppers are at your service."

A lightness hit my chest. Maybe things would work between the PRF and the Liberty Enclave.

I shook my head as soldiers marched to my left. The PRF was about to leave the bunkers permanently after a decade of hiding.

When my father got news of this battle, he'd send more troops in for sure. We couldn't stay.

As for the spy, we still didn't have a clue who it was and could only guess they hijacked our system and got that information out somehow. Nina had reinforced our security system even more after the attack, but we needed to stay vigilant.

At least there was something positive in all this—my father was blind to our plans of attack. The strategy meetings had been kept private. The soldiers would be briefed when the attack was imminent, and once inside Promissa, they'd take action.

Our people back in Promissa and Electi had their instructions as well as Constantine's people. We'd already sent a coded letter to our agents inside Electi and had let Frank know of our plans.

Peter had already left orders for the troops allied with us inside. They'd wait for the signal.

Now we only had to determine what the real goal of the Liberty Enclave was and if they'd help us.

I let out a quiet exhale when the choppers came into view. Lucas, along with the rest of the enhanced soldiers, were drugged and moved via helicopters early in the morning. The decision had been his—to take the sedatives alongside them to show he trusted us. So they'd know we weren't the enemy. Abraham had helped Faez build a prison deep within the cavern. Multiple gates and a security system had been created inside the chamber. It held twenty enclosed spaces in total. It wasn't much but was enough to hold them. Abraham also created an interrogation room like the one we had in farming.

Other than Lucas, we now had nine other reapers in our hands, five of whom presented behavior like his. Abi insisted on building some common rooms and a sort of lounge area where they could relax. Abraham was working on those preparations.

Matt and Michael, even with all that was happening, took the time to study the blood samples from the reapers taken during the attack. They discovered some kind of synthetic neurochemical agent, one they hadn't seen before. They extracted it and found that once it went into the bloodstream, it flooded it immediately. They thought it hijacked the brain's aggression center, stimulating the amygdala and suppressing rational thought. It was also highly addictive and rewired the dopamine receptors and manipulated the serotonin levels, creating from the user a sense of loyalty toward the giver.

Our team of experts believed the NWG scientists somehow combined stimulants with some kind of hallucinogen and then somehow manipulated it neurochemically to have this result—a highly obedient being prone to violence and without a moral compass. Our job now was to wean them off this stuff and see where that took us.

I rubbed my eyes, willing them to stay open. I just wanted to lie down, but that wasn't an option. I had to focus.

I drew in a deep breath, urging the clean forest air to fill my lungs with renewed energy, then looked at the only person who could give me the comfort I desperately needed.

I tucked one of Abi's rebellious curls behind her ear, grazing her neck gently with the back of my hand. "Are you sure you don't want to travel with the Liberty Enclave?"

Goosebumps rose on her neck, and she turned her shiny hazel eyes toward me, gifting me that sense of calm only she could.

Abi tilted her head, a small smile plastered on her face. "I want to travel with you."

I wanted to get her to the safety of the caves as soon as possible and had insisted on her hopping into one of the choppers. I was about to argue, but she raised a hand, cutting me off.

"Don't start." Abi pulled on her huge backpack. "I'm feeling much better, and both Zachary and Matt said I could make the journey."

I let out a sharp exhale. She was so stubborn.

We hadn't told anyone else about the pregnancy. Only a few knew about it, Matt, Zachary, and Aoki included. As for Sarah and Deb, Abi wanted to wait till we were safe inside the caverns.

Abi turned to the empty field where a chopper was about to depart. "So he's leaving with them?"

There were five helicopters in total. David hopped into one, following Sinclair. He'd asked permission to keep a close eye on her. They didn't see eye to eye, but from what happened during our meeting, I sensed they were more like two sides of the same coin. Both vigilant of each other without enough trust to make their relationship amicable. I couldn't blame him for it. You could never be too careful with a force like them.

After David was inside, Matt pushed Shirokuro's kennel in, then climbed in and took the baby from Aoki. David helped Aoki up, and they settled in. Abi waved at David. He smiled back, then he caught my stare and nodded.

Mark was placed into another one, as were many of the most critical cases. The rest of the injured were moved by land in vehicles, and the rest of us would walk.

The transfer was dangerous, but there was nothing else to be done.

Deb and Sarah went into Mark's chopper, followed by Aspen. Sarah had come in very late on the night of the attack but was silent as a ghost. She had not talked since but had stayed by Deb's side.

Abi watched Deb and Sarah. "Do you think they'll be okay?"

I took Abi's hand. "I don't think any of us will be for a while."

She stared at the ground, keeping one step in front of the other without pause. "I'll miss sitting with Connor. He made me think we'd make it. I..." She sniffed. "I always thought he'd be there with us in the end."

I swallowed hard and nodded. "I thought the same. It never crossed my mind that we could lose him."

The heaviness in my heart was ruthless ever since I'd lost my brother. I couldn't even remember my last words to him. There was so much chaos. He'd fought valiantly but then ran ahead when he heard a commotion not far from us.

Matt and I were engaged in battle and couldn't follow him fast enough. Then it was too late.

I let go of Abi and pulled my hair back into a ponytail. I was fidgety, my body itching to fight. To take them down for killing him.

Our group made it just before nightfall. Abi had pushed through.

There was nothing on site. I'd instructed for the helicopters to be settled in a valley far from the caverns, then covered with massive camouflage tarps designed to blend in as rolling hills.

There were no signs of life when we entered the massive cavern opening, which arched in the rear of a mountain.

The walls within were damp and cool to the touch. Ceiling openings let the last rays of sunlight inside, throwing shadows and bathing the dark environment with a warm glow. Moss and lichen grew in patches, bringing life into otherwise dead scenery.

The air carried a mild, earthy aroma that was soothing to the senses. It was like stepping into another world.

Just as my eyes adjusted to the dim lighting, we stopped in front of an iron door, its surface painted to blend in with the surrounding walls.

Abi searched with her flashlight. "Here."

An intercom was hidden behind a cover that imitated the wall of the cavern. Anyone who was not used to this type of hidden mechanism would have missed it. I punched in the code Faez had given me, and the door clicked.

I covered my eyes as the door opened. Embedded every few feet along the rocky walls, LED lights created a soothing illumination that transformed the dim cavern into a welcoming refuge. We followed them deep into the cavernous halls, their light reflecting off mineral veins and the occasional trickling of water down the rocks.

I spotted cameras hidden within the rugged walls. No corner was shrouded in darkness, creating a sense of safety and direction as we passed through.

Not more than five minutes passed until we heard them.

Our people.

Chapter 19

Davon

May 10, 2214

"We're gathered to discuss what our next step will be." I glanced around the table.

The councilmembers' attention was set on me, their new general of the army.

An assembly had taken place last night, and the people chose me as their new leader, with Matt, as general, at my side. I'd fight for them till the end.

I drank some water and took in every one of them.

Katherine and Seth sat at the far right, with Faez and Steven beside them. Dani and Michael were opposite Katherine, and Jess and Abi were to my left. General Sinclair sat at the other end of the table, facing me, while Matt took my right. David and Corporal Mathews were by the door. Lavigne was to my left, whom I'd appointed as my advisor.

The room had a natural feel to it, as did every other location inside this complex. Rock formations protruded here and there, forming alcoves and ledges for the wires and equipment required to run this sanctuary.

I sipped some water, taking a moment to compose myself. "We've lost many, including my dear friend General Harris, and today I sit humbly at this table in his place." Talking about Connor's death still shook me.

Abi looked down. Matt and David closed their eyes briefly, but most waited and darted their eyes toward Sinclair, who, unmoved, kept her stare set on me.

"War is ahead. We no longer have time to sit idly. Our country is in peril. Its citizens are suffering even more at the unmerciful hand of our enemy, who, as you have seen, is ten times stronger than us. Nevertheless, we had our victory, thanks to our unexpected guests."

I gestured toward General Sinclair. "The Liberty Enclave answered our call and aided us in destroying our enemy. This is General Jules Sinclair."

Sinclair stood. "I'd like to extend my sincerest condolences on the loss of General Harris and your citizens. We stand at the edge of war and share a common enemy—the New World Government. The Liberty Enclave is a bastion of the republic you all were part of once, and we aim to take it back."

I flinched. Such a statement was a dangerous one to make at this table, and I secretly hoped I understood her wrong, because if not, this meeting would take a turn for the worse.

David stepped forward. The others kept their rapt attention on Sinclair.

I cleared my throat, and David retreated, taking his place by the door.

I put my palms on the table. "Just to be clear, we fight to take back Promissa. We do thank you for your aid and hope to have your support in the difficult times ahead, but we are not letting go of what is ours."

Sinclair nodded. "I understand. As I explained to the envoy your general sent to Empire City, we believe we can reach an agreement. Our military aid in exchange for your intel and assistance in understanding what we'll face in Halcyon. You see, Halcyon was our capital, our greatest city. They not only destroyed our government, but they took our people and enslaved them." She paused. Her eyes seemed lost, and for the first time since we'd met, I faced a different person. One who'd suffered as much as we had.

She clenched her fists. "I'm not sure if you're aware of what's happening in Halcyon. Of the way General Thorne Steele has run his rule."

What Halcyon faced was a different reality of what we were going through in Promissa. They'd been under the regime for twenty years, and theirs was a predicament of what we'd meet in our future. I remembered my father's words. The purge and how Grace Orville had already started killing off the elderly so they wouldn't waste their precious resources on them.

And, no, I had no idea how Steele was running Halcyon, but from what Sinclair stated, it was hell and one we'd be subjected to in no time if we stayed put.

"If I may." Peter waited for my consent before answering.

He'd gained the respect of everyone after the attack, having taken down dozens of reapers with our soldiers. He went in without rank, donning the same uniform we all did. And he fought valiantly.

I nodded.

"I'm General Lavigne." He shook his head and raised an eyebrow. "Sorry, force of habit. I'm former General Lavigne of the New World Government."

Sinclair widened her eyes. "*The* General Lavigne?"

Peter bowed.

"But you..." Sinclair's hands shook for a moment before she eyed me. "What the hell is he doing here?"

I straightened. "He's one of us."

She flinched. "But—"

I didn't let her continue. "He's the one who aided our escape. Thanks to him, we have the intel you need. So please try to look past all you've heard or think you know about him, and show him the same respect as all the people in this room."

She took a moment but relaxed her posture and nodded.

Peter frowned. "I can't even express how sorry I am for the things I've done for the New World Government. I only wish, with the time I have left, to make up for it in any way I can. I do know how things are in Halcyon and the tyranny and violence that reign over the citizens there. General Thorne Steele is a dangerous man and one set on destroying us all. Whatever intel you need, know we will help you. But please understand we need all the help we can get against our enemy. If you can spare it."

The way Peter managed the situation showed his experience with working with powerful people. His resolve and self-control were two of the things I admired most about him. He always used the right words. The correct tone to get a person to do what he needed. This was why his presence on this council was vital. Not only because of the intel he could bring to it but because of his experience as a seasoned general.

Sinclair sat and propped her elbows on the table. Her intertwined hands covered her mouth as she studied Peter.

Was she weighing her options?

The tension in the room was palpable, all waiting for what the enclave could offer us.

I clasped my hands together, willing them to still. We needed their alliance. We needed it desperately.

Sinclair sighed. "We can give you weapons, two helicopters, and enough troops to give you a chance. That's all we can offer for now because what awaits us in Halcyon is hell."

I controlled my urge to scream for joy. That was more than I expected. *Armed helicopters.*

"But we have some stipulations," she said. "We want to attack in unison. You enter through Promissa as we rush into Halcyon. Our council believes an attack from both fronts is our best chance to defeat them."

An attack from both sides was risky, but as Sinclair said, the NWG would be forced to divide their army, and that could very well tip the scales in our favor.

We needed to act soon, but we were also aware that as we planned our strategy, my father and General Steele would be doing the same. Both Peter and I suspected that by this point, the NWG jets should be almost ready, and we feared the military trains were more dangerous than we thought.

Sinclair drummed her fingers on the table. "To be honest, I fear with the enhanced soldiers and the threats from the air and land, it may prove difficult, but if we play our cards right, we might have a chance."

"The attacks will be different. We'll come from the tunnels and the forest, using stealth as our ally. But you..." Abi watched Sinclair intently. "They'll see you coming from afar. They'll be ready. You need to make sure to hit them with all you've got. No mercy."

Sinclair raised an eyebrow and smiled. "I plan to do just that."

Goosebumps rose on my skin at Abi's words. She was proving to be the councilmember Connor saw in her. The one the rebellion needed. One who would fight to the end without hesitation. Without refrain.

Connor would be proud.

We had to become like them because neither my father nor Steele would show mercy. They'd annihilate us all.

The discussion went on as we evaluated our options.

I rubbed the back of my neck and cracked it. There was so much to cover. "I leave the table with Councilmember Davis and General Anderson. They will give us a progress report on a project they've been working on."

Abi opened a file and passed it over to Sinclair, then stood. "For the last week, we've been working on a project to understand the enhanced soldiers and their nature. Our main objectives are to know how the NWG controls them and to give them a chance for a new beginning."

Sinclair, who was ignorant of this investigation, scooted forward, her rapt attention on Abi.

"All the soldiers are highly intelligent and capable of problem solving. They are incredibly strong and heal faster than us. They feel no pain. Some show signs of cognitive problems and seem to have issues rationalizing friend from foe. This makes them prone to distrust and violence, joined with bursts of extreme agitation and aggression. We believe this is mainly caused by a drug they've been given. It's still under investigation, but our scientists are making progress. Six out of ten soldiers have shown progress during the interview process. They are aware they've been given some kind of stimulant and have agreed to work with us if we help them manage the withdrawal and recovery from such drugs."

"And how do you know they're being honest and not manipulating your system?" Sinclair asked.

Abi shrugged. "We don't." She gestured toward the file in Sinclair's hands. "Vitals appear normal during interrogations, and we believe they're telling the truth. These are humans who have suffered at the hands of our enemy. Victims just like us. I know it's hard to see them as such with all the damage they've done, but now that we have evidence of how the NWG has been controlling them, I believe they deserve a chance. So did Connor."

Most faces around the table became unreadable. Seeing the reapers as fellow humans after such violence was hard. It would take time.

Sinclair studied the file. "Have you found out more about these drugs? Can we use them in our favor?"

I swallowed hard and turned my attention to Abi, who clenched her jaw before taking a deep breath.

Sinclair was treading on dangerous waters.

Abi rolled her shoulders back and looked into Sinclair's eyes. "We won't use them as the NWG has. We will not become our enemy. If they decide

to fight with us, it'll be because they want to, not because we make them."
Her tone was firm, leaving no place for retort. "Now I will give the table to
General Anderson."

Sinclair gripped the file hard before letting out a long exhale and handing
it back to Abi, who in turn, passed it down the table to Matt.

Matt cleared his throat. "We recreated the supplements as best we could
based on what my father, Minister Frank Anderson, sent us."

There was a gasp from the end of the table.

Sinclair's mouth was agape for a second before she frowned. "You mean
to tell me you're the son of the minister of health, the man responsible for
all this?"

Matt nodded. "I am. He's been working against Jordan Niles for years
now."

Sinclair cocked her head. "Explain."

"My father tried to sabotage the Elysium Project, the one used to create
the enhanced army in Halcyon years ago. He failed because of General
Steele. He'd taken an interest in the project and was keen on following my
father and learning all about it. He even got his own scientists once the
government center moved into Promissa. My father lost control over the
project in Halcyon over a decade ago. We believe that's when Steele created
the drug that controls the reapers, a drug my father had no knowledge of."

Sinclair frowned, then turned to me. "I don't understand. Wouldn't
your father want all the enhanced soldiers under the drug's control? Why
wasn't this implemented in Promissa?"

I closed my eyes briefly. "General Steele does many things on his own,
and Father lets him as long as the results are favorable. I believe Father has
been losing control over Halcyon for years now. His trust in his general is
too blind for him to notice. I don't know the true intentions of General
Steele, but this last year, something happened without my father's knowl-

edge, including the commencement of the purge by none other than Grace Orville."

"The president's daughter?" Sinclair said.

I slumped back. "The one and only. She's Steele's lover."

The situation in Halcyon sometimes kept me up at night. Since Father told me, I couldn't let go of the idea that there was something else brewing over there. That maybe Father should be questioning Steele's loyalty.

Sinclair shifted forward. "And what is this purge?"

I took a deep, calming breath. "It's what we're trying to stop. We were never part of the NWG's future. Their plan has always been to use us to create a genetic pool large enough so they could create their own army to take over the continent. Now that they're so close to the numbers they wanted, we're no longer needed. They plan to execute each and every one of us."

Sinclair drew back and covered her mouth. "Where did you get this information from?"

I darted my eyes between Matt and Abi, recalling our time in the city. "From my father during our time in Electi."

She shook her head. "This is worse than we imagined."

"It is," Matt said. "That's why we need to learn as much as we can from these soldiers and maybe get them on our side."

Matt opened the file. "We've been maintaining their supplements. Of the four who have shown cognitive problems, two are showing progress. We're using other stimulants in lower doses to wean them off the drugs, and they appear calmer. The other two act like animals. No conscience. Just raw violence. The cuffs don't seem to work on them. We're trying to find out why."

Sinclair propped her elbow on her armrest. "Do you think we can turn most of them against the NWG?"

Matt let go of the file and clasped his hands on the table. "We stand with Councilmember Davis on this. Her work has proven successful in getting them to see the NWG was using them, but I don't think they'll be ready to fight with us. At least not now. I do see the potential in helping them and turning them to our side after we win the war."

"It's a start." Sinclair relaxed back.

"For now, we fight on our own." I hoped with the Liberty Enclave and Constantine's cells that it would be enough.

Sinclair nodded. "You're no longer on your own. As I said, we came to help. I'm confident if we attack together, we'll have a better chance."

I sighed. "Thank you."

"I have a question." David approached the table and stood a few feet from Sinclair. "What happens if we lose and you win? Will you continue fighting or abandon us after getting your city back?"

Abi threw him a side glance.

Ever since Sinclair arrived, David had been edgy. They didn't see eye to eye, and even though Abi had urged him to stand down, he wouldn't back away.

But there was something else I couldn't put my finger on, some kind of tension between them.

Sinclair stood to face him. "And what if you win and we lose? Will you stand by us? Will you fight?"

David didn't back away. "Of course we will. I would go out of my way to stand against oppression. The NWG has to be stopped."

Sinclair smirked. "At last we see eye to eye, Captain Martinez. We have a common enemy, and we will end their regime, whatever it takes."

Something sparked between them before both nodded.

"Then we fight," he said.

Sinclair's eyes flashed. "Then we fight."

The meeting was intense, and we had little to no privacy inside the caves, so after dinner, Abi and I took a stroll outside. Now it was time to turn in.

As we walked through the cavern, I couldn't help but remember Jimmy. He started this project, and to see it to its completion was a tribute to his dedication to our cause.

I swallowed the lump in my throat. He died without seeing it finished. Without knowing how he, in his own way, saved us all.

We were deep inside the cave system and reached the administrative area, one built with extra security after the events at farming. We couldn't risk the spy having access, so we had extra security. Our room was there, as were the rooms of the higher-ups, including one for Sinclair.

The cavern had ample rooms, all bestowed with at least a small table, a bed, and lights. Some had extra spaces to have some privacy, but the restroom area was shared. In the depths of the cavern was an underground lake. Its water was conducted through pipes toward the shower rooms and cleaning area, and the rest was used for drinking after passing through a filtration system.

"Come here." I threw my arm around Abi's shoulders when we reached our room.

I pushed the code and put my finger on the scanner. The door opened.

"You're back," Matt yelled the moment we opened the door.

We shared our room with Matt, Aoki, and Doug.

Doug was crying while Matt sang him a lullaby.

"Why won't he stop crying?" He rocked the baby in his arms.

Aoki followed him with his gaze. Shirokuro took a nap on his lap.

"I don't think he likes your singing," I said.

Aoki burst out laughing from the table.

Matt side-eyed Davon, then shifted his emerald eyes Abi's way. "Help. This nephew of yours won't stop crying."

"Give him to me." Aoki put the cat down and walked to Matt, using one crutch. He cradled his son.

Doug immediately stopped crying.

"See?" I gestured toward Matt. "I told you. He just can't take your singing."

Matt humphed.

Deb had given Doug to them after the attack, and he was now officially their son. We shared the care between the four of us.

I snaked my arm around Abi from behind and rubbed her belly. It was hard to believe we'd have our own baby soon. I kissed her nape. "I love you, baby."

Her skin rose in goosebumps, and she shuddered. She gave me a soft kiss. Scorching heat radiated from our contact. God, I wanted her. I deepened the kiss before remembering we were not alone.

Matt covered his eyes. "Would you please stop? We know you're all lovey-dovey over there, but have some decency toward your friends who haven't had a moment of privacy in weeks."

Abi stepped away from me and grabbed hold of Matt's hands. "Okay. We'll spend the night in the bunkbed common room so you can have your privacy. Doug will come with us."

I grunted.

"Oh, come on. Don't put on that face." Abi winked. "If we do this, they'll have to do the same for us."

My heart skipped a beat, and warmth traveled down my body, stirring my desire.

That's my girl.

"So we'll finally have some time alone." I gave her a sultry smile. "Perfect. We'll have a system, then."

My mind went over all the things I wanted to do to her. She was the only one keeping me grounded. Her love and touch were like a balm in all this chaos.

Aoki lifted one eyebrow, checking out his husband. "I see no problem with that."

Matt flushed beet red.

"It's settled, then." Abi took the baby's backpack.

I prepared a bag for us, took the baby, and waved goodbye. "Have fun, guys, but remember the deal. Tomorrow it's our turn."

As I shut the door, I caught Aoki pulling Matt toward him and kissing him deeply. I smiled.

When we reached the common room, it was full to the brim. We found a bunkbed, and Abi settled in the bottom with Doug.

I put our bag on the top one, then sat beside her.

Doug munched on his little hand. It almost seemed like he was teething. He already looked like a two-month-old baby. His accelerated growth, twice as fast as a normal human, caught us all by surprise. We knew it would happen, but to see it with our own eyes was unreal.

I tucked one of her rebellious curls behind her ear. "How are you feeling?"

"I'm all right." She beamed. "I had my first coffee today in weeks."

"I saw you." I brushed her chin softly. "I'm relieved. It was weird having an exhausted, non-caffeinated Abi around."

She smacked her shoulder against mine. "It wasn't that bad."

I smirked. "Just joking. But I'm happy you're back to being the same old caffeinated you. I was worried."

Doug took hold of her finger, and she smiled. "Zachary says everything's good. Our baby will be all right."

I kissed her temple. "I can't wait to have a mini you running around. She'll be a warrior just like her mother."

My heart grew with hope for our future together. But it suddenly shifted to the reality we faced. What if we didn't make it?

No.

I pushed those thoughts away and covered her cheek, tilting her face toward me. "We'll be all right. We'll make it through. I'll protect you both with my life."

May 20, 2214

Lucas had completed his detoxifying treatment a couple of days ago and was going through the last of his withdrawal symptoms, which included hand tremors, nausea, and dizziness.

I was in charge of the interrogations of the six enhanced soldiers who'd shown signs of progress, and Seth and Katherine had taken over the others.

Voices reached me the moment I entered the hall that separated his room from the outside, a security measure taken in case any enhanced soldier rebelled against us. I looked through the small window in his door.

Rachel and he appeared to have dined together, their plates forgotten on the side table. She'd been key to understanding and getting through to Lucas and was my right hand, especially after the attack. As long as it wasn't on the battlefield, she said she'd help us any way she could. Nevertheless, I noticed that when she interacted with Lucas, there was something between them that seemed more intimate, and tonight was not an exception.

They faced each other on his bed, and he cupped her cheek in an intimate way. She covered his hand with hers and leaned into it, closing her eyes.

Were they...? I took a step back and collided with a trash bin.

Rachel scooted away from Lucas, who withdrew his hand and made a fist on his thigh.

She whispered something the mics that connected outside didn't catch, then patted his knee.

His fists relaxed.

She waved at me. "Abi? Is that you? We just finished."

I pressed the intercom. "We need to talk."

She stood, squeezed his shoulder, and walked out.

I bit my lip. "What's going on between you two? You and I both know this isn't part of the protocol. You need to stop."

What she was doing was dangerous. There was a lot we didn't know about them. What if he was using her? Manipulating her into creating this false sense of security around him just to pounce whenever her guard was down? I had to protect her.

She lifted her chin. "Why? Why should I stop? Aren't we supposed to treat them the same as any of us?" Her tone was hard, her voice a pinch louder than her usual caring one.

I gently grabbed her arm. "Do you care for him?"

She pressed her lips together, then looked inside. Lucas's blue eyes were raptly set on the small window, his eyebrows drawn together.

"We both do."

Their gazes searched for each other across the window.

I was stunned into silence. There was no denying it. They'd fallen for each other. Lucas's gaze no longer carried the anger I once witnessed. It was soft. Loving.

What if he was ready? What if Lucas had finally broken away from the chains the NWG had thrown around him?

I had to find Davon.

"Come in!"

Walking into the acting general of the army's office and finding Davon inside still surprised me. Connor had always been the one we went to. The one who helped us through these tough decisions.

Davon didn't look up, his attention set on the files that covered his desk.

"Can we talk?" I asked in a low voice.

He dropped everything and stood. "Is everything okay?" His eyes darted from my face to my stomach.

I sighed. "You have to stop this, Davon. You need to relax and know I'm okay."

Lately, he was always on edge in terms of the pregnancy, unable to let go of what happened after the attack.

He let out a heavy breath. "I'm sorry."

He was about to walk to me, but I raised my palms. "Please. I don't want to take you away from your responsibilities."

He smirked. "I'm the general of the army, so if I want to hug the woman I love, I will."

In three strides, he came around the desk and embraced me.

I melted in his arms. His warmth gave me the calm I needed. The peace I craved.

He held my shoulders. "Now, tell me, love, what is it that has you this riled up?"

I dropped my shoulders. "It's Lucas."

His grip became hard.

"And Rachel."

He shook his head. "What happened? Did he attack her?"

I looked into his eyes. "Quite the opposite."

He frowned. "You're losing me, love."

I sighed. "I think they're falling for each other."

He flinched. "In love?"

I nodded. "I went to check on him today and caught Lucas caressing her cheek. She responded to his touch. I confronted her, and she didn't deny it."

He lowered his hands. "And him? Does he feel the same way?"

"The way he looked at her." I dropped my gaze, then met his. "Yeah. I believe so."

Davon paced back to his desk, then slumped into his seat and bent over, holding his hair back with both hands. Then he started laughing.

My mouth hung open as I walked to his side and crouched. "Why are you laughing?"

He straightened, arching his back with his hands still locked over his head, wearing a beaming expression I hadn't seen in a while. "The psych evaluation just came through." He pointed toward the files. "They believe because these soldiers were psychologically and physically conditioned from a young age, they were deprived of emotional development. The doctors are sure they can relearn to be human. To feel again."

I opened Lucas's file, and a fluttery feeling entered my belly. Adrenaline tingled through my body. It was true.

"Don't you see? This is what you wanted all along—to prove they aren't monsters. If what you say is true, it further evidences they're neither sociopath nor psychopath."

I held the file up. "This changes everything. We can actually save them. We may be able to convince Lucas and the other five who have shown progress to join us. The others will take more time, but it can be done."

Davon pushed his chair back, grabbed my waist, and pulled me onto his lap.

I giggled as he peppered kisses up my neck.

"You're a genius, Abigail Davis," he whispered next to my ear, sending goosebumps all over my right side. "I'm sorry I ever doubted you."

May 21, 2214

"I need to tell you something."

My pregnancy was still a well-kept secret, but I wanted to tell David before we trained today. With my council responsibilities, the nonstop training, and his assignment to continue preparing the sniper team and to safeguard the passage to the caves, we had little time to sit and talk.

After him, I'd tell my sisters. We planned to spend the afternoon together and have a sleepover in their room. Jess and Rachel agreed to bunk elsewhere temporarily so we could have some time alone.

David narrowed his eyes at me. "If it's about Jonathan, there's nothing going on." He took a bite from his sandwich.

I'd met Jonathan for the first time a couple of nights ago.

His gray cat was following a lizard down a hall, the same one Shirokuro had been hunting. I was on Shirokuro duty. He'd been exploring the caves nonstop, but Aoki wanted him safe inside our apartment, so we took turns finding him every night.

Jonathan's cat caught the lizard first, to which Shirokuro hissed.

"Come on, Shadow. Time to go home."

The cat went to Jonathan, lizard in mouth, and rubbed against his legs.

Jonathan extended his hand. "Hi. We haven't been properly introduced. I'm Jonathan."

I shook it, trying to hold on to Shirokuro, who fought to scurry away to hide God knew where again. "I'm Abi. Nice to meet you."

"Dave told me about you." He smiled, and two dimples formed on his face. "It's good he has a friend."

He was striking, slightly taller than David. His hair was cut short and bleached blond, almost white. His dark skin and mesmerizing green eyes were eye-catching, and his smile carried a mischievous gleam.

"I hope all was good." I smiled back while Shirokuro fought for his life.

He chuckled. "Too good. I almost got jealous." He winked. "We have our history together, you know." He bit his lower lip.

I nodded. "Yeah, I do." I looked down at Shirokuro, who had calmed down for a moment, biting on Bonnie's thread bracelet. "Well, I guess we should go."

"Yeah. Us too." He patted his thigh, and Shadow followed him, the lizard long gone.

Today I met Jonathan again. This time it was right here in the mess hall. He was having coffee with David and left as soon as I arrived.

I sipped from my coffee and shrugged. "If you say so."

He was lying. The day I first saw them together I was assigned to scout the area. A branch snapped in the distance, and when I went to investigate, I caught Jonathan pressing David against a tree, claiming his mouth in a kiss that was anything but subtle. Then the other night, Jonathan and David came out of a storage room just as I was about to pass by. I ducked around a corner as Jonathan reached for David's shirt—fingers deliberate, adjusting the fabric with an intimacy that told me everything I needed to know.

David liked to keep his life private, so I respected his wishes and didn't bring it up. But now that he did, I wanted to know more.

He put his sandwich down. "We're just hooking up. It's nothing serious."

I lifted an eyebrow. "What about not forgiving him?"

"I haven't," he said flatly and kept eating.

If he was with Jonathan, what the hell was happening between him and Sinclair? I'd seen the looks between them. It was like they hated each other one moment and wanted to strip each other naked the next. They were training together, and once in a while, I'd catch them sharing a private conversation here and there. We'd all seen it. Matt said it reminded him of Davon and me before we hooked up. For once, I understood how he felt when it was just the three of us.

I edged closer to him. "Then what's going on with Sinclair?"

He choked, and I passed him some water.

I patted his back. "Don't say anything. I'm sorry. That wasn't what I wanted to talk to you about. It's something else. Promise you won't overreact."

David furrowed his brow. "What the hell happened?"

I lifted an eyebrow. "See?"

He took a deep breath, then put down his sandwich and shifted his chair to face me. "Okay. Tell me."

The mess hall was almost empty midmorning. Only about a dozen soldiers shared the spacious room with us, none close enough to overhear our conversation.

"I'm pregnant."

His eyes went so wide I thought they'd pop out. "You're..." His mouth wouldn't move.

"Pregnant, David." I smiled. "Davon and I are having a baby."

He raked his hair back. "Wow, that was unexpected."

"I just passed my first trimester. We didn't plan for it, but we're keeping her."

He brushed my upper arm. "A girl?"

I beamed and instinctively touched my mom's silver bracelet, which rested beneath my long sleeve. I never took it off. "Yes. We'll name her Elizabeth after my mom. Lizzie for short."

David took my hands in his. "Is that why you were sick last week after the attack?"

I nodded.

His gaze dropped. "Are you both okay?"

"We are." I pressed my lips together. "Losing Connor was just too much. But I'm good. Zachary says I'm in no danger, and neither is the baby."

The pain of losing Connor was still too close to the surface, and my throat burned with unshed tears.

David squeezed my hands, and his eyes clouded. "I still can't believe he's gone."

"Me either. Sometimes I swear I can hear him around. His sure step. His strong presence. It's like he's walking with me even though I know he's gone." He was with me like a memory, one I could almost touch.

Was he waiting for the end? For the conclusion of this nightmare we were thrown into?

The voices at the other end of the mess hall fell silent, but it was only us who'd fallen into this void.

"Are you all right?" David's soft tone called back my attention.

I nodded.

"Do you think it's a good idea?"

I squished my eyebrows. "What do you mean?"

He gazed at our joined hands. "I mean." He shook his head and grazed his thumb over my hand in an intimate gesture. "Do you think it's a good idea for you to be out there?" He clenched his jaw. "Fighting?"

I jerked back. If anything, I wanted to fight more than ever. To stop this nonsense so we could have our life back, so *she* could have a normal life, if it was even possible.

David tightened his grip on my hand before I could pull free. "I'm just worried. I can't bear to lose you."

I let go of him and glanced down at my interlaced fingers. "I can fight." I captured his honey-green eyes. "I need to be out there. Now more than ever."

"I understand." His hands covered mine, and I noticed the thick, rough callouses that had formed at the base of his thumb and on the tips of his fingers where he gripped the rifle. A testament to our countless hours spent training. A silent mark of his commitment to the PRF. "I will protect you with my life."

Each step we took toward our goal was so unclear that it was hard to imagine. I hoped we'd all make it and find our own path to freedom in the midst of this chaos. Because winning this war would demand all of our strength, yet it could also call for the ultimate sacrifice—our lives.

Loud grunts greeted us the moment we entered the training area.

I widened my eyes as Matt dodged Davon's attack, then slipped to the floor. His low kick landed on the back of Davon's legs. Davon hit the matted floor with a heavy thud.

We assembled our engineers after last week's council meeting to discuss adding protection to our armor based on what we faced in the attack. After I painfully narrated the events that resulted in Connor's untimely death, they decided to create some enhancements to make up for the armor's flaws, all without compromising mobility.

We'd started to train with the new armor a couple of days ago.

Matt clicked his tongue at Davon, stretching his hand to pull him up. "Our general of the army defeated by his second-in-command. What would the masses say?"

Davon swatted Matt's hand. "As if." He sat and shifted his head from side to side over the new plate that had been fitted to protect the back of his neck.

A memory of Connor's last moments flashed through my mind, but I shook it off.

Breathe.

Davon got up, rolled his shoulders, and adjusted his armor before assuming his fighting stance.

It was a great design, and it wasn't as heavy as it looked.

Matt chuckled and mirrored him. "Feeling brave, General?"

Davon took out his khukuri and made to hit Matt, who used his arm to block the slash with a resounding clang that echoed around the training area. The interlocking plates glistened under the cave's light, each meticulously designed to deflect blows and absorb impact.

Matt kicked him hard in the chest, but he stood firm. The breast plates and ballistic material beneath his chest provided an added buffer against frontal strikes.

Davon pivoted and turned his hips and shoulders, picking up enough momentum to throw a round kick against Matt. The edge of his boot hit Matt's left side.

Matt lost his footing and struck the floor hard.

Davon rushed him and pinned him to the ground, holding his khukuri against his throat. A half ponytail held his hair back, his loose waves hiding part of his face. His glistening brow evidenced how long they'd been at it. Sweat dripped onto the floor as he kept a strong hold on Matt, who was tirelessly trying to get Davon off by using his lower body, which was now trapped beneath the massive body of his best friend.

Back in Electi, Davon trained day and night to get stronger. He said the battle to come would be hard and he wasn't strong enough. Now, four months later, his bulging muscles were bigger than Matt's, and his strong legs held him down in an unbreakable hold.

Matt tried to use his legs to push him up, but Davon wouldn't budge.

David clapped at their display and stepped toward the center of the training area. "Time's up."

Davon and Matt turned in unison toward us.

They must have been too focused on sparring to notice they had spectators.

Davon stood and helped Matt up. They shook hands and patted each other's backs.

Within seconds, Davon was sharing my space, his hand nestled tenderly on my hip as he took me in a gentle embrace.

I rose on my tiptoes and pressed my lips against his in a warm kiss.

He lightly rubbed his stubble against my cheek, peppering kisses until he reached my neck. "God." He groaned and held me tight against him. "You smell so good."

Even after training, his unique scent woke every cell in my body—like leather mixed with whiskey and musk. It ran through me like a balm easing my fractured soul.

Davon stepped back and started taking off his armor. "Did you tell him?"

I pocketed my hands. "I did."

He looked over to where Matt and David exchanged words. "How did he take it?"

"As expected. He asked me whether I thought my fighting was a good idea or not."

He chuckled. "I can just imagine what happened next."

I slapped his shoulder, and he raised his palms, feigning innocence.

"Okay, okay. I know you have all the right to go out there, but cut us some slack here. We care about you. You can't just expect us to sit idly and not worry."

My heart ached for them both, but I needed to do this. It was the only choice. If I didn't fight, I'd regret it forever.

Davon secured the straps of my armor. "Your turn to train."

I stood motionless as he finished checking my chest piece. "Remember, tonight I'll sleep with Deb and Sarah."

He nodded. "It's about time. You should have told them earlier."

I dropped my head. "I know. It's just...after Connor's death, I wanted to give them some time to grieve."

He gave me a sweet smile. "I'm sure Connor is smiling upon us now."

Matt cleared his throat beside us. "Lunch later?"

Davon side-eyed him.

I giggled. "Sure. What are we having?"

Matt held his chin with two fingers, looking up comically as if in deep thought. "How about some curry for old times' sake? The one Aoki makes."

My mouth watered. "I'm in."

Davon grunted. "So much for you telling me we'd spend the afternoon alone."

I put my hands on my hips and stared at him.

He held his hands up. "Okay, we'll have lunch together."

"I knew I could count on you both. Two at our place. You can make yourselves at home." Matt chuckled, then winked at me.

We still shared a room, but Matt insisted it was theirs, and we were just guests. It was a joke intended to annoy Davon, which always worked.

I laughed, then waved goodbye.

Davon stroked my cheek and moved his hand slowly down the side of my neck. "See you at two." He pulled me in for a swift but intimate kiss.

A shiver shot down my body at the promise his touch made. "How about after lunch we ditch them to have that time alone? We can go to the cave you told me about."

It was a cave neighboring this massive system, one he'd found empty. He hinted at us visiting it.

His roguish smile was the death of me. "And that's why I love you." He brushed my lips with his thumb, then kissed them again ever so slowly. When I was sure I was about to melt right then and there, he stepped away. "See you later."

And with that, he left.

I shook my head and faced David, ready to get the training over with.

Davon and I set up the table.

He turned to Aoki. "How are you feeling today?"

Aoki stirred a pot of curry over the portable stove they'd brought from farming. He was still using his crutch to move around. "Good. I'm more mobile by the day, and, apparently"—he glanced toward Matt—"Doug is too."

Matt was changing Doug's cloth diaper, and the baby was damn strong for being only a month old. It was comical to watch Matt struggling to close it around him.

I had many questions about how this whole genetic enhancement worked, but at least Matt knew and was taking care of the supplements and nutrition.

I placed the plates on the table, then went to get some water.

I missed beer. David promised after training he'd work on a nonalcoholic formula for me and Lizzie.

Matt sat with the baby at the table and fed him. We grabbed our seats and allowed Aoki to do his thing.

When we arrived, his exact words were, "You all make me feel like I can't do shit, so you'll sit and let me do the rest."

He walked slowly but steadily, and we all ate dinner.

Matt gripped the baby's bottle in one hand while holding his spoon with the other. Aoki smiled sweetly at him while he ate.

"Who could believe you guys would make such good parents? I mean, of Aoki I could believe it, but Matt?" Davon shrugged. "It just blows my mind."

Matt threw him a menacing glance before getting back to his food.

I chuckled.

Matt dropped his spoon on the plate, then pressed his hand against his breastbone. "So you're taking his side?"

I raised my palms in innocence. "I was laughing at an inside joke."

"Yeah. Me." His bright-green eyes widened, and I choked.

Davon patted my back, feigning worry.

"Well." Aoki cleared his throat and bowed slightly. "Thanks for your words, but"—he clasped Matt's hand—"Matt's truly a wonderful dad."

His eyes glazed, and Matt's skin flushed.

Davon's lips curled into a smirk. "You know I'm joking. You're both great."

"I can't believe you'll also be a father. That, I never saw coming," Matt said.

Davon looked at me, then at my stomach. He squeezed my thigh. "I can't either, but I'm the happiest man alive." He glanced at his brothers. "No joke there."

My chest swelled at the love around the table. If it weren't for the threat of the NWG, I'd say we had a perfect life at this very moment.

The conversation went on as we finished Aoki's curry. Its warmth and taste brought me back to the night I learned about Davon's true identity. Of his first reaction when I wanted to go into Electi. Who knew at that moment that we'd actually go there, that we'd infiltrate the deepest part of the government and discover so much? And now we were preparing for war.

Matt ran his hand across my back. "Are you okay?"

I twisted to him and found Aoki was now holding the baby, with Davon quietly staring as he cooed and smiled.

I shook my head. "Sorry for zoning out."

Matt pulled at my ponytail playfully. "No need to apologize." He winked. "We haven't made time to talk. Want to train tomorrow for a bit, maybe even go out?"

My heart jumped at the invitation. I still hadn't adventured outside much. We had time to do so in pairs, but with everything going on, I only went with David for training purposes, not really to relax.

Matt grinned. "I see that's a yes. I'll tell the big guy so he doesn't go berserk when he can't find you."

"What do you need to tell me?" Davon raised an eyebrow.

"What makes you think I was talking about you?" Matt grimaced. "You think too much of yourself."

A carrot hit Matt square on his nose, and he flinched. "Fucker!" He was about to throw it back when Aoki shushed us.

Doug was so used to their bickering that he fell right asleep.

Matt beamed at his son, then frowned at his brother. "I'll get you later. Your girl and I are going outside to train tomorrow, just so you know."

I caught a small dent in Davon's jawline as he clenched his teeth slightly, then breathed out and nodded. I noticed those small gestures, almost imperceptible, whenever my training was brought into conversation. Even as I pulled on my uniform each morning, he'd spare a look at me and then continue with his own, thinking I wouldn't notice, but I did.

He was making a huge effort, and I was thankful. He'd changed so much since that first night at Janus Peak. Then he'd used his rank to prohibit me from even thinking about fighting at his side, but in reality, he was worried about what would happen to me.

"Thanks for letting me know." Davon fixed a loose strand behind my ear, then took my hair band and used it to tie his hair back.

My hair cascaded down the sides of my face. "Hey!"

"For old times' sake." He smiled. "Be safe out there."

I brushed his thigh. "Always."

Aoki went to put Doug in his crib, with Shirokuro following behind.

Matt hurried to their bed and crouched. He took out a box from underneath it.

Davon and I exchanged looks.

Matt brought the box to the table and opened it. It was a carrot bundt cake with a white candle on it. He shushed us silently and lit the candle.

Davon grimaced. "Aoki's birthday was on the eighth, the day after the attack." He sighed. "With everything going on, I forgot."

I covered my mouth. The attack had rocked the PRF, and Connor's death had especially affected our little group. Not only that, but Mark, Aoki's brother, had been at death's door just hours before his day, and he just went on as if nothing had happened.

"Hey, what's burning?" Aoki hugged Matt's waist and kissed his neck lovingly.

Matt sighed. "I can never surprise you."

Aoki stood by his side and lifted his chin. "Thank you, baby." He kissed Matt and then blew out the candle. "This means the world to me."

We ate, talked, and listened to some soft rock before Doug woke again.

Davon talked to Matt as he fed the baby.

I was left alone with Aoki. "Happy birthday. I'm sorry I forgot."

He cupped my cheek. "Honey, there's nothing to be sorry about. It's hardly time to celebrate, but I'd be lying if I said I wasn't happy you took this time to be with me. I kind of missed this part of Davon and Matt." He glanced back as Matt warmed the milk and Davon rocked the baby. "I know you'll all leave for battle soon."

As a civilian, Aoki didn't know much of what would happen, but living with the general of the PRF gave him an idea. Matt was easy to read, and it was in his eyes. The certainty that time was up.

Aoki looked down before capturing my gaze. "I'm grateful for this moment and can only hope after it all ends, we can meet again but back in Promissa."

I hugged him. "I'm sure we will."

Davon passed Doug to Matt and walked to my side. "Time to go, love."

I patted Aoki's shoulder. "I have to go. See you tomorrow."

Aoki winked. "Whatever you're doing, have fun."

Outside, Davon put an arm around my waist and kissed my temple. "Are you ready for an adventure?"

I smiled. And what an adventure it was.

Chapter 21

Davon

May 21, 2214

After a soak in the spring I discovered and giving Abi a thorough body inspection, we returned to our hall.

I waited outside our room while Abi grabbed her stuff to leave for her sleepover.

When she came back out, I seized her before she walked away. I kissed her neck, drawing a sigh from her. "See you tomorrow."

She pulled me to her. "I can't wait." She pressed her delectable body against mine, then kissed me until we were breathless.

I waited till she was out of sight and slumped against a wall.

I closed my eyes as I recalled her searing caresses and her fingers tracing every inch of my body. Her mouth, as she nipped my skin, languidly reaching that place where her control over me was absolute. She carried me to heaven, as wave after wave of pleasure burned through me.

We took our time, both eager to indulge in each other, to immerse ourselves in every touch. Every scent. Every taste.

I savored her silky skin, taking my time to reach her core, where each taste and touch turned into ecstasy as I delved into her deepest desires.

We lost track of time, memorizing every inch of each other's bodies until we were one.

Nothing compared to being inside her. To the softness and warmth of her body. To the feel of her walls closing around me as I lifted her to the highest peak.

My body turned to fire in that moment as another round of ecstasy took over me, and I let myself fall with her. It was enough to render me powerless.

God, I loved her.

I gathered myself and entered our room.

Matt sat at the table with a bottle of whiskey.

"Aoki went to visit Mark and Carol. Little D planned a tea party for him." He lifted his mug. "Want some?"

"Sure." I chuckled inside.

Little D always cracked me up with her antics. I imagined it all. Diane dressed in a cute dress and cups and mugs of whatever she could find set up on the table with sweets for everyone. I'd been invited to those before, and they were a blast. She'd be a great party planner, like Mom.

A sudden pang hit me at not being able to protect my mother. When Father mentioned her in the video, I couldn't help but worry. My father was a crazy son of a bitch, and betraying him was a punch to his ego. I just hoped his love for Mom was enough to keep him at bay.

"You're taking it well." Matt put a mug next to his and poured whiskey into it.

I suspected where he was going with that comment, so I let it pass.

I grabbed the mug. "I'll have just one. We have a strategy meeting."

"Davon?"

I took a calming breath. "Say whatever is on your mind. You'll do it whether I want to hear it or not."

He traced the rim of his mug. "You're doing the right thing by letting her go. She's strong. She'll make it."

As general of the army, I could order Abi to stay and guard the caves. But I knew she'd have my head for it. She was stubborn as hell, and whether I allowed it or not, she'd go.

I touched my leather bracelet. "You don't know that."

I tried to keep a calm countenance, but whenever I was reminded of Abi going out there and walking straight into danger, I wanted to lock her in a room and keep her safe.

"What? Do you think she'll be safer here? It's the same. We don't know Jordan's plan. He's unpredictable. Do you think I don't fear for Aoki's and my son's lives?"

It was the first time I'd heard him call Doug his son. My chest swelled at the realization that my brother would be loved. Then I remembered what we were talking about, and whatever peace I thought I found went to shit.

It was true. My father could easily make his move if the spy found a way to tell him. The security was high, vigilance 24/7, and soldiers hid around the perimeter at the ready. But what if he already had his planes ready? What if they attacked again but this time by air? What if he waited until after we all went to war to send an attack and annihilate our people?

Nothing was short of what Father was capable of. *No one opposes me and lives to see through it.* He would not rest until he squashed the rebellion and every single soul in it.

"I'm sorry." I shook my head. "I know it's hard for you too."

Matt propped both elbows on the table. He took a swig, set the mug down, then buried his face in both hands. He raked his golden curls back and grabbed the back of his neck and exhaled hard. "Fuck, man, why did it all come to this?"

I took a sip from my drink, letting it burn through my everlasting frustration at my father and all he'd destroyed. "A question I ask myself every day."

Why did Father do what he had to these people? Why couldn't we live in peace?

I downed the rest of my whiskey in one shot, then stood and put on my vest. "Let's go. We have a war to plan."

I gave Abi the afternoon off, but that didn't mean the council wouldn't meet, as it did every other day. Times were precarious, and getting everything ready was of the utmost importance.

I browsed through the strategy files Jules had passed over when the meeting started. She'd just come back from a virtual meeting with the Liberty Enclave's council. A huge area was marked on a map, taking up most of the northeastern part of the continent, running kilometers into the country. The Liberty Enclave had a larger area than I would have imagined, almost as big as the one the NWG had control over.

I learned from her that they had a socialist democratic government, a system where economic and social policies prioritized equality and the people chose their leaders, ensuring they had a voice in the government's decisions. The essential services like healthcare and education were free, and the government guaranteed their citizens freedom of speech, press, and assembly, allowing the common people to participate in shaping policies.

They had a council and a president. Their constitution ensured there was no abuse of power and that the government could be held accountable by the people. She was part of that council.

I closed the files. "When will your president make the attack?"

Sinclair sat across the table. "A week. We already started moving our forces to the south. We'll take Halcyon by air and ground."

We'd need to alert Constantine so he could prepare his people to strike the supplement facilities and get the signal out to the citizens. I was confident he'd handle it. He'd even come up with a plan to tell friend from foe. NWG defectors willing to fight by our side would wear a black cloth on their shoulders and wrapped around their waists.

The late Lieutenant Davis, Abi's uncle, had assured us the same. The rebellion was rooted deep within some NWG ranks.

But something still bothered me. Getting our troops ready and down there in a week would prove difficult.

I rested my brow on my hand. *Fuck.* One week to get half of our troops across the tunnels and inside Promissa, then to move the rest of our forces across the forest.

"One week doesn't give us much time to organize our soldiers, but we'll try our best." I glanced at Matt. "We need to start moving our forces in the next couple of days, and they need to be alert. I'm sure the NWG will be ready to attack the moment they see us."

Matt nodded. "Mark and I will start working on that as soon as the meeting is over."

"We've prepared our soldiers for this type of eventuality. If the NWG troops are waiting inside the forest, we can create a diversion elsewhere to get their attention away from our main forces so they can cross over." Mark had recovered and retaken his position.

I darted my gaze around the table. "Can we work with that?" I could make the decision then and there, but I wasn't my father. This was a council, and I was just another one of them.

Katherine rose. "Yes, and I think all the members will agree with me."

Councilmembers nodded across the room.

She nodded and sat back down. "It's about time we took back our city."

"Can we count on your aid?" David asked Sinclair.

He always sat by her side. They'd become close lately even though most of their time was spent bickering.

She held her chin high, staring right into his eyes. "I never back down on my promises. You will have the helicopters and part of our troops, but our main focus will always be taking back our capital."

David watched her for a moment before turning to me. "I'll start the preparations to leave as soon as possible. Either tomorrow or the day after, we *will* be ready."

My heart wrenched at the realization that I'd have to let Abi go. I was part of the forces that would enter the city through the forest, while the snipers and soldiers did their sneak attack from within the city. I knew she could make it, but still...

Matt's troops would infiltrate Electi through the tunnels for a surprise attack once we took down the government center in Promissa.

It was a sound plan, and with the help of the enclave and the attack in Halcyon, the NWG forces would be forced to divide their army.

"Moving on." I took another set of files, these ones about the enhanced soldiers' interrogations and psych evaluations. "The psych evaluations of the enhanced soldiers are back."

Sinclair leaned forward. "Is it how we feared?"

"No." I passed the files to her. "They aren't psychopaths or sociopaths. The psychologists believe they're victims of extreme psychological conditioning. That mixed with a lifelong exposure to drugs and the fact that they were made into weapons has created some sort of identity crisis in them.

"The doctors believe that once the detoxifying process is completed, they will eventually 'relearn' to be human. Having their emotions suppressed for so long could make the process long and difficult, but we have reason to believe it's possible and that the key is to let them have contact with others, at least in a controlled fashion."

Sinclair raised an eyebrow. "You say you have reason to believe it's possible. Has there been any development with the subjects being studied?"

I swallowed hard. For the first time, I found the word *subject* in referring to Lucas offensive.

This morning before training, I went to find Rachel. We both went to see Lucas. I sat with them at a table and exchanged words with my aggressor. He was a different person. Highly inquisitive and with a gentle nature I hadn't seen before.

I stretched my hand toward him. "My name is Davon Niles. I'm the general of the army of the People's Revolutionary Front."

Lucas bowed. "I remember you, and I'm sorry for the way I acted on the battlefield." He hesitated a bit before shaking my hand. "I understand the situation much better now even though it's tough to see my creators as the bad guys." He glanced at Rachel. "Rachel has helped me see."

What Abi said was true. It was in the way he looked at her. He felt something for Rachel.

"Miss Davis told me you've improved. Do you still have symptoms of withdrawal?"

He lifted his hand, palm parallel to the table. It was shaking lightly. "Tremors. Sometimes I get a headache, but they go away."

Now for the question that would tell us if we could take him with us into the fray. "Do you still get violent thoughts against us?"

He dropped his gaze and clenched his jaw.

Rachel covered his hand.

He interlaced his fingers through hers. "They're not as frequent as before." He stared at his free hand and the cuffs he still wore. "These help."

His blue eyes locked with mine. "Rachel told me about the possibility of being accepted into your group. Of fighting by your side."

I stilled.

I let Rachel come in before me to talk to him. To ask how he felt about being part of us. If there was someone who could ask him about this, it was her. I let them have a moment before I came in, so I had no idea how he felt about it or what his answer would be.

"I want to fight by your side." He smiled at Rachel. "I want to fight for her so she can be free." He let go of her and showed me his cuffs. "But with these on, I don't think I'll be able to fight out there. If I want to be of help, if you want to use me against them, I need to be the monster they made me into."

I cringed. "That's not what we want. We want to give you a normal life. Whatever you choose to do with it, whether it's fighting or just having a normal life like many of our citizens is your choice. You don't have to fight if you don't want to."

"But I want to. I want to fight the motherfuckers who did this to me." He eyed his cuffs, tilted his head to the side, then took a long, shuddering breath. "But for that, you're going to have to trust me and take these off."

I propped my elbow on the table and rubbed my stubble. That was a risk I couldn't take. Not after he told me he sometimes had violent thoughts. But maybe there was a way. "They'll stay on but be deactivated. I'll ask my scientists to create some kind of remote control. It's not that I don't trust you. I don't trust what they did to you or your capacity to control what they've programmed you to do."

Lucas nodded. "If you feel safer that way, I understand."

"So you'll fight with us?"

Lucas nodded. "If you'll let me."

"Good. I'll talk to the council. If they accept, you'll fight by my side."

"Niles?" Sinclair's words broke through my thoughts.

I darted my eyes around the table. "From now on, we'll refer to them as humans, not subjects."

The councilmembers, along with Sinclair, all bowed in understanding.

I cleared my throat. "I talked to Lucas this morning. He showed remorse for the attack against me and is the first enhanced soldier who showed progress. He asked to be permitted to fight alongside me."

The room erupted into chaos. Seth and Mark were against it, but Katherine and Matt took my side. Sinclair watched in silence.

Seth stood. "What if he turns against us on the battlefield? They're unpredictable."

Katherine grabbed his arm. "You don't know that. Each of them has responded to treatment differently, and even the violent ones have shown some kind of progress."

Seth huffed. His gaze softened toward Katherine, then he took his place beside her.

"Have you seen progress in the aggressive soldiers?" Matt asked.

Seth turned his head to Katherine. "Just yesterday, one of them talked to Kathy." He clenched his fists on the table. "I thought he'd become aggressive, that he was manipulating the situation, but they actually talked."

Katherine covered his fisted hand. Their eyes met for a moment, and I could swear something passed between them.

Were they together?

She let go of his hand. "I've been able to talk to two of them. They have shown interest in knowing more about the NWG. Their withdrawal symptoms have also lessened these past few days."

Mark shook his head. "But how will we control them out there? We don't know how deep the influence of the NWG is."

"I've got that covered. Matt already confirmed that he and Michael can create a remote device to control the cuffs. They will be deactivated during battle, but at any sign of insubordination, you and I will be able to activate them to restrain the soldier."

The whole room turned toward Matt.

"It will work," he said. "We need to use this opportunity Lucas is giving us."

Mark rubbed the back of his neck. "It's a risk."

Matt nodded. "It is, but we need to try."

It was the least we could do.

Mark grunted, then turned to me. "And I'll have one of these devices?"

I nodded. "You will."

Mark relaxed. "Then I'm in as long as we have that control. Will he be training with my soldiers?"

"Yes. Today, after Michael gives us the devices, he'll start training as part of your troops. He's willing to share what they taught them and how they fight, which may prove invaluable during battle."

"Understood," Mark said.

"If there are no other objections." I swept my gaze around the room.

When no one said more, the load on my chest lightened. Having Lucas with us would be an advantage, one I would use against my father.

I raised an eyebrow as Nina entered the conference room.

We'd waited for her before starting but couldn't lose more time, so we began the meeting without her.

"Sir. Madam." She dipped her chin to both sides of the table. "I'm sorry for being late. I was decoding a message from our spies in Electi." She sat to my right.

Did something happen?

I widened my eyes at her news, clenching my fists over the map I'd been studying. "Why wasn't I alerted of this earlier?" My voice came out harsh, much like Father's when talking to his council.

Nina jerked back, and I swallowed hard.

What was wrong with me?

She hurriedly tapped her tablet. "Sorry, sir. The decryption took longer than I expected." Her hands trembled.

What the fuck? I glanced around the table.

Some rubbed their necks, while others avoided my gaze and organized their files. They were acting just like Father's councilmembers. Matt stared at me, shaking his head slightly.

No. I'm not my father.

I took a calming breath and softened my features. "It's okay. What did they say?"

She searched my eyes, then relaxed. "They're ready to take over the transportation system that connects Electi to Promissa. They found a way to get to the minister of transportation."

Once the minister was in our hands, we'd have control over the trains.

I nodded. "That's good. Was there anything else in the comms?"

Nina lowered her head, her eyes hidden behind her blue bangs. "There's been a lot of commotion lately inside Electi. Miss Lisa Johnson and a group of women have been giving out information to the people. Booklets that explain what's truly happening inside Promissa. People are enraged about this situation and have taken to the streets."

My heart was about to burst out of my chest. Lisa had done it. She'd taken on gathering allies in our favor.

"This is great." I frowned. "Why are you acting like it's bad news?"

She dropped her gaze. "Because Lisa and some of these women disappeared two days ago."

"Fuck!" I raked my hair back.

Father had them.

My world turned upside down, and I suddenly couldn't breathe. Lisa was like a second mother to me.

Matt's chair screeched as he stood. "My mother is missing?"

Nina met his eyes. "Yes."

Matt clenched his jaw, then sent his steady gaze my way. "He'll kill her."

He would. There was no question about it.

Determination wasn't the only emotion I detected from Matt. There was also fear. Unadulterated, raw fear.

My stomach twisted. I couldn't shake the feeling that my own mother was surely kept prisoner inside our home, and she was the woman Father loved. What would he do to Lisa?

Jordan Niles was like a time bomb, and we were pushing all his buttons. There was no telling when he'd snap, and with Lisa in his grasp, he could kill her just to spite us. He'd always hated her.

I stood, eyes set on my best friend. My brother. "Get everything ready. We'll attack in a week."

Chapter 22

Abi

May 21, 2214

The caves were a maze, so it would take a while to get to my sisters' room. I'd just started figuring out which way to go after getting lost so often.

I walked down another hall, but images from our afternoon together kept flashing through my mind, as my body felt the aftermath of our lovemaking.

I could still feel his calloused hands on my body. He was gentle but fierce. Loving but brimming with passion. My body yearned for him, for the scorching heat only he awakened within me.

In that cave, he possessed me in every way, giving me round after round of pure ecstasy before finally taking me.

His fullness brought me pleasure beyond measure. The press of his body against mine as he pushed deep inside me, pounding me with all his strength, melted me from the inside out and took me to immeasurable heights. The feel of his muscles straining beneath my touch as I pulled him deeper made me crazy with need.

When his rhythm became erratic, almost violent, we both shattered in pure bliss. My core throbbed in pleasure as his heat pulsed inside me, giving me everything.

I couldn't believe he was mine.

I took a deep breath to calm my blazing heart as my body reacted to those memories.

There was nothing but him. He was my everything.

I went around a corner and found Sarah talking to Lavigne in front of her room. I'd seen them together a couple of times after the attack.

Davon assigned Lavigne to assist Sarah as the link between the council and our people, and they'd become close very fast. Since then, Sarah had changed. She'd been training with the soldiers, both in fighting and in shooting, especially the latter.

I was glad for it. To see Sarah at last take control over her life gave me ease.

After Connor died, she'd stayed silent for days. I let her deal with her grief as Davon suggested but visited her daily. Then one day, she seemed focused for the first time in ages, set on going to war with us. Whatever turmoil I once saw in her had turned into a strength I never imagined she had. And I had a hunch that Lavigne had something to do with it.

The caves were full of naturally formed crevices. I slowed and hid behind one when Lavigne took Sarah's hand between his.

"I can't find the words to express how sorry I am for all you've been put through. I hope you can find the peace you seek."

"There's no need to apologize, Peter." She bit her lower lip and shook her head. "Life has just dealt these cards for me, and you, you just gave me the truth I sought. So I'm the one who should be thanking you."

"No, Ms. Davis. I don't deserve your gratitude. Nothing will ever make up for the suffering my people put you through. Nothing." He spoke in a hushed tone. "You take care and take the afternoon off to be with your family."

Sarah smiled. "Please call me Sarah."

He nodded. "Okay. Sarah."

"See?" She tilted her head to the side. "That wasn't that hard."

He chuckled, then let go of her. "I'll see you around."

I rested my head against the cool surface of the cave wall and waited for Sarah to enter the room.

What was he talking about? What truth?

I shook my head and pushed the thought away. It was not my place to ask, so I'd let it go. Sarah would tell me in her own time.

When I knocked on the door, Deb opened it. Aspen threw herself at me.

"Hello, beautiful! How are you?" I ruffled her fur, speaking in the same childish tone I used for Doug.

Deb stood behind her. "Come on, girl. I told you not to jump on people."

Aspen went to her side, her tail wagging wildly.

I hugged Deb. "How are you doing?"

"As well as can be." She shrugged and stepped away. "Sarah just came back from a meeting. She's in the bathroom."

I followed Deb to the table. She walked slowly, like a robot, with Aspen shaking her tail after her. Since Connor's death, her situation had worsened. At least she talked to Davon, and she did try to get out, but most of the time she stayed in this room.

"Canvases?" I widened my eyes with glee. "We're painting?"

I caught a small smile from Deb. "We are. Sarah got the materials before we escaped Janus Peak. This is all she has left of her old life."

It was what drove us all forward—the hope of having our lives back. I touched the rough canvas and studied the paint and brushes at the table.

"I see you made it." Sarah, same as me, wore the army uniform.

She'd taken off the buttoned vest with our symbol, one we kept even after we learned a traitor had created it. We'd show Leslie that she only rekindled the fire within the rebellion.

It had become the norm to always have our uniforms on in case of an attack.

Sarah adjusted her gray pants, her long-sleeved black V-neck the same as mine. "Did Deb tell you? We're painting, just like old times." Her smile was contagious.

Very old times indeed. It was before the regime, before it all went to shit. I was a little girl, and Sarah and Deb would teach me how to paint. Deb and I did simple things, like flowers and houses. Sarah...she was something else.

"Can't wait." A strong aroma reached me, and I opened my eyes wide. "Coffee?"

Deb smiled. "Want some? I'm having a cup just now."

I lowered my shoulders. "Um. No. Thanks."

Sarah and Deb stared at me like I'd grown horns.

"You're saying no to coffee?" Deb furrowed her brow.

I shifted from one foot to the other. "It's..." I was trying to cut my intake because of Lizzie. "I just had some at my place."

"Strange." Deb eyed me for a moment before turning to get a mug.

I stood beside her. "What about you? You're drinking coffee again? Connor told me you'd stopped."

The moment I said his name, Deb stopped pouring the coffee, but then as fast as it happened, she continued.

Shit. "I'm sorry. I..." How could I be so thoughtless?

Deb shook her head. "Don't be. We should be able to talk about him." She sighed. "I started drinking coffee after the attack on farming. It makes me feel like he's still with me."

When I reached out to her, Sarah grabbed my hand. "Let her be," she mouthed.

I took a deep breath and noticed Deb was looking at something. Their wedding picture was on top of the counter.

Sarah and I sat at the table, then she joined us.

I couldn't wait to see what Deb was painting. She always did stick figures, blaming it on her lack of artistic skills, but it was quite the opposite. When she was a teacher, I once caught her doodling in a notebook. She'd made a beautiful horizon filled with mountains and an evergreen forest. Now that I lived here, I understood why she hid those drawings from Uncle Scott and Aunt Annie. She was drawing her home.

Hours passed as we sat in silence, each of us concentrating on our work.

I made three yellow tulips and a small red one. A flower for each of us and one for my baby girl. Flowers were the only living thing I could paint. The color of friendship and happiness. It was what I longed for. For us to find joy again. Sarah came from my right. "Hey." She elbowed me playfully. "That's actually pretty good."

I grinned and painted the point of her nose green.

She jerked back, then took some of her black paint and threw it on my face.

Deb started laughing, a sound we didn't hear much, and we both attacked her.

She took her canvas and turned it around. "No! You'll ruin mine."

My senses dulled at the sight.

Sarah stood frozen, her black paint falling on the table.

There we stood, facing forward, with the city of Promissa behind us in all its splendor. It was us in the same pose as the family picture I cherished. We were our current age, and Mom and Dad looked older. Now more people joined us. Connor had his arm around Deb's shoulders, and Carlos stood next to Sarah on the other side. A boy about ten stood between them. They each covered one of his shoulders. Davon stood behind me, his hands over my belly, holding me close. Jimmy sat in the middle with a joyful expression on his face. It was black and white but clear as day. She'd painted a picture of us as if nothing had happened. If no one had died. If no one had gone missing.

I dried my wet cheeks with the sleeve of my uniform, and Sarah stood motionless, touching Charlie's outline.

Sarah's tears fell on top of the table as Deb put the canvas down.

Deb's face was stained with the charcoal she'd used. "I'm sorry. I..." Her lips trembled, and her eyes glazed. "I wanted to have a picture of all of us. To be able to have a glimpse of what might have been. I don't want to forget."

"It's beautiful." My heartbreak at seeing us all together was immense. To see us as a family, this happy, was a sight to behold.

Sarah hugged Deb. "Thank you."

After taking a moment, Sarah showed us her painting. It was the city of Electi in ruins. Everything was black and white except a woman who stood in the middle. The wind ruffled Sarah's long, blond hair as she danced with Carlos. His dark hair swept over his face, hiding his features. She wore a short red dress that swayed around her as Carlos, wearing casual blue jeans and a burgundy shirt, made her twirl around him. A little child was by their side, jumping, his blue denim shorts and burgundy T-shirt the same as his father's. His smile was bright.

My soul cried for all she'd lost. For the family she yearned to have back. For her long-lost son.

"It seems we had the same idea." Sarah smiled at her canvas.

Deb grabbed her hand. "It seems we did."

I held her other hand. "When we win, we'll make sure to find Charlie."

A flash of pain crossed her face, but she continued smiling. "I'm sure we will."

Deb moved in front of my painting after wiping away her tears. "So when were you going to tell us that you're pregnant?"

I let go of Sarah and faced her, my eyes bulging out of my head.

They knew.

"Did you really think we wouldn't notice?" The corner of Deb's mouth curved up. "Abi, you were sick, and you ate like a baby. That's not you. You love food."

Sarah chuckled. "And coffee."

I dropped my head, pushing my hands into my pockets. "I'm sorry. With everything going on, I wanted to take some time to adapt to the idea. Then the attack happened, and I didn't have the heart."

Deb hugged me. "We're here for you, and we're happy for you both."

I held her close, and Sarah joined us.

My heart was full. I never thought I'd have this again.

After some time, we sat to have some of Aoki's cake leftovers. I explained what I painted and that the little flower was Lizzie.

"A girl," Sarah said. "And you're naming her after Mom."

I nodded, a smile plastered on my face.

Deb took a bite from her cake. "I bet Mom and Dad are smiling down at us at this moment. Connor and Jimmy too."

We spent the rest of the night reminiscing about our days in Promissa—moments shared with Mom, Dad, Carlos, Connor, Jimmy, Maria, and all the others we had lost along the way. We laughed and cried as we celebrated their lives and held on to the hope of a brighter future. Of having our freedom back.

Chapter 23

Davon

May 24, 2214

"Ready for your orders, sir." Seth saluted the moment I entered the armory. "I finished the inventory. There's enough to arm all the troops. General Sinclair expects another group of soldiers to arrive before the week is over. Captain Martinez also confirmed the sniper rifles and ammunitions are ready for use. He'll leave with his team as soon as you give the order."

I shuddered, realizing I'd be the one to send Abi away, but I quickly pushed the sentiment aside. She was a soldier, and we were on the brink of war. There was no doubt in my mind that we'd find each other out there. I had all the strategy plans and exactly where she'd sit in wait for the signal. I'd find her no matter the cost.

"Arrange for Matt's and David's troops to leave in two days. Your mission—to take down any enemy you encounter and clear the way for us. The drones are ready, and comms will be up until you reach the tunnels. We'll follow you closely. Once we reach the forest perimeter, we'll wait for the signal and meet you in Promissa."

Seth nodded. "Understood."

I walked along the crowded halls, making a stop at the mess hall. I continued deeper into the cave and reached Deb's room. I was about to knock when Abi opened the door.

Her eyes widened, and her smile reached her eyes.

To see her smile again, really smile, was an unexpected surprise. My pulse quickened, and a need to touch her stirred inside me.

I cupped her chin. "God, you're beautiful."

She went on her tiptoes and gave me a swift kiss, then played with my hair. "I love when you wear it down."

She was so cute when she was happy.

I raised an eyebrow. "I'll keep that in mind." I peeked inside. "Did you tell them?"

She pressed her lips together. "They already knew."

I widened my eyes. "Since when?"

She shrugged. "Since I stopped drinking coffee."

I chuckled. "That's understandable." It was a given. Abi couldn't live without coffee. "So everything's good?"

"Yeah. I was on my way to get breakfast." She glanced at the bag I held. "But I see you already covered that."

I lifted the paper bag between us. "BLTs."

Abi's eyes gleamed. "Are you staying?"

I nodded, then pushed the door wider, finding Sarah and Deb sipping some coffee. "Morning! I brought food." I strolled to the table and took out the sandwiches.

"Thanks." Deb smiled up at me.

I nodded.

My chest lightened. It was good to see them like this—carefree. It was all I could hope for.

Abi sat beside me. They cracked jokes about last night's games. Apparently, they played Pictionary until the early hours of the morning. Abi showed me their drawings, and they were so bad I couldn't guess half of them.

After a while, the commotion outside was too much not to notice.

"What's going on out there?" Abi glanced at the door. "Did anything happen at the meeting?"

I swallowed dryly. I couldn't meet her stare. "Yeah. We're preparing to leave."

She covered my hand. "When?"

I spared a glance her way. "The day after tomorrow."

We both knew what that meant. We were part of different teams, and she had to go ahead of me with the sniper team and wait until Nina hacked the broadcast system to alert the citizens after Aleczander gave the signal.

At that moment, troops would come out of the tunnels in different parts of the city, while the snipers began taking down NWG soldiers in strategic points around the area. Then I'd go in with my troops through the perimeter of the forest.

The thing was there was no guarantee we'd meet until the war was over, and that thought alone was driving me insane.

She squeezed my hand. "Everything will be all right. We'll make it."

"What do you mean you'll make it?"

We both turned toward Deb.

Her tone was stern, her eyes guarded. "Are you thinking of going out there?"

Given all Abi's family had lost under the regime, Deb's reaction was no surprise.

Abi closed her eyes briefly. "Deb, I can't stay here and watch others fight for me. I want to finish what you started. I need to see Jordan break down and all that he built crumble into nothing."

"But what about the baby?" Sarah asked.

"I'm doing this for her. For you. For our people in Promissa. Don't you see? This is our moment to take back what's ours, and I'm not staying here in wait. I want to fight."

Her tone showed more than her words could. Abi would stop at nothing to free herself and the ones she loved from the chains of oppression my father had built around them. There was no stopping her, and it broke my heart.

I understood her reasons, but that didn't stop my soul from being ripped right out of me. I could lose her out there.

Deb punched the table and stood. "So you're willing to sacrifice everything for this? We're finally together, and now you have someone to take care of."

Abi spread her hands over the table and faced her sister head on. "Yes, Deb, I'm willing to sacrifice everything. I've been clinging to hope for years, and now, at last, I've been given this opportunity. I will make it through." She covered her belly and took my hand. "*We* will make it through."

Deb watched her for a moment before turning and leaving the room.

Abi let out a long breath and sat.

Sarah's gaze darted between us. "She'll understand. Give her some time." She sighed. "Even though it hurts, you're doing the right thing. I want to be out there with you."

Sarah seemed different. I'd seen her training with Peter during their free time. A sharp shooter and a good fighter. "Peter told me about your training. He said you want to be part of our troops."

She nodded.

"We'll leave in less than a week, then make our way into the assigned areas. You'll be part of my team." By my side, I'd make sure she made it. Abi couldn't lose another member of her family.

We sat in silence after that, each lost in our own thoughts.

"So Davon's troops will come from this side and join us here," David told Sinclair.

They were hunched over a map of Promissa at the conference room table.

She turned toward David, and I swore she flushed when he caught her stare mere inches from her face after pointing at a location on the map.

As if suddenly realizing how close they were, David jerked back and retook his place behind her.

I shrugged. Maybe I was imagining things.

I shook my head and faced the map. "And where will you be?"

Abi pointed to the east. "Here in a building close to the government center."

I narrowed my eyes at David.

"She'll be safe from the blast there," he said. "You know I'd never put her in danger."

A shiver ran through me, and I rolled my shoulders back.

If anything happened to her...

He cut through my thoughts. "Trust me. I'd never risk Abi."

I sighed. "I'll trust your judgment." I turned to the map.

Aleczander Constantine would blow up some facilities around the city. He would launch the attack on Saturday, focusing on the supplement facilities' storage sections to minimize civilian casualties.

Some would die from the bombs, but there was no other option. We needed to send a clear message to the NWG and make that signal strong enough to reach our soldiers and those in the NWG who would join our ranks.

This was our last meeting before David's team left. If everything went as planned, after the government center was dealt with, we'd move into Electi and meet the rest of Matt's troops inside. By that moment, we should already have control over the council and President Orville, so the only one left was my father.

Matt pinpointed some X's on the map. "This is where my soldiers will come out of the tunnels and into Electi. I marked down where Constantine's groups will be. Once chaos breaks out, they'll arm the citizens who answer Connor's broadcast and attack."

My breath caught at the mention of his name. Before his death, Connor created a video that would be broadcasted in the government plaza and in each home inside Promissa once the attack started. All the evidence and videos we had of the atrocities the government had committed would be made public. The citizens would have the choice to fight with us or wait for it all to be over.

War would break out, and we didn't want any unnecessary casualties. Aleczander's teams would be at the ready around the city to protect those who stayed or arm those who came out to fight with us. With the reign of terror Father had implemented inside the city, we hoped the latter would take place, and many would join our ranks.

After everyone studied the map, I stood and clenched my fists on the table. "Once Constantine makes his attack, I'll set off the bunker bombs from Nina's tablet and take out all the NWG troops that have taken over them."

Bombs were set inside all the bunkers after the energy bunker attack. The only one with the codes to set them off remotely was Connor. After his death, I found his journal and took on the burden. I'd be the one to destroy all we'd built.

"General Sinclair will use the enclave's helicopters to make sure no reaper troops are left alive after the bombings and to take down any NWG soldiers that remain alive. She'll move into Promissa and take care of any troops that could block our advance, then destroy the government center."

"We're hoping their jets aren't ready, but the threat is still there." Sinclair looked at David, then faced me. "After conversations with Captain Martinez, I've decided to only send one helicopter back to Empire City. The enclave has enough air power to take on Halcyon. I can't leave Promissa unprotected."

I stilled. "That means we'll have four helicopters on our side."

Sinclair nodded. "And a better chance to take down their government center, which is something both our countries aim to destroy. I don't see why my superiors wouldn't approve, so I took the liberty to make the decision myself."

A jolt of adrenaline ran through my body, and I dared hope everything would be all right.

Taking down the NWG center of operations was crucial. Not only as a symbol of the fall of the regime but to take from my father his safe haven and most treasured possession in Promissa. Father and his council would not be there during the attack, but we had a plan. We'd corner him and then strip him of his power.

My heart raced at the thought of finally being able to face him, not as his son but as his sworn enemy, the general of the People's Revolutionary Front. He'd pay for all he had done.

David shifted in place. "What about the transportation system? Will we be able to control it?"

"We will." I took a coded note from my pocket. "Mark, I need you to get this out to checkpoint one."

"Yes, sir." Mark pocketed it. "I'll send my soldiers out immediately."

The coded message carried an order to kidnap Minister Fernandez in two days. Once we had her and used her codes to open the system, Joe would hack it.

"With control over the trains, we'll make sure no reinforcements can come in from Electi. Half our troops will infiltrate Electi via the tunnels and the other half via the trains." I locked my hands together on the desk.

This could work.

It was a long meeting. Sinclair sent back a helicopter with some soldiers to relay our plans to her government. It was imperative they attacked the same day we planned to but a couple of hours earlier. That way Father would be forced to send additional troops toward Halcyon, giving us a chance back in Promissa.

The Liberty Enclave had a greater army than the NWG, but we still worried about those jets and whatever plans my father could have strategized that we were ignorant of. We had no idea what the trains' capabilities were or if he'd reached out to his allies in other parts of the continent. Hell, we didn't even know whether we'd make it or not. He could be planning an attack as we spoke. We just hoped he didn't do it before the week was up.

Chapter 24

Abi

May 25, 2214

"God, these are good." Abraham ate the last piece of his cookie.

I chuckled, my plate already empty.

Abraham and I had seen each other a couple of times during our time here, but we both had so much on our hands that it was always a passing moment. A short conversation.

Today, after a coffee and some of Rosa's chocolate chip cookies, we finally got to talk.

Abraham turned his chair to face me. "Be careful out there." His gentle eyes settled on my belly. "Especially now."

I took his hand. "I will. You too. I know Yuxuan and his troops will stay behind to protect you, but please promise me if anything happens, you'll run. Save yourself and the civilians who stay."

He patted our joined hands. "Don't worry about us. Leith and I have been working nonstop on securing the cavern system. If anything happens, we'll do whatever it takes to protect our citizens."

I furrowed my brow. "Leith?"

Abraham chuckled. "Sorry, force of habit. I mean Faez."

I lifted my eyebrows. "Oh." I smiled.

Abraham was a different man, no longer the history professor I'd met. With every passing day, it was clearer why Jacob carried himself the way he did. He'd gotten it from his father.

Abraham had become a leader. A man who would defend his people's freedom to the end. He still wore his suits and had this elegance about him that made him singular among all of us soldiers, but he was a leader. Faez's right hand. If he said the citizens were safe, there was no doubt about it.

Abraham squeezed my hand. "We'll do whatever is needed, and we will not fall."

We stood.

I rubbed my nape, then circled my shoulders back. Hours of practicing with a sniper would do that to you. Our morning training had been hard but necessary. Tomorrow we'd march to battle, and a lot depended on us.

He grabbed my shoulder. "Take a break today. You deserve it."

I smiled. "Yeah. Davon just ordered us to take the day off. We leave tomorrow before dawn."

Abraham nodded. "You'll make it out there. There's no doubt in my mind. We'll retake what they stole from us."

His words brought back memories of Jacob. Of our conversations before they took him from me. Tears stung my eyes.

Abraham cupped my chin. "Are you thinking about Jacob?"

I widened my eyes.

He tilted his head, and his gaze softened. "Thank you for still loving him. Thank you for bringing me peace. I do this for him. Not for revenge because I already forgave those lost souls. I do it because I know this is what he wanted. What he dreamed of. And this victory will also be his."

Tears ran down my face at the memory of Jacob and Bonnie. At the goodness of this man, who'd forgiven what I could never do.

I never told him about what happened out there. I didn't want his memories of Jacob to be tarnished by my need for vengeance.

I looked up.

Abraham's eyes glazed with unshed tears. "I guess this is goodbye."

I wrapped my arms around him, and after a moment, he did the same.

He caressed the back of my head. "My sweet Abigail. You've done so much for us. I'm sorry for all you've been through at such a young age. They robbed you of your youth."

A whirlwind of emotions ran through me. I sobbed, no longer caring about the people who might see us. About being a councilmember. About having to be strong.

Abraham held me tighter. "That's good. Let it all out."

Those three years out there came rushing back. I cried for the innocence I'd lost. For the friends they'd murdered. For the cruel way in which my whole world was taken from me.

By the time I stopped crying, my chest had lightened, and my heart didn't hurt as much as before. I took a couple of breaths, then wiped the tears from my cheeks.

Abraham nodded. "Make these the last tears you shed for what you lost. The next time we meet those will be tears of joy because we'll have back our freedom."

"Deb, we don't want to go with you being mad at us. Please understand. We have no other option," I said to Deb, Sarah by my side.

Deb wouldn't meet my stare as she huddled in her bed with Aspen.

I'd just come back from the mess hall and joined Sarah in their room. We didn't want to leave with Deb angry at us.

My heart broke for her. She'd lost so much, but to give up now wasn't an option.

I stood beside the bed. "I'm leaving tomorrow. I need to know we're okay."

Sarah would stay with Davon's troops, but Matt, David, and I would leave before the sun was up tomorrow. My heart was already broken into pieces for having to leave Davon and my family behind. I just wanted to know we'd be all right. That Deb understood this was what I needed to do.

Sarah sat on the bed, brushing Deb's hair gently. "We're a family, and we stick by each other no matter what. We have no idea what our future holds, so every minute counts."

A sob escaped Deb, and I crouched by her side. She hid behind Aspen.

"Come on, baby." I petted Aspen's head, and her blue eyes settled on me. "Let me be with your mother."

Aspen didn't leave, but she did go to Deb's feet, giving me the space I needed.

Deb covered her face with her shirt. "I won't survive this. I can't lose you two."

I swallowed the lump in my throat and hugged her. There were no words I could say to ease her worry. There was no guarantee we'd make it. Just the hope we all guarded inside our hearts.

"I wish I could go with you, but I can't. I can't go in there again. I'm sorry." Deb's anguished cries filled the room. "I'm sorry this all happened. I just wanted our people to be free. I thought we'd make it out together and have our family. Now he's gone, and you're going out there. I never thought it would be this hard."

Deb's pain matched my own. We'd lost so many.

I touched her cheek. "That's why we have to do this. We have to finish this. For them."

Deb blinked twice before throwing her arms around me. "Promise me you'll be safe. Promise me you'll come back alive."

I couldn't promise what I didn't know, so I just held her. "I love you, sis. Thank you for making this possible. Davon, Connor, and you gave us hope when there was none, and we *will* fight for it till the end. When we finally reclaim our city, it will be only because of your dream."

The silent fight they started. The hope they'd given so many. The light they offered when all else seemed to swallow us whole. That was what pushed us to this moment. A dream that a couple of teenagers thought impossible was coming to its completion. We would win.

I rested my brow against hers, then kissed it. "I have to go make the final preparations before we leave. I'll come by tonight to say my goodbyes."

Deb nodded.

When I was about to leave, Sarah caught my arm. "Come by the mess hall at six. Let's have some dinner together."

I kissed her cheek. "Take care of Deb while I'm gone."

"Will do. See you at six?"

I nodded. "See you at six."

I let out a pent-up breath. "God, that was long."

We trained for hours, then made the final preparations for our journey.

David chuckled as we walked down another winding hall. "At least we're ready. I think this might work."

I nudged him. "Always the optimistic one."

He smirked. "I'm realistic. If it weren't for Jules, I'd still have my doubts."

I lifted an eyebrow. *Sinclair.* "So it's Jules now?"

David rolled his eyes. "Please, Abi, don't start with this again."

Whatever they had they'd kept secret, but there was no doubt in my mind that something was going on. Their furtive glances. The way their bodies gravitated toward each other whenever they were in the same room. The gleam in their eyes whenever they met.

I stepped in front of him. "I've seen you with her. It's...different."

He shifted left and went ahead of me. "You're talking nonsense. We're just working together toward a common goal."

I ran, trying to keep up with his long strides. "But, David."

He stopped, then pocketed his hands and looked down at me. "Why do you have to be this annoying?"

I grinned. "Because you're my friend and I love you."

He leaned into my space. "These past two weeks have been hard. You know how I feel, and you can't imagine how hard it is for me to watch you be with him day after day. To know you'll have a family that won't be my own. Do you have any idea how hard it is for me to stay away?" He straightened and took a step back. "Jules is just..." He shook his head. "She knows I'm having a tough time and gets me. We're both adults, and we connected. That's it." He closed his eyes and turned his face away.

"So you're telling me she's just a hookup, like Jonathan."

He was in my face in mere seconds, his lips pressed in a hard line.

I didn't back down. "It's okay to feel, David. I know you. You've been happier lately. Don't let go of something good because of me. You have a big heart, and I truly believe there's someone out there for you. If she understands you better than I do, maybe you should give her a chance."

He kept my stare for a moment, then his eyes widened.

"General." David bowed and left.

"What's with him?" Davon held a smiling Doug.

"I think he has feelings for Sinclair, but he's confused."

"Because he still loves you." Davon brushed my cheek lovingly. "Don't force it. When we fall for a woman, we fall hard." He played with one of my loose curls. "I've seen it also. There's something between them, but he has to be the one to take that step. He must be the one to let you go and move on."

"I know." Being the source of David's sadness clawed at my heart because I did love him and I wanted him to be happy.

Doug stretched his arms toward me, and I took him from Davon. He looked so much like his brother.

I tickled the baby. "We should get going. Diane must be driving Mark and Carol crazy, asking for Doug."

We had a playdate to go to. For Diane, having a baby cousin was an adventure. She loved taking care of him, and we visited whenever we could.

When we arrived, Peter was just leaving, with Diane giving him one of her signature hugs.

She hung from his neck. "Are you coming back tomorrow? We can play hide-and-seek."

Peter laughed. "Sure, and I'll bring more cookies." He unclamped her hands from his neck and put her down.

"The baby is here!" She jumped around me.

Davon grabbed him from me. "Come on, Little D. Doug is anxious to play with you." He crouched and took her with his other arm, balancing them.

Doug giggled as Diane made faces at him.

Our fight was not only for our freedom but for their future. Our children deserved a better life. A home to come to. A safe place to grow up in.

"They'll be all right." Peter's reassuring voice settled my heart.

I turned to him. "I want them to have a future."

He clasped my shoulder. "They will. You *will* make it. We *will* be free. Believe it. Make it a reality. Do not doubt. Do not fear. Be strong, and set your mind on your goal. There's nothing else."

I took a deep breath, taking his words to heart. Peter was my mentor in Electi, but he'd become so much more. A person to look up to. Someone I could count on, no matter what.

"We'll make it through, Abi." He smiled, then patted my back. "I'll see you out there."

I nodded. "Of course."

He ruffled my hair, reminding me so much of Connor. An ache pressed at the back of my throat, but I smiled and watched him retreat, praying we'd see each other again. That we'd celebrate together after everything was over.

Peter was on Davon's team. They'd enter through the forest without a clue of what they'd encounter inside.

"Are Matt and Aoki saying their goodbyes?" Mark asked the moment I closed the door behind me.

"Peekaboo!"

I turned toward Diane's sweet voice. Doug lay on a sheet on the floor and stared wide-eyed at Diane, a beautiful smile on his face.

"Yeah." Davon sipped his coffee. He'd grown accustomed to having a second cup with me after lunch. "But they should be here after lunch. Matt wants to give Abi and me some time also."

Both Matt and I would leave tomorrow. Matt commanded the troops that would enter Electi through the tunnels, and I'd follow David with the sniper team to the center of Promissa.

I couldn't let my mind slip into the uncertainty of war or all the possible ways things could go wrong. I couldn't bear to think of anything happening to Davon. Of him not being there when it all came to pass.

The weight on my chest made it hard to breathe. I closed my eyes for a moment, willing myself to center, then focused on Peter's words. On Connor's last moments.

There was no space for doubts. The plan was set. The only thing left was to do our part and make it work.

Carol bumped my shoulder. "Are you okay?"

I glanced at Davon. An emptiness had started growing inside me since he told me the time had come. "I'll be okay." I patted my belly and smiled. "We'll be okay."

We'd told the rest of our friends about the pregnancy. They deserved to know before war broke out.

Carol played with her wedding band, eyes downcast. "I wanted to thank you for saving Mark."

I choked up, remembering that private moment with Mark. That instant when we both believed he wouldn't make it. When he asked me to say goodbye to his family. "I didn't save him."

She moved in front of me. Her blue eyes were soft, filled with an inner glow I hadn't seen before. "You did. Michael told me how you ran to get David. Even after losing Connor, you pushed your pain away and acted just in time. It's thanks to you that he's still here. It's thanks to you he survived."

Diane ran to Mark and tugged at his uniform. "Daddy, look! I made him smile!"

Mark crouched carefully and picked her up.

She grabbed his ponytail and started brushing his brown strands.

Mark kissed her temple. "I see. Did you know Uncle Davon and Aunt Abi are having a baby girl? You'll have another cousin soon."

Her eyes brightened toward Davon. "Are you really going to be a dad?"

Davon smiled sweetly. "I am."

Diane extended her hands to him, and Mark passed her over to her uncle.

She cupped both of his cheeks and watched Davon seriously. It was comical. "But you'll still come visit me, right?"

Davon touched his brow to hers. "Always. Nothing will change between us."

She pushed away and offered her pinkie. "Promise?"

Davon interlaced his finger with hers. "Promise."

I rubbed my belly. Lizzie would have a wonderful family, one I'd protect with all my being.

Diane hugged him tenderly, then shimmied her way off him and came to me. "Aunty A?" She grabbed my hand.

I bent over. "Yes?"

Her eyes sparkled as she moved closer, bouncing from foot to foot. "Can I touch your belly?"

"Of course." I placed her hand on my stomach. It was starting to grow.

She moved her hand over my belly. "What's her name?"

"Elizabeth." Every time my mother's name slipped past my lips it was like she was right there with me. Watching over me and my family.

My heart swelled at Diane's beautiful smile.

"Don't worry, Baby E. Grandpa told me when Daddy comes back, we'll all be together again and live in a city. I've never seen one, but he says it'll have schools and parks." She glanced at Doug, then back at my belly. "I don't know what they are, but he says we can play there. We just have to be patient and do what Mommy and Uncle Aoki say." Diane looked at my uniform. "Wait. Are you leaving too?"

I leaned down till we were the same height. "I am."

She frowned. "With Baby E?"

I brushed her arm. "Yes."

"But you'll come back, right?"

I held up my pinkie. "Promise."

She gave me a huge smile and hooked her finger through mine. "Promise."

Half an hour later, I went to go check on Matt and Aoki, who had not arrived. When I opened the door, Aoki was grabbing the collar of Matt's black long-sleeve shirt while Matt fisted Aoki's white button-down shirt at the waist, holding him flush against him. They pulled away from their kiss.

"Oh. Hi!" Matt waved as if nothing had happened.

Aoki adjusted his black slacks, giving me a wink as he entered, followed by Matt.

I tilted my head as they passed by me. "Hey, why are you all dressed up?"

Matt shrugged. "Don't know." He signaled at Aoki with his thumb. "He told me to, and I decided to oblige." He whispered in my ear, "Believe me. He deserves my reverence, if you get what I mean."

I chuckled and followed them inside.

I walked to Carol. "I guess it's goodbye for now."

Carol hugged me. "I prefer to say until we meet again. Be safe out there."

My eyes filled with tears as I turned away from her, then went to Mark, who held Diane. "Remember to play a lot with Doug while I'm out there."

Diane nodded happily. "Will do." She caught one of my tears. "Why are you sad?"

I wiped my face with my uniform. "I'm just going to miss you all."

Mark kissed my hand just like his brother did sometimes. "See you out there."

I stepped away and into Davon, who waited for me by the door. "I'll see you then."

I stretched next to Davon's naked body, trailing my fingers over his chest muscles and down his marked abs. The flames from his phoenix tattoo added to his strong physique. Nothing covered his lower half, and I took a moment to appreciate what was only mine.

I glanced up when he stirred, as if he felt my eyes touching him.

I never tired of watching him sleep. His calm breathing and relaxed features were rare to behold. I cuddled him, my head on his left shoulder, then stroked down his right arm and over his bulging biceps.

His arm tightened around me, and he leisurely trailed his fingers down my side in a sinful caress, igniting my skin. "What time is it?"

I glanced at my watch. "Five."

He shifted sideways and moved his hand down until he grabbed my hip and pressed me against his impressive length. He took my breast into his mouth, and I was done for.

I wrapped my left leg over him, trying to complete our connection, but he had a different plan.

He pulled me on top of him.

I lifted an eyebrow as I straddled him. "Are you sure you can handle it?"

He threw me a mischievous smile. "Why don't you find out?"

I kissed him and slowly sank onto him. He met me halfway and pushed up, eliciting a gasp from me as he filled me to the brim. He grabbed my hips and let my core adjust to him like always.

I moaned as liquid heat flowed down my body to where our bodies joined. I placed one hand on his pec and held the other against the wall. "Are you ready?"

He raised an eyebrow. "Surprise me."

Reapers corner me between two buildings.

I fire my gun, but they don't budge.

Connor is there. A dagger juts from his throat, and I scream as blood covers his uniform.

"Love?"

Someone was shaking me.

I pushed him away and jumped from the bed.

Davon kneeled on the bed, hands up. "It's me. You were having a nightmare."

I darted my eyes around the room, and once I gripped onto reality, I sat on the bed. "I'm sorry."

He cradled me in his arms. "It's okay. Want to talk about it?"

My body trembled. It was the first time I'd dreamed of him, and seeing his last moments again was too much. "I was out there, fighting reapers. Then Connor was there and..."

Davon hugged me tight, and I let myself sink into the comfort only he could give me. The whole world went silent as his warmth enveloped me. "It's okay. I'm right here with you."

I don't know how long he held me, but it was long enough for my tears to dry and my cries to calm down.

He kissed the top of my head. "Are you better?"

I met his gaze. "I am. I'm sorry. Going out there has me on edge."

He cupped my face with both hands. "You're the strongest woman I know."

My chin trembled. "I'm scared, Davon."

He kissed me, then focused his dark irises on me. "I am too, but if there's something I know for certain, it's that there's no force strong enough to keep me away from you. I will fight for you and our child." He touched my belly. "And you will too. We will make it out. We will win."

I let myself relax and took a couple of deep breaths until my heart calmed and my chest lightened. Fear was our enemy, and I would not let it take me down that dark path. Never again.

Sometime later, I jerked back and snatched my watch from the side table. "Shit! We're late!" I grabbed my clothes and jumped from the bed. "She said she'd be at the mess hall at six, and it's almost seven."

Davon leaned back, crossing his arms behind his head. "They can wait."

"But we're just going to meet Sarah." I remembered what Matt said and how they were dressed. "Wait. What's going on?"

He shrugged. "Don't ask. Just trust me."

Something was up, but I'd follow his orders. After all, he was my general.

I buttoned my blue jeans, then fixed Davon's sapphire necklace over my red tank top.

Davon slid his black leather jacket over a white T-shirt. His torn blue jeans and black boots completed his dangerous look. He brushed his hair into a half bun.

Heat radiated through me. "I wish we could stay."

He captured my chin. "Then we'll come back early. Matt still owes me the extra hour he spent with Aoki."

I smiled sultrily, wrapping my arms around his lean waist. "And what will you do?"

He brushed his lips against mine like that first time in the clearing of the forest. "I'm going to strip you and indulge in your sweet taste." He took a deep, shuddering breath, then stepped away from me, leaving me breathless.

I pressed a palm to my chest, willing my roaring heart to calm down.

Davon opened the door. "After you."

Chapter 25

Davon

May 25, 2214

Sarah had planned everything. We just had to be there by six, but it was seven.

As we neared the mess hall, Abi stopped mid-stride. "Is that music?"

I opened the door, and music boomed outside. The tables had been bunched into a corner, and lights filled the cavern space in a beautiful array that brushed over the bodies on the dance floor.

Her eyes were wide. "It's amazing." She hooked her hands around my neck and kissed my cheek. "What are we celebrating?"

Her dazed look and gleaming eyes made me wonder what I had done to deserve her love. I ran my finger down the edge of her collar and placed my palm over her heart. "Our coming victory. A night between friends. It's whatever you want it to be."

She played with my hair, wrapping a long strand around her fingers. "Did you plan it?"

Her gentle touch sent a shiver down my body.

I pulled her closer, then tipped my head toward the dance floor. "She did."

When Sarah saw Abi, she ran to us and grabbed her hand. "Come on!"

Abi laughed as Sarah pulled her away from me, but she jerked to a stop. "Is Deb here?"

Sarah gestured toward a table in a corner, her face taking on a solemn look. "She won't come onto the dance floor."

Abi lifted an eyebrow. "Like hell she won't. Let's go get her."

Abi pulled her toward Deb. They each took one of her hands and dragged her into the writhing bodies.

Deb wasn't moving much, but then Aoki and Matt came to her side, and they started dancing together. It didn't take long for a smile to cross her face.

This was worth fighting for.

David passed me a beer. "Thanks for this."

I clinked my mug against his and smiled. "To getting Promissa back."

David smiled. "Por acabar con esos cabrones. Salud." He took a swig from his brew. "So what's this about?"

I shrugged. "One last night of carefree fun before the battle. We've all lost so much. Sarah thought this was a needed reprieve to lift everyone's spirits, and I couldn't agree more."

David smiled. "I suspected something was up when Jules stopped our training session halfway through and told me to change into something fresh. Do you know how long it's been since I wore normal clothes?"

I glanced his way. His thumb rested in one of the loops of his khaki slacks, which he combined with a black V-neck. He wore a couple of rings and a necklace with a miniature flag with three horizontal lines: one magenta, one lavender, and a wide blue stripe at the bottom. Aoki had one just like it. It was a bisexual pride flag.

David shook his head. "You guys really need to learn how to do surprises. May as well just tell us next time."

I raised my mug to the dance floor, where Sarah, Deb, and Abi danced their hearts out. They were grinning and swaying in sync with the music.

Sarah seemed like a different person. I asked Peter about it since they were close, and he said he couldn't say much but that he appreciated her and they'd built a nice friendship. That they were helping each other heal. I was glad.

"Hey." Sinclair bumped David's shoulder. "Having fun?" She clinked her mug against his, and some beer spilled on her black slacks. She tried to dry it with the sleeve of her red silk blouse to no avail. "Fuck, why did I wear this?"

David crouched and used the hem of his T-shirt to dry her pants, then he stood close to her ear. "Because I said you looked sexy as hell in it."

I stifled a chuckle when Jules gasped and hit his shoulder.

Maybe David thought I couldn't hear with the music so loud or maybe he didn't care anymore.

"Come on." Sinclair grabbed his hand. "Let's dance."

"Davon!" Abi waved for me to come to her.

Carefree Abi was a joy to behold, and I wouldn't miss this chance for anything.

I finished my beer and went to her.

Aoki and Matt danced much slower than the rest, but they were all over each other.

Sinclair danced with David, and Jonathan grabbed his hips from behind, swaying to the rhythm. They danced like no one was watching, lost in the music.

I laughed as Abi jumped and twirled around me, her sisters by her side. Tomorrow we'd go to war, but today we'd dance like there was no tomorrow.

May 26, 2214

I buried my nose in Abi's hair and branded her scent in my mind. "I'll see you in a couple of days."

She buried her face in my chest. "Tell me everything will be okay. Tell me we'll take him down."

I tilted her chin up. Her eyes were red, her lips trembling.

I closed the distance between us in a tender kiss. "We will make it through. Together."

"I love you."

I hugged her one last time. "I love you too."

My watch beeped.

"Time to go." Abi wiped her tears away with the sleeve of her uniform. "I'll see you on the battlefield."

And with a salute, she turned away and joined the rest of the soldiers. She stood next to David.

"Attention, troops! General Niles is on the grounds." Matt's voice was firm.

My chest tightened. More than a thousand soldiers saluted me, and a deep silence settled among them.

I summoned strength from memories of Connor. From all those moments we shared and everything he taught me. These soldiers would go out there today, and it was an honor to stand with them as their general.

"Today we start our journey to freedom. We face a formidable enemy, but our will is stronger than theirs. Sure, they have the reapers and thousands of soldiers in their army, but what do they fight for?

"Their strength is based on fear, not love. Their army follows orders, not their hearts.

"With courage and will, we have the upper hand. We go out there, and we don't back away no matter what we face.

"We fight against oppression no matter who it comes from or who it's directed at.

"The New World Government thinks we're weak. They think we'll stand by and do nothing. They're wrong.

"So go out there. Fight with all you have. When this is over, we will have Promissa back, and the New World Government will be no more."

The soldiers cheered, their shouts echoing through the mountains.

Warmth traveled through my chest. All doubts and fear left me, and a new sense of hope filled my soul.

I saluted my troops just as David and Matt gave their orders. Without a glance back, fifteen hundred PRF soldiers marched to war.

I watched the footage as our drone followed the troops. They were reaching the halfway point of their journey and still hadn't encountered the enemy. My fingers twitched as I zoomed in. There she was, with David by her side.

I touched the monitor. *See you soon, my love.*

My heart ached at being so far from her. At the fucking reality that if anything happened out there, I wouldn't be able to do a thing. I just had to trust they'd make it.

"How long until they're safe?"

I jumped as Sinclair entered the office. Multiple screens covered the wall, with two computers up front on a long desk. Nina sat by my side.

"Two, three hours at most." Nina turned the drone back.

Sinclair stood by her.

"Comms will be off until they reach the next one," Nina said.

Sinclair sighed. "Now we wait." She raked her hair back.

I huffed and closed my eyes. It would be hours until they reached the next drone.

Connor had set this all up before he died. The drone was tethered to a power source and functioned as an antenna. Once it reached its 250-foot height, it would extend the network and comms range for more than eighteen miles.

Nina managed to create a jamming signal. Even if the enemy found a way to intercept it, they would only hear our scrambled comms. When our soldiers reached it, we'd have a better picture. But for now, they were on their own for a couple of miles.

Sinclair, palms on the desk, watched as our troops disappeared from the video feed, her nails scratching the wood below them.

I turned the screen off. "Want to train?"

Sinclair nodded. "Anything to get my mind off this shit."

We sparred for over an hour until we were both breathless.

"Who taught you to fight?" I wiped the sweat off my face.

This woman fought like a devil.

Sinclair grinned. "I've been training since I can remember. We have an academy and train in martial arts, melee combat, air defense, whatever you can think of. We've been preparing for this for a long time. And you?" She sat on a bench.

"Many. Major General Yuxuan Li trained me here. He's a kung fu master. Lavigne trained me in Electi."

"And what about your father?"

I threw the towel over my shoulder and started toward the door. "I don't want to talk about it."

"What did he do to you?"

I sent her a side glance. "He killed me inside."

I had to burn off some steam, so I left the cave and ran. I only told Peter about it in case of an emergency and took a talkie with me. We still had a couple of hours until the comms were back up.

My legs moved on their own until exhaustion took over. My lungs burned as I doubled over, willing myself to breathe deeply. The sky was tinged with orange and red. I had to turn back.

A sharp burst of static crackled from the walkie, and a garbled voice emerged. It sounded urgent.

"Falcon to Den. Do you copy?" I asked.

Another crackle was followed by a high-pitched hiss.

The hairs lifted at my nape, and my hands shook as I tried in vain to recover comms. Something had happened.

"Fuck!" I raced back as fast as I could, my throat aching from the effort to keep up. "Falcon to Den. Falcon to Den." I pressed the button again and again until it crackled to life.

"Den to Falcon. Do you copy?"

It was Nina.

"I copy. What the fuck happened?" I struggled to keep my tone calm.

"They're in trouble." Her voice shook.

My heart faltered.

"There are reapers out there. Sending backup." Sinclair's order leaked into our conversation.

"Don't!" I said.

The walkie crackled, and white noise came back.

She turned it off!

"Fuck!" I yelled at the top of my lungs and put the walkie away. I could still make it in time.

Ten minutes later, I arrived.

Black-and-red uniforms filled the space in front of the caves.

Seth was bringing in the Hummers from the valley where they stood with the helicopters.

Soldiers grouped around Sinclair.

"Two Hummers will go out there. A helicopter not far behind."

"No!" I ordered. "Whatever the emergency, we can't risk getting noticed."

She rolled her shoulders back. "They could get massacred out there. You're saying we should ignore our people? Let them die?"

I swallowed the urge to go out there and save Abi. I was the general of the army, and I had to put our mission first. "I am the general of the PRF army, and my order stands clear. You will back down and let them respond to this on their own."

She turned her violent gaze toward me. "I am a general of the Liberty Enclave, and I will give the orders to my soldiers however I want."

Peter brought my vest and stood by my side with about a dozen of our soldiers. "I tried to talk some sense into her."

I nodded. "General Sinclair, you're standing on the People's Revolutionary Front grounds, and I won't stand for your insubordination. My troops knew what they were signing up for. They have sufficient weapons and artillery to fight out there."

"So you'll let them die? You'll let your precious Miss Davis die?" Her words were like venom, but I stood my ground.

Each word that left me was like a shot to my heart, but above all, I needed to protect my people. I'd have to trust Abi would survive. I would not let Sinclair tempt me.

I held my place. "We will not risk the element of surprise. It's the one thing we have in our favor. I ask you again to stand down or face the consequences."

General Jules Sinclair didn't back down but stayed silent.

I approached her with my soldiers, her own taking on a fighting stance. I raised an eyebrow and watched each one, ending with their general.

"Stand down," she said.

I nodded. "Let's talk inside."

Sinclair threw her hat on the conference table. "What the fuck, Niles? Do you have any idea what's going on out there?"

Peter had explained our troops' prerogative on the way here. When they sent up the drone, we captured various troops of over fifty NWG soldiers waiting inside the perimeter of the forest. Some were between our troops and the tunnels. Reapers were with them.

I stood at the head of the table. "They're prepared to fight them. We knew this could happen. That's why we sent out so many."

She punched the table. "But you saw what happened in the last attack. How many will you let die before sending backup?"

I pulled out a chair and sank onto it. "I know how you feel. Believe me. Abi's out there too as well as my brother, but I promised Connor I'd see this through, and we can't risk it. They will make it. They've been training for this."

She laid her palms on the table and closed her eyes. "Fuck. This is why I didn't want this. I shouldn't care. This is…" She looked up. "How do you do it?"

This was definitely about David. She was hurting just like I was, but Abi and I had been apart before, and I trusted she'd make it.

I pressed my lips together. "I just trust they'll make it." I pictured Abi out there, fighting. I wanted to run. To get on a helicopter and attack them. To burn everything down. But I couldn't. "This is all we have, Sinclair. If they figure out we're sending in our troops, everything we've done and every sacrifice that has been made will have been for nothing."

She slumped into the chair next to mine and covered her face. "I didn't want to care. I was just supposed to come in and help you. Nothing else. A treaty between countries. But this. I didn't sign up for it." She put her hands down in defeat.

I gave her a small smile. "A wise man once told me that one doesn't choose when or with whom it happens."

Matt would never let me forget it if he found out I called him wise.

She let out a heavy sigh. "And he was a wise man indeed."

Chapter 26

Abi

May 26, 2214

"Understood." David pressed the button on his helmet.

I fixed my boot lace after resting for a bit.

We reached the drone and turned it on, then David ordered us to take some time to rest when he received a call from the base. He put some distance between us. He was pacing and doing hand gestures. I mean, he always used his hands when speaking, but this time it was different.

"Mierda!" he yelled before coming to us. He sat between Matt and me and raked both hands through his hair, leaning over his knees.

A chill swept through me. This couldn't be good. "What happened?" I passed David my canteen.

He took a long swig. "That was Lavigne." He kept his stare on the horizon. "We have a problem."

We listened as he explained what we were facing. It appeared Jordan had allocated troops inside the forest, all around its perimeter. Not two miles away from us and right between our location and the tunnels, there was one NWG troop of about fifty soldiers, half of them enhanced.

I clasped my knees together and rocked my body slightly. *Reapers.*

David touched my back, and the tremors lessened.

"We need a diversion." Matt ran a hand over his brow and stayed silent for over a minute. "I'll send a troop north. Once they're a safe distance from us, they'll set up bombs every half-mile and detonate them when they're farther west, then they'll repeat the process in different directions. They can regroup with the rest of the troops when they start their advance toward Promissa. The important thing is that they think we're still in the forest. I'll talk to Davon." He pressed his comm.

I brushed Matt's knee. "Tell him we'll be okay. That he shouldn't endanger the mission."

Even though I trusted Davon's good judgment as our general, I feared he might do something crazy because of Lizzie.

Matt nodded, then walked away and started talking.

"How are you holding up?" I asked David.

He covered his face.

I hunched over. "Tell me."

"It's nothing." He blinked, avoiding my gaze.

"David?"

He humphed. "It's Jules. She was there, and she kind of lost it."

He didn't say anything, but then I remembered last night. How they danced together with Jonathan. How they looked at each other. "Oh."

He leaned back, looking at the heavens. "Oh, yes. She wants to send in a helicopter."

I stilled. "But that would sabotage the mission." If they sent in any vehicle, by air or land, everything would be fucked.

He sighed. "I know. I told her. She...wasn't herself."

So that's why he looked so agitated. Jules must have gone crazy with worry. "When you care about someone, sometimes you can lose logic." I touched my sapphire necklace through my vest.

Davon.

What would I do if he was the one in danger? My pulse rose at the thought. I would stop at nothing to save him.

"It's just..." He shook his head. "It wasn't supposed to be like this."

"Things sometimes don't go as we expect." I never imagined I'd fall in love with Jordan Niles's son. Never in my wildest dreams. It just happened.

My mind wandered to last night. "Isn't Jonathan around? Can't he talk to her?"

"I'm sure she already spoke to him." David took a deep breath. "He must also be crazy with worry."

I leaned back with him. "So it's polyamorous?"

He looked north. "Yeah, but not like most think."

I nudged his shoulder. "Enlighten me."

"Jonathan and I have history, and we enjoy each other. I mean, I do care about him, but I'm still trying to come back from what happened between us. Then Jules came, and I don't know when I started to fall for her." He took out his necklace from under his uniform and fiddled with the little flag that hung from it.

A soft smile was painted across his lips, and for a moment, he seemed to have forgotten our current predicament. "We have a vee dynamic. There's an emotional connection between the three of us, but I'm the one romantically involved with both." He bit his lower lip. "It's working well, and they are good to each other and to me, but still..." He darted his eyes toward me, then away. "I'm confused." He slumped forward.

I gripped his hand for a second. "Give it time, David."

He nodded.

Matt returned. "Answer that."

My comms beeped in my ear.

Matt shrugged. "The boss wants to talk to you."

I moved away from Matt and David, then answered.

"Abi? Are you okay?" His voice shook.

A familiar rush stirred inside me, but his desperate tone tugged at my heart. "We're okay. You?"

His hard exhale came through the walkie. "Crazy with worry but hanging on. Be careful out there. Matt already told me about the plan. Corporal Mathews will go with his troops. He knows the area."

I was unable to speak for a moment before I summoned a confident tone. "We *will* make it." I was glad he wasn't here to witness my quivering chin. My trembling hands. But I needed to reassure him, or else I feared what he might do. "You don't have to worry."

"I can, and I will. That doesn't mean I'll endanger our mission. We'll continue with the plan. We prepared for this. You know how calculating he can be."

My stomach heaved. His father. "I know."

There was a moment of silence.

"Keep safe. Fight with your heart. You can do this."

His words gave me the strength I needed to move forward. "I love you."

"And I you, love. Be safe," he whispered.

The comms crackled and died.

Now it all depended on us.

"Position one. Ready."

"Position two. Ready."

We were taking our positions around the forested area. After Mathews left, Matt and David split the troops into different zones. We'd wait until the bombs went off.

Our drills proved to be useful earlier than expected. We'd practiced nonstop against our own using stealth. After all, once inside Promissa, we'd need to get to our positions, and for that, most of us had to go out into the streets.

"Position nine. Ready," I said.

"Position ten. Ready."

I let out a pent-up breath at David's confirmation. He was farther up the hill.

Body flush against the ground, I blinked twice to relax my eyes, then peered through my scope and adjusted it. The NWG troop I was observing had stayed in formation for the last twenty minutes. I'd counted seven reapers.

My body twitched. I flexed my hands to quiet the tingling in my fingers and cracked my neck from side to side. My muscles were tight, but I kept my breathing even and my eyes on the target.

A reverberating explosion boomed through the forest. The reaper I had in sight grabbed his machine gun and got into a fighting stance. He touched his helmet and nodded, waving for the others to follow. He signaled two other reapers, then they dispersed.

"Four stayed behind." I fixed my scope on one. "Awaiting orders."

David's voice came through. "Let's wait for the next one."

My heart was pounding so loud that if someone stood next to me, they'd probably hear it.

The forest groaned, and the branches swayed in the wind. The deep silence marked each passing second. Time moved slower than usual, as if the whole world waited for what would come.

The ground shook a bit closer, and the stillness was broken. The last four reapers dispersed.

The comms crackled to life.

"The NWG troops have moved north. Only one-third remain." Matt had a video feed from the drone. "There's an opening near position nine about half a mile west. Another south of position four. Do not engage. Avoid the enemy at all costs."

"Snipers, stand at the ready," David said. "Guard the troops, and await further orders."

"Copy." I steadied myself.

I rolled my shoulders and stayed in place. Being pregnant had made it a bit more exhausting but not enough to affect my performance. We trained for months like this before I left for Electi and after the attack. David was ruthless and would leave me for hours in the same position so I'd understand what being a sniper encompassed.

At first, it was painful. My muscles would spasm and hurt for days. But now I took on the pain with honor. It was our job to guard those fighting and to ensure they could move by the enemy without being harmed. To eliminate any threat in their way, engaging again and again until it was no more.

The bright afternoon was swallowed in shadows. I frowned and looked up.

Dark clouds covered the clear skies. Water beads slid off my rifle's ceramic coating as a relentless downpour hit the forest. Science had developed the PRF weapons to ensure they'd work under any condition, so even the optics stayed clear as I kept my position.

Every few minutes, an explosion echoed across the forest. My ears tweaked at the sound of distant gunfire, and I exhaled to maintain my calm.

Mathews's troops had engaged the enemy.

About an hour passed before Matt's voice came through. "My troops are in."

My tension eased. Matt was safe.

My radio clicked.

"Snipers, start moving," David said.

Without hesitation, I narrowed my eyes and adjusted my scope for one final scan, then followed David's command. With practiced precision, I disengaged and slung the sniper across my back.

A loud crack stopped my retreat. I was nearing the tunnel, but I couldn't ignore the sound. Either I was being followed, or someone's position was no longer secure. And there was only one person behind me.

My stomach dropped.

David.

No. I couldn't lose him. I had to go back.

Another crack.

Adrenaline shot through me, taking away the heaviness of the last couple of hours. I took out my khukuri, letting its comforting sensation flow through me. One foot after the other, I walked back toward David's position.

A grunt.

I rushed toward the sound, no longer caring if someone heard me.

A reaper had her arm pressed against David's throat. His eyes bulged as he desperately clawed at the reaper's hands, his legs swinging wildly.

Shit. My body froze for a moment before my mind realized the gravity of what was happening.

A sinister laugh escaped the woman who had him pinned to the tree. "You'll die here, soldier, but not before telling me how many of you are out here."

I had to save David, then figure out how to stop her from getting any intel out. Her hand moved to press the button on her helmet, and I had a second to act before she revealed our position. Without hesitation, I sprinted toward them.

The reaper jerked back, and David reached for his belt.

I was about to reach her when she made a gurgling sound. Blood sprayed all over her chest.

Bones cracked as David twisted the dagger, breaking her neck. With a sickening slide, he extracted his weapon and fell to the ground with her.

I crouched to check him, but he put his hand up.

"I'm okay." His voice was coarse, as if sand filled his throat.

"Here." I passed him my canteen.

He took a small sip and rubbed his bruised neck. He held my hand to stand. "We need a place to hide her."

I squeezed his hand. "Are you sure you're okay?"

He covered mine, his eyes soft. "I am."

I nodded, then turned around to study the area.

It needed to be somewhere easy to dig and hard to find. We had to be fast, or we'd lose our window to enter the tunnels.

"There." I pointed to a heavily forested area where a puddle had formed.

I breathed heavily as David and I dragged her massive body into the mud hole.

I was massaging my muscles and preparing to hide the reaper when David grabbed a rock and shattered her helmet with a horrible thud, damaging her comms device.

He gripped my shoulder. "I'll get a boulder to cover her. You go ahead to the tunnels."

"Like hell I'm going out there without you." I shook my head. "We go together."

Never again would I leave someone behind.

I went to a huge rock that rested a few feet away. "Are you going to help me or not?"

He groaned, then pushed with me. Once we were done, we continued our retreat.

We blended into the forest and slipped away, the rain muting our footsteps. We were so close.

A loud crack echoed ahead, then another one, similar to a branch snapping in two. We stood guard and listened. Footsteps splashed toward us.

Not another reaper.

David and I cocked our guns and aimed toward the sound.

"It's me!" Matt put up his arms. "What took you so long?"

We put our guns down as another explosion boomed over the storm that was now pouring violently.

"Did everyone make it?" David asked, his voice still hoarse.

Matt nodded.

"Perfect. Let's get inside."

We followed David into the camouflaged hatch that connected to the tunnels.

Matt tapped the button on his helmet. "Everyone's in. Comms out." He closed the hatch behind him after we entered.

Until we reached Promissa, we were in the dark.

Now there was nothing else to do but execute our strategy and trust that everyone would do their part.

Davon's face flashed through my mind. *I'll see you on the other side.*

When I took the final step down, the damp air hit me, and I gasped as my boots struck water.

Matt patted my shoulder. "Don't worry. The hatch is lined to prevent any more water from getting in. It took longer than we expected to get everyone inside, but the drainage system will take care of it."

I'd heard about the preparation that went into the tunnels. Not only did they spend about a month clearing the rubble, but they also put a lot of work into making them safe for this moment. They covered some sections with a geocomposite drainage system in case water came in and also created an air filtration system.

Lights were scattered along the tunnel, draping the area in an oppressive gloom. The three-meter-wide space stretched for miles ahead. The heavy thuds of our soldiers echoed through the space.

Matt's troops had already started heading into Promissa and would only stop once they crossed into the city. Then they'd await Matt's orders before going into Electi.

After walking for more than an hour, my legs screamed for a rest.

Matt stopped. "Let's rest here."

I sagged against a wall and let myself slide to the floor.

Matt sat to my right and David to my left.

Matt passed each of us a beef jerky and leaned forward. "Mind explaining what the fuck happened out there?"

David took a swig from his canteen, then wiped the sweat from his brow. "A reaper followed me, but thanks to Abi, we took care of it."

Matt darted his eyes to me. "Are you okay?" .

I nodded. "Just tired."

In truth, my arms and legs hurt like hell, and I was fucking hungry. That jerky didn't do the work, but I was grateful for it. "I'd kill for a cup of coffee."

David chuckled. "I'd do anything for you, but I'll give you a raincheck on that coffee." He passed me half of his jerky.

I put my palm up. He needed his energy.

He shook his head. "Take it. I'll be fine."

"Thanks." I ate it.

"Did you take your vitamins?" Matt said after a moment.

"Uh, I almost forgot." I searched my pocket for a packet of my prenatal vitamins and swallowed them.

"Did you hide the body?" Matt asked David.

David nodded.

Matt let out a hard exhale. "The important thing is you're safe."

I rested my head against the wall and closed my eyes for a second.

A warm caress slid down my cheek. "Abi?"

I sighed and opened my eyes.

David was crouched in front of me. He took his hand away.

"We need to go." His voice was no longer raspy, more the normal, soft tone he always used for me.

I squinted, adjusting to the dim tunnel. "How long was I out?"

"Just half an hour." He helped me up.

My legs were stiff, and I grunted.

He narrowed his eyes, then glanced at my belly.

I yawned. "I'm just tired. We're okay."

I frowned. Matt was nowhere in sight.

"Where's Matt?"

"I told him to go ahead, but we should be able to catch up. You needed your sleep." He tipped his head toward the tunnel. "Ready to go?"

I nodded.

Soon we'd be inside Promissa.

Chapter 27

Davon

May 26, 2214

"Copy that." I grabbed the edge of the desk. "They're in."

"God." Sinclair slumped back in her chair. "That took longer than expected."

I bowed over the desk, willing my breathing to slow. The last couple of hours were the hardest I'd had in a long time.

A soldier came into the room. "Sir." He passed me a note.

The heaviness in my stomach eased. "Constantine is ready." I straightened. "Our spies too." I turned to Sinclair, who had moved to the edge of her seat. "They'll take the minister of transportation hostage tomorrow night."

She let out a heavy breath. "Good."

Now it was all in Matt's and David's hands. They had to make sure everyone was in place by tomorrow because in a day and a half, everything started whether we were ready or not.

I went to the door. "It's time to go. We leave by sundown."

"Deb?"

Her sobs reached me the moment I opened the door.

Time seemed to slow as I approached her. She sat by her table, facing the canvas she'd drawn.

I crouched by her side as she wiped away her tears.

"Hi." Her voice shook.

It was such a beautiful picture. I swallowed the lump in my throat. We'd never be whole again, but I'd fight with my everything to keep us alive.

I covered her hand. "Are you okay?"

She shrugged. "I'm not sure if I ever will be again."

Her words were a punch to my heart. I squeezed her hand. "We started this together, Deb, and I won't rest until we achieve what we swore we would. We'll all be together in no time."

She bowed her head and shook it. "You don't know that, Davon."

I didn't, but I had to believe. "Deb, look at me."

She did so. The dark shadows under her eyes evidenced her sorrow.

I made a silent vow to erase it. I'd give my sister the freedom we pledged to give our people the day we created the People's Revolutionary Front. I would not fail her. "Don't lose hope. Not now. Hope is what has driven us since the beginning."

She blinked. "Do you think it's possible? Do you truly believe we can defeat *Jordan*?"

Her voice trembled when she mentioned his name.

I cupped her face. "I not only believe it. I know it."

She threw her arms around me. We hugged for a long time until her cries quieted.

She sat back. "Please keep them safe. Bring them back to me."

Her sisters.

I cradled her hands in mine. "I'll protect them with all my being."

She nodded. "You too. Come back to me, big brother."

A tear slid down my cheek at her endearment. I never thought she'd use it again, not after all we'd been through.

She gave me a soft smile. "Promise."

I kissed her temple. "I do."

"Once the facilities blow, Davon will activate the trigger mechanism in the bunkers, and the bombs will go off seconds after the first explosions inside Promissa. That's when you come in with the helicopters." Peter showed us the maps and plans on his tablet.

We were outside, our troops in formation and the helicopters refueled and armed for war.

Sinclair pocketed her hands and looked at her choppers. "We'll take care of any troops left around the forest, then clear any that lie in wait around Promissa so you can enter. After that, we go to the government center."

I rubbed my nape and cracked my neck. This would be a hell of a ride. "Okay."

Sinclair left to give the orders to her troops.

Peter patted my back. "Everything will be all right, son. I'll be right by your side."

I released a pent-up breath. "I just hope everything goes as planned."

He clasped his hands behind his back with his usual air of authority. "If there's one thing I've learned in my twenty years of service, it's that something always goes wrong. The key is to know how to deal with it and fix it. You have a good strategy and an army willing to give everything for their goal, which is more than Jordan could ever have. You will be victorious."

He saluted, wearing the same PRF uniform as any other soldier. "It's an honor to fight for you, General Niles."

My eyes prickled at his words.

This man taught me all I knew and, more than that, treated me like his son when I lost my father. Seeing him standing before me, calling me his general, shook me deeply.

I saluted back. "The honor is mine, General Lavigne."

With that, he joined the rest of the soldiers.

"Sir, my unit is ready for your orders." Mark fastened his strap over his shoulder, securing his M72 LAW across his back.

"We'll leave in thirty. Your unit will follow the main troops. Try to use high places to cover for us if we encounter reapers. Remember, inside Promissa, we aim to paralyze. Kill only when necessary. Constantine's people will take as many enhanced soldiers alive as they can."

I looked at his soldiers, who were organizing to our left. Lucas was among them, carrying the metal mace Connor had once used and his own M72 LAW.

Rachel was looking at him, their hands interlocked as they talked.

I lifted my chin toward him. "How's he doing?"

Mark followed my gaze. "Good. He's following orders. His skills are magnificent. His strength's well above our finest soldiers'. The problem is getting the soldiers to trust him."

I darted my gaze to the rest of the troop. Some were minding their own business, but most kept their eyes on Lucas.

I narrowed my eyes. If they turned against him on the battlefield and he felt threatened, it could be disastrous. "Will that be a problem?"

Mark shook his head. "No, sir. They will follow my orders. I was quite clear. They wouldn't dare."

I swallowed hard. "I'll trust you, but remember, if anything happens…"

Mark patted his chest. "I'll activate the cuffs."

I nodded. "Also, refrain from using any rocket or missile until Constantine's signal, then you're free to engage however needed."

"Understood, sir." Mark left.

I'd asked him to stay because of his recent operation, but there was no way in hell he wasn't going into Promissa. He had his mind set on winning the war and finding his parents.

"We'll make it work."

I turned. "Katherine."

She hugged herself. "Whatever happens out there, we don't stop, we don't retreat, and we push even if we lose our lives in the process. Better dead than slaves to their cruelty."

These last months, Katherine had proved again and again what a remarkable human being she was. I'd hurt her, and I had to right my mistakes. If I was to prove myself worthy of Abi, this was something I needed to do.

I touched her shoulder. "I'm sorry for all the pain I put you through. I'm sorry you had to meet the asshole I was during our time together. You deserved so much more."

When I let her go, her brown eyes brimmed with tears. "Thank you." She wiped away a tear. "I knew what I was getting into. You were always clear. I just didn't expect to fall in love."

I stepped back at her confession. I was an asshole.

She shook her head. "You don't need to worry, Davon. I've moved on." She looked at the forest, and Seth waved at her when their gazes met.

I'd wondered about them and asked Seth about it. He said they'd been together for some months. That they cared for each other.

To know that Katherine had found someone who would treat her right gave me peace. She deserved so much more than what I'd given her.

"Abi and you deserve happiness. You were meant to be." She adjusted her vest and straightened. "My troops are at your command, sir." She saluted and left.

I spied Yuxuan and waved for him to approach. His jian hung by his side as he made his way across the battlefield. He saluted.

I sighed. I'd never get used to this shit. "At ease, Major General."

He put his hand down. "Do you need anything?"

I shook my head, then grabbed his shoulder. "Just wanted to say goodbye to a friend."

A smile spread across his face. "We *will* see each other again."

I looked down for a moment, then caught his stare.

"We will, Davon, and I will keep everyone safe until your return." The strength in his voice moved something within me, a trust that my people would be safe. That we would win.

I bowed to my mentor. "Thank you. You've done more for the rebellion than I could've asked for. And I'll forever be grateful for your teachings."

Yuxuan chuckled and patted my back. "Boy, there's no need for that. You're the one I should be bowing to. After all you've been through, you've kept your promise to us." He bowed to me, and my chest tightened. "I'm proud of you. You will do great things for your people."

My eyes welled up, and I couldn't hold back my tears. I dried them with my sleeve.

He gave me another salute. "Until we meet again, General Niles."

I nodded and returned the gesture. "We'll see each other again, Major General Li."

The words left my mouth with a certainty I hadn't had before this moment. We'd meet again.

Yuxuan left, and I took a moment to behold our army. We had about five thousand strong in the PRF, and a third of them had gone with Matt. That combined with the three hundred the Liberty Enclave had sent would have to be enough.

The captains and lieutenants of the People's Revolutionary Front took their places in the valley with their troops.

A welcome warmth radiated through my body. My people waited for my orders with only one thing in mind—to take back their freedom. It took me a moment to quiet the drumming of my heart enough to be able to speak.

"Tonight we leave our home and begin our journey toward Promissa. In two days, we enter Promissa and fight with everything we've got. The New World Government will fear us, and we won't let them walk over us ever again. We will become their judges and justiciaries, and they will pay for all the suffering they've put us through. For every life they've taken from us. We will fight together, and we will win." I raised my hand. "May we never forget our mission."

The ground shook as thousands of soldiers raised their hands and said in unison, "May we never forget our mission."

The blood vibrated inside my veins, and adrenaline rushed through me, breaking my last restraints like a river destroying a dam. The roar of the People's Revolutionary Front would send anyone to their knees. And with that shout, we started our journey south and marched to war.

May 27, 2214

"Take the rear. We'll cover for you, and when they follow, you attack from behind. Keep it low. Do it fast." I crouched close to the floor and started my approach.

We started bumping into enemy forces the closer we got to the mountain where Janus Peak once was. Most were normal soldiers, but every troop had at least two reapers with them.

We couldn't take them hostage at this time, as we couldn't spare anyone. Inside the city, Constantine's people had agreed to aid in the retrieval of the hostages once they were paralyzed so we wouldn't lose our numbers.

One by one, we took them down but not without our own casualties. We'd lost about a dozen soldiers during the first attacks, but once we picked up this strategy, we rushed through the forest. It was the same one Connor and our troops had used when clearing the forest after the first attack, and it still worked. An ambush.

Half the people attacked headfirst with a melee attack, while the others came in from the other side to take down the rest. The only problem was evading the reapers' hits, especially if they fired. Stealth was key because at close quarters, their firing skills would be greatly affected.

I signaled the soldiers near my location to attack. The six of us went out in unison. Two of us glided through the wet ground and slashed the back of the reapers' knees. The other four charged in, wielding metal maces we had taken from others.

The rest of the soldiers came from the other side, and the confused officers started going down.

After slicing through the reaper's tendons, I jumped to his chest and used my body to hold him down, then drove the khukuri into the side of his neck. I looked around. A soldier was down, but the rest were winning the battle.

I let out a huge breath.

A cocking sound disturbed the thuds from our hand-to-hand combat. "Everyone, down!"

The hiss of the bullets went over me, but someone fell with a grunt.

Fuck.

A reaper had come from the east. She viciously opened fire against us, uncaring about her fellow soldiers. She took them all down as well as half of my troop. She continued firing even when we all played dead, then stopped. A hissing sound was all we heard before she exploded into pieces.

A grenade launcher.

I looked up and sighed.

Mark strolled in and offered his hand. "I know you said to keep it down, but with the ruckus this one was causing, I decided it was no big deal."

And it wasn't. We were still far from the city.

He pulled me up.

"How many are down?" I wiped chunks of reaper remains from my uniform.

The scene was horrific as, one by one, my soldiers stood, bathed in reaper blood and innards.

"Jones?" A soldier shook a fellow officer, but there was no response. She checked her pulse and shook her head.

One down.

"Beta to Falcon." Peter had taken the lead with over half our troops.

I pressed the button on my helmet. "Falcon here."

"Is everything good? We heard gunfire."

We still had nine more hours to go before the signal. We needed to make sure the majority of our troops made it to the city limits before nightfall to rest before all hell broke loose.

I checked one last time to make sure our enemies were down. "The problem has been taken care of. Keep moving."

"Understood."

I changed the channel. "Falcon to Eagle."

No answer.

I rolled my eyes and used the complete code name Sinclair had insisted on taking. "Falcon to Iron Eagle. Please respond."

"That's more like it."

I humphed. "We're twenty klicks away from going dark. Keep your comms up. We'll meet you on the other side."

The comms crackled for a moment before she answered. "Roger that. Be safe."

I pressed the button one last time. "You too."

I sheathed my khukuri and checked my HK416. "Grab everything you can." I closed my eyes for a second before moving on. "We continue south."

We camped a few miles from Promissa, a safe distance away from the NWG troops that were now between us and the city.

The howl of the wind sang of the upcoming battle as the tree branches languidly swayed through the night. Our army was scattered across the perimeter at this point, all on the ground and covered by mud or leaves. We couldn't make a move or be seen, so we stayed as quiet as possible.

Right about now, the Liberty Enclave army should be starting their attack north of Halcyon. A diversion to divide the NWG forces. A trap to puzzle Father.

A heaviness swept through me, but I pushed it away. It would work.

I touched Abi's leather bracelet. *Be safe out there.*

I glanced to my side. Sarah and Nina had followed Peter when things started going bad. I had a promise to keep, and I entrusted them to him. Sarah had fallen asleep about an hour ago, same as Nina, who now hugged her side. It was a chilly night.

Peter had kept his promise and protected both.

Nina was not a trained fighter, but she was essential to our plan. Joe should have already hacked the system and now waited for the signal to open up comms. Once they were up, Nina would broadcast the video to all the homes in Promissa and Electi, then we'd attack with full force.

"In a matter of hours, we'll be entering the city." Peter was next to me. He rested his head on his arm and gazed at the stars. "My forces will take the prison, and we'll find Lisa. I promise."

Ever since we learned Lisa had been captured, he'd taken over the mission to get her and our people out of the prison. We weren't sure where Father kept her, but Peter was hopeful he'd find her there. We prayed Father hadn't removed Peter's fingerprints and codes from the system because he was our only way in.

"I know you will."

Peter searched his pockets and stretched his hand over to me. "Here."

I frowned.

"Take it."

I opened my palm, and he dropped something into it. It was the obsidian ring my parents had given me on my twenty-seventh birthday. My heart skipped a beat. Even though I threw it away in a fit of rage, it reminded me of my mother, but I couldn't help thinking about *him* too.

I closed my fist around it. "What's the meaning of this? I don't need a reminder of him." Ever since the attack, I'd refrained from calling him my father in front of others. He was a bastard. An irredeemable monster.

"Rebecca gave that to you. You need a reminder of what you're fighting for because it's not only for Promissa but also for Electi. Most of our people have also been kept in the dark and will be scared when tomorrow comes. You gave the instructions not to attack civilians, but once we're inside, once our soldiers see what the elites have, they *will* attack. You've read the books. You know how war is." He faced me. "Don't forget who you are. Don't forget our people. You are their general, and they will listen to you. Make them see before we enter Electi."

A barrage of emotions hit me. Even though elites lived above Promissa's citizens, most, like my mother, didn't know what was truly going on. As long as things didn't affect them, they'd prefer ignorance over knowledge. They'd choose to stay put over doing something about it.

This was how it always worked. That's why justice was overrated because the system didn't care about the ones who were down and, in many cases, rebels were seen as the ones in the wrong. But what would the world be if we didn't stand against oppression, against injustice, against evil?

We were in the right, and even though my people were innocent, I couldn't stop the rebels from raging in. If I was in their place, I would hate them as much as they did.

The problem was knowing when to stop. When enough lives were taken. When we were becoming the same evil we were fighting against. And that was hard.

That's why Peter had given me this ring.

I took a deep, cleansing breath, then opened my hand to study my initials.

I was part of both worlds and had done terrible things against the rebellion and against elites. I was right in the middle of this war, and if someone could stop things when they went too extreme, it was me. That was what Peter was asking of me. And it was a mission I would accept.

I sighed. "I can't promise I'll be able to stop them."

Saving both sides could prove difficult, but I'd try my best.

Peter nodded. "I know. And I wouldn't judge them either. But you need to try."

I put the ring back on, not for my father but for all the innocent people out there. And for my mother.

Chapter 28

Abi

May 27, 2214

A gentle touch on my cheek stirred me awake.

"It's time, Abi. You need to wake up," Matt said.

He hadn't left my side since we caught up with him.

I rubbed my face, trying to shake off sleep.

The troops had split across the sections of the tunnel that led to different parts of the city.

We were the last in this branch that came as far as the soldier residences near the government center. From here, Matt and his troops would move into Electi through the tunnels, while David and I would take the branch east and reach the limits of the government buildings, far enough that we could hide among the apartments pinpointed by Constantine's people.

Now that the moment was here, a dropping sensation fell over me. I had to say goodbye to Matt and David with no idea of what I'd face out there or if I'd ever see them again. After losing Connor, nothing was certain anymore, and with each moment that passed, it was more difficult to focus on the positive. We could lose it all.

Matt stroked my back. "I know what you're doing. Push those thoughts away. You can't go out there with fear. Focus on the plan, execute it, and use all that you've learned to push forward." He put a hand on my belly. "Fight for what you love."

I hugged him tight. "You always know what to say."

He shrugged. "Of course. I'm the wiser one, remember?"

I hit his chest playfully. "I love you."

He kissed the top of my head. "I love you too."

Matt stood and helped me up.

I raked my hair back and fixed it into a high ponytail, then hugged Matt. "Be safe out there."

Matt tightened his hold. "I'll see you later." His voice carried a weight that wasn't there before.

The ache behind my throat became unbearable, and tears sprang from my eyes. Matt was my brother, and for the first time since we'd met, we'd be going in separate directions.

I looked up from his chest. "You'd better be there at the end of the day, or I'll kill you myself."

He dried my tears with his thumb and chuckled. "I'll be sure to make it, then."

I pulled him down to kiss his cheek, which was also wet with tears.

We both nodded in a silent understanding that we'd do everything possible to see each other again.

The pressure in my chest was excruciating, but I breathed in and out, just like Matt had taught me, until he disappeared from view.

God, please let him survive this.

I entered the tunnel to my left. David slouched against the wall, one foot resting casually against it, just beside my way out. His gaze was fixed on the floor.

"Hey." He shifted his weight and pushed himself upright, stepping closer. Taking my hand, he brushed his fingers against my cheek. His gaze darted restlessly, never landing for long. "Are you sure you want to go out there? You could stay here if you want."

I squeezed his hand. "I'm ready."

He curled over me and, in a swift move, pressed me to him. "Be safe out there."

His tone shook me to the core. I had never heard him this scared.

We were the only ones left, and the silence that surrounded us was almost deafening. I could hear his heart thumping against my ear.

"Please don't break my heart. Stay alive out there. Think before you act. Use all the training I put you through, and be the soldier I know you are."

I nodded. Words wouldn't form against the knot in my throat.

He grabbed my shoulders and leaned down so our eyes were level. "Fight for him and the baby you're carrying. Fight for your family and all we've lost. Don't lose control. Stay vigilant. Stay strong."

"I will." I ran my hands down his arms. "You too. You'd better make it because I'm not the only one who will be waiting for you when this is all over."

He shook his head.

I traveled back to our first real conversation when he told me there was no one left for him. No one who cared.

Things had changed. Now he had so many people by his side. I shuddered at the thought of losing him. A man who had become part of my soul.

I stroked his chin. "You need to remember there are others out there who care for you. That you matter. So fight and survive."

He closed his eyes and leaned into my hand. "I will." His hazel eyes searched mine. "Remember it too. I don't know what I'd do without you."

I nodded.

He did the same, then stepped away. "Have you eaten anything?"

I shifted my feet. The last thing I'd eaten was the beef jerky he and Matt shared at the first rest stop.

"I'll take that as a no." He removed something from his backpack. "Turn around."

He unzipped my pack. "Eat this when you get there. It's the sandwich I told you about. The one my mom used to prepare from my island. I made it for you with Rosa. It'll give you the strength you both need for what's ahead."

He had such a good heart. Sometimes I asked myself what I'd done to deserve having him in my life.

He tucked the package inside, then zipped it shut.

I smiled at him. "Thank you." I put my palm over his heart. "I'll see you out there. Okay?"

He seized my chin, and for a moment, I thought he'd kiss me. I kept my breathing even. This was David, and he'd never cross that line.

His hazel eyes were soft. "I can't go out there without getting this off my chest. I know you don't feel the same way, at least not the way I do, but..." His thumb grazed my lower lip in a fleeting, intimate caress. "I love you, Abigail Davis, and that will never change. No matter how many people I meet or if I ever grow to love them too, they will never come close to what you mean to me."

My world was rattled by his words, by the depth of his feelings for me, and it hurt. It seared my soul because I couldn't give him the love he deserved.

I wanted to tell him so much. That I loved him too. That he meant the world to me, just not in the same way. That I didn't want to lose him and would always be by his side no matter what. But I couldn't say the words.

He gave me the sweetest smile. "You don't have to say anything. I understand the kind of love you have for Davon because it's the same burning inside of me. We..." He shrugged. "We're just not meant to be. At least not in this lifetime." His smile faded.

With that, he moved away and opened the door.

I hesitated before stepping through it and into the darkness.

"Abi." His voice was but a whisper.

I turned to him.

He drew his eyebrows together. "Take care out there. I'll be watching over you."

My chest grew heavy. I couldn't stop thinking this might be the last time I saw him. I clutched my dad's watch, then threw myself into him, holding on tightly. "I love you too. You know I do."

He nodded, wrapped his arms around me, and buried his face in my neck. "This won't be the last time we see each other, so help me God. You and your baby will make it. Davon too. Push whatever you're thinking out of your mind, and be the strong woman I know you are."

His words reached the depths of my soul, taking away the last of my doubts. I would see my loved ones again. We would not lose this fight.

I stepped away. "See you soon."

He grinned, then nodded. "I'll see you tomorrow."

I left the basement of the apartment building. My heart pounded furiously as I rushed through an alley.

The safe location David had assigned for me was on the other side of the street. The building would give me a clear view of the plaza that surrounded the government center. My mission was to take down as many soldiers as possible from the plaza and clear the way for our troops.

If the helicopters were unable to destroy the government center, I'd cover for Davon's troops so they could set up bombs around the area.

If everything went as planned and the helicopters completed their mission, I was to meet with Davon's forces a block south and seize control of the train station.

David was the one in charge of taking down officers protecting the station so it was ready for the taking when we arrived.

Numerous NWG officers marched between me and my post.

Just cross the street, Abi. You're so close.

I hid behind a dumpster, and all the memories from my attack barged into me. I closed my eyes and pushed away the feeling of his hands on me. The unbearable pain he put me through as he took me against my will. The metallic taste of his blood as I slit his jugular. No matter how much time had passed or how I'd moved on with my life, being here was like a strike to my gut.

I took three deep breaths until my heartbeat slowed. He was dead. I killed him.

I hugged the wall and took tentative steps until I reached the street.

The troop was about a block away already. It was now or never.

I dashed across without a glance back, then pressed my back against the side of the building.

You made it. Just a few feet, and you'll reach the door.

It was an office building. According to Constantine's and Joe's intel, due to renovations, it was empty.

I went to the back door and pushed. It didn't budge.

My stomach churned. Wasn't it supposed to be unlocked?

Fuck. This can't be happening.

Davon had showed me the basics of picking locks, but the smallest thing I had was my pocketknife. I pressed it inside, holding my ear close. Two clicks, and I'd be in. I just needed to push the pins down.

Click.

I let out a breath. Now for the other one.

I glanced over my shoulder.

Shit.

Footsteps were fast approaching. I attempted to hold the knife steady, but my hands shook.

Just one more click, Abi. You can do this.

I didn't dare look back. The shuffling coming from the street became clearer. Stronger.

A bead of sweat slipped down my face and onto my chin. I could almost hear my heart thumping against my chest.

"Hold it there!" an officer yelled.

I froze. The weight of the world crashed over me. I was done for.

I was about to stand when another voice called from farther away. "Over there! They went that way!"

"Damn rebels. You two, follow Sanders. Phillips, come with me."

It had to be Constantine's people.

They had our positions, so they'd cover for us once we entered the city.

I slumped against the door and closed my eyes. Tears welled against my eyelids.

God.

I blinked twice and straightened, then took a calming breath and brought my ear to the lock.

Click.

I crossed the threshold and closed the door behind me.

Gun cocked, I turned on my flashlight and started up the stairs. After twenty floors, I'd reach the room.

The dark stairwell seemed endless. The minutes passed, and the echo of my footsteps was the only sound across the empty space.

Five more flights, and I'd reach my floor.

My lungs hurt, and my legs were killing me, but I'd made it.

Office 232. I closed the door and slid to the floor.

After drinking enough water to replenish the hellish climb up here, I unwrapped the sandwich David had given me in the tunnels. If I remembered right, it was a *tripleta*. A sandwich his mother made that was very popular in their homeland. He told me it was one of the few things he remembered from before the regime. By God, it looked good.

I took a bite and moaned as the rich flavor of mayonnaise mixed with tender meat melted in my mouth.

I patted my belly. "Enjoy, Lizzie. Today we rest. Tomorrow all hell breaks loose. We need to be strong."

Chapter 29

Davon

May 28, 2214

"Peter, once inside, go straight to the prison, and take control of it. Medics will go with you to care for the prisoners. If any of them insist on fighting with us, arm them. We need as many soldiers as possible."

Peter nodded. "Understood."

Once the day broke, I called a meeting to make sure everyone knew their tasks before the battle started.

About a dozen PRF officials surrounded me.

"Katherine?" I said.

Mathews and Mark parted to make way for her.

I straightened. "Your mission is to continue west and gain control of the western outskirts. Stay there, and secure the area."

Katherine nodded. "It will be done, sir."

The strategy was to take control of each area of the city as we moved south. Half the troops would stay in Promissa, and once the government center was destroyed, the other half would move into Electi.

The meeting ended fast, and everyone retook their positions.

Hours passed. Still no signal.

If Constantine's attack was compromised, then it was all over.

I loosened my hair, then slicked it back into a half ponytail. What the fuck could have happened? A headache was threatening to hit me, but then I saw Sarah.

She was eating a beef jerky next to Nina, who tapped her tablet furiously. There was as much on her as there was on me.

I sat by Sarah. "Stay close to Mathews and me once we enter the city."

Sarah swallowed the last piece of her jerky and wiped her hands on her trousers. "I will. Do you know if your father will be in the government center?"

I raised an eyebrow. "He won't."

We didn't talk much, but she never asked about my father.

Constantine had been watching the government center for a couple of weeks now, and there was no sign of Father. Whether as a security measure or to keep an eye on Mom, he was inside Electi.

"What do you intend to do with your father once you find him?" she asked.

A slight chill ran through me. Something about the way she asked didn't seem right.

I shifted to face her. "You know that's confidential, Sarah."

Sarah was not part of the council, and this information was kept from the citizens to ensure the mission went off without a hitch. We still didn't know who the spy was and couldn't be too careful.

As for Father, Connor wanted to keep him alive as a bargaining chip and to ensure he'd sign his surrender. This was something he'd decided a long time ago way before Deb was taken hostage. I was sure he wouldn't cooperate, but Connor was set on trying to get him to, and I would honor his wishes. Also, he said death was too fast for him, too easy. On that, we agreed.

Sarah picked up a rock and threw it, then lifted her chin toward the city. "He should die for all he's done, as should all of the elites for all I care. He and his people are too dangerous to be kept alive."

The finality of her words sent a shiver down my spine. She'd kill everyone? This was why Peter had talked to me last night. These were the people we needed to keep under control. She had suffered immense losses, and her child was still missing, but that didn't give her the right to attack the innocent. That would make her just like Father.

She put her hand on her vest pocket, her gaze on the horizon. "And Electi too. Their city must be destroyed."

Long gone was her sweet, passive voice. This woman was set on vengeance.

I frowned. Electi? We aimed to protect the city and wouldn't endanger its resources in any way.

I needed to do something about Sarah once we went in. There was no way I would let her inside Electi.

A shock wave hit us, then blasts erupted around the city, shaking the earth. We stood. Smoke rose throughout Promissa.

The signal.

"It's time!" Sarah ran to get her weapons.

Nina came to my side. "Joe and I are in!"

She hit the screen, and Connor's face appeared.

My breath hitched. A final act of rebellion from the man who had been not just my general but my mentor and my family. "Is it transmitting?"

Nina smiled at me. "It is! All around the city."

My body vibrated with something new—a euphoria I hadn't felt in a long time. We'd hacked their system. Our people would see their general.

I shifted, unable to stay still. Once the video was over, it was my turn.

I stood guard, my senses heightened. "Now we wait."

War is about to start.

I pressed the trigger mechanism.

The distant rumble indicated our bunkers were no more. A huge void grew within me when black plumes traveled into the heavens, turning the clear skies into a dark, dreary reminder that all we'd built was gone.

I closed my eyes, took a moment to let go of that past, and breathed deeply. Today we'd start building our new future.

Abi's face came to mind. *I'm coming.*

The comms crackled to life.

Nina packed her tablet. "Comms are up."

I pressed my comms. "Falcon to Iron Eagle. Do you copy?"

Nothing. My stomach turned. We needed them to enter.

"Falcon to Iron Eagle. Do you copy?"

"Take cover! We're coming in hot!" Her voice was followed by the hissing sound of not one but multiple missiles.

"Everyone, down!" I said through the shared channel.

The ground shook, and I almost lost my footing.

Peter grabbed my arm. "You all right?"

I nodded. This was it.

"Soldiers! Ready yourselves for battle. Time to fuck up these sons of bitches!"

The roar of the army swept through the perimeter of the city, a call for war that renewed my courage.

A wall of fire and smoke rose before our eyes, with clear areas for our troops to pass through, a strategy Sinclair had devised.

With the entrance clear, we rushed inside our city and into the unknown.

Chapter 30

Abi

May 28, 2214

The silence was unbearable. I was positioned, sniper at the ready, facing the government center plaza. Not many elites were coming in or out.

I cracked my neck. Dawn had hit four hours ago and still nothing.

I had a feeling Constantine had pushed the time in case we ran into trouble. Or maybe something had happened. My heart stammered as I thought of all the people I loved who were out there. Being in the dark was driving me mad with worry.

I shook my head. *Focus, Abi. They're okay.*

I rolled my shoulders back. When I was about to position my face to my scope, it hit me. It was as if a wall of air slammed into the building, reverberating around me a second before the explosions started. The roar echoed across the city like a monster. The crack of glass and the rumble of the structures as they collapsed were enough to shake me to the core. The ground shook beneath me for a moment before everything settled and chaos erupted.

My heart thundered. I tried to focus against the screams that filled the streets below.

People ran through them, and hundreds of NWG soldiers burst into the city.

Seconds later, the huge screen by the government plaza crackled to life. Connor's face popped up.

The pain of his loss resurfaced. I'd seen the video before, but in this moment, it was gut-wrenching. He died before he could see this day, and I wished it could have been different.

"Citizens of Promissa. My name is Connor Harris, general of the People's Revolutionary Front. Today I speak to you as another citizen of Promissa, one who, like you, has lost everything to this regime. The day of retribution is here. Today we push away our fears and free our homeland. We take up our weapons and make our oppressors face justice. The New World Government has made us prisoners inside our own city under the pretext that resources were scarce. These are all lies."

The frame changed, showing visuals from the Electi Entertainment District. Their cars. Lakes and parks. Restaurants and schools. A visual of a concert at night, of the fountains and plazas that covered the city. Videos of the opulent mansions and luxury apartment buildings.

Connor came back into view. "We've been fighting in silence against the regime for a decade. Ten years in which we've lost hundreds of our people who defended our cause. But we won't back down. Our army is already inside the city. We've just taken down multiple facilities made to maintain an enhanced army they built from our own children."

The feed showed the video the drones had taken after Janus's attack, the one Nina shared with the council. Elites by the plaza held their hands over their mouths in shock.

"We are many, but we invite you to join us. If you're capable of fighting, grab whatever you can, and fight with us. Our soldiers will march with you and arm you if necessary. If you can't fight, lock your doors, and stay inside. War is about to start."

The screen crackled and shut off.

My chest swelled at his words but with something new—hope. This was our time. Our moment. And nothing would stop us now.

I turned toward a distant rumble from the north.

The bunkers.

I held a palm over my heart and let out a huge exhale. Davon had done it. Soon the rest of the army and the choppers would enter the city.

I shifted back into position.

NWG soldiers went into formation around the plaza, weapons at the ready.

A commotion from the west caught my attention. Armed citizens poured into the street, firing at the officers who tried to subdue them. People in black uniforms marched with them.

Constantine's army.

I tightened my muscles in readiness. This was our moment.

The enemy started shooting them down.

I settled my raging heart and fixed my scope. The piercing snap from my sniper rifle cut through the silence as I took down the first officer. A direct hit to the head.

Energy surged within me as he went down, but then a hollowness swallowed me. His blood mixed with that of a citizen he'd taken down, staining the pristine marble floor of the plaza.

Why did it have to come to this?

I exhaled.

You need to go on.

One down, dozens more to go. Without hesitation, I tracked my next target and breathed out.

Crack.

I couldn't dwell on the lives I was taking. This was war, and if I didn't act, they'd massacre my people.

I'd taken down about twenty soldiers, then my heart stopped.

A wall of reapers rampaged into the streets. They ripped the citizens apart, painting a gruesome canvas with their vicious attacks.

I swallowed down bile and tried to focus my scope, but it was in vain. They were too fast.

The hissing sound of a missile broke through the chaos and hit the reapers. Many died on the spot, but the rest continued as if nothing had happened.

Hundreds of black-clad people came from the alleys. With light armor, Constantine's soldiers fought like devils. They attacked in groups, their agility and speed aiding in taking the reapers down one after the other, while others took the wounded citizens away from harm and into buildings.

Nonetheless, many died. A single hit from a reaper was enough to rip a body apart, especially if it was unarmored. Bodies flew across the square, lying in odd positions across the ground. Some tried to run to no avail. Their guttural screams as they were torn apart made my stomach churn. I turned away from the sniper and retched, then wiped my mouth with my sleeve and retook my aim.

I swallowed hard. If the rest of the PRF army didn't arrive soon, we'd lose this war.

A rapid succession of fire came from the west. I bowed over the scope as troops of PRF soldiers came into view. Those hidden in the tunnels had emerged.

I dropped my head over my rifle. *Thank you, God.*

A high-pitched sound pierced the air, and a jet passed beyond my field of vision. Two more followed.

My stomach plummeted. *The choppers.*

I took a deep breath and tried to stay positive. If one made it, it would be enough.

I'd already changed magazines twice and counted thirty officers down. I slammed in a new mag, released the bolt, and kept firing, but I was running low and needed to save the rest, just in case.

I secured the sniper rifle to my back. It was time.

I grabbed my gear and bolted down the stairs.

Outside, it was chaos. PRF and NWG soldiers clashed in the streets, gunfire echoing all around me.

"Grenade!"

Someone shoved me back inside the building. A heavy body pressed me against a wall.

Boom!

The building groaned.

I pushed, then recognized who had saved me. "Jonathan?"

He grabbed my arms. "Abi? Are you okay?"

I nodded, then noticed blood running down the side of his uniform. It came from his shoulder. "You're hurt!"

He waved my hand away. "It's okay. It was a clean shot, went right through."

"But..." I tried to check it, but he stepped away.

He crouched, and when his gaze locked with mine, he smiled. His green eyes held me as he shook his head. "I'm all right. Let's get out there. There's a war to win."

I nodded, taking in a deep, calming breath. "Okay." I sneaked a glance at the street, then drew my khukuri and trench knife in an iron grip.

Following Jonathan into battle, I held my blades close. They'd been with me through it all, and today they'd taste the blood of my enemies and bathe in the glory of our victory.

May 28, 2214

Lucas sent another reaper flying into a building. The concrete cracked under its weight. He'd been instrumental in the battle, ramming his way first into it.

We wanted to save the reapers, but there were too many, and they were too strong. It couldn't be helped. Many would die.

"Take cover!" Lucas yelled from across the street.

A second later, a distant roar reached me. Three jets came into view. They tore through the skies toward us.

"Fuck, no!" Father had finished them in time. For a moment, the whole world seemed to stop, then something dropped from one.

My heart stopped. "Bombs!" I ran into an alleyway.

Soldiers dispersed, but the jets were too fast. Dozens of bombs fell onto our troops.

I radioed Mathews. "Everything okay?"

"We took cover in time." He paused. "But dozens died."

I exhaled. Sarah had made it.

I risked a look around the corner of the alley. Two jets continued north, and one turned to the southeast.

The choppers.

I pressed my comms.

"Falcon to Iron Eagle. Two jets are heading your way."

Her response was immediate. "We see them. The troops?"

I swallowed hard. "Many died. Don't know the numbers yet."

"We'll take them down," she said before a deafening boom reached us, then a resounding crash. "One down! Fuck!" Her comms died.

She needed our help. But who...?

I darted into the street. "Mark?"

He was close to me when the jets came in.

Soldiers started emerging from their hiding spots, but Mark was not with them.

"Mark!" A heaviness crashed through my chest. No. It couldn't be.

I searched through the rubble. Hundreds of PRF and NWG soldiers were gone. Their broken bodies covered the pavement in a sea of death and gore. It was sickening. Barbaric. The stench of bodily fluids and waste hit me, and I fought back nausea. So this was war.

"I'm here!"

I stumbled before doing another take around the street. "Mark?"

"Here." His voice was muffled.

I followed it and found Lucas. He was covering someone against a wall. His burnt skin was visible through the unarmored parts of his body, but he still stood. He straightened to reveal Mark. He was unscathed.

I gasped and ran to them.

If ever I had doubts about the humanity of these soldiers, today it was erased. Lucas had risked his life to protect Mark.

I grabbed Mark's shoulder. "Are you all right?"

Mark nodded, then darted his gaze to Lucas. "You saved me."

Lucas straightened. "It's my duty." He turned to me. "Awaiting orders, sir."

"You're burned." I shook my head. "You need a doctor."

There was no way he could fight like this.

Lucas rolled his shoulders back. "No need. It doesn't hurt, and it will heal. I can go on."

The burns were third degree. The skin on his arms was peeling off, and his bones were almost exposed. Yet he was talking as if nothing had happened. What the fuck had Father created?

I nodded, my mouth dry, then faced Mark. "Get to a safe location, and set up the antiaircraft artillery. We need to help the choppers."

Mark pressed his comms. "Everyone, follow Lucas and me. We need to take down those birds."

They ran off.

I touched my headset. "Peter, a jet is moving north. Stay alert."

"Copy that. We secured the prison. Lisa isn't here, and Anna...she's in bad shape. The soldiers too."

I dug my fingers into my right palm to the point of pain. "Secure the prison, and keep everyone safe. He must have her in the facilities inside Electi. Await further orders."

Peter sighed across the radio. "Understood. Keep me posted, and remember what we talked about."

Protecting the elites. I traced my right thumb across my ring. "I will."

Mathews's and my troops had been fighting for over an hour when I received a communication from Joe.

The reason why the signal took so long was because my father set up a system to ensure his most precious project was not harmed by any attack and Constantine's people couldn't get in. Frank was in the hospital as instructed in our last communication and was the only one who could help us get inside. Joe took him step by step to turn off the security system so the rebel cells could set up the bombs.

He was now back in the hospital, but it wouldn't be long until Father connected the dots.

I had to ensure Frank's safety. He'd done too much for us.

I left the building I was huddled in, then ran back into the melee, bathed in the blood of the enemy.

"Mathews?" I yelled. "Sarah?"

Not only were hundreds of soldiers engaged in battle, but smoke was everywhere. I dodged my way into an area filled with reapers who'd just been hit by our paralyzing agent.

Ugh.

A reaper slammed into my back and shoved me to the ground.

I tried to push him off, but nothing worked. He was too damn strong.

I caught his knife as he was about to slash my throat. Blood dripped from my hand as I fought to draw it away from my skin.

Was this it? Was this my last moment? Was I never going to see her again?

Abi's face flashed through my mind. I couldn't die. Not now. Not when I was about to have my own family.

Tears burned my eyes, but I pushed through the pain. I used strength I didn't know I had and heaved him off of me. He stumbled over a body. Sarah jumped onto him and buried a blade through his neck.

She helped me up. Her gray uniform was covered in dust and blood, but she appeared unharmed.

"I was looking for you." I panted, then pushed her to the right and kicked an oncoming reaper.

They were slower than usual but still moving. Once down, I pinned him to the ground and grabbed the lower edge of his helmet. I pulled up, then drove my elbow into his throat. He choked and, after a few seconds, passed out.

I took out my mace. We'd used all the weapons we could, but as expected, they'd prepared after the last attack. With their gas masks on, we had to shift to melee combat to break their helmets so the paralyzing agent would take effect. But they were still hard as fuck to take down. Even with our armor, each one of their hits was agony.

"Where's Mathews?"

She pointed to the right.

He was fighting a half-paralyzed reaper.

Another one ran toward him. In a flash, I made for the kill. My mace connected with her neck with a crunching sound, and as she lost her footing, I threw her down with a roundhouse kick. Brain matter sprayed over me as I shot my HK416. I was not losing Mathews. Not on my watch.

Mathews looked over his shoulder. "Thanks."

The reaper he'd been fighting was already unconscious. I looked around. The battle raged to the south, but our area was clear. Constantine's people were already taking the reapers away.

Mathews and Sarah faced me.

I rolled my shoulders back, then secured the mace by my side. "I'm going to the government plaza. Once you finish here, take the troops to the hospital. Make sure Frank Anderson is safe, then secure the building."

Mathews nodded. "Understood."

Sarah frowned. "But the deal was I'd go to Electi with you and Abi."

Her attitude rubbed me wrong. "This is an order. You are to take control of the hospital, and guard it."

"But..."

I gripped her shoulder. "Don't make me pull rank."

She wasn't wrong. We'd made a deal at the caverns, but at the risk of her losing it out there, I preferred to keep her away from Electi.

She hesitated but stayed with Mathews as I darted south. I needed to get to the government center. Sinclair was taking too long.

The last hour had passed in a blur as we fought our way to the government plaza, but the enemy seemed to multiply by the minute.

I smashed into a soldier, then cut his throat and grabbed his grenade launcher. I aimed it at an enemy troop that marched toward us and fired.

"Iron Eagle to Falcon." Sinclair's voice filtered in through my headset.

I dropped the launcher and exhaled. She was safe. "What's going on?"

"We took the second jet down but not before it eliminated two of ours. There's one jet..." The radio went silent.

What the fuck? "Sinclair, do you copy? I repeat. Do you copy?" My thunderous heart pounded in my ears, and I watched the skies.

A rush of wind hit the street. The choppers were here.

The buildings around us rumbled as two Liberty Enclave helicopters flew across the city and into the government center area. We were still about two blocks north.

"There's someone on our tail. We'll try to lose it, then go for the government center." Her voice was rushed.

"Roger that." My hands shook, but I focused on the task at hand.

We had to destroy that last jet.

I pressed the side of my helmet. "Mark, there's still one of those fuckers left. Are you in position?"

"I am. I'll get back to you once it's down." He ordered his soldiers to be at the ready before turning his comms off.

A sharp hissing sound crossed over me. I stumbled back into an alley and called Mark. "It's here."

The missing jet.

In the distance, the choppers climbed in altitude, then split. One went west, and the other headed east. They skimmed the buildings, making sharp turns, with the jet close on their tail.

I clenched my fists. The air was so thick it was choking me. We couldn't lose the helicopters. We couldn't lose Sinclair.

A sharp crack split the air, followed by a deafening roar that rattled my bones.

My headpiece crackled.

"It's coming down! Take cover!" Mark's voice was marked with excitement.

I hid behind some debris just as a jet crashed into a building a block south. It shook the ground. If we won, we'd have to rebuild because as it was, the city was in ruins.

"The fucker is down!" Mark whooped through the radio.

I couldn't suppress a smile. "I can see that. We move south."

"Copy that."

Cheers reached me before I cut the comms.

I sighed. One thing was for sure, if it wasn't for the attack in Halcyon, we'd be fucked. These three jets were the only ones we'd encountered so far and hopefully would be the last.

The government center was up ahead. I secured my firearm and mace and sprinted toward it, my heart screaming to get to Abi.

The clear thumping of our helicopters' propellers approached. The distinct hiss of a missile passed through the skies. A wave pushed me back. A huge blast shook the buildings around me, and smoke and debris filled the sky.

At last.

As dust and debris settled, the cracking sound of metal beams bending under the high temperatures of the fire reached me. Then another hiss.

Boom.

This second one tilted the government center's tower to the side. My breath bottled up in my chest as my father's floor collapsed to the ground. Half the building came down, and a jolt of energy shot through me.

We did it. My father's legacy was no more.

Alarms buzzed everywhere, the streets swarming with soldiers from both sides.

"Iron Eagle to Falcon. Mission complete." The rush in her voice was gone.

My chest expanded. Would we even be here without them? "Thank you for everything."

Sinclair's sigh reached me. "I gave you my word, and I'm glad I was here to fight by your side." She paused. "I received a disturbing message from my people."

Halcyon.

I clenched my jaw. "Is there anything we can do?"

"No, General, you have your own battle to win." Her voice dropped.

I frowned. "What happened?" From her tone, I feared the worst.

"Half of our troops were decimated. The train served as a mobile strike platform. They launched missiles that hit precise locations between Halcyon and the Liberty Enclave before our attack even started. Many of our incoming troops were taken out before they got to the city."

Fuck. My fingernails bit into my palms as I tightened my fists.

The radio crackled to life again. "The last report says we took down the NWG air base, but their jets are still airborne, and the soldiers aren't enough to fight the thousands of reapers Steele sent our way. They need all the help we can spare. I'm taking both helicopters and my troops. I'm sorry I can't do more." Her voice quivered.

A sudden cold hit me. This wasn't supposed to happen.

"Go. You've done more than enough." I watched her choppers as she turned east. "When this is all over, we'll meet again."

"Have you heard from them?" It was but a whisper.

David and Abi. I chose my next words with care. Leaving us broke her, especially with how much she cared about David.

"Still nothing." Not knowing about Abi and the others was drilling a hole through my chest, but I kept my tone steady. "They're strong. They'll make it."

Something must have happened to the comms because we should have been able to reach the rest of the army. I just hoped Joe would fix it soon because I was about to lose my shit.

All was silent for a moment, then her voice broke through. "Take care of them. I'll contact you soon."

After everything was over—win or lose—we'd meet again.

I closed my eyes. "Take care, Jules."

We were on our own.

"You too, Davon."

I stepped out of the alley and grabbed the hilt of my khukuri. My heart stammered. NWG soldiers fought by our side against the reapers. They still wore their white uniforms, but a black cloth hung from their arms and wrapped around their waists.

My chest expanded. Davis's men.

In the middle of the chaos, Abi moved like water, flowing and strong. Like a hurt beast, she slashed across her path. Vicious. Relentless.

I broke into a run, and without a word, I took her side. With a brief glance, we both fixed into a fighting stance and faced our enemies.

We moved as one, destroying our foes in a dance of gore and carnage. Our blades struck flesh, and with each hit, we reset, ready for the next. We sliced through reapers and soldiers until none remained standing but us and our people.

Mark's troop was instrumental in taking care of the reapers with their rocket launchers, and with Lucas by their side, they were unstoppable.

Jonathan's crew fought alongside Constantine's, tearing through the enemy ranks and taking down NWG officials by the dozens.

By nightfall, it was over. Battles raged in the distance, but we'd vanquished the majority of the enemy forces, and the government center and train station were ours.

I removed my helmet and pulled her into me. "Are you hurt?"

She took hers off, then shook her head. She stroked my cheek. "You?"

Warmth spread through my body, filling me with the strength I needed to move forward. "I'm okay. Did Matt get through the tunnels?"

"Last time I saw him, he disappeared in the distance with his troops, but ever since comms came on, I haven't heard anything from him or David." She grabbed my arm. "But we knew this could happen. Maybe Jordan set up something to scramble comms."

Matt could be hurt or worse. I pressed my palm to my chest. I couldn't lose him.

I shook my head.

No. This kind of thinking was dangerous. It could break me. We'd predicted this, so the only option was to go ahead with the plan.

I sighed. "Ready to face whatever awaits us out there?"

War had already begun in Electi. Even before the signal went off, our people started working on their mission. Whether they were successful or not was a question that would only be answered once inside.

She stood next to me, staring at the darkness between Promissa and Electi. "Do you think he'll be waiting for us?"

A chill ran through me. "He will."

He'd face us. I was sure he had a plan.

Abi's intense gaze shifted to the blazing fire of the government center. The bastion of the NWG was no more. "Whatever he has planned, we'll overcome it. Today we break the regime."

Renewed hope ran through me, and I touched my headset. "Mark."

The comms buzzed. "General? Is that you? Comms seem off."

So it was as Abi thought. They seemed to be scrambling our comms now that we were closer to Electi.

"It's me. You're in charge of Promissa. Keep the perimeter."

Silence met me.

"Do you copy?"

White noise reached me for a moment, then his voice came through. "Copy that."

I glanced down at Abi. "Gather the troops. We go into Electi."

The smell of human waste and burnt flesh swept through me as we crossed the space between the plaza and the station. My boots crunched over the rubble, grinding through shards of glass and debris. A thick layer of dust settled over the white and gray uniforms that lay across the now crimson marble of the plaza. What once was a symbol of power for the NWG now served as a mausoleum for all the lost souls.

A tall black man donning the black uniform of the rebel cells stood in front of the train station, David by his side.

I clasped his hand. "General Davon Niles. Great to finally meet you."

His hold was strong. "Aleczander Constantine." He grinned. "I would have preferred to meet over some wine or whiskey." He shrugged. "But this is the hand we were dealt."

I liked him. Down to earth and to the point.

I lifted an eyebrow. "I know from a good source that Minister Niles has a wine cellar in his mansion. Maybe when this is all over, we can check it out ourselves."

Aleczander chuckled. "Sounds like a plan. And please call me Alec."

"You can call me Davon." I tilted my head toward Abi. "This is Abigail Davis, councilmember from the PRF."

Alec took her hand. "Great to meet you, Miss Davis."

"The pleasure is mine." Abi smiled.

"David?" Jonathan rushed between us, pressing both hands against David's chest.

Right, I'd seen them at the party, and Abi had told me about their relationship blossoming again.

David's lips parted, and he hugged Jonathan. "Thank God you're alive."

Jonathan winced.

David pulled away and scowled. He reached for Jonathan's shoulder, which had gauze wrapped tightly around it. "What happened to you?"

Jonathan waved his hand away. "It's nothing, Dave. The medic already saw to it."

Medics were all around the area, helping the injured. I told Jonathan he could stay, but he insisted on going with us into Electi. The doctor stitched it closed after clearing him. She said Jonathan was lucky.

David's gaze softened. He ran his hand down Jonathan's side where his uniform's dark stain ended. "It doesn't seem like nothing." He squeezed Jonathan's hip and pulled him closer.

Jonathan flushed. "I told you, I'm good. I got shot, but it was clear. It hurts, but I can go on."

David shifted his feet.

Jonathan's gaze flitted down David's body. "God. You're bleeding."

David took his hand. "I'm okay."

David's thigh was covered with bloody gauze.

I studied his face. David was alert and standing. He'd be okay.

Abi stepped forward, but I held her hand, then bent to whisper in her ear. "Let his boyfriend take care of the problem."

Abi's watery gaze met mine, and she nodded.

"You're obviously not okay." Jonathan wrinkled his brow. "Come on. I'll take you to a medic."

David shook his head, giving Jonathan a comforting smile. "Alec already took care of it."

Alec and David shared a look.

"He found me on the battlefield and took me to safety. Then cleaned it and stitched it up."

Jonathan studied Alec, then pressed his lips together and stretched his arm toward him. "Thank you for taking care of Dave. Name's Jonathan Miller. And you are?"

I raised an eyebrow at Abi. She shook her head and elbowed my side. This was turning into quite a scene. Jonathan obviously didn't know who he was talking to, and his jealousy permeated through his pores.

Alec smirked. "I'm Aleczander Constantine."

Jonathan's eyes widened, and he took a step back. "A pleasure to meet you, sir."

Alec nodded. "The pleasure is mine."

Jonathan brushed David's arm. "I have to go, but after all this is over, promise me you'll take care of that."

David tilted his head. "I will, with you by my side." He stroked Jonathan's cheek. "Be careful out there."

"I will." Jonathan went back to his troop.

Abi approached David. "Are you sure you're all right?"

David nodded. "I am."

Abi looked toward the wall that separated Promissa from Electi. "Have you heard from Matt?"

David shook his head.

I was done with this shit. I needed to reach Matt. I pressed the button on my headset. "Get me Joe."

There was a scrambled signal from Nina's side.

The response was immediate. "Joe here."

"What the fuck is happening to the comms?"

Tapping noises hit me.

"We're working on it, sir. It looks like they found a way to hack our network, but it's only in this area and Electi. Give me a few more minutes, and we'll have it back up."

My fingers twitched. This had better be fixed soon.

Abi touched my arm. "Be patient. Joe can do it."

I closed my eyes, focused on her touch, and squeezed her hand, letting the calm she gave me push back the darkness that threatened to swallow me whole.

There was a high-pitched buzz, then Joe's voice came through. "We did it, sir. Comms are back, but the network doesn't reach Electi. They must have their own security measures."

So we're in the dark.

I grunted. "Do you have visuals on the train tracks?"

Our drones were airborne, but their range only got halfway to Electi, not inside the city.

"I do. How can I help, sir?"

"Do you see enemy troops on the way here?"

We had control over the train, but soldiers could walk long distances, and they could be on their way.

"It's too dark to know for sure."

The battle had taken longer than expected, and because the government systems were down, the way into the city was cloaked in shadows.

"And our people, did they get the prize?" I held my breath for his answer.

Getting control over President Orville was one of the most important parts of our plan. Without him, things could get a lot more difficult.

"They did right before we lost the signal. And the others too. They're secure."

I bowed my head. "Good. What about the prisoners?"

We needed to get our people out of the Electi facilities. I owed it to Aoki and Peter and all those harmed by this initiative.

Matt was supposed to take control of Electi's side of the station, then send troops into the prison system inside the city.

"We're blind."

I huffed and raked my hair back. "Did you catch anything before comms went down? Do you at least know if our troops made it into the city?"

Joe took too long to answer.

I paced and pushed the button again. "Tell me!"

The comms buzzed to life. "No, sir. No communications came in, and the drones can't reach that area. I'm sorry."

I had to trust that Peter's soldiers would aid us once inside. We hadn't been able to communicate with them, but Peter had left orders and trusted them completely. With them, we might have a better chance of taking down my father.

I squared my shoulders. There was no time. "Turn the system on, and get us halfway through. We'll walk the rest of the way into Electi. Once we're off the train, turn it back, and get the others."

"Got it. Systems are up."

Power hummed around us, and the train came to life.

I stood on a platform and faced my troops. "Everyone, in. We have a city to take."

Chapter 32

Abi

May 28, 2214

The air seemed thicker than usual inside the train. Our forces were crammed into the space. The brakes shrieked as the train came to a stop just as we crossed the wall.

I breathed evenly, Davon holding my back against his chest.

His breath caressed my neck. "Breathe with me, baby. Everything will be okay."

I let the back of my head fall onto his chest.

He kissed my temple, then smiled. "It will all be over soon."

I closed my eyes. David and Alec had stayed behind to make sure the place was secure. Considering David's condition, it was for the best.

Davon lowered his arm to my belly. "Stay by my side," he whispered near my ear.

A shiver ran down my spine, and I focused on what lay ahead.

Davon put his helmet on. "Helmets on, weapons out and loaded. We don't know what awaits us out there."

We followed suit, and the doors opened.

A black-clad soldier, one of Constantine's, was the first to go out, two hunting dogs with him. He crouched. "Cerberus. Athena. Go ahead. You know what to do."

The two golden-haired dogs bounded into the valley, their muscular forms as large as Aspen's. Their black snouts stretched forward with purpose, ears perked high in alert.

I followed Davon out.

He pulled down his night-vision goggles. "Did you train them?"

The man shook his head. "Alec did. He had them when it all started."

Davon stood beside him. "Are they part of Halcyon's canine special unit?"

The soldier nodded. "These Belgian Malinois specialize in finding mines. We'll know in a few if the valley is clear."

I wrapped my arms around myself. Mines.

A couple of minutes passed until Davon pulled his goggles up. "He's coming back alone."

Cerberus grunted and stared at where Athena sat about half a kilometer away.

"There are mines out there." The soldier took out a whistle and called Athena back.

Davon faced our forces. "Soldiers with RPGs and grenade launchers will arrive on the next train. When they do, meet us in Electi, and finish the NWG troops inside the city. Tonight we end this regime. But remember, no matter our rage and our thirst for revenge, we will not harm the innocent. Most elites were lied to, just like us. We won't repeat what they did to us. If we learn to live together in harmony, we all win."

It was the way to go. After living in Electi for three months, I found most people didn't have a clue of what was happening outside. Like us, they'd been educated to believe what the NWG said and encouraged not to ask any questions. They didn't deserve to die for what the government did. For what they created.

Davon left about a hundred soldiers under the supervision of Constantine's man and Jonathan. They would stay by the train tracks to alert the next group about the mines and the mission objective.

The train left with a low hum.

"Stay close to the rails." Davon walked out front.

Hundreds of soldiers followed us in silence.

I shivered as darkness met us. What would be waiting for us out there?

Joe confirmed the hostages were secure—the councilmembers of the NWG. Now we needed to infiltrate the city and find Jordan. If we got to him, it would all be over.

Bile rose in my throat at the thought of facing Jordan again, just like when I was in Electi. At the end of our time there, it had become unbearable to be in his presence. A hate that was almost physical.

I lost my footing when an earthquake hit us.

Davon grasped my arm as I was about to stumble to the ground.

"The tunnels," was all he said before shouting orders.

"We're under attack." He pointed at the soldier with the dogs. "Take half the soldiers north. You'll see a compound with two buildings built like a prison. Wait for us there, then take them down, and free our people." He touched his helmet. "Jonathan?" His gaze shifted across the field. "Did the rest of the soldiers make it?"

Davon nodded. "Good. Make haste, but once you're close, keep your distance. If anything goes wrong, wait till the coast is clear to follow." He closed his eyes. "Be safe."

A silent boom made the ground shake again.

Davon faced the soldiers. "They've collapsed the tunnels, and our people need us now more than ever. The time has come to take our freedom back. We'll get our people out and find the man who took everything from us—Minister Jordan Niles. Half of you will go to the prison facility up north. The rest, follow me. Be ready for battle."

Jordan had made his move, but we were ready. Soon we'd find out who was stronger—the ruthless leader of the New World Government or his unwilling apprentice, the general of the People's Revolutionary Front.

I gripped the handle of my khukuri and followed my general, ready to face whatever Jordan had in store for us. Whatever it took, today we'd take it all back.

The perimeter of the city was about fifty feet away. The power went out, and a shroud of darkness met us. We moved forward, knowing it was only a matter of time before we were hit by whatever Jordan had planned.

Guns cocked all around us the moment we entered Electi's train station. All lights were turned on. In the center of it all was him, donning the black uniform of the NWG high ranks. A five-star insignia rested on his collar, and the NWG emblem took up the center of his hat.

My stomach roiled. Jordan.

Four enhanced soldiers loomed to his right and left. Behind him, dozens stood guard.

A line of PRF soldiers kneeled in front of Jordan, with a beaten man stooped by his feet.

I gasped.

His shoulders slumped forward. His golden curls hung over his face, and thick drops of blood fell from his hair onto the polished marble floors. A huge gash marred the right side of his temple.

No.

I stepped forward. "Matt."

His green eyes met mine. His nose bled, and his right eye was swollen shut with a purple bruise around it.

Jordan forced him down with the butt of his gun. The thud brought a pained groan from my brother.

My chest caved in, and I dug my nails into my palms, controlling the urge to run to him. To get him away from that monster.

Jordan's sinister laugh crawled under my skin, sending a shiver through my body.

"Oh. If it isn't my prodigal son and his girlfriend. You can't imagine the joy it brings me to welcome you back." His tone was bathed in sarcasm. His suave voice would make anyone back away in fear. "Now, if you please, put your weapons down."

I stood still.

There was no escape, and we were outnumbered. About fifty soldiers came with us to the station, and for each, two NWG soldiers stood strong.

Jordan shot the two soldiers to Matt's right, then cocked his gun and aimed it at Matt's head. "I said, drop your weapons."

We did so.

"Gaby. Oh, sorry. Abigail. Did you get the video I sent you?" He shrugged, a half smile curving his lips. "You see, I'm a good father-in-law and knew you'd appreciate the message. Your uncle fought hard before his body gave up, but I'm glad I could give you something to remember him by."

I stepped forward. By God, I would rip that smile off his face if it was the last thing I did.

Davon held me back. "Don't let him bully you."

My blood boiled at the memory of Uncle Scott's battered body hanging from that post. I clenched my fists.

Davon whispered, "You're giving him what he wants."

"Tsk tsk. Aren't you the brave one? Learn your place, little one. You're in my turf now." Jordan pointed the gun at my face. "Arms up."

NWG soldiers stripped us of the rest of our weapons and helmets, then tied our wrists.

I hoped to hell Davon's earpiece was still in place. It was hidden behind his ear, and before getting out of the train, I'd seen him activate it. It was made as a precaution, and all ranked officers had them. He'd predicted something like this could happen.

I shivered when one soldier forced his hand inside my waistline, pressing Jacob's trench knife against me. "Do as we say." He patted the knife but left it there. "All clear."

I wanted to look at Davon but stayed as still as possible. These had to be Peter's men. Still, about fifty soldiers stood behind Jordan.

Jordan sneered. "You may have taken Promissa, but you can't have Electi. I'll let you have this small victory, but it's only a matter of time before we put you back where you belong. Only this time your little rebellion dies with you."

Jordan yanked Matt's hair, jerking his body sideways so he'd face him.

Matt's nostrils flared, and his breathing was hard.

My heart shattered at seeing him this broken. His usual smile was twisted into a grimace, and the gleam in his eyes was drowned by a storm.

"What a family of troublemakers. The audacity of your mother to take to the streets surprised me. But she's learned her lesson, hasn't she?"

Matt's steely glare promised revenge.

Jordan stretched his arm toward us, gun dead set on us. "How the fuck did you get Frank on your side? And getting rid of the supplement facilities?" He sneered, but his eyes gleamed. "Good move on your part, son."

Was he proud?

Matt struggled against Jordan's hold, eyes darting to us now and again.

Jordan hit him again, blood now dripping from Matt's temple to the floor. He bared his teeth. "You're trash, Anderson."

Jordan's gaze shifted from Matt to us. It wasn't possible for his eyes to darken further, but in this moment, I could sense a storm brewing inside them. I'd seen it before in his study when I told him Deb was the leader of the rebellion. When she escaped from his grasp with his child.

My whole body vibrated with rage and something else—fear. Fear at what this man could do to my friend, who was at his mercy.

"How the fuck did you forgive him? Did you know he's the one who convinced me to carry out the genetic projects?" He laughed maniacally. "Fuck. This whole regime is based on his ideas. His intellect. And you fucking forgave him!" He was yelling now.

He drove his knee into Matt's face. "Fucking traitor."

With his hands tied back, Matt fell to the floor.

I fought against my ties. My wrists burned. I had to save him, but a soldier held me back.

Matt's battered face no longer looked human.

"Is this why he took your side? Did he miss his dear son?" He kicked him again, this time in his stomach, and Matt spit blood. "Well, after today, he'll no longer have a reason to defy me. I'll take away what he treasures most and leave him with nothing to fight for." He cocked his weapon and shot Matt's shoulder, the same one he'd fought for so long to recover.

Matt's piercing scream boomed through the empty station, tearing through my soul.

"It's time for you to learn your lesson." He stepped on Matt's face, moving it to the side so their eyes met. "Your corpse will be reunited with Lisa's in no time, and I'll bring Frank to you so he can bear witness to my power." He stepped away. "Soldiers, you can have all the fun you want with this one."

Some soldiers stood in watch, but about a dozen sneered and made their way to my friend.

Tears slid down my cheeks when the first blow landed on Matt. I dared to look back at Davon.

Veins popped out in his temple, and his chest moved up and down firmly. Contained rage threatened against his intense gaze. He was hanging by a thread.

Jordan's voice rose above the thuds and Matt's anguished cries. "Lisa's ideas are like a plague that needs to be eradicated. She'll pay for poisoning my people. Poor Suzanne fell victim to her. It's a shame she'll die as a nobody for defending your people, while Peter died a hero." His tone sobered when he said Peter's name.

I froze. He still didn't know Peter betrayed him, but Suzanne... God. She must have been captured with Lisa.

"Bring them." Jordan holstered his gun and walked away.

Reapers surrounded him.

The soldiers grouped around Matt. Thuds and grunts echoed from where he lay.

"No!" I screamed, struggling against my captor's hold.

They'd kill him.

Davon pushed a soldier with his shoulder and charged through the group, using only his body as a weapon.

When he was about to reach Matt, the cold barrel of a gun pressed against my temple.

"One more step, and she dies."

I gasped and stopped struggling.

Davon went still as a rock. It took three soldiers to move him away.

"Stay strong, brother." Davon staggered toward me as soldiers forced him to comply.

Matt nodded.

One kicked his ribs. "Time to pay for your friend's little outburst."

Matt's life was now in Jonathan's hands, and I prayed his troop made it before it was too late.

The gun shoved against my back. "Move!"

I followed Jordan.

We walked two blocks to what could only be the holding facility for Promissa citizens. It was a gray building with no windows. No markings. Nothing to hint at what lay inside.

How many injustices had been done within those walls? How many lives lost? How many souls broken beyond repair?

"I have a surprise for you." Jordan faced one of his reapers. "Get Ms. Leslie Gibson. Let her know her friends are here and to bring us Lisa Johnson."

"Tammy." Davon growled beside me.

My blood thickened at the mention of her name.

A couple of minutes later, Leslie came out, her long hair hanging loose and a sinister smile plastered on her face. "Oh, it's you! I was quite impressed you made it." She held a machine gun to Lisa's back.

I inched forward, my fists itching to break that smile off her face. "I'm going to fucking kill you, bitch."

Leslie forced Lisa to kneel.

Lisa's eyes were sunken, her skin ashen, just like me all those years ago. I shuddered at the memories. At the living hell I went through during those three years. No one deserved to live this way.

Jordan's steps were measured, his gun still secured at his side. He bowed and gripped Lisa's chin, forcing her to look at him. Her spit hit his eye.

His back slap reverberated through the air, reaching us where we stood just a few feet away. Lisa's crumpled form lay sideways.

"Get up!" Leslie kicked Lisa. "Get up, you fucking bitch!"

"Leave her!" I snapped.

She kicked Lisa's ribs, then stormed toward us. "And what are you going to do about it?"

I tightened my muscles. "I'll make you pay for them both."

She raised her eyebrows. "Oh!" She chuckled. "This is precious. Did you lose your precious little dog?" She pouted. "Jimmy was always following you around, and look where that got him."

My ties snapped.

"Now!" the soldier behind me yelled before giving me back my weapons.

The others followed.

In a matter of seconds, chaos erupted.

I looked toward Jordan. Four NWG soldiers stood behind him and pushed syringes into the enhanced soldiers who stood by his side. The reapers crashed to the ground before they could respond.

Davon dashed to his father, gripping his khukuri.

Adrenaline surged through me. I grabbed my revolver and headed straight for Leslie.

She raised her machine gun, but I dodged and slammed into her with my shoulder, sending her stumbling.

She dropped her firearm. I kicked it away, then shot both her knees.

Her guttural scream cut through the raging battle.

I sat on her chest, pinning her arms beneath my legs.

Her blue eyes bulged. She fought my hold, crying desperately, but she wasn't getting away.

An image of Maria's battered body came back to me, and I drew my trench knife.

I slashed Leslie's right cheek. "This is for Maria."

Jimmy's sweet smile flashed through my mind.

"And this is for Jimmy."

Her cries were music to my ears as I cut her other cheek. Tears flowed down her face, mixing with the blood that poured from the deep gashes I'd carved.

I sliced her obliques. "This is for Carlos." Her hot blood wet my uniform as I cut the other side. "And this is for Richard."

"Please." She howled. "Please stop!"

I kept her gaze and dragged the blade from the top of her chest to her navel. Deep enough that it would hurt, not kill.

Her breaths were short, her voice muffled by her sobs. "I can tell you whatever you want. Just let me live."

Smiling, I held the knife to her throat and bent so my face was inches from hers. I could taste her fear the moment I pressed down enough to open her skin. "There's nothing you can say that will make me stop. You die now."

She gurgled. "But it wasn't just—"

I slit her throat.

"No more will die by your hands."

Her eyes dulled.

I smirked. "See you in hell."

A dark cloak lifted from me the moment her body went limp.

I wiped the blade on my uniform and looked around.

Davon and about a dozen PRF soldiers fought a group of men who encircled Lisa and Jordan. Davon grunted as one of them sliced his face, leaving a gash that ran down his left eye. Blood splattered the left side of his armor.

"Davon!" I cried.

Davon growled, then slashed his way to his father, gutting every soldier who dared get in his way.

I sprinted to Lisa the moment there was an opening. She looked at me and pushed herself to her knees. She headbutted Jordan's crotch.

Jordan staggered back, then turned his weapon toward me. Davon cut through his arm, eliciting a pained grunt from him, before using his weight to throw him to the ground. He placed his khukuri against his neck.

Davon snarled. "Bet you never imagined I'd use your precious gift against you."

The defectors from the NWG turned their firearms against their own.

The soldier who had spoken to me moved forward, aiming his gun at one of the NWG soldiers who had been protecting Jordan. "Stand down." He shook his head. "It's over."

I crouched over Lisa. "Are you okay?"

She nodded, then looked to the west. The sound of many footsteps came from the shadows. Our troops pointed their guns at the rest of the NWG troops, friends and foes. It was a standoff.

Constantine's man was up front, his dogs barking at the enemy.

I gestured toward Peter's men. "They're with us."

He nodded. "Do you have everything under control?"

I looked around. Davon had his father pinned to the ground, and the rest of the officers had their hands up.

"I think so."

"Then we go into the prison."

His troops stormed inside. Rapid fire erupted from within, and alarms rang all around us.

I helped Lisa up. "It's okay. You're safe now."

She hugged me. Her body was so thin that it seemed like I was holding a child. The tension eased from me but then came bounding back when I remembered Matt.

"Go with them. They'll take care of you." I let the soldiers take her.

I aimed my gun at Jordan. "You've lost. We took the president hostage, and every member of the council has been detained except for one." I shrugged. "Our soldiers shot the minister of labor down when he attempted to kill one of ours."

His face paled, and beads of sweat fell from his forehead. "Impossible. How?"

Davon smirked. "Peter."

Jordan's eyes widened in shock. "But..."

"He's been with us since the beginning, covering our tracks long before we even knew of his true allegiance. It wasn't until I came back to Electi that he told me." Davon pushed the blade down.

Jordan flinched as the sharp edge cut through his skin.

There was fear in his eyes, and I savored every moment of it. I wanted him to suffer. I wanted him to hurt for all he'd put Davon through.

Davon bared his teeth. "That's what happens when you force people to fight for you through fear."

Jordan's eyes glazed with fear. "Son." His voice trembled. "Please."

Blood seeped onto Davon's blade. "I'm going to ask a question, and you will answer me truthfully."

Jordan swallowed hard.

"Is Mom alive?"

Pain etched his father's eyes. "I'd never hurt her. She's at home, safe."

I sighed in relief. Rebecca was alive.

Davon removed the blade from his neck and grabbed hold of his black uniform. The silver chains of his epaulets clinked at the force of the pull. "Take me to her."

Chapter 33

Davon

May 28, 2214

I disarmed my father, then tied his hands behind his back.

"Watch him for a moment," I ordered one of my soldiers and went to look for a medic or someone to help me with the stabbing pain behind my left eye.

I wiped it and blinked hard. Fuck. I couldn't see shit. It was all cloudy and unfocused.

Abi came over with a piece of cloth. "A medic gave me this. Your eye..." She frowned. "It doesn't look good."

"What do you mean?"

She pointed her flashlight at it.

I winced and covered it.

"Sorry. It looks..." She shook her head. "There's too much blood, and I can't quite see it. There's something..." She waved her hand. "It doesn't matter. Just crouch for me so I can tie this."

She wrapped the cloth over my eye and secured it. "All done." She cupped my cheek.

I drew my gun at a noise that came from the shadows.

"General." Jonathan saluted. "As ordered, the troops went into the city and are fighting their way in as we speak."

"Good." I nodded, then looked behind him. I felt elated, but I couldn't keep Matt off my mind. Had they made it in time? "Captain, did you find...?"

My heart raced as two soldiers came into the light. Matt limped between them, gauze tightly wrapped around his shoulder and his leg at an odd angle.

I ran to him, but Abi got there first.

She kissed his hand. "Thank God."

One of his eyes was swollen, but the other smiled toward her. "I'll be okay." He winked at me. "What do you think about this new look? It took a lot of hard work." He studied my face. His eyes flickered with concern before he shook his head. "You fucker. You just had to get a pirate look. How am I supposed to compete with that?"

He coughed up blood, and I furrowed my brow. How the hell could he joke at a moment like this?

"Ease up. You look like you're seeing a dead man." He looked over my shoulder into the raging fires and screams that swallowed Electi. "We'll have the city in no time."

Lisa barged into Matt and touched his chin.

"Mom?" A tear slid down his cheek. His arm trembled, but he grabbed her shoulder and drew her to him. "God, I thought I'd lost you."

"I'm here." She pulled away. "We need to get you to a hospital." She checked him over, then went to Father and kicked his ribs. "What the fuck did you do to my son?"

Unable to move, he sneered her way. "He deserved much worse, just like you."

Lisa stood motionless, her breathing hard. "You'll soon get to see what it means to lose everything." She turned toward the allied soldiers. "Do you have a van? A way to get to the medical center?"

An NWG soldier stepped up. "We do, ma'am." He faced another of his group. "Simmons, take five soldiers, and get Dr. Johnson and her son to the hospital ASAP."

I watched the city, which had devolved into chaos. "Lisa, give me a moment. It's dangerous for you to go out there in an enemy van."

They could get shot or worse.

I pressed my earpiece. "Joe. Joe. Do you copy?"

Abi came to my side, but I shook my head. Her shoulders dropped.

"Joe. Do you copy?"

My earpiece crackled to life. "Joe here. Comms are up, sir." His tone was giddy.

I exhaled. At last I'd be able to reach my people. "Thank you. Is it safe to talk through the general channel?"

"It is, sir. We hacked the government's network. They're in the dark."

I rolled my shoulders back and cracked my neck, getting a sort of relief from the stiffness. "Thank you for your work. Can you patch me through to my troops?"

There was a click.

"You're connected, sir."

"Soldiers, we have Jordan Niles in our custody as well as the president and his council. Soon the city will fall without the need for more violence. Fight any resistance you encounter, but remember, whoever surrenders is to be spared."

I looked at Matt and Lisa. "Whoever is between the holding facilities and the hospital, a NWG van will be passing through. General Anderson is inside. You're to protect its path at all costs."

A couple calls of "yes, sir" came through.

I grabbed Lisa's hand. "The way is clear."

Lisa reached for my eye, but I flinched back. "You should go to the hospital, Davon."

I shook my head. "There's no time for that. I need to get Mom."

Her gaze flitted east toward Eden Gardens, where my childhood home stood. "Does he have her?"

I lowered my head. "He does."

She nodded and took me in her arms. "It will all be okay, son."

I couldn't control the burning sensation at the back of my throat or the tears that threatened to leave my eyes. Lisa had always been like a mother to me, and her comforting embrace made me realize how scared I truly was. How fucking terrified I was of losing my mother.

Lisa stepped away and held me at arm's length. "Go to her."

Abi was letting go of Matt when I turned to face him.

I wrapped my arms around him with care. "Be safe, brother."

Matt patted my back with his good hand. "You too. And when it's all over, get that eye looked at. You may look cool, but an eye injury is no joke."

I nodded. "I will. See you later."

Lisa and Matt got into an NWG van and waved goodbye.

The soldier who had called for the van took off his helmet and secured it by his side. He fixed his black tresses back into a short ponytail, then saluted. "Captain Cruz at your service."

I tipped my head. "At ease, Captain." I extended my hand to him. "A pleasure to meet you. I understand you're from Lavigne's troops."

"We are. How is our general?" Cruz's dark eyes were vibrant. Alive. Full of hope.

I smiled. "He's alive and well. Will you walk with me?"

Cruz nodded. He was a slender man about as tall as me, and his gait screamed of his leadership.

"I wanted to thank you for aiding us. You saved us today."

Cruz shook his head. "The honor is ours. We've been silent for too long. I should be thanking you for giving us this chance."

I waved his words away. "Nonsense. We're all victims of the NWG, and we stick together."

We reached my father, and his body went taut. Could it be fear?

A huge commotion came from the facility. Frail bodies of all ages filtered out of the prison. Pregnant women. Children. Elders. Their faces appeared gaunt and haunted by terror. Their bodies beaten and their gazes lost.

Some wept in joy. "Are you here to save us? Is it over?"

Then Suzanne came into view. Her face was full of hematomas, her eyes swollen shut.

What the fuck did that bitch do to her?

"I'm going to help her." Abi darted her eyes between my father and me. "Will you be okay?"

I kissed her temple. "I will. Go."

Abi went to Suzanne. They started talking.

I watched as Abi killed Leslie, and I couldn't be prouder. It was her vengeance. Her right. And Leslie deserved all she got for what she did to us.

Everywhere I looked, there was someone in need. Too many to count.

My heart grew heavy.

All were victims of the New World Government's system. I wondered if Aoki's parents were around. I had no idea what they looked like, but I'd make sure to search when all was over. I'd find them.

A group of prisoners approached me.

"We want to fight," one said.

I nodded. If they wanted to fight, who was I to deny them?

Soldiers and armed captives charged into the streets.

I swallowed the lump in my throat and faced Father. "Is this what you call progress?"

Father's gaze seemed detached. He hardened his features. "I don't see a problem. Some must fall for others to rise. It's part of life."

I yanked him to his feet. "That's part of life?"

A teenager, not older than thirteen, was full term. A man was on the ground, his legs full of ulcers. Soldiers carried body bags out, their stench indicative of days of neglect.

I threw him to the ground. "Guard him."

NWG soldiers surrounded him.

I clenched my jaw and walked away. I had to get away from him, or else I'd lose it.

Connor's plan was never to kill him unless we were forced to. He was to live out his days in prison, enduring the same life he'd subjected these citizens to. So I'd wait. He'd get his punishment in due time.

I pressed my earpiece. "Joe, are you still there?"

There was a buzz, then his voice came through. "Yes, sir. I'm here."

"Have you heard from Sinclair?"

He didn't turn off the comms as he asked the room if there had been any word from Halcyon. "No, sir. We broadcasted the president's arrest via all channels, and he asked the citizens to stand down. Promissa and the surrounding areas are following his orders, but we haven't heard from Halcyon."

The president, even just being there for show, had power over the NWG. His voice was law. I hoped the Liberty Enclave had gotten the upper hand. We needed to take down General Steele and Grace Orville.

I walked to Father, where Cruz waited.

"What are your orders, General?" Cruz asked.

"We go into Eden Gardens. You are to clear our way and take down any enemy troops. If they surrender, have your soldiers bring them back here and lock them up. Once we're in Minister Niles's house, guard the premises."

Cruz straightened. "Yes, sir."

Half an hour later, Abi and I strode across the district, Jonathan's and Cruz's troops guarding our way.

The battle had dwindled, and the streets were almost empty except for the occasional PRF troop marching by.

A message kept playing around the city: "Citizens of Electi. Stay in your homes. We will take care of the insurgents and transmit a message once it's safe to go out."

People watched from their homes as we passed, holding the most powerful man in the NWG. We passed Lake Egregie to our right and headed through the gardens of our estate. What was once my childhood home now gave me a sour taste in my mouth. I wanted to turn away, but I needed to know if Mom was still alive. To hold her and take her away from this nightmare.

"You will pay for this," Father said when the house came into view.

I ignored him.

Abi stopped midstep. "Davon...the garden."

The estate was in a sorry state. Deprived of life. The gardens were neglected, and the conservatory my mom loved so much was in the dark.

Every muscle of my body tightened. "Where are you keeping her?" I pulled my father's collar. "What the fuck did you do to her?"

He gritted his teeth. "I told you she's safe."

He had to have her prisoner because she'd never let her home fall like this.

I shoved him away and let Jonathan take him in. I lifted an eyebrow at the bio scanner by the door.

That's new.

"How do we enter?" Jonathan asked.

I grimaced. "That's a bio scanner. Put his face to it."

Jonathan grabbed Father's head and pushed it in front. The door clicked.

Abi and I followed in silence. The foyer was empty. Our butler was gone. Had Father gone mad with paranoia? Did he let everyone go, thinking he'd be betrayed? And where the fuck was Mother?

I looked around, my heart thumping wildly. She was nowhere in sight. "Where are you keeping her?"

My father was silent, his face unreadable.

I grabbed his lapels and hauled him face-to-face. "I said, where the fuck are you keeping her?"

A bead of sweat slid down his temple. "She's in the basement. The key is around my neck."

I searched inside his vest. *The key.* I pulled the chain off and passed it to Jonathan.

I growled. "I swear, if I find you've harmed her in any way, you won't see the light of day, and I'll be the one to kill you." I pushed him out front.

"Cruz, search the house for anyone else."

He saluted. "Yes, sir."

I gave Jonathan the key. "Once we enter the study, get to the basement. Call me when you find her. If my mother is unharmed, tell her you're with me, and get her to a safe place. Don't let her come inside."

When we reached the study, two soldiers stayed outside, guarding the room, while I dragged Father in. I guided him to one of his settees.

Abi followed.

I turned to Jonathan as he was about to close the door behind us. "Find my mother. Keep her safe."

Jonathan nodded.

I glanced out the glass panel behind Father's desk for a brief moment, taking in the pristine forest. It was so silent in here that one could almost forget war raged outside.

"I see we're back to being a big happy family," Father said as Abi took my side. "So you did it. You took your precious city back. Now what? Do you think you can keep it? Do you truly believe your people will be able to keep mine from getting it back? We still have Halcyon."

I stood behind his desk and punched it. "The Liberty Enclave will take it back today."

"The Liberty Enclave lost, son." He chuckled.

Abi frowned. "You're lying. They're still at war."

She didn't know about Sinclair's last communication. Could it be? Could they have lost?

Father smirked. "Believe what you want, but this whole thing... This rebellion as you want to call it will be lost in the blink of an eye. You have no idea what you'll be facing. Steele will retaliate, and I'm an angel compared to him."

We planned for this scenario. Even if we lost Halcyon, Promissa was ours, and I'd make sure it stayed that way. As for Halcyon, if what Father said was true, we'd promised Sinclair to fight with her, and we would. But I sure as hell hoped he was bluffing.

I clenched my fists. "We'll see."

He angled his head toward me. "When was the last time you heard from your precious allies? I know you planned all this together. When I didn't hear back from my soldiers after the last attack, I knew something had happened. I received intel of large explosions and then nothing. You went into hiding." He raised an eyebrow, looking at my uniform. He scoffed. "Did your precious General Harris die? I saw him on the broadcast, but I see you're wearing his insignia. I knew you had it in you to rise, son, but I would have preferred for you to do so by my side."

In a second, I rounded the desk and punched his face. "You have no right to say his name." I gripped his hair, yanking it till his eyes were on me. "And I would never have joined you."

He sneered. "But you did, son. How many of your rebel friends did you kill on my orders? Or did you forget?"

"Davon?" Abi's voice was but a whisper against the raging of my blood against my ears.

Scorching rage spread through me. I wrapped my hands around his neck and squeezed. His eyes watered and turned red, and my heart danced at his fading pulse.

Abi's hand gripped mine. "Davon, we need him alive."

I shook my head and let go.

The strain in my teeth was unbearable.

He coughed dryly. "Why did you close the door? What are you two planning to do with me? Are you going to torture me? Oh." He smiled. "I forgot you're the good guys. I bet you have some paper you want me to sign. A surrender note or maybe a peace treaty." He shook his head. "What have you become, son? I raised you better."

Abi grabbed my arm before I hit him again, then she crouched before him. "We're giving you an opportunity. Surrender the NWG. We'll make a treaty so your people are safe and can live within our borders."

The president had already signed, but they shared power, and having Father's signature could help advance the transition. Especially if what he said about Halcyon was true. He was the only one who could possibly convince Steele to give up. To surrender his city.

"And what happens to me, my dear Gaby?" He flinched. "Oh, sorry. My dear Abigail."

She backed away from him and shrugged. "You get to live."

He tilted his head and watched her closely. "And what life would that be, my dear?"

I stood by her side. "I'll make it simple. If you don't sign this, we'll let the people do whatever they want with you, but I'll never let them kill you. I'll let you recover, then do it again and again until you sign. You know I'm a patient man."

Father's pupils dilated for a moment, and his lips twitched before he regained his composure. He was afraid.

"General Niles."

I pressed my earpiece. "Jonathan?"

"Rebecca Niles is safe and unharmed."

I let out a huge breath.

"But there's a problem, sir."

I frowned.

There was some noise before the radio went silent, then clicked to life again.

"Son?"

"Mom?" My stomach fluttered, and I stumbled.

Abi caught my arm. "Is it Rebecca?"

I nodded, tears already pooling behind my eyes.

I widened my eyes as the door banged open and one of our soldiers barged in, followed by Mom.

She ran to me, her complexion clean but pale.

I wrapped my arms around her. "You shouldn't be here."

She buried her face in my chest. "Nonsense." She held my shoulders and reached for my eye. "Are you okay?"

I smiled. "I am."

"Love?" His voice was but a murmur.

Mom tensed in my arms. She stepped away from me and went to Father. *Crack.*

She slapped his face, leaving a red mark on his already swollen cheek. "You don't get to call me that ever again. You destroyed our family." She opened her arms. "And for what? Power. Riches."

Father watched her, his eyes pained. "I did it for us."

She walked away from him. "You're nothing to me."

We turned at a screech on the wooden floor. The soldier who had entered with Mom barricaded the door with one of Father's settees.

My stomach roiled. A chill slithered down my spine. Who was this soldier? What the fuck was happening?

Abi guarded Father as I approached the soldier, pushing Mom behind me. "What are you doing?"

The soldier took off their helmet.

I froze. *Sarah.* "What are you doing here? You're supposed to be with Mathews."

She turned, gun in hand. "Step away from him."

Abi gasped, still by my father's side. "Sarah?"

Sarah aimed her gun at Abi.

What the fuck?

I took a step forward. "Put your gun down. That's an order." My hands trembled. Was she mad?

"If you try to stop me, I'll shoot her." Sarah didn't flinch. She cocked her gun at Abi. "Step away, Abi. Now."

A raging storm brewed within me. Had she finally lost it? "Abi, come here."

"I don't understand." Abi put her hands up. "What's going on?"

My heart thrummed wildly.

Sarah's eyes were intense. Would she shoot her own sister?

"Come here, love." I gestured for Abi to come to my side. "She's not well."

Once Abi was safe, I took another step.

Sarah aimed her gun at Mom. "Don't move, or I'll kill her."

"Who is she?" Mom asked Abi.

"My sister." Abi pulled Mom behind her. "Sarah, what the hell is going on?"

Father dragged himself into a kneeling position, then rolled his shoulders back. "I thought you'd never come, Ms. Davis."

What the fuck did he just say? I stood still, but my mind ran wild through all the memories it guarded.

Abi darted her eyes between them. "Sarah, what's he talking about?" Her voice was broken.

Sarah looked down.

"You still haven't put the pieces together, have you?" My father chuckled. "Oh, this is precious."

"Shut up!" Sarah yelled.

Father's laughter vibrated around the room. "Oh, my dear daughter. It seems you weren't the only one living a double life."

Abi trembled violently. I reached for her, but Sarah raised her gun.

"Your sister here is a spy. She's been working for us for almost a year now."

Abi backed into a bookshelf. "No, it can't be."

My heart pounded in my ears. I stared at Sarah, and the pieces started fitting together. Some things about her escape always perplexed me. How easily Deb got her out after Connor had never been able to form a plan that would work. Why the soldiers didn't shoot Connor or Sarah as they ran into the forest.

It was all part of a plan. They let Sarah escape.

How could we be so blind? She was right under our noses.

How much was her fault? Why would she betray her family? This would destroy Abi.

"Oh, I see your mind working, son. You know, she even killed for us. Her hands are as tainted as mine or more. How did it feel, Sarah, to take that innocent boy's life? Leslie told me how it went, how you told her the boy had come to you after seeing a runner leave with a coded letter. I didn't know you had it in you to murder someone in such a way."

Abi gasped. "You killed Richard?"

It all made sense. She was the only one missing at the party. The only one without an alibi. I thought she was crazy, but it was guilt. She'd murdered an innocent boy.

Heat flushed through my body. She'd done it in cold blood.

Sarah closed her eyes and shook all over. "I'm sorry. I had no other choice."

"Sarah, please." Abi inched toward her sister, her neck corded, her stare pained. "Please tell me it's all a lie."

Abi's desperate pleas broke me.

How could she survive this, knowing Sarah's hands were in everything that had happened? I wanted to hold her, to shield her from it all, but Sarah...Sarah was not herself. Or maybe, for the first time, she truly was.

Father looked at me. "When I received those letters, I thought it was you. I believed you were helping us and even made you part of my council. I never suspected you could betray me like this. I mean." He shrugged. "You were difficult sometimes, but you kept your mask well. When Leslie escaped, she told me everything. After Richard's murder and your imprisonment, Leslie found out Sarah had kept your true identity secret, I imagine because of sentimentality for her sisters. You see, Leslie didn't have access to the cypher, so it was Sarah's job to send the intel out."

Abi sobbed. "But Carlos. How could you?"

Sarah flinched but kept her gun up. "He wasn't supposed to die." Her hands shook.

An empty feeling swept through me as images of Christina's and Carlos's bodies came to mind. Then of Maria's body sprawled on the floor. All those deaths.

Father cleared his throat. "Sarah told Leslie about your escape plan. Leslie insisted it was time to let me know about you so we could capture you as soon as you entered the city." He glared at Sarah. "But you didn't want that, did you? You thought to give him a chance and didn't get the intel out." He sighed. "In the end, Leslie got it out. I never expected her friendship with Deborah Davis would get her a chance to join the tech team. Once there, it was only a matter of time till she got the information out, not only about your treason but about your base."

Everything was falling in place like a puzzle. Piece by piece until the image was clear. It all made sense now.

His gaze returned to me. "You barely made it out of the city, but I made sure you paid for what you'd done to me. How many people did you lose in that first battle? How many more after?"

A swarm of memories hit me. Of Pedro impaled to the tree. Of the forest floor bathed in our people's blood. Of Anna suffering his relentless torture.

"Shut up." I gritted my teeth.

He looked at Sarah. "By the way, thank you so much for the intel on that second base. I was saddened to learn you misled my soldiers by a couple of kilometers. Was it a mistake, or did you want the rebellion to have a chance? Your little game cost me a lot, my dear." He smiled. "But I forgive you.

Now, will you please unbind me so we can take care of these two? Don't worry. They won't be mistreated."

"Connor," Abi whispered at the same moment I'd put Father's words together.

Sarah was responsible for his death. I swallowed the bile that rose into my mouth.

Sarah shifted her aim to my father. "Just as no harm came to Carlos, Deb, or Connor. You promised! You said my family would be safe."

"My dear, Connor isn't your blood. As for Carlos, the soldiers had orders, but he shot at them first. They didn't have a choice. I'm sure your sister is in wonderful health. My son here made certain she fled unscathed."

Sarah's nostrils flared. "Did you call her whole when you tortured her? When you made her part of an experiment to carry a child who's not her own, a genetic experiment made for your own benefit?"

"Ah, I wasn't the one who tortured her." He jerked his head toward me. "You can take that up with my son." He frowned. "By the way, did my son survive?" He shrugged. "Just curious. It'd be a shame if he didn't—he was quite the masterpiece."

I clenched my fists. "Son of a bitch."

"So he did?" Father sneered before turning his gaze back to Sarah. "Ah, don't tell me your sister isn't happy. At least she was able to have a child. I'm the one who lost a magnificent specimen thanks to my son here. If she had stayed, she would have been taken care of. And my son would be in my arms. I'm the victim here."

I was about to rush to him when Sarah shifted her aim. "This is between him and me."

Abi's breathing was fast.

I took her hand. "Breathe, baby."

Her hazel eyes were glued to her sister, as were Mom's.

Sarah turned her gun back to Father. "She would've been safe? After what you put her through to get our location?" Her eyes burned with rage.

Father lifted an eyebrow. "Well, you were the one at fault for not giving us that intel. That was your mission, or have you forgotten?"

Her chin quivered. "How could I have known they would blindfold me? I couldn't give you what I didn't have. It was impossible."

Father humphed. "Impossible? No, you just couldn't handle what you needed to do. If it wasn't for Leslie, we wouldn't have taken down your center of operations. You were useless."

"Useless?" She stepped toward him, her arms trembling. "Useless?"

She hit him with the butt of her gun, and he fell sideways. Blood seeped down his face.

"You made me betray my family. Every day I suffered, knowing I was lying to them. You promised you'd give me my son if I did what you wanted, but it was a lie. My son is dead. He's been dead for years." Tears streamed from her eyes.

So this was all about Charlie. Father promised him to her.

Father's eyes flashed with fear. "No, that's not true. I have your son. He's safe."

"Liar." She stood next to him. "Peter told me. You gave Charlie to him, but he got sick when he was a child and died. But you knew. You fucking knew and made me betray them. You took away my parents, my love, my child, and my brothers. You made me into this."

She glanced at me. "I'm sorry." Her tearful gaze moved to Abi. "I'm sorry, little sis. I guess I truly was unhinged at the end. But you don't have to worry about it anymore. It will all be okay. I love you."

Before we could stop her, she shot Father in the head.

Mom let out an anguished sob and ran to him. Her cries echoed around the study.

She still loved him.

My soul wept for her.

Sarah held the gun to her temple. I sprinted toward her.

Crack.

Blood sprayed over my face. Her body slumped to the floor.

"No!" Abi's scream reverberated around the study.

Abi reached her and hugged her tight, her cries heartbreaking.

I crouched and put my arm around her. She leaned into me.

The world darkened around me.

I closed my eyes and embraced her, praying we would pull through.

We stayed there in our bubble as her cries were drowned out by the chants outside: "Promissa is ours. We're free."

We had done it. We'd won. But at what cost?

Chapter 34

Abi

June 17, 2214

The sun streamed through Davon's penthouse. I was wrapped in his arms, his black silk sheets caressing me warmly. The orange and pink hues of dawn should have brought me a sense of peace and joy, but since that day, I'd lost a piece of myself.

I couldn't wrap my mind around what happened, about all the deaths that could have been avoided. Sarah's trauma had won over her reason at the end. I should have known.

When I looked back, there were signs. All those conversations. She was screaming it to the world. Her betrayal.

Our victory over the New World Government was stained by Sarah's treachery. Her name would be forever remembered for the deaths of hundreds of rebels. Our family broken with no possibility to be mended.

Davon and I were the ones to tell Deb. It had been one of the hardest things we'd ever done. Harder than war.

Deb yelled and rampaged through Sarah's stuff, which still lay around the room in the caverns. She kept asking why in uncontrollable sobs and didn't quiet down until she found a yellow rag, one Sarah had been holding the day she'd made the painting. It was taped behind the canvas with the phrase "We'll be together soon" written next to it.

Deb held that rag for a while in silence, a silence that lasted a week. I came by daily, but she just stayed like that, with Aspen by her side.

Aoki was the only one who could get through to her and brought her back, but she was not the same.

A funeral service was held for the hundreds of soldiers who died during the war. The area where the government center once stood would become a memorial center for both PRF and NWG soldiers.

As for the enhanced soldiers, hundreds were saved and held inside facilities where they were receiving the help they needed. Many were responding to treatment already. Others would take more time, but Rachel and Lucas had taken it upon themselves to rehabilitate them. To give them a chance at a normal life after all their trauma.

Davon helped Rebecca push through after Jordan's death. The council had approved of incinerating his body and burying him in the gardens of their home in Eden Gardens.

As for Davon, he had nightmares but wouldn't talk about them. I let him be. He'd tell me when the time was right.

Davon's breath caressed my nape, and he kissed me softly. His stubble tickled my skin, sending goosebumps all over my body.

I pressed myself against him and twisted to reach his lips. The kiss was loving. Gentle. Deep.

He brushed my hair back, capturing my gaze. "I love you."

I traced my fingertip across the scar over his now cloudy, sightless left eye. He'd lost vision completely but carried his scar with honor.

"You're beautiful," I whispered.

He chuckled. "And you're blinder than I am."

I giggled at his pun and took his lips in an ardent kiss.

Our bodies melted into one, letting our love drown away the pain that was always present. Always constant. Never-ending.

It was midmorning when we left the bed. I looked out into the city.

President Orville had signed the treaties after being sent to Electi's medical center and treated for arsenic poisoning. It seemed Jordan had been right and his own daughter had been trying to kill him from the start. The poisoning had caused his stroke. That was how much she wanted to take over.

The Liberty Enclave had lost the war but not before destroying the war train and Halcyon's air base. In the end, they were forced to retreat after losing two-thirds of their forces to the enhanced army.

Still, there were no comms coming from Halcyon. They'd closed their borders, and we believed they were rebuilding. Both sides had lost a lot.

Minister Jordan Niles's death was proclaimed all throughout the continent, and most of the NWG cities followed President Orville's mandate to stand down.

Halcyon was standing alone, but it didn't mean they were helpless. As far as the Liberty Enclave knew, they were preparing to attack them. As Father said, Steele would retaliate, with Grace by his side.

The PRF and NWG councils met regularly, trying to reach an agreement. For now, we'd taken over Promissa and Electi, and the NWG would bear the costs for the restoration of our city to its past splendor. We agreed to let them live within our cities but under our rule.

Most of our people moved into Promissa, but the council insisted on Davon and me relocating into Electi. Even though they requested we take residence in Eden Gardens with Rebecca, we moved back into the penthouse, as did Matt.

The aroma of coffee hit me just as Davon offered me a cup. "Here, baby. Are you all right?" He caressed my belly.

I nodded and took a sip.

"Take your time. I'm going to change and start prepping for brunch."

About fifteen minutes later, our door unlocked, and in came the woman who had become like a mother to me. One whose eyes carried as much pain as I did. To lose her true love, the man she adored, in the way she did. To lose him even before he was dead was a pain I couldn't understand. Her vivid eyes were now sunken, but she still smiled when she caught her son's frame in the kitchen.

I gave her a huge smile. "Rebecca, so glad you could come."

She kissed my cheek. "How are my two girls doing?"

I chuckled.

"I think she'll grow as addicted to coffee as her mother." Davon took his mother into an embrace.

There was a knock on the door.

"Come in!"

Now that everything was over, we could leave the door open. It was surreal.

"Hi!" Aoki's mother entered with countless bowls of food.

"We come with the goods." Aoki's father, who looked just like Aoki but older, brought in a porcelain jar.

"Thank you." I bowed.

She went right into the kitchen.

Aoki had taken after his mother. She was a chef before all this happened.

"What did you bring?" Davon took the jar from Aoki's father. It bore a traditional carving of bamboo stalks. Delicate and elegant.

Aoki entered behind them with Doug in his arms. "It's a sake. I've been preparing it for the last couple of months."

Doug had grown quite a bit and looked to be about four months old. Matt and Frank had taken over the care of the other six babies as well as the ones growing inside the Electi facilities, which were also part of the Prometheus Project. The natural-born babies were to be returned to their mothers if they wanted them or given up for adoption to a caring family. The costs of maintaining them would be covered by the NWG.

"I can't believe he saved it." Aoki's father took the jar from Davon. "It's been in our family for years."

They moved to the kitchen. Matt entered with Lisa and Frank.

Davon opened his arms in question. "Did you all plan to get here at the same time?"

Frank shook Davon's hand. "The Itos live next door, and we decided to stay over. With all the rebuilding going on, we wouldn't get here on time."

"Hey." Lisa kissed my cheek and stepped back so Frank could kiss my hand.

"Beautiful as always, my dear." He winked.

Matt dragged his father away from me. "Hey, you know she's off-limits."

Frank held a palm to his chest, then furrowed his brow and gasped. "You wound me, son."

I giggled.

"You two will never change." Lisa chuckled and led her husband away. "Come on, love. Let's have some sake."

Matt hugged me, then patted my belly. "Is your man feeding you right? You look thinner."

I'd lost some weight since the incident.

"I'm working on that." Davon hugged his brother. "Come on." He pulled him into the apartment.

I grabbed Davon's arm. "I need to call Deb."

Davon kissed my temple. "We'll wait for you inside."

I went into the hallway and dialed Deb's number. She lived in Promissa now and had taken over the reconstruction with Peter. Suzanne and he had moved out of Electi and into a house in the same neighborhood as Mark, Carol, and Diane. We dined with them just two nights ago at Mark's, and they were doing great.

The phone clicked. "Deb?"

I'd invited her over, but she said she wasn't ready to deal with anyone. That's why she was working nonstop. She said it helped her mind stay at ease.

"Hey, sis. Give me a second."

The rumble of machinery filtered through.

"I'm sorry. Did something happen? Are you okay?"

I smiled. "I'm fine. Just wanted to hear your voice."

The line stayed silent for a moment, and I thought I'd lost the signal.

"I'm sorry I can't be there with you. I promise I'll work on it."

I nodded. "I understand. I just... I love you."

"I know. I love you too."

I swallowed the lump in my throat. "Talk to you soon?"

"Sure. I'll call you tonight."

"Okay." I hung up.

I wiped my eyes.

Would we ever be able to move on from this?

I fought the heaviness that took over me each time we talked. The pain at not being able to mention her name. A name that carried so much loss and agony. It was like she was erased from our lives, the only reminder a nameless grave in the Janus Peak area, one only our closest friends and the council knew of.

The elevator's ding caught my attention. There was only one person left to arrive.

I smiled wide. "David!"

He caught me in an embrace and swung me in a full circle before letting go.

I glanced over his shoulder. "Where's Alec?"

They'd grown very close since the attack. David's eyes brightened whenever Alec was near, and there was a softness in his voice whenever they talked. I saw it in Alec too, something unspoken, a hesitant affection. But David was still with Jonathan even though he spent most of his time with Alec.

"He's at a meeting."

My pulse accelerated. "A meeting? What happened?"

"Jules arrived yesterday with an envoy from the enclave."

Sinclair decided to stay in Empire City to aid the wounded and start preparing for war. Just as we moved most of our army east as a precaution, they were also planning, set on taking back Halcyon.

"Are they in trouble? Did Steele attack?"

David cupped my cheek. "Everything is okay, but Alec and I are leaving with her."

My heart faltered. "What do you mean?"

He exhaled, then met my gaze. "Alec is taking his troops with him to the enclave. He ran it by Davon this morning. I want to go with him, and I miss Jules. She needs me by her side. I must keep my promise and save the people in Halcyon."

I swallowed my tears. "What about Jonathan?"

David smiled. "He's coming too but not today. He's still working with the enhanced soldiers and should join us in a month or two."

I was happy for him. He'd found people to care about. But I couldn't bear seeing him off to war again.

He gripped my shoulder. "You knew this would happen. You stay here. Safe. With your family. I'll go with mine."

I nodded. "I understand. Please don't be a stranger."

He grinned. "Never."

He kissed my cheek and was about to enter the elevator when Davon came out.

"You're leaving already?" Davon asked.

"Yeah, they're waiting for me."

Davon clasped his hand and patted his shoulder. "You have my complete support. Tell the enclave that whatever they need, we're here. We will take them down."

David saluted. "It's been an honor fighting with you."

Davon returned the gesture. "The honor has been mine."

When the elevator door closed, Davon pulled me into his arms. "I'm sorry for not telling you, babe. You seemed to need a moment this morning, and when Aoki's parents arrived, it slipped my mind." He held my shoulders. "Are you all right?"

I looked up into his dark eyes, the ones that had captured me from the moment we met. "I will be." I cupped his face and pressed my temple gently to his. "We will be."

He hugged me tighter, then threaded his fingers through mine. "Let's go see our family."

My heart swelled as we followed the sound of laughter into the room. Promissa was ours, and we had united our people. There was no doubt in my heart—we would keep this peace and protect our family, no matter what.

The End

What happens next?

Thank you for reading Breaking the Regime: Third Book of the Promissa Trilogy.

This has been quite an adventure, and as you might already have figured out, the story doesn't end here.

Promissa is free, and Electi is theirs, but Halcyon is still under the tyrannic rule of General Thorne Steel.

Follow David, Alec, and Jules into the Liberty Enclave, as they find in each other the strength they need to take back the city.

Live alongside Xavier, Issy, and Marcus as they struggle to survive in the depths of Halcyon and protect their love as they look for a way to go back to their loved ones and finally be free.

In the ashes of oppression, a different kind of love will blaze.

David and Xavier will take you deep into the Flames of Halcyon, where love doesn't just survive—it fights back.

Please follow my author pages. Reviews are greatly appreciated.

Goodreads:

https://www.goodreads.com/author/show/49079198.E_R_Phoenix

Amazon:

https://www.amazon.com/author/erphoenix

Acknowledgements

This is a dream come true, and I want to thank everyone who believed in me.

It was hard—years of writing and creating—but it was so much fun. These past two years have been extraordinary, and I couldn't be prouder of the result.

The Promissa Trilogy is more than I could've ever imagined. And now, two more trilogies are already forming. It's mind-blowing.

To my husband, David—thank you for standing beside me through every up and down. For being my number-one fan and for always pushing me forward. I love you with all my soul and being.

To my son, David, who listened patiently to all my ramblings and offered the best advice.

To my daughters, Karina and Mariana—thank you for knowing when I needed quiet, for turning down the TV, and for respecting my writing space. I'm sorry for every postponed K-drama episode and video game session. Your patience and love have meant the world.

To my fellow authors—there are too many to name, but each one is equally important. Your support, your presence, and your encouragement made this journey worthwhile. I wish you all the best in your own stories and endeavors.

To my readers—your words lifted me when the doubt crept in. You showed up in the darkest moments and helped me find the light again.

Meeting you has been a blessing beyond words. Thank you for walking with me through each chapter—the sad, the joyful, and everything in between. You've kept me grounded.

And lastly, and most importantly, to myself—from twelve years ago.

Thank you for believing in me. For holding onto my dreams.

For leaving behind that letter... and that first chapter...

That ended up being a complete trilogy.

About the author

E. R. Phoenix is a full-time novelist born and raised in Puerto Rico. She's enthusiastic about the environment, freedom, human rights, and societal justice.

Dystopian fiction is her favored reading and writing genre. She combines this with romance, particularly when love appears suddenly in a dangerous setting and is impossible to resist. Her tales are filled with action, danger, suspense, steamy romance, and individuals who would stop at nothing to defend their cause.

She's worked as a middle/high school science teacher and as a personal trainer. When she's not writing, she spends most of her time reading and being with her family. She loves dancing, hiking, watching anime, going to the beach, and playing videogames.

E.R. Phoenix is best known for her dystopian novels, but she will dive into the LGBTQ+ and polyamory contemporary romance genres in the near future.

She currently lives in Vega Baja, Puerto Rico.